# TO EARN SUBMISSION

by
Evelina
# CORTEZ

# TABLE OF CONTENTS
# IN ORDER OF PRESENTATION:
Chapters are numbered in chronological order.
First time readers are recommended to start on page 1, Chapter 6.

## ACT 1:
| | | |
|---|---|---|
| 6: | BLINDSIDED | 1 |
| 4.0: | LABOR WEEKEND | 5 |
| 1: | CASE CARDS | 15 |
| 4.1: | LABOR WEEKEND, FIRE AND ICE | 18 |
| 2: | CASINO | 39 |
| 4.2: | LABOR WEEKEND, THE THAW | 48 |
| 3: | COURTING | 68 |
| 4.3: | LABOR WEEKEND, END | 88 |

## ACT 2:
| | | |
|---|---|---|
| 8.0: | THE TURKEY CLUB, "NO" POWER | 109 |
| 5.0: | DENIAL | 125 |
| 5.1: | DENIAL | 134 |
| 8.1: | THE TURKEY CLUB, CONTINUED | 137 |
| 9: | HOLES IN THE DESERT | 145 |
| 8.2: | TURKEY CLUB, JEALOUSLY INSANE | 155 |
| 10.1: | MEN ARE TALKING | 171 |
| 10.0: | CIELITO LINDO | 176 |
| 12.0: | ISSUE AT BAR | 180 |

## ACT 3:
| | | |
|---|---|---|
| 12.1: | HURDLING THE BAR | 192 |
| 15: | THE CASE | 203 |
| 16: | ACCEPTANCE | 218 |
| 17.0: | THE DEPOSITION | 223 |
| 18.0: | OFFICE PARTY | 226 |
| 17.1: | DEPOSITION DEBRIEFING | 233 |
| 18.1: | FOR THE KIDS | 239 |
| 14, 13, AND 11: | HONEYMOON, WEDDINGS, PROPOSALS | 243 |

# ACT 1

# Chapter 6

# BLINDSIDED

It was supposed to be date night. She was supposed to leave her house. He was supposed to wait in his car.

Edward viewed her duplex through his passenger window. The only light was the glow of out-of-season Christmas decorations on the adjoining unit. That was how he saw the three silhouettes of her neighbors standing on the walkway to her door, watching him.

His concern grew as the minutes passed. He texted again. Still no response since yesterday. Against her wishes, he exited and started up the path.

As he approached her three neighbors, he gave an acknowledging nod. "Gentlemen."

The tall, skinny one spoke in a Cholo-accent. "Katrina won't see you tonight."

Edward stopped and looked at the speaker. "Perhaps not," he replied with a congenial smile. "But I'm sure she can tell me herself. Thank you." He diverted off the walkway the men were blocking.

The skinny one side-stepped to obstruct Edward's ingress. He stopped again.

"We know you have a gun."

This put Edward on alert.

Under normal circumstances, he would leave at such an utterance, armed or not. But these were not normal circumstances. One factor prevented his departure: Katrina's safety. What if she was in danger?

Though he had not given his surroundings his full attention, his mind kicked into tactical overdrive as he had been trained. From left to right, he thought of them as "Flaco", "Négro", and "Gordo" because they were skinny, dressed in all black, and overweight, respectively. They were all at least ten years younger than him, late teens to early twenties. If worse came to worst, he knew the order in which he would isolate and nullify the threats, while hoping it would not go that far.

"What's the matter, white boy?" Flaco asked. "Afraid of something?"

"Yep," Edward returned, resting his arms at his sides. The three grinned, looking back and forth at each other.

"Afraid we gonna hurt you?"

"Nope," he countered with equal frankness.

Their smiles turned to gritting teeth.

Edward stood tall as he scanned them. "Do you quarrel, gentlemen?"

Their eyebrows lowered in confusion.

Négro chose to break, or perhaps exacerbate the tension by pulling a butterfly knife out of his pocket to perform an opening trick for intimidation. Before he was halfway through the gimmick, Edward put one foot behind the other and placed his right hand behind his back, prompting Flaco and Gordo to step back with hands in front. It was that moment at which the trio had shown their cards.

With their slack jaws and wide eyes, Edward recognized the fear on the faces of Flaco and Gordo was the realization the three had brought one knife to a potential gun fight. And by the way Négro almost dropped it, Edward knew he was no warrior.

To him, they were youth with no leadership. Though it was easy to influence one young man with no direction, three of them together could compound their mob mentality and dare each other to psychosis. Edward would attempt verbal de-escalation.

"What seems to be the problem, gentlemen?"

"We know what you did to my cousin," Flaco answered.

"Who is your cousin?" Edward asked, though he could have guessed.

"Katrina, cabrón!"

"Exactly what did I do to Katrina?"

"You beat the shit out of her, motherfucker!"

"Is that what she told you?"

"That's what her mom told us, homes."

Edward drew deeply through his nose to keep himself calm. "Do you know what 'consent' is?"

"I know this word. I don't give a fuck if she gave *consent*. She's a woman! Only a piece of shit hits a woman! Do you know what a 'machista' prick is?!"

"Yes, I know what a 'misogynist' is. I'm openly sexist. So consent doesn't matter because she's a woman?"

"Fuck you! You're not talking your way out of this!"

Edward saw the eyes of Négro and Gordo dart back and forth between Flaco and himself. They weren't following the conversation in English. So he made another attempt to reason, this time in Spanish.

Although some may have found Edward's Spanish laughable, nobody was laughing. The trio understood the message of his statement. He noted their common interest in Katrina's well-being and made it clear that either he or the police would be verifying her safety. He said he would not be leaving until he had accomplished his goal and ended with an offer to teach them how to handle a butterfly knife if he may proceed unobstructed.

All four men stood in silence until Edward said, "Qué quieres hacer? Es sus opción. Yo o la policía. Me or the police."

Gordo said something to Flaco in a street Spanish that Edward did not understand. His deep voice gave the impression he might be the senior of the three.

At that, Flaco jutted his chin. "Okay, asshole. Give me the gun and you can see my cousin for a minute."

Edward spoke in a jovial tone. "Of course! I told you tomorrow, the wall outside my childhood home can only support a 50-inch TV and nothing more!"

Flaco's eyes narrowed as they dropped to the ground. Something was lost in translation. By the time he had processed the hypnotically confusing statement, Edward was already behind him. "Hey! The gun!" He turned in pursuit but Edward was walking backwards toward the front door, right hand steadfast behind his back.

He stabbed the air in Flaco's direction with his left index finger causing a stutter in his step. All three walked in line at Edward's pace but dared not close the gap between them. If combat were to ensue, he had them arranged in the order he wanted to take them: Flaco, then Négro, then Gordo.

As Edward crept up the two steps of the porch, he stated, "We can all rest easily in the knowledge that there will never come a day when I give you a gun."

He knocked on the security screen. Katrina quickly opened the door but not the screen. It was difficult to see her face through it with her hand over her mouth. But he kept his head on a swivel, with most of his attention on the trio waiting at the steps, trying to look tough.

"Hello," Edward greeted.

"Hello, S-," she stopped herself.

"Are you okay?"

"Yes."

"Is something wrong?"

"No, Sir," she slipped. "I cannot see you."

He craned his neck down and spoke softly and simply as though she were a frightened child. "Would you like to tell me why?"

She shook her head.

"Are you in danger?"

She shook her head again.

Then he spoke in a voice loud enough for the three to hear. "If you are in any danger," he turned to look at them, "I can get you out of it right now."

Flaco looked at his partners who were now flanking him. Négro held one hand over the other, trying not to reveal the accidental cut on his knuckle as a drop of blood landed on the walkway.

"No! No, Sir. No danger. Please don't hurt them."

"I won't hurt them," he said. "They're not bad people, just misinformed. But I don't know where they got their information."

Edward couldn't tell what was happening. Did these knights in shining armor become privy to a false accusation and decide to come to Katrina's rescue? Was she attempting to end the relationship by enlisting the help of these would-be warriors? Is that how they were aware of his affinity for, and proficiency with, firearms? Or were there more factors at play?

Uncertain if she was telling the truth or if she was being coerced by some malevolent force that was listening to their conversation, he lowered his head and voice again. "If everything is okay, say our safeword and tell me what you want. If there is a problem, say a different word, and lie to me."

"'Exonerate'. Please go, Sir." She inhaled sharply, trying to stop herself from crying.

Edward did not visibly react beyond a hard blink as he stared at her. "As you wish."

# 4.0

# LABOR WEEKEND

They were both excited, but for different reasons and in different ways. Her excitement came from a combination of desire and fear for this man as he would be guiding her through a series of activities for her first time. His excitement came from a combination of the pleasure of training yet another submissive, and his trepidation at the possibility that she could be his last one. But the one reason they had in common: they both knew the events of this weekend would either fully define the nature of their relationship, or end it forever.

"Are we going to sign a contract?" Katrina asked.

"So you *have* done some research!" Edward replied.

"A little."

"You're going to make a good attorney," he said. "I think of every word from my mouth as a contract. We can have one if you want to write one, 'counselor'. But I think the video should suffice. If you want to add any clauses, addendums, or codicils, feel free. Do you want to write a contract?"

She shook her head.

Edward stepped to the entrance of the master bedroom to raise the light level. Katrina's eyes followed as he walked to a video camera on a tripod. Her vision dropped when he glanced at her. He peered down at the image of Katrina from the waist up wearing a black blouse, arms crossed. "Look at the camera."

Though it was through the screen, Edward stared at her for the longest amount of eye-contact she had made in the short time he had known her. He could feel his pupils dilating at the sight of this unmolded clay. Or perhaps it was the final product of his artwork he envisioned.

"What! …is your name?" he asked in a playful voice.

She attempted to hide her anxiety by answering with a tone like a song: "Katri-*na*!" But her crossed arms and hunching posture betrayed her true feelings over what was about to happen.

His eyes rose. "Are you here on your own volition?"

"Sí. Yes," she returned with a nod, trying not to be distracted by the memory of when she learned that word. *Volition.* Her eyes followed Edward as he stepped around the room. But again, she looked away when he looked at her.

"Are you familiar with the concept of 'safewords'?"

"A little?" she said hesitantly. She was proficient enough at English to know what "safe" meant and what "words" meant. But she had never heard the compound word before.

"Okay, I'm going to give you a quick lesson on the concept. What we are doing is commonly referred to as a 'power exchange'. You expressed your interest in allowing me to help you reach your personal goals through training in the 'submissive arts'. In order to do that, you will be giving me complete control over your body and hopefully your mind as well. The words 'no' and 'stop' will not be respected if you say them."

She watched him standing off camera through the tops of her eyes with her chin down.

"But we are going to have a couple of words to replace them. We might have more personal safewords in the future but for now we are going with the standard 'red' and 'yellow'.

"If we are in the middle of an activity and you want it to stop, you will say the word 'red'. At that point, we will stop whatever we are doing, you will have your power back, and I'll speak to you as an equal. Do you understand?"

"I understand?" she said, her voice rising at the end, giving her statement a questioning inflection as she sometimes did.

"And if we are in the middle of an activity that you don't want to stop, but you just want to slow down a little, you will say the word 'yellow'. Do you understand that?"

"Yes?" she said, once again sounding like she was asking a question.

"Now let me tell you what 'safewords' are *not*: You are going to be experiencing a combination of pleasure and pain, confusion and clarity. But it's not going to be like I am just torturing you until you say the safewords. The idea is to allow me to challenge you and for you to challenge yourself; to take the experience as far as you can go and refrain from using the safewords if possible. We are going to go pretty far this weekend for your first time, but we will go slowly. All right?"

"All right," she said, trying to hide that she was starting to feel her own accelerating heartbeat.

"Remember, there is no shame in using the safewords. Remind me, what are the safewords?"

"'Yellow' and 'red'?"

"Are you asking me a quest*ion*?" he asked, with extra emphasis on the last syllable. "Or are you making a statement, period."

She straightened her posture ever so slightly and stated, "'Yellow' and 'red'."

"Good. You sound more confident already."

"Thank you."

"Do you have any bodily injuries or sore spots I should know about?"

"I don't think so."

"When do these activities end?"

Slightly squinting, "I don't know."

"This ends whenever one of us wants it to end."

"Okay. What are we going to do?"

"It is important that you don't actually know what is going to happen."

Katrina's eyes widened. "But I read to talk about what we are going to do."

"I doubt your internet research did much to prepare you. That's not how I work. You don't get to know what happens next. You only need to know that you can stop it at any time."

Her vision dropped in thought.

"And half the time, *I* don't know what's going to happen. I'm just making it up! A girl who claims to like '*surprises*' should be okay with that," he mocked. "After all, you can only experience the unknown once."

Her heart pounded a little harder as she nodded.

"Are you ready to begin?"

"Let's begin!" she answered, attempting to squeeze some enthusiasm from her apprehension.

With a quieter voice, Edward concluded, "Katrina, no matter what, remember that you are in a safe place with someone who cares about you and wants this to be a positive experience for you."

For reasons she didn't understand, she liked the rare occasion she heard her name from Edward's mouth. She took solace in his words as she took a cleansing breath. She had been looking forward to this experience, though she didn't know what the experience would be. All she knew was that it was an opportunity to grow. And if it would help her grow closer to this man to whom she was already attached, all the better. She did not want to disappoint him.

Edward moved the camera to the corner, revealing a spacious master bedroom with Katrina standing in the center, arms ever crossed, eyes down. She was wearing a black blouse with a matching knee-length skirt and heels. Above her head was a metal bar suspended by chains at the ends from two points in the ceiling. Behind her was a neatly made bed with a towel spread on a corner. It was evident by the lumps that it was covering a few foreign objects with which Katrina would become familiar.

Wearing a dark purple ensemble of flannel pajama pants and a robe, Edward walked into the camera frame and stood directly in front of Katrina. He stared at her with a warm smile until her eyes finally rose to meet his.

"Here we go! First rule: You will address me as 'Sir' at all times. You will end all sentences or at least put that word into every statement you make. Understood?"

"Yes, SiR!" Katrina replied with the same spirited tone as Edward. She thought matching his level might help hide her fear.

He liked how her accent made her accentuate and hold 'r' sounds a little longer. He particularly liked how the 'r' in "SiR" sounded from the back of her tongue.

Seemingly from nowhere, he produced a black chain about fifteen inches long with a combination lock. "While we are working together in my house, you will wear my chain. Think of it as a 'training collar'."

*A 'training collar'? Like a dog?*

Edward placed the collar around her neck and closed the shackle of the lock. She concentrated on the physical weight of the chain while trying to ignore the emotional weight of the control it would give him. She had resolved to take a chance and trust this man. The collar would be her faith made manifest.

"We are going to start with the basic positions: The first position, we will call it… oh, I don't know… Let's call the first position, 'position number one'. Sound good?" Edward asked with a whimsical grin.

"Sound good!" she replied, returning the smile. But she was too far in her own way to recognize Edward's humor.

Edward's gaze froze on her. "Sounds good…"

"Sir!" she corrected herself. "Sorry, Sir."

"Say the entire sentence. Sound good?"

"Sounds good, Sir!"

"Good, now… I never want to hear you say the word 'sorry' to me. Instead, you will say, 'Please forgive me, Sir'. Understood?"

"Understood, Sir. Please forgive me, Sir." Since this wasn't the first time she had been told not to say the word, she wondered what was wrong with it. But she didn't have much time to think.

"Atta' girl," he reassured. "So, position number one: You will stand with feet shoulder-width apart…"

She placed her feet, regretting her choice in high heels for footwear.

Edward walked around behind her. "…and your arms will be crossed behind you."

She uncrossed her arms in front and crossed them behind her back.

"Whether you are able or not, you will try to touch your elbows with your fingertips behind your back. Understood?"

"Yes, Sir."

The stretch in her back and the front of her ribs made her wonder how much she had been slumping over. She noticed how this position made her stand straighter and made her open her chest, thrusting her breasts forward.

From behind, he adjusted her arms and was pleased to find she was almost flexible enough to hold her elbows in her palms. "Impressive!" he encouraged as he held her fingertips on her elbows.

"When I give you a compliment, you say…"

She completed his sentence, "Thank you, Sir!"

"How do I say 'impressive' in Spanish?"

"'Impresionante', Sir."

"Tu eres 'impresionante'."

"Gracias, Señor!"

"Good girl."

She was getting used to hearing him say that phrase to her. She liked the sound of it but didn't know why. It was condescending and respectful at the same time, with a protective quality.

He continued, "Your arms crossed behind your back is the standard location for position one. But a variation will have your fingers interlocked behind your head. Show me what that looks like."

She uncrossed her arms and lifted her hands to demonstrate the position as instructed.

"Good. But keep your elbows back," he directed. "This is called, 'position one, inspection'. Understood?"

"Understood, Sir."

"Go back to position one."

"Yes, Sir." She dropped her hands and crossed her arms behind her back.

Still standing behind her, he placed the fingers of both of his hands under her cheeks and traced her jawline, pulling her hair back. He gathered it in a tie from his pocket. She liked how he lightly yanked her hair as he tied it high on the back of her head. And although she had enjoyed the pleasure of his touch in modest amounts before, she liked how he assertively helped himself to her body as he pleased.

"So, one of your goals, you said you wanted to work on your confidence. We are going to start by making you *look* more confident, even if you don't *feel* confident yet. Your head will always be facing forward, up, with confidence," he said as he adjusted her head with his left hand around her ponytail and right fingers under her chin like he was posing a model. With his right hand he pointed over her shoulder. "And your eyes will stare a mile toward the horizon, with confidence. Understood?"

"Understood."

He pulled his hand back and rested it on her shoulder. There was a loud silence, like he was waiting for something.

She remembered. "Understood, Sir!"

"There you go," he reassured as he patted her shoulder.

She was determined to get this right, but distracted by the number of times he used the word "confidence". She wondered if it was intentional, an attempt to hypnotize her. *Even if he does hypnotize me, at least my own thoughts will be out of my way.* She decided to stop trying to see through his methods or ascertain his purposes for the time being.

His fingers unclasped the top of her blouse at the nape of her neck and unzipped it to the bottom. "Take this off," he gently ordered. The light fabric slid off her shoulders, down her arms, into her hands.

"Fold it, place it on the bed, and return to this position." He remained still, feet planted. He decided to ignore her failure to give a proper verbal response for the time being.

She obeyed, bashfully keeping her body turned away from him with an arm over her brassiere, before resuming position one with her back to him. Her efforts to hide in his sight were unsuccessful. He noted the bra was a front-closure before taking a moment to touch her unclothed shoulders and neck. She was grateful that at the very least, there was no way he could tell that the soothing warmth of his palms and the stroking of his fingers caused her nipples to point into the soft padding.

"Now focus," he said with more depth. Standing behind her gave his voice a disembodied quality.

She concentrated on her mile-long stare, though it barely felt like it was ten inches. With hands resting on her shoulders, he leaned forward. His warm breath filled her right ear. "This body belongs to me."

"Yes, Sir."

"To whom does this body belong?"

"This body belongs to you... Sir." She tried to speak nonchalantly, hoping to fool herself into believing this was a casual exchange.

"Say it again." He knew she didn't quite believe it. But he knew she needed time to process.

"This body belongs to you, Sir?"

"Is that a question?"

"This body belongs to you, Sir."

He delicately held her earlobe between his thumb and forefinger, saying a bit quieter but just as deeply, "This is my right ear. Say that."

"This is your right ear, Sir," she said with a calm that matched his.

He released her right ear and leaned over to her left ear. Holding it the same way, he asked, "What is this?"

"This is your left ear, Sir."

"Good girl," he whispered, giving her a light pat on the bottom, causing her buttocks to flex, followed by a tingling between her legs.

When he stepped around in front of her, she looked up to associate his face with his voice. "No," he corrected. "I like looking at you too but your focus and vision remains on the horizon. Look *through* me. Understood?"

Her eyes dropped back down, "Yes, Sir." She wasn't sure if this made the activity more impersonal. *Is there some greater purpose to all these rules?*

"I asked you to trust me," he said. "Do you trust me?"

"Yes, Sir," she replied as she tried to stare through the exposed middle of his chest where his robe was coming loose.

"Trust that there is a reason for everything I am doing with you. Can you do that?"

"Yes, Sir." *How did he know what I was thinking?* She couldn't ruminate much longer before her mind was directed to his next actions.

He knelt to her feet and unbuckled her left heel. Holding the shoe with one hand and supporting her ankle with the other, he ordered, "Step out." She did so, stepping down as he guided. Her curling toes were enveloped by the thick carpet.

With a bare left foot flat on the floor and a right foot still wearing a heel, she stood with her right knee bent. He took a moment to caress her right leg from her ankle to the warmth of her inner thigh. "I like my leg like this," he complimented. "Nice and smooth."

"Thank you, Sir," she said, trying not to dwell on the fact that he was claiming her body.

She was feeling objectified; like the leg that Edward was exploring was just an object that now belonged to him. And she wasn't allowed to be involved with his examination or even watch, as her eyeline remained on the horizon. For personal, and perhaps linguistic reasons, she never considered her body to be her own in the first place. But she never thought of it as belonging to someone else either. She did know one thing for certain: the ever abiding tingling was undeniable.

After doing thusly with the right shoe, he slid both to the side before rising back to his feet, kissing her on the forehead on his way up. As he stood, his hands stopped at her sternum and he unhooked her bra. But he didn't pull it off. He left it there. She wasn't given time to think about how close her breasts were to being exposed to him.

Returning to task, he said, "Listen carefully." Standing in front of her, reaching his left hand up to hold her right earlobe, he said, "This is my left ear."

Her eyes flashed a glance at his but they immediately dropped back down. He repeated, "This is my left ear. Say it."

She spoke tentatively. "This is your left ear." *Does he know what he is saying?*

He walked around behind her and held her right earlobe again. "This is my right ear."

"This is your right ear."

He walked back around in front of her, holding the same ear and asked, "What is this?"

She paused before answering, "This is your... right ear?"

"No." He insisted, "This is my left ear."

She took a breath and said, "This is your left ear."

Again, he walked behind her. Holding the same ear, "What is this?"

She pondered. "This is your... right ear."

"Good." He walked back in front of her, still holding her right earlobe. "What is this?"

"This is your left ear."

"Gooood," he said darkly. He dropped his left hand from her right ear and held her left earlobe with his right hand while facing her. "What is this?"

"This is your... right ear?"

"You're catching on!" he said, his voice getting lighter.

She noticed herself starting to breathe again. *How long have I been holding my breath?*

His right hand dropped from her left ear to her left shoulder. "What is this?"

"This is your right shoulder."

"Atta' girl."

She was unaware the cup on her right breast had fallen away; hanging to the side.

He took her right nipple between his thumb and forefinger. Her breathing quickened at the sensation. The tingling below intensified as though she was being touched in both places at once.

"What is this?"

"This is your... left nipple."

"Good girl!" he praised. He walked around behind her and uncrossed her arms. He pulled her bra off her shoulders and down as casually as one would give a handshake. She crossed her arms again without prompt. He grabbed her left breast from behind and asked, less formally, "What is this?"

"This is your left breast!" she stated with certainty.

"I think she's got it!" Edward announced. She smiled briefly, not sure if smiling was allowed. But Edward didn't see anyway.

"Now, whenever I touch any part of my body, you never do anything to impede my access. You aid my access. For example..." He walked back around in front of her, put his right index finger under her chin, and ran his thumb across her lips. "If I touch my lips, you open my mouth." She opened her mouth.

Her tongue welcomed his thumb as she closed her lips around it and lightly sucked, looking up into his eyes. He didn't think about her eyeline. His own lips parted for him to inhale and give a smile at the eagerness of his subject. "That's a good girl," he murmured.

Upon the withdrawal of his wet thumb, he drew a spiral from the edge of her left areola to the center, making her nipple point like a diamond. Then he opened his palm and massaged her breast with his whole hand.

"If I grab one of my breasts, you push my chest out further." She did so, leaning into his hand. "Atta' girl."

He walked back behind her and took an unabashed grope of both of her breasts. She tightened her crossed arms so her back would arch even more, pushing her bust into the warmth of his hands. This also caused her to stick her butt into his crotch where she detected his erection through his pajamas. He made no effort to hide, asking, "Can you feel how hard I'm getting?"

"Yes, Sir," she breathed.

"Take it as a compliment."

"Yes, Sir! Thank you, Sir."

He took a knee and unzipped the back of her skirt. She shimmied her hips to help it slide down, revealing a black thong that matched the bra. Once the skirt was to her ankles, he ordered, "Step out." She did so. He tossed it on the bed where it laid in a tangled heap next to the blouse she had neatly folded.

As he rose to his feet, his fingers traced her left leg. She subtly opened her thighs a little more before his hands came to rest on her butt. His left continued up to grab her ponytail, steadying her. His right remained to give her a few smacks on both cheeks, inducing the tiniest jiggle from each one.

Katrina's eyes widened at the simultaneous humiliation and exhilaration.

He stayed his hand to ask, "Do you like being spanked?"

"Yes, Sir." she replied. Her words were more of a surprise to her than to him. She had never thought of it as something to be enjoyed.

"Would you like some more?"

"Yes, Sir," she said with a shy grin, as though it were a confession.

"Harder or softer?"

She had to think. "I don't know, Sir."

"I order you to choose. Harder or softer?"

"Harder?"

"Request it."

"Harder, Sir."

"Give me a full sentence. Include the word, 'please'."

"Please... *pao-pao* me harder, Sir."

He released her ponytail and walked in front of her. "What did you say? 'Pow pow'?" he asked with a chuckle.

"'Pao-pao'. I don't remember how you say, Sir."

"The word is 'spank'. But I like 'pow pow'. Ask me again."

"Please give me pao-pao harder, Sir!"

He leaned down and kissed her on the forehead again. "I adore you."

"Thank you, Sir."

This time, instead of returning behind her, he spun her around by the shoulders, grabbed her hair, and proceeded. As the repeated smacks grew in intensity, she tried to take a small step forward but she was held in place by his hand on her ponytail. She struggled to resist the urge to uncross her arms and block his spanking hand. She felt herself panicking as her heart started to race, causing her to pant. *How much more of this is... Oh, he's done.*

It was over as quickly as it began. *It couldn't have been more than twenty smacks. Why was I scared? ... And why did I like it?* She savored the sting as she clenched, revealing a cute dimple on each cheek.

"Now that's one fine ass!" he announced as he rubbed the rosy red areas he was once smacking.

"Thank you, Sir!" she said with a smile in her voice.

He yanked her ponytail, almost causing her to lose balance. But her body fell back into his as he wrapped his arms around her front. He lifted her chin until her head rested on his shoulder as she closed her eyes. His robe had fallen open so her back was in contact with his warm bare chest. She felt and heard his breath in her ear as he tickled her cheek with his fingertips. He placed his right hand over her pliant lips and put his index finger into her mouth as he had done with his thumb. She sucked on it as if to invite more. But he pulled his finger out and found her right nipple and once again spread the water from her mouth around her areola, certain to give it at least as much attention as he had given her left. They reveled in the delectation of her nipple projecting into the air as he rubbed and tweaked it.

His left hand joined to massage her left breast until that nipple erupted again. The contrasting temperature between his hands and the air deepened her arousal. She pushed her chest out further in a desire for her breasts and his hands to melt together.

"I've got a fantastic body here!" he proclaimed.

She leaned lower into him to get a better sense of his arousal on her bottom, employing the same shimmy she used to get her skirt off to rub his erection. He uncrossed one of her arms and placed her hand on the front of the flannel. "Can you feel what you are doing to me?" he whispered in her ear. She nodded as she explored him up and down.

They were immersed in the moment. She grinding on him, he massaging her. His hands ran from waist to collar and back. She clenched her abdominal muscles when he traveled over her stomach in an attempt to tighten the area. But she didn't know if she was successful. *I hope he likes my breasts enough to ignore my belly.*

Without warning, he grabbed her hair again and pushed her an arm's length away, halting their activity. She naturally returned to position one. "Whew!" Edward said with a deep sigh. "I'm getting a little carried away with you! We have an agenda... tasks to perform... training to complete!" he declared. He turned her back around.

She was also out of breath. But she maintained her position. *All this and he hasn't even fucked me yet! Why did he stop?*

"Ah, what the hell," he said as he groped her breasts again, now from the front. He took a moment to admire the handfuls; how her dark nipples seemed to stare right back at him. He released one to place a hand on her heart and heeded the wild tattoo it beat. All the unreserved and unapologetic touching and staring not only brought physical pleasure to the two, but it also served to cement his claim over the body she was gradually giving him.

Years had passed since a man had seen her in any state of undress. And she could not recall a time when she had been touched with such a balance of passion and perversion. She didn't have time to think about whether or not she was ready. She was relieved she didn't have to look at his face or start a conversation. She wouldn't know what to say anyway. There was no pressure, none to do anything or be anything more than what she was.

If her breasts were not big enough for him, if her butt was not fit enough for him, if her stomach was not tight enough for him, there was nothing more she could do about it in this moment. But judging by his state of arousal, she was sufficient for his pleasure. *And he doesn't even seem to notice my stretch marks!*

She took comfort in the fact that all she had to do in order to please him was obey and allow him to do whatever he wanted to do. As long as she did that, there was no way to disappoint him. It was that simple; He could be a man. And she could be a woman.

# 1

# CASE CARDS

*Congress shall make no law respecting an establishment ooff religion, oorr prohibbitting the the ffree eexercisee therereoff; or or abridging abridging the the freeedomm of of speeech...*

Katrina caught her eyes crossing as the words doubled. She tried to force more knowledge from the book into her mind. But once her fatigue caused her to read the same paragraph for the third... or maybe fourth time, there was no use continuing. Even the music of Michael Jackson in her headphones was not enough to keep her alert. Her law studies would not be resulting in any more retention tonight. And besides, she didn't want another lecture from her mother about coming home late. So she would return the copy of *Conventions of the Constitution* and go home.

Her flats slapped the marble floor as she made her way through the office lobby, past the aquarium, to the law-brary. She stopped in the doorway upon the discovery that she was not alone in the building.

"Katrina!" Shannon greeted. "What are you doing here so late?"

Under the only light in the room, Katrina observed Shannon Smith, Arnold Kalish, and three men that she did not recognize sitting around a table with cards, poker chips, beverages, and snack food. All conversation abruptly ceased at her entrance. All eyes were on her as she lifted the book to her chest.

"I am study upstairs," she mumbled.

"What were you doing?" Shannon asked again. "I can't hear you."

Still hugging the book, Katrina shuffled forward. "I am study," she said a little louder, though self-conscious that her Spanish accent was obscuring her words.

"What about her?" Arnold asked Shannon as they exchanged a nod.

"Come! Play poker with us!" Shannon invited.

Katrina continued her journey to the edge of the light. "I don't know how."

"Even better!" one of the strangers joked. "We'll teach you!"

"I don't have money here," she said, not wanting to reveal the fact that she didn't have much money anywhere, not to mention her student loans among other debts and charges.

"This is Katrina Gomez. She's a new clerk here," Shannon told the table. "She'll play on my money."

"How much money?" Katrina asked.

"Don't worry about it," Shannon replied. She pulled an empty chair out to her right. "Have a seat!"

Katrina was uncertain if her mentor was making a request or giving an order. So she set the book atop a nearby stack and sat. She could not say 'no'.

If she was honest with herself, Katrina wanted to go home before it was too late to spare herself from an argument with her mother. But she understood this was one of those "networking opportunities" they tell you about in law school… or in every school. It was a chance to be social with both her boss and a founding partner of the firm. *Mamá will want to fight no matter what time I get home. Don't let them know how scared you are. And don't mess this up!*

Shannon told Katrina to find a "rank of poker hands" on her cellphone. But when she saw Katrina only had an old flip phone, Shannon put her own smartphone in front of her displaying a chart that would help Katrina understand the value of her cards.

Katrina noticed her tired mind was catching a second wind. Her eyes did not cross at the sight of this chart.

Shannon explained the basic rules of the game. She used the chart to show Katrina what kinds of decisions she should make. And the three strangers were all too happy to volunteer pointers to the lovely young clerk. They played a few practice hands until she had a grasp.

Once the game began, Katrina did everything she could to blend in. She consciously thought about trying to strike a balance between the action and the banter. She wanted to be conversational without making any big mistakes in her play in spite of her limited English. She folded most of her hands. But when she looked down to find pocket aces, she slow-played them perfectly to take a hefty pot off of Arnold.

"I'm sorry, Mr. Kalish," Katrina said as she timidly gathered and stacked her new chips.

"Don't ever apologize for winning a poker hand," Arnold gruffed.

Katrina wasn't sure if she was being chastised. *Don't cry you baby.*

But she felt better after he lifted a scotch glass to his lips and appended, "And at the poker table, call me 'Arnold'."

"Arnold," Katrina said, keeping her eyes on the task at hand.

"When are we going to make an attorney out of this girl?" Arnold asked Shannon as she started to deal the next hand.

"Why the hell would we want to do *that* to her?" she replied dryly.

"One more year of school," Katrina volunteered. "And then I 'faithfully and honestly discharge the duties of an attorney at law to the best of my knowledge and ability'." She delighted in the opportunity to employ a portion of the longest and most impressive English phrase she had memorized.

The whole table smiled at the statement from the aspiring litigator. Shannon said, "It's good that you know the oath but you won't have to recite it from memory. You just repeat after the judge."

"Maybe we all should have it memorized," Arnold suggested, to some nods of agreement. He directed his attention back to Katrina. "You can learn more about human nature at a poker table than you will ever learn in a courtroom," he said. "…or law school, for that matter."

Shannon added, "And it will help you know when you are being lied to."

...
    About an hour later, the tournament was down to two players, Arnold and one of the strangers. After a few more minutes of play, the stranger had all the chips on the table. Every player reached into their pockets or purse for money. Each of them slid a $100 bill to the winner except for Katrina and Shannon. Shannon slid $200 to the winner to cover Katrina's buy-in. This made Katrina uncomfortable.

    "Is too much," Katrina said to Shannon in a hushed tone. "You can't pay for me $100."

    "It's nothing, really," Shannon replied at equal volume. But Arnold still heard them.

    "Yeah," he agreed. "You're the one helping *us* out. We lost some of our players from another firm this week to a corporate retreat or some shit. You're doing us a favor filling the seat."

    Katrina still wasn't comfortable with the idea of Shannon paying for her. But with her boss' boss framing the circumstances as though she was the heroine, she agreed to sit for another tournament and play on Arnold's money this time.

    Between the two tournaments, Katrina improved from fifth place to third place. This resulted in some words of encouragement from the other players.

    Once the table broke, most, including Katrina and Shannon, stepped outside to smoke by the front entrance. Katrina learned this was a weekly occurrence. And they usually played three tournaments, but she missed the first one this night. They talked about what it would be like next week with more participants as though Katrina's attendance was a foregone conclusion.

    Shannon noticed the guys seemed to clean up their language as they conversed in Katrina's presence.

    Katrina was careful not to verbally commit to another tournament since she didn't want her bosses to pay for her. But her apprehension was assuaged the next afternoon when she went to the firm's mailroom.

    She received a manila interoffice envelope. The name line above hers was blacked out by a marker, rendering the sender anonymous. Inside the manila envelope was a standard white envelope. Handwritten on the front were the words: "For poker, buy a book, practice in a casino, get a better phone." She peeked in and counted thirty $100 bills. *$3,000! They must really want me to play. They each bill hundreds of dollars hourly. I guess the money isn't an issue to them.* It was evident that some of her study time would now be devoted to poker.

# 4.1

# LABOR WEEKEND, FIRE AND ICE

Katrina stood in position one, eyes forward, feet at shoulder width, arms crossed behind her back. Standing in front of her, Edward lightly pinched her left nipple with his right thumb and forefinger and asked, "What is this?"

"This is your right nipple," she replied.

He paused before reminding, "And how will you be ending your sentences?"

She corrected herself. "Sir!"

"Say the whole sentence."

"This is your right nipple, Sir."

"I've been a bit lax about the way you address me so far. I've given you a few orders and compliments and you have made a few statements without ending your sentences correctly. But here is what is going to happen when you forget."

With his left hand, he delivered a brush to her face that was… like a slap. It only caused the tiniest bit of pain. But it was nonetheless surprising to Katrina. Her mouth opened to take in a breath as her eyes darted about.

"Kind of hurts, doesn't it?" he said with a sympathetic smile.

"Yes, it hurts," she whispered, once again abandoning her submissive bearing as a result of the physical discomfort.

His right hand immediately repeated the action, hard enough to make a soft clap. He encouraged, "Come on, Katrina! What do you say?! Does it hurt?"

"Yes it hurts, *Sir*!" she shouted back.

"Good girl!" he said, rubbing her cheeks. He held her face to steady her wandering eyes and spoke with kind assurance, "I'm going to help you with this. You are going to get really good at addressing me. I am determined to help you earn your degree in the submissive arts."

"Thank you, Sir," she mumbled. She was confused in ways she did not know how to articulate in any language, not even to herself. Though this was not nearly as severe, a man had not caused her physical pain in years. And she had not been *punished* with pain since childhood. She was feeling memories.

Edward could see the disconcertment on her face as she stared forward, tears welling. "Would you like a hug?"

"Yes, Sir," she said with voice breaking.

He wrapped his right hand around the back of her neck and pulled her head to his chest. With his left arm, he reached behind her and held her crossed arms together so he was hugging her but she could not hug him. She could only feel the affection that he was conveying to her with his arms and robe entangling her in his warmth. Her tear ran down his chest as he listened to her breathe and sniffle. There was no need for words.

Once the pace of her breathing steadied, he lifted her chin until her eyes met his. Her mascara was running but there was nothing she could do about it, and he didn't care.

He spoke with sensitivity. "You're getting a rush of emotions right now, aren't you?"

She nodded. He ignored her lapse in verbal protocol for one more moment.

"Remember what I told you. You are in a safe place with someone who cares about you. Remember?"

She nodded.

"Remember your goal: to not cry so easily in public?"

She nodded.

"You will cry with me anytime you need for any reason. ...or for no reason! You will give me *all* of your tears. Even when we are not together, your tears are mine."

At that, her eyes filled again and she buried her face in his chest and robe once more. *Does such a man exist that I may be given permission to feel?*

Edward listened as her stuttered breathing turned her weeping into sobbing. He held her tighter and stroked her back and neck. When he released her arms, she tucked them into his robe around him.

As a man, he didn't know exactly why she was crying. He did know however, that she also did not know. But it didn't matter.

Once her breathing resumed its pace, he asked, "Remind me, what are the safewords?"

"'Yellow' and 'red'."

He lifted her chin again. "Remember, this ends whenever you want. But I hope you will keep going. Do you want to continue?"

She nodded.

He held his right hand to the side of her face as a warning, repeating with a mischievous twinkle in his eye, "Do you want to continue?"

"Yes, Sir!" she said, returning a smile.

"I'm glad you are not giving up," he said with relief. "Let me ask you this: Is there a way I can discipline you that would work better than slapping my face?"

Katrina's eyes looked down in thought. "I don't know, Sir."

"I could pinch a nipple or smack my fine ass," he suggested. "Or I could make you do push-ups."

"Maybe smack your fine ass, Sir?" she said with a shy grin, embarrassed at her own words.

He smiled. "No, that was a trick question. I know you *like* being spanked!"

"Yes, Sir!" she said through her lilty laugh, impressed that Edward caught her ruse.

"The point is to *discipline* you when you make a mistake, not reward you."

"Yes, Sir."

"I'll spank you all you want. No problem there!" he said. "But in order to discipline you, what should I do?"

"Maybe… pinch your nipple, Sir?" she muttered.

"Request it."

"Will you please pinch your nipple, Sir?"

"Why?"

"For to discipline, Sir?"

"Ask me in one sentence."

"Will you please pinch your nipple for to discipline, Sir?"

"Gladly," he said as he kissed her forehead. He took a deep breath to renew the energy of his voice. "Here we go! Position one."

She took a step back under the bar and resumed her position as ordered.

He clamped onto her left nipple with much greater force and said, "That was an order!"

"YES, SIR!" she yelped, with a cry in her voice. The pain caused her to dance like she needed to pee. But she denied her urge to uncross her arms, holding her elbows even tighter behind her back.

Still clasping her nipple between his knuckles, he put his left hand on her right shoulder and leaned down until his eyes were on the same level as hers. Through raised eyebrows, he half yelled and half reaffirmed, "I'm going to be a bastard about this! I'm going to help you learn how to address your Dominant! Okay?!"

"Yes, Sir!"

"I'm not going to let you down! I'm *not* going to fail you! You are going to learn this! I promise!"

"Yes, Sir!!! Thank you, Sir!" she shouted as she locked her knees in an attempt to keep from struggling against her agony.

"Do you want my help?!"

"YES, SIR! PLEASE, SIR!"

"Do you want me to train you in the submissive arts?!"

"YES, SIR! PLEASE TRAIN ME, SIR!"

"Do you want me to help you with the goals we discussed?!"

"YES, SIR!"

He released her nipple and rubbed her breast to soothe the ache and kissed her on the forehead. "It will be my honor."

"Thank you, Sir," she said between panting breaths.

Something about the pain felt different than before. The initial emotional shock was replaced with determination. Now she had his promise that he would not give up on her. This was the first time she had ever been given such an assurance. His revelation that he felt a responsibility to her made her want to please him more than ever.

"Here's what I'm going to do." He lifted her left breast with his left hand and wrote on her with a marker that appeared in his right. While writing, he said, "This is now my 'Sir nipple'. Every time you forget to address me correctly, I will punish my 'Sir nipple'." He tossed her breast out of his hand just to see it jiggle. The marker disappeared into his robe. "Look at my Sir nipple."

She peered down and remembered to say, "Yes, Sir," just in time to avoid more discipline. Though it was upside-down from her perspective, she observed the word "SIR" written just above the poor, ailing nipple with a red halo around it. Edward writing on her with impunity made her feel even less her own and more his. But it did not feel like a loss.

"That will also serve to remind *me* what to do when you forget because I can forget too sometimes."

"Yes, Sir?" she said, not knowing if his comment warranted it.

He heard the uncertainty in her voice. "It's okay. I will not discipline you for anything you say …within reason, as long as you put the word 'Sir' in it. So in an abundance of caution, take advantage of every opportunity to respond: 'Yes, Sir.' 'No, Sir.' 'Please, Sir.' 'Thank you, Sir.' 'Permission to… do whatever, Sir?' Understood?"

"Understood, Sir."

"You have the potential to be great at this. You wouldn't be here if I didn't think you could do it."

"Thank you, Sir!" His praise was nourishment to her heart, a drink of water in a desert of self-doubt.

Continuing the lesson, he reached out, "What is this?"

"Your right breast, Sir!"

"What is this?"

"Your right shoulder, Sir!"

He surprised her when he stuck his index finger in her mouth and pinned her tongue to her lower jaw with his thumb under her chin. "What is this?"

"Yo tun, thir!" she slurred.

Edward laughed out loud causing Katrina to laugh as well while her eyes and cheeks dried. She started to double over but he grabbed her by the chain, stood her up straight, and said with dry sarcasm, "Nope! No laughing! I don't allow fun here!"

"Yeh, thir!" she said, still snickering, struggling to retain her composure and not bite Edward's finger.

Holding her by the chain and her jaw, he kissed her cheek and whispered in her ear, "The sound of your laughter is like a song to me."

"Tank ou, thir," she replied warmly, grateful for the levity.

He withdrew his finger from her mouth and dried it on her chin. Her hand rose to wipe but he blocked it. "Nope."

"Yes, Sir." Her hand returned behind her back. *I guess the spit on my chin will go with the mascara down my cheeks. ...his cheeks. ...his chin.*

"Alright. What is this?" he said, sticking his finger in her navel.

"Your… 'ombligo', Sir?"

"Belly button," he enunciated.

"Your 'belly button', Sir." The brief language lesson made her forget to think about how much she disliked that area of her body. Not to mention his hand dropping between her legs.

He felt the humid warmth of her thong, stealing her breath. The tingling returned like a flash flood. In a lower tone, he asked, "What is this?"

She thought about a Spanish word for it, inasmuch as the flood would allow her to think. *Concha? Coño?* But she settled on, "Your... your pussy? Sir?" she asked with her accent that sounded as sweet as her laughter to Edward.

"'Pussy'... works for me," he replied. "I never really thought of it as an offensive term anyway. I've always kind of liked the word."

"I agree, Sir." Though English was her second language, she never found it to be a distasteful word either. But she knew to avoid its use in the course of daily speech.

"By the way, you will watch your language in public like a lady. But here, when we are alone, there are no bad words. You may say anything as long as it is the truth. Understood?"

"Understood, Sir."

"When we're alone, we can let the expletives fly like Kramer at the dentist's office!"

"Yes... Sir?" She didn't get the reference.

"Nevermind."

"Can I ask a question, Sir?"

"This is how you ask:" He articulated: "'Permission to ask a question, Sir?'"

She repeated, "Permission to ask a question, Sir?"

"Permission granted."

"What do I call... yours, Sir?"

"I usually just call it my 'cock'. But I'm open to suggestions."

"Yes, Sir. Maybe I suggestion later, Sir."

He reached his hands down around her and grabbed her behind with both. "What is this?"

"That is your ass, Sir!" she replied, trying to maintain her balance.

"No, that's my *fine* ass!" he corrected.

"Yes, Sir!"

"Say it!"

"That's your *fine ass*, Sir!" she said with a skeptical chuckle, still unaccustomed to saying nice things about her own body.

He placed his right hand on the small of her back and his left above her crossed arms, pulling her to him so her bare chest was flush with his. "What is all of this?" he asked as he rubbed his hands around.

She pondered. "Your body, Sir?"

"Say it better."

"This is your body, Sir!"

"Yes. This is my body," he said with a hug.

"Yes, Sir," her voice softening with his.

"Say it again."

"This is your body, Sir." She sounded more convincing, and convinced, with each declaration.

As he lifted her off her feet, he said tenderly, "This is my good girl."

With her head over his shoulder, she exhaled with contentment. "This is your good girl, Sir."

He gently placed her back down and kissed her on the cheek.

...

Though Edward was not prone to thinking out loud, he vocalized his thoughts so Katrina could stay involved in the process. "We have covered position one, spatial orientation, verbal protocol… There are six positions. We probably won't get to all of them tonight. But we will get to as many as we can."

Katrina listened carefully for opportunities to contribute a "Yes, Sir" or a "Thank you, Sir".

"Let's continue with 'position two'."

"Yes, Sir."

"Position two is the same as position one from the waist up. Arms crossed, eyeline and facing is the same. But you will be on your knees."

"Yes, Sir."

"Show me what that looks like."

She started to lower herself but Edward grabbed her SIR nipple between his knuckles, lifting her back to position one. "That was an order."

"Yes, Sir!" she squealed, holding her breath, trying not to react to the pain or show frustration in herself.

He let go. "I'm about to order you to show me position two again. Think about exactly what you are going to do."

"Yes, Sir." *Address my Dom, lower to my left knee, then my right. He probably wants my knees apart…*

"Show me position two."

"Yes, Sir."

She lowered herself and looked up at Edward.

"Good girl."

"Thank you, Sir."

"Eyeline on the horizon."

"Yes, Sir."

He walked all the way around her, inspecting his subject. A foreign object like the end of a stick poked the balls of her feet. "You are going to keep my toes pointed behind you."

"Yes, Sir."

"I like those legs spread like that."

"Thank you, Sir."

Stopping in front of her: "Tits out."

"Yes, Sir."

"Now I'm about to tell you to return to position one. When you do, address me properly, maintain your eyeline, and do it faster."

"Yes, Sir." *Don't look at whatever that is in his hand.*

"Position two."

"Yes, Sir." She jumped up and almost lost her balance. A startled Edward took a quick step and put his hands on her sides in case he needed to catch her. But she recovered, still unable to identify the object in his hand on her side.

He said, with a chuckle, "Good eyeline! Good speed!"

"Thank you, Sir," she said, relieved she did not fall.

"Now, quickly but carefully, go back to position two."

"Yes, Sir." She dared to try something, dropping back down in a different manner than before.

"Good job. I like the way you did that, with both knees at the same time."

"Thank…"

"I always appreciate initiative."

She paused to make sure he was finished speaking before saying, "Thank you, Sir."

"Like position one, there is a variation on position two. We will call it 'position two, resting'."

"Yes, Sir."

"It is just like this position but you are sitting back on your feet. Show me what that looks like."

"Yes, Sir." She obeyed.

With a thin wooden rod, he tapped the inside of her thighs back and forth, saying, "Open my legs."

"Yes, Sir." *Carajo! I knew that!*

"What position is this?"

"Position two, resting, Sir."

"Go back to position two."

"Yes, Sir."

"Do not move."

"Yes, Sir."

"You know position one."

"Yes, Sir."

"And you know position one, inspection."

"Yes, Sir."

"If you had to guess, do you think you could demonstrate 'position two, inspection'?"

"I think so, Sir."

"Do it."

"Yes, Sir." Katrinas arms rose from behind her back and her fingers interlocked behind her head with elbows pulling back.

"That's my smart girl!" Edward praised.

"Thank you, Sir!"

"Show me… 'position two, resting, inspection."

"Yes, Sir." She maintained her posture from the hips up and sat back on her feet.

Edward bent down to kiss her on the forehead as he cradled a breast. "You are going to be great at this."

"Thank you, Sir!"

"Show me position two again."

She leaned forward and balanced up on her knees. He went from fondling her breast to pinching the SIR nipple harder than before. "Yes, Sir!" she said, trying not to wince.

He continued to squeeze and spoke conversationally, "It's okay. We're going to get you there. You are getting better but we are going to get you all the way. I won't let you down."

"Thank you, Sir," she said. *I won't let him down either.*

He released her nipple and said, as he massaged her breast, "To add another rule, when I give you any kind of rewarding pleasure or corrective pain… or rewarding pain, for that matter... What do you think you should say?"

"'Thank you', Sir?"

"Good. Gratitude is very important. It builds character."

"Yes, Sir."

"What kind of 'rewarding pleasure' would you like me to give you?" he asked as he continued to massage her breast.

"I... I don't know, Sir."

He watched the eyelids of his subject droop while he handled her breast. "Do you like this?"

"Yes, Sir."

"I'll ask again: What kind of pleasure would you like me to give you to reward you?"

Her lips parted in an attempt to control her breathing. She repeated, "I don't know, Sir."

"I want to give you pleasure but I want you to ask for it. So tell me, how do I reward you?"

"I like you to touch me, Sir."

"Touch you where?"

"I like you to touch my breasts, Sir."

"What do you mean? You don't *have* breasts," he stated.

"I mean, I like you to touch *your* breasts, Sir."

"That's good. I like touching my breasts too. Anything else?"

"Maybe…" she began. "I don't know, Sir."

"What about here?" He took a knee and dropped his hand directly to her undercarriage, pulled her thong to the side, and rubbed. "Does that work?" he asked as he watched her face.

Her jaw dropped as she inhaled sharply. Her eyes looked as though she went blind as her awareness retreated into her mind.

Edward knew something important was happening. He withdrew his hand and sat on one foot to look up at her on her knees. "What's going on? Where are you going?"

"I don't know, Sir," she whispered, eyes forward but face blank. The truth is, she really did not know. She just knew that the pleasure she had experienced there before always led to bad places.

"Come here," he demanded as he stood and grabbed her by the collar around her neck. As he walked, she started to stand but he held her head down and led her, crawling on her hands and knees to the front of a recliner. She didn't know if she was in trouble. But she wasn't able to think about it.

After resetting her in position two, he sat on the recliner and placed his hands on her hips at her thong. He took a moment to think about how he was going to explain a new concept to his fledgling submissive, staring between her breasts at a freckle before establishing eye contact. "Give me my eyes."

"Yes, Sir." With Katrina on her knees and Edward sitting on the edge of the chair, her eyes looked up to his, just above the level of her own.

"The pleasure of this body," he said as he placed his hand on her chest, "is as important to me, or perhaps even more important than the pleasure of this body," he said as he replaced his hand on his own chest. "I already know how to please *this* body." Referring back to her body, "But I need your help to make sure *this* body gets what it needs. And in order to do that, I need you to communicate your desires to me." He said, "There's something in you, like a wall in your mind that is blocking you from being able to do that. I want to get you through that wall."

She was struck by how apropos the illustration of this "wall" was in her situation. Were it a real object, it would be painted with graffiti depicting every person she had ever disappointed in her life and every time she was ever used or victimized. Her late husband blaming her for his own impotence; her mother's voice telling her how she didn't put enough effort into her appearance; her failure to keep her father in her life and her unworthiness of his protection; being forced to ...do things... at a time when she was too young to understand what was happening, let alone give consent. And how could she enjoy any physical pleasure whatsoever when her earliest sexual activities were used as punishments by a "relative" she was supposed to be able to trust? None of these trials and traumas were things she wanted to think about. She didn't even *want* to understand how these experiences affect her to this day. And she definitely did not want to *talk* about them now and risk scaring this man away.

Edward and Katrina shared a moment of silence. She didn't look like she was about to cry. Through her eyes, he could see she was processing something deep in her mind. He did not want to interrupt her contemplation.

Eventually, it was Katrina who spoke. "Permission to sit, Sir?"

"Permission granted. Would you like to sit on the floor or in my lap?"

She had the floor in mind, but when given the option: "In your lap, Sir."

He helped her up into his lap before pulling the lever, causing the chair to recline. She rolled on her right side on top of him and he held her with her head resting on his left shoulder and her hand on his chest. "Talk to me. Tell me why you have difficulty asking for what you want."

She was relieved she was not looking him in the eye. That made it the slightest bit easier to talk. She explained the sum total of her difficulty, employing as few words as possible, speaking slowly, putting space between each word: "I can not ask because... is not important. Is selfish."

Edward listened intently to what she was saying. He wanted to keep her talking. "Why do you think it is selfish?"

"I don't know... I... It make me feel... 'verde'," she said. "Like whore, Sir."

"Physical pleasure makes you feel like a whore," he said with the succinctness of a man.

"Yes, Sir."

"Okay. We're going to talk more about why you feel that way in the future. But for tonight, we are going to change the tune in your head. Give me my eyes," he said.

Her head pivoted on his shoulder. He placed his right hand on her cheek, assuring her undivided attention.

Speaking bluntly: "You are *my* whore." Then he articulated word for word, "You. are. *my*. private. whore."

She was conflicted, uncertain if she was supposed to like being called a "whore". But she did like it: especially being called "[*his*] private whore".

He continued, "You will have pleasure at *my* will. Your satisfaction will come only with my permission. You will not orgasm unless I order you to have one. You already know that all of your tears belong to me. And now, all of your orgasms will belong to me as well. Even if I'm not around, you will not orgasm without my permission. Your pleasure will be my pleasure. It will not be selfish because you will be enjoying pleasure in my name. Do I make myself clear?"

"Yes, Sir. Very clear, Sir."

"Are you ready to get back to work?"

"Ready, Sir!"

"No, wait. I want to hold you for a few minutes."

"Yes, Sir." Her hand moved from his chest to his side, under the robe so she could hold him too.

"Position two, resting."

Edward's voice brought her to consciousness. *Was I asleep? I don't think so. What was that?* Her body started rolling off of him before her mind knew what she was doing. "Yes, Sir."

He leaned the chair forward and sat on the edge with his hands on her shoulders. "Now tell me, what can I do to reward you?" He recounted, "Play with my breasts. What else?"

"Well," she started. "Will you please touch my pussy, Sir?"

"What pussy? You have no pussy!"

She amended with a laugh, "*Your* pussy, Sir! Will you please touch *your* pussy, Sir?!"

"Oh, MY pussy. Of course! But ask again because I like hearing you say it in that cute, sexy, accent."

She let out an exasperated sigh. "Will you please touch *your* pussy, Sir!"

"With pleasure," he said as he inched his right hand down the inside of the thong. "But not for *your* pleasure, *my* pleasure!" he clarified.

"Yes, Sir!" She was eager to see if thinking of it that way would help her put a crack in that wall.

She pushed up a little higher, helping his hand find its way to the warmth between her legs. He was impressed by how wet she was. Though *she* was a bit self-conscious about it, *he* was proud of the effect he had on her.

"That's a wet pussy!" he declared.

"Yes, Sir," she said, eyes dropping.

"Take it as a compliment."

"Yes, Sir. Thank you, Sir." *Does he think getting wet is a good thing? This man is the opposite of... every other man!*

"Remember, you ask permission to orgasm."

"Yes, Sir."

With his index and ring fingers, he parted her petals and found her clitoris with the middle. He journeyed a bit further in to get some more lubrication before he started running it back and forth, slowly at first, and gradually faster, making minor changes in the motion in accordance with her vocalizations.

Mouth open, eyes closed, and face relaxed, her breathing was shallow and rapid. It was striking how good he was at what he was doing. She breathlessly asked, or at least tried to ask, "How do you..." But her voice failed.

He continued by wrapping his left arm around her and drawing her toward him. Her grip on her own crossed arms behind her back tightened. As his finger continued pleasuring her, he reached his left hand up and grabbed her hair, pulling her head back, forcing her to thrust her breasts into him. He leaned down and took her right nipple into his mouth and used his tongue to mimic the way his finger was stimulating her clitoris, occasionally punctuating the pleasure with some pain by tweaking her nipple with his teeth or yanking her hair. Feeling her muscles contract inside, she knew she wasn't going to last much longer.

"Sir?" she whispered.

"Mmmm?" he replied, his low voice vibrating her breast.

"I..." Her panting made it impossible for her to speak.

He dropped the nipple from his mouth. "You are about to cum for me when I say. You are not cumming for yourself. You are cumming for me. Is that understood?"

"Yes... Sir."

"You will cum in 3... 2... 1... Get me that orgasm girl!" he said before taking her nipple back into his mouth and smacking and groping her butt with his left hand.

She pressed into him, moaning. Her arms uncrossed and found his shoulders for support. He released her nipple and leaned back. She started to fall onto him so he picked her up and draped her across his lap on her arching back, her head and legs spilling over the arms of the recliner. He wasn't entirely certain her short climax had reached its full potential. But he was not finished.

To Edward, this woman was a finely crafted instrument that was singing under his skillful touch as he exercised the same muscles between his fingers that he used to play guitar. Of course, he did not get as much pleasure out of the sounds of his guitar as from the sounds of her whimpers and squeals that helped him find exactly where she was in the song. He sensed her approach. With perfect timing, he growled, "Cum!"

She concentrated on the points of the most intensity: the pain of her hair being pulled back, the warmth of his mouth on her nipple, and his hand... oh that hand between her legs. She surrendered to a conquering force as the sensations overwhelmed her. But what really inspired her to sing her song, was this man who was coaxing it out of her: *forcing* it out of her. It was his desire and his effort for her pleasure that gave her two consecutive orgasms for the first time in her life.

Coming down from the peak of her ecstasy, her thighs tightened on his fingers, halting his performance. She melted onto the floor at his feet.

He rested his elbows on his knees and drank in the sight of his conquest, breasts heaving for air, making no effort to cover any part of her exposed body as though ignorant of her nakedness. Once her breathing steadied, he reached down to bring her to her knees by the collar and rested her head on his thigh, right by his turgid member. He put his finger in her mouth for her to suck the flavor of her own juices. His left hand gently stroked the cheek and hair of his pet, causing her to let out a sigh like the purr of a cat.

He reflected on the experience, taking pride in her satisfaction, noting that if he were to make her sing multiple songs in the future, or perhaps torture her with ceaseless orgasms, he would have to see to it that she not have the ability to close her legs on his hand, voluntarily or involuntarily. After a few more moments of rumination, he removed his finger from her mouth and tapped her on the ear causing her to open her eyes and sit upright. "Remember your gratitude."

"Thank you, Sir," she said with a hoarseness in her voice.

"Thank me for what?"

"Thank you for the orgasms, Sir."

"No. Let's make sure you have the right mindset about this: I didn't give you orgasms. I *made* you orgasm. I *allowed* you to orgasm… *for me.* Do you understand?"

"I think so, Sir."

"So thank me again."

She selected her words more thoughtfully, "Thank you for allowing me to orgasm…"

"For whom?" he helped.

"…for you, Sir."

"Getting better. Who did I make orgasm?"

"Me, Sir?"

"And who are you? Rather, *what* are you?" He had a couple of ideas for answers he wanted to hear to this question. But he was going to let her be creative.

She took a moment to think about her next words knowing what she was going to say. But she was not accustomed to such language: "I am your whore, Sir."

As with the word, "Sir", he liked the way her accent caused her to slightly over-accentuate the 'r' in "whoRe". "Good. Now take these elements, and formulate an appropriate statement of gratitude."

"Thank you for allowing me to orgasm for you, Sir."

"You already said that. Try again. Tell me who I made orgasm."

"Thank you for allowing your whore to orgasm… for you, Sir."

"Better. Now make it even dirtier."

After thinking for a moment, "Thank you for allowing your pussy to orgasm for you, Sir," she said a bit louder.

"I like it! Say it again!" he yelled through a smile.

"Thank you for allowing your whore pussy to orgasm for you, Sir!"

He whispered, "Good girl."

Looking into his bright, warm eyes like her reflection was on his face, she replied, "Thank you, Sir."

Her head laid back down on his lap. In the silence, she felt his member soften as he continued to brush her cheek and hair. She thought upon her words and was determined to improve and internalize the lesson. There was no way he could know what was about to happen next.

With a jolt, Katrina lifted her head, looked up at Edward with a naughty smile, and said, "Thank you for allowing your slut, whore pussy to orgasm for you… TWICE, Sir!"

A wide-eyed Edward burst into laughter and beamed with pride in both himself and the adorable monster he was creating. She buried her face between his thighs, unable to stop giggling. He enjoyed the sensation of her laughing face in his crotch that was inspiring tumescence once again. As their laughter subsided, she put her hand on his lengthening cock through his pants and asked, "Can I do for you, Sir?"

"You are already doing so much for me... But not yet. We still have work to do."

*Oh yes. There are at least six positions. And I have only learned two!*

\*   \*   \*

Observing herself in the master bathroom mirror, her face was a mess with mascara running everywhere. She did her best to clean up in the running water of the sink.

Her mind was unwittingly coming down from the clouds of the submissive bearing in which she was being immersed. This gave her the opportunity to take mental stock of the activities in which she was participating for the first time this evening. She thought about how she had never allowed a man to see her so exposed or touch her the way he had been doing all night.

*Why do I find it so easy to trust him? Is he manipulating me? Does he really enjoy the sight of me naked as much as he says?* She looked through the open door. *Why won't he let me close the door? Is he trying to make sure I don't smoke? Does he like to watch girls in the bathroom?* Just another bit of privacy that was not afforded to her as she stood naked in the mirror, save her black thong and the chain locked securely around her neck.

But he wasn't watching her as far as she could tell. His voice called from the master bedroom: "Would you like some wine?"

"Yes please... Sir," she answered as she wiped off the remainder of her makeup. She finished up and walked to the doorway to find Edward by the desk with his back to her.

"Join me!" It sounded like an invitation but she knew it was an order.

"Yes, Sir."

She walked up beside him and suddenly remembered she was naked. Trying to hide in his sight, she stared down at her crossed ankles, leaning with one arm on the tall desk and the other crossed in front, covering a breast like Botticelli's Venus.

He turned to her with a bottle and corkscrew and shook his head with disapproval. "You will never do anything to hide my body from me." He released the corkscrew, took her hand that was covering her breast, and dropped it to her side. "When in doubt, assume one of the positions."

"Yes, Sir," she said as she uncrossed her ankles and crossed her arms behind her back, eyes forward for position one. Although this position was physically taxing at long periods of time, it was comforting. It helped her regain the submissive mindset.

Of course, she knew this position, like all of the positions she was learning, was for the visual pleasure and utility of her Dominant. His staring bothered her less as the night continued. And she liked the fact that he took such pleasure at the sight of her naked body. *At least I'm not expected to stare back at him in this position. And I don't have to worry about what to do with my hands without a cigarette!*

Being a self-proclaimed oenophile, he led her through a crash course on how to present and serve wine starting with how to select the appropriate glass for the type. He told her about the number of ounces in a standard bottle, the number of ounces a glass will hold, and the number of ounces one is supposed to pour into said glass. He showed her how to analyze the color, texture, and smell before tasting, finally asking, "To what shall we drink?"

"To anything you want, Sir!"

"Nope. Don't deflect. I order you to answer. It doesn't have to be complicated. To what shall we drink?"

She thought for a moment before lifting her glass and saying, "To new experiences, Sir."

"I'll drink to that," he said as they tapped glasses.

Her eyes were fixed on her glass from the contact with his glass to her lips.

His eyes were fixed on her, observing her apparent pleasure with the taste. He knew what her next lesson would be. "Set your glass on the desk."

"Yes, Sir." She did so, keeping her eyeline on the horizon.

"You may look at me for this lesson."

"Thank you, Sir."

He was transfixed by her dark eyes for a few seconds before a deep breath and a hard blink broke his contact. "I feel like I'm going to fall in."

She wasn't sure what that meant but she liked the poetry of it.

"Here we go. Do you know how to shake hands?"

After a pause, "I think so, Sir."

"Show me."

She offered her right hand, looking at it in front of her.

He didn't move. "Don't look at your hand. Look me in the eye."

Her eyes met his again and she straightened her posture even more than before.

"That's better. Now keep this eye contact with me," he said as he took her hand with his own, locking the web of his thumb with hers before applying equal pressure from each finger around her hand. She did the same. "Squeeze my hand a little tighter."

"Yes, Sir."

"Tighter."

"Yes, Sir." She squeezed even tighter.

Edward yelled, "Ahh! Too tight!" And he withdrew and cradled his hand as though it were broken.

She covered her mouth with both hands, wide eyed, holding her breath.

Edward went silent, face burning with knitted brows. Then seeing her panicked face, he burst into laughter.

She sighed with relief and started laughing as well. "Edward! Sir!" she shouted.

He reached for the chain and pulled her to him for an embrace and another kiss on her forehead. She had forgotten she was naked again.

"Let's try again!" Edward said, rejoining her hand. "That's good. Firm but not *too* firm, good eye contact. This is how you shake hands. Not just with me but with everyone you meet in business or social settings for the rest of your life. Understood?"

"Yes, Sir." *Why don't they teach this in school? ... It's more fun learning like this anyway.*

"Now, take your glass."

She complied.

"You are going to tap glasses with me the way I just taught you to shake hands. We won't tap the glasses very hard but you will look me in the eye when we do it. Show me what that looks like."

Their glasses made contact again as did their eyes. And the eye contact endured until the sweet wine reddened their lips once more.

Edward swallowed and said, "That is how people in other countries toast. And they think Americans are rude when they don't make respectful eye contact. It's like offering a weak handshake."

"Thank you for the lesson, Sir."

"You are welcome, my charge," he said warmly.

Neither of them said anything as they enjoyed their wine. Two office chairs went unoccupied as he leaned on the desk, shifting back and forth between staring at her and losing himself in his musing. She thought about this name he called her: "charge". She wasn't sure what it meant. But his affectionate tone suggested that it was special to him... *assuming he doesn't call other girls the same thing.*

For this moment, they felt like they were having a normal date; like they were not in the middle of some kind of radical life coaching session; like they were just getting to know each other; as if she was not standing naked before him; as though he did not already know how to make her orgasm more satisfyingly than she could make herself.

She liked him in control. There was no obligation to fill the silence with any kind of small talk. She could enjoy simply being in his presence, awaiting his next command.

Halfway through his wine, Edward was the first to break the silence by thinking out loud again for Katrina's benefit: "So you learned the first position which we call 'position one'. And then you learned the second position. As you know, I affectionately refer to that position as... 'position two'." She smiled at his playfulness. He continued, "So what position do you think I should teach you next?"

"Ay, I don't know, Sir," she said with a coy smile. "Maybe you can teach to me 'position three'?"

He looked at her as though she was being ridiculous and scoffed. "No way! Are you crazy?!" his tone dripped with playful sarcasm as he shook his head. "You are *not* ready for position three."

She laughed at him.

He continued to smile but his voice came down to a more serious tone. "Actually, I'm not kidding. We are going to skip position three and go to position four first," he said as he took her glass and placed it on the desk. "But first, we are going to bring back the focus we had before our wine break. Ready?"

"Yes, Sir."

"Go stand under the bar. Position one."

"Yes, Sir." She returned to her place under the bar and thought about what it might be used for. *Am I going to learn about that thing tonight?* She heard him walk up behind her to adjust the way her arms were crossed behind her back. Then he draped his left arm over her shoulder and supported her right breast. With his right hand, he used a finger under her chin to level her head and then pointed toward the horizon, reminding her to stare miles into nothingness.

"Think of the point at which you are staring as the focus you seek. Clear your mind, breathe, and search," he said as he kissed her ear.

She let his words echo. *Clear your mind...*

He walked around in front of her. "Show me position two."

"Yes, Sir." She dropped to her knees where her face was directly in front of the button and hanging draw strings on his pajama pants. *Clear your mind... search...*

He held her face and brushed a few loose strands of hair behind her ears and let his cock touch her nose through the pants. She took a chance and broke her position, leaning forward and rubbing her face on the flannel until he started to get hard. With a hand behind her head, he pulled her even further into his crotch. "You are going to be magnificent."

"Thank you, Sir," her muffled voice replied.

He took a step back and regained his composure. Before she reestablished her eyeline, she snuck a glance to see the wooden rod was back in Edward's left hand.

Starting as though he were lecturing a class, "Position four is just like position two from the waist down. The difference is, my hands will be on the floor in front of you. So in position four, you are essentially, on all fours. Show me what that looks like."

"Yes, Sir." Her hands pushed into the floor before her. She felt her breasts hang from her body, reminding her to flex her stomach in an attempt to keep it from doing the same.

He stepped over to correct a few things about the position. With his hand under her chin, "My head will still be up and facing forward." Poking her hand with the rod, "Fingertips together and toes still pointing."

"Yes, Sir."

Edward stepped around behind her. Katrina felt one of his hands at the small of her back and the other between her legs to her pubic bone. He tilted her hips forward making her feel even more exposed from behind.

"Don't move," he said before he removed his hands.

"Yes, Sir."

"You are getting really good at remembering how to address your Dom."

"Thank you, Sir."

Edward walked over to the desk and refilled the two glasses, almost to the brim. "I haven't had to pinch my SIR nipple for a while. I'm afraid she is going to feel neglected."

"I think she is okay, Sir," she said through a smile. "But maybe you can do anyway."

"Oh, believe me. I will."

He carried the two glasses over to the recliner, placed one on the small table next to it, and brought the other back to Katrina. Turning his back to her, he sat in front of his subject who obediently remained in position four. He laid back with his head on the carpet looking up at her chin, careful not to spill the wine. "Crawl forward and get those titties in my face."

"Yes, Sir." She did so, maintaining her position on all fours, hanging her breasts over his face.

He admired the way they took a different shape as they extended from her ribs. He cupped her right breast with his right hand, played with it, jiggled it, traced the outside of the areola with his nose, and flicked it a couple times with his finger before sucking it.

The tingling between her legs returned as she tried to control her breath. It wasn't just the combination of pleasure and pain he was inflicting on this sensitive point. It was also the fact that her position and the distant stare she was practicing left her uninvolved in the administration of her sensations. Her use for his unencumbered amusement made her feel both objectified and valued. She never knew she could find a submissive status to be so stimulating, both physically and mentally. *Is a woman supposed to enjoy this so much?*

Though she dutifully kept her eyeline, she noticed she was not the only one getting aroused. The button in the front of his pants was straining to stay closed.

He lifted the glass to her lips though he couldn't see her face. She took a couple of sips, spilling a few drops down her chin to the bottom of his sternum.

"I'm sorry, Sir!" she said, panicked.

"Don't say 'sorry'."

Remembering, "Please forgive me, Sir."

"It's okay. It's probably my fault too. My view is blocked by these pretty titties!" he said with a chuckle. "Now, lick it up!"

"Yes, Sir!" she snickered. She bent her elbows to lower her head to his chest and licked the wine off of him as though she was kissing him with her whole mouth. Relishing this task, she took a little more time than she needed to get her Dominant clean. When she lifted back up, she heard Edward inhale sharply. That's when she realized she had been smothering his face in her bosoms. "Please forgive me, Sir! Do I..." She didn't know the word in English. "Do I stop you breathing?!"

He caught his breath before replying. "Yeah!" he snorted. "But now I know how I want to die!"

She shrieked with laughter at his declaration while he watched her breasts shake.

"Why don't you stop me, Sir?"

"I didn't want to risk getting a wine stain on this carpet. We're playing with fire here!"

He pulled the glass from his side, positioned it under the word "SIR", and lifted it until her whole left areola broke the surface. Withdrawing the glass, he licked and sucked the wine off her nipple.

Katrina fought to control her breathing so her chest would not interrupt his activity or interrupt the fascinating new sensation she was experiencing as a result.

After a few moments, he carefully brought the glass back down to his side and laid still. His warm breath cooled on her wet, erect nipples as he relaxed, crossing one foot over the other, aroused as ever. She couldn't tell what a motionless Edward was doing beneath her. But she reminded herself that she didn't need to know. She only needed to be.

Edward eventually broke the silence by ordering, "Position two."

"Yes, Sir." She switched positions, concentrating on her eyeline and speed.

He sat up and ordered, "Position four."

"Yes, Sir."

He stood up and turned around. As before, he grabbed Katrina by the collar and led her, crawling over in front of the recliner.

*And now he thinks I'm his dog! But is he wrong?*

He sat and positioned her on all fours so her head was to his left and her behind was to his right. "Among your many uses, you will serve as my table and footstool."

"Yes, Sir."

"How does that make you feel?"

"Good, Sir…" She wished she had given a less perfunctory answer. So she changed her answer and spoke with sincerity: "I feel honored, Sir."

"I'm pleased to hear you say that," he replied with equal sincerity, kissing the back of her shoulder. "I can't get enough of this body!" he said as his hands continued to explore her most personal parts.

She was getting accustomed to his examinations and seemed to like it more with each new position. Her head started to droop, so he corrected her with a tug on the ponytail in his left hand. He slid his right hand down her back to her butt, groping and slapping it a few times until it recouped its red hue. Now the spanking was less terrifying and more exhilarating. But it was about to go to a new level.

She felt him place the rod on her back. "Would you like a mark?"

"A 'mark', Sir?"

"Yes, a mark. On my fine ass!"

"I don't know, Sir."

"What I do, is I hit this fine ass with this dowel rod and leave a mark."

She felt him roll the rod up and down her backside and thighs. "It will hurt?"

"Oh yes," he murmured. "It will definitely hurt. The pain, I can assure you, will be exquisite."

This intrigued her. She had already been surprised by how much she liked being spanked. While she didn't believe she would truly enjoy being in pain, she wanted to try it, especially if it meant further losing herself in submission to her Dominant. "Please let me try, Sir," she said with a quaver.

"To new experiences!"

"To new experiences, Sir!"

He began with light, rapid taps on her rear with the rod up and down across both cheeks. The stick started making slapping sounds, louder and louder as Edward gradually tapped harder and harder. When he saw her toes curl in an effort to keep from squirming, he said, "When you are ready, you will say, 'Please hit me, Sir.'"

She took a deep breath. "Please hit me, Sir."

The tapping stopped... and there was silence, immediately followed by a sharp, stinging impact across her ass that sucked the breath out of her lungs with a whimpering squeal. Her vision went dark as her head dropped again. But Edward's hand quickly retrieved it from under her chin and held it steady while he pressed his lips hard against her cheek. His other hand was rubbing her backside, helping the pain subside as her eyes slowly reopened. A welt rose under his fingers as his rubbing turned to a caress.

"Now that's incredible! You just received your first mark and you are still in the proper position! You hardly moved!" He kissed her on the cheek a few more times. "What an impressive submissive!"

"Thank you, Sir!" she said, still uncertain what was happening. A few tears were welling. But it was not like before. This time, the pain was a release. It was like she had overcome an obstacle of fear. And she was experiencing a rush of endorphins that made her feel invincible!

Edward leaned toward her backside and admired his art, tracing the line with his fingers. "I think you are going to like this. I'm excited for you to see it later." He shifted back from his work and turned her face to meet his eyes. "How do you feel?"

"I feel... accomplished, Sir."

He turned her ear to his lips and whispered, "I'm so proud of you."

These words caused even more tears as her eyes rested on the horizon. A man she wanted to please was proud of her.

The line across her butt was starting to throb. But if she was honest with herself, she wanted to do it again but did not know how to ask. So she was relieved when Edward asked, "Would you like another mark?"

"Yes, Sir!"

"Request it."

"Please, Sir. Will you please give me another mark?"

"Ask better. Think about it."

"Sir, will you please give another mark on your ass?"

"What kind of ass'?"

"Sir, will you please give another mark on your *fine* ass, Sir?" she said with her lilting titter.

"It would be my honor to give you another mark on my *fine ass*! But first..." He lowered a glass of wine in front of her face. She opened her lips as he tilted the glass. Her stare deepened as the wine rolled down the back of her tongue. After taking a drink for himself: "We are going to add to the challenge. Hold... very... still."

"Yes, Sir."

He placed the glass on her spine at the bottom of her ribcage.

"Sir?" she started to protest, doubting she could balance a top-heavy wineglass on her back.

"Shhh. Silence, my charge. Eyes front."

"Yes, Sir."

She was holding as still as she could, trying not to breathe. The rapping began as before. It was light at first, then harder and louder. But this time, she let it get much more intense.

She was not enjoying this experience. In fact, she was terrified of spilling the wine. Though she had concern for her Dominant's carpet, the dread of disappointing him was paramount. *What if I fail him? Will he leave too?*

Finally, the pain became too severe for her to bear. It was time to face the inevitable. She cried, "Please hit me, Sir!" In the subsequent silence, she could almost hear every muscle in her body audibly tense in an attempt to hold still. And then… there was a sharp cracking impact accompanied by a liquid covering her back, followed by a loss of vision. Her nerves were so overloaded, she felt like she was freezing. She curled up in the fetal position, wailing into the wet floor, repeating, almost screaming, "Please forgive me, Sir! Please forgive me, Sir! Please forgive me, Sir!"

Edward reached down and grabbed her by the ponytail as before. He tried to pull her up, but she barely moved. Not wanting to pull any harder by her hair, he stood up and put his arms around her torso, picked her up and dropped her into his lap as he dropped back into the recliner. She continued to cry and repeat, "Please forgive me, Sir!"

"Shhh…" He rocked her like a baby. Her repeated words and crying became softer and softer as he rested his chin on the crown of her head. "Shhh…" he soothed. "You have nothing to be sorry for."

"Please forgive me, Sir," she whispered.

"You have nothing that needs to be forgiven."

"I fail, Sir." She sniffled. Her breathing stuttered when she inhaled.

"You did no such thing. I think you are amazing!"

She didn't believe him. Her sobbing subsided as he continued to rock her. When she began to shiver, he pulled a part of his robe over her and attempted to get as much of his skin to touch hers as possible. "I'm so cold, Sir."

"I know you are, baby. We will get you warm."

She nestled into him under his robe as far as she could as he rocked. Her breathing regulated as her body warmed. She may have fallen asleep for a few minutes before she was awakened by her own words. "Permission to clean my mess, Sir?"

"That won't be necessary," he replied.

She wasn't sure how to take that. She didn't know if he meant that he would clean it up himself, or if he meant that she was no longer worthy to be his submissive and therefore was not *allowed* to clean. Either way, she needed to figure out how to make the wet carpet her responsibility.

"Please, Sir." She started to weep again. Looking up at him through teary eyes, "I fail you. Please permit me to clean my mess, Sir."

"Oh sweetheart," he said as he held her tighter. He was appreciating what a deep impact this experience was having on her. "Are you afraid I'm disappointed in you because of the carpet?"

Unable to bring herself to a verbal response, she buried her face and began to weep again.

"My charge," he said softly in her ear. "The fact that you are here with me right now makes you one of the bravest women I have ever known. You are a *heroine* to me. I want you to be a very important part of my life. And no amount of spilled wine will change my desire to have and keep you." He lifted her head and waited for her to open her eyes. Gazing deeply into the dark tear-filled pools, he concluded, "And besides… it was ice water."

# 2

# CASINO

The drone of slot machines was sporadically punctuated by the outburst of a crowd of patrons cheering for the outcome of the roll of a ball, the toss of dice, or the turn of a card. The music of a live band playing classic rock covers pounded as she passed by a lounge. Cocktail waitresses in low-cut attire offered beverages to gamblers through row after row of tables and slots like gleaning a wheat field. Though she couldn't smell the cigarettes, she did get the occasional whiff of marijuana, making the very air in her lungs feel like a drug. The ugly, disjointed carpet pattern and the flashing lights just above her eyeline kept her head raised and her posture uncharacteristically upright as she made her way across the gaming floor, into the poker room. The atmosphere was both energizing and intimidating on this, her first time playing poker in a casino.

The cashier exchanged Katrina's money for an equal amount of poker chips. Holding a rack of chips in front with two hands, she was directed to one of the tables on the edge of the bustling room.

Observing it reminded her of the many conference tables at which she had taken a seat for arbitrations, depositions, moot courts, and other legal proceedings. Although the number of tables was great, the experiences did little to ease her initial angst every time she attended a table of mostly men, who rarely let her get a word. This anxiety was usually fleeting at a conference table. Katrina hoped that would be the case at the poker table.

As she took her seat, the dealer asked if she had a "player's card" she would like to use. Though she understood the words themselves, she did not understand what he was asking. *Shake your head. He will think you know what he's talking about. Do what the book says.*

Following the advice of a poker book she had been studying, she looked around the table at the other players in an attempt to abide by decorum. As none had their chips in racks, she thus pulled her chips out of her rack and placed them on the felt of the table.

They each held their cards differently. But none of them picked their cards up off the felt or held them in a way that would allow anyone else to see them. She acted accordingly using both hands.

Among the more obvious of her observations: with the exception of one small elderly Asian woman seated to the right of the dealer, she was the only female. She felt the eyes of the men on her from time to time. They would dart away the second she glanced in their direction. She shrugged it off as she often did. In no way did she consider herself to be a model of contemporary beauty. And she believed that the use of what little aesthetic clout she may have would be a tasteless exercise, whether in her daily life or at a poker table.

Katrina was unaware the man sitting to her left, between herself and the other woman, was searching for an excuse to talk to her from the moment she sat down. So once it was her turn to post the blind, he was all too happy to remind her the amount.

"You're the two-dollar blind," he said, trying not to sound too enthusiastic.

"Thank you," Katrina responded as she flashed a shy smile, even though she already knew of her obligation. She slid a red chip of $5 forward and asked the dealer for $3 of change. She gave the same shy smile if someone told her the amount of a previous bet or reminded her when it was her turn to act. Some of the men were eager to help her fit in. Or perhaps they were eager to help relieve her of her money. Either way, she was content to fold until she felt like she was ready to play.

The men fit into two categories: Most of them were tourists wearing t-shirts and/or a hat that displayed a sports team from their home or some type of 'Las Vegas' logo. But there were a couple of players who wore thin hooded jackets with solid colors that exhibited a small label from one of the city's casinos. The latter players were much less conversational than the former who were discussing everything from poker strategy to the daily top ten sports plays being shown on the many televisions around the room. Katrina surmised the quiet players were the professionals and the talkative players were the tourists. She decided that once acclimated, she might try playing against the tourists while avoiding the pros.

About every half hour, a new dealer approached and tapped the seated dealer on the shoulder, relieving him or her and taking their place. Though Katrina saw the dealer changes, she was not cognizant of the timing thereof. She was getting comfortable watching the other players while the minutes passed much faster than she perceived. There was a similar, more randomly timed turnover among the competitors. Players would leave the table, sometimes with a rack or more of chips, sometimes with no chips at all and their seat would soon be occupied by another player.

Katrina did not know she had been seated for a little over two hours when a tall, thin new player wearing sunglasses, a baseball shirt, and cargo shorts arrived at the table with two full racks of his own. He stood across from the dealer while a hand proceeded. As with the others, Katrina watched this man in an attempt to learn about him.

He set his racks down and reached into his back pocket for his wallet with eyes fixed on a television across the room. He pulled his player's card out and placed it on top of two of the community cards before looking back at the TV. The dealer looked at the players in the hand and shook his head with an apologetic chuckle, pushing the obscuring player's card off of the community cards toward him and continued the action.

When the hand finished, the dealer framed the winning cards and pushed the pot to the elderly Asian woman who won and tipped generously.

While this was happening, the new player picked up his player's card, replaced it in his wallet, returned his wallet to his back pocket, and sat down, still paying more attention to the TV than his surroundings. No sooner had the new player taken his seat, than the dealer asked if he would like to use his player's card as he gathered and shuffled the deck.

He took his sunglasses off to reveal his bushy furrowing eyebrows. "I just set my card down on the table!" he said, a decibel under a shout.

Looking the player in the eyebrows, the nonplussed dealer answered, "I didn't scan it. I was dealing a hand of poker at the time."

Sensing condescension from the dealer, challenging the alpha status to which he clung, the player ordered, "Call the floor!" He was determined to show the dealer who is in charge.

"Floor on three!" the dealer yelled before cutting the deck, initiating the next hand.

A moment later, the floor supervisor, wearing a gray pinstriped suit and red tie, walked up behind the dealer.

Motioning to the dismayed player, the dealer said, "This gentleman requested an audience with you."

The floor man looked at the player with attentive visage as the dealer attempted to go back to directing the action. But it was no use. The rest of the table sat in distracted silence in contrast to the noise of the other tables, still not knowing why the floor was getting involved.

"Yeah!" the player started. "I pull out my card for the dealer to scan, and he tells me he didn't run it after I already put it back in my pocket and sat down!"

Some of the tourists looked at each other with confusion, expressing how ridiculous they thought this man was being. The pros went back to the TVs or their cellphones, dismissing the antics. Katrina did not know what to think. But it was clear the hand would not resume until the angry player was pacified.

"You didn't run his card?" the floor asked the dealer.

"No, I was in the middle of a hand," the dealer replied, his tone even, and his face impassive.

"Then why did you move my card?" the eyebrows demanded.

Realizing the action would not recommence until the issue was resolved, the dealer turned his head over his shoulder to the floor supervisor. "If I may state on this gentleman's behalf," he said as though addressing a courtroom. The perturbed player leaned into the table, not knowing where the dealer was going with the following speech:

"In his defense, he probably didn't notice that there were players sitting here at this table," the dealer said, looking around at the amused faces of the jury. "And he probably didn't notice that these players were in the middle of a hand when he pulled his player's card out and placed it…" He established eye contact with the disgruntled player and articulated, "…directly on top of the community cards of the aforementioned hand in progress."

The player exhaled and went from leaning on the table to leaning back in his chair, glaring at the dealer.

With a mellow voice, the dealer concluded, "I pushed this gentleman's player's card off of the community cards, so it would not obstruct the view of the active players, whom this gentleman failed to observe. Once the hand was over, his card was no longer on the table. I asked him if he would like to use his card. He requested the floor. And now you know… *the rest of the story.*"

The dealer's speech was so dry at points and blunt at others, Katrina wasn't sure which parts were intended to be sarcastic and which were not, since she didn't understand the reason this player was upset. But she was not the only player who didn't understand this man's behavior.

The Asian woman next to the dealer pointed a crooked finger at the offending player and spoke up, "He put card on cards in hand! I win hand!"

The dealer looked over and down at her with affection in his eyes and a smile on his face with, "It's okay mom. I appreciate you but you don't need to defend me from him."

She laughed and grabbed his shoulder. They apparently had a rapport that was previously established. Unless he was adopted, this Asian woman was certainly not the mother of this white man.

The floor man turned to the player. "Is there anything you would like to add?" he asked with courtesy.

The player, jaw slack in disbelief, shook his head as he continued to scowl at the dealer.

"I'd be happy to scan that card for you at the *conclusion* of *this* hand if you wish," the dealer said with composure.

The floor man walked away once it appeared they had reached a resolution. But Katrina could see by his beady eyes that the contrarian player was scouring his brain for something he could say or do to agitate the dealer. Her read was confirmed when he pulled his player's card out and threw it at the dealer's chest right next to his name badge.

The dealer was unaffected, ignoring the player's childish action. Once the hand was over, the dealer pushed the pot and picked the player's card up out of the table bank in front of him where it landed, scanned it, and then slid it back to the child without so much as batting an eyelash.

The table remained subdued in comparison to the rest in the room. But it didn't take long for the player to start criticizing the dealer. "You're the worst dealer I've had in Las Vegas," he muttered.

"Yeah, I get that a lot!" A couple other players smiled as they enjoyed the free show.

The eyebrows continued, "I don't know how you survive on tips when you are so horrible at this."

The dealer replied as though having a friendly, casual conversation. "Well, I'm fortunate to have players here who are generous enough to sustain my lifestyle in spite of my shortcomings as a human being. But the truth is, I don't talk about my tips." Then making intense eye contact with the player, he said, "It would be rude and classless of me to discuss my income, or that of anyone else, at this table."

One of the pros said with a snicker, "Well that's an intelligently veiled 'go fuck yourself' if I ever heard one!" He tossed a chip to the dealer as a tip. Most of the table broke out in laughter, including the dealer and Katrina.

A moment later, one of the tourists lost all of his chips and slid some cash over to the dealer to exchange for chips in the table bank. The childish player complained. "Don't sell him chips! Let the chip runner get them!" he said. "Didn't they teach you in dealing school not to slow down the game?!"

Choosing not to point out the hypocrisy of the player's statement, the dealer counted out chips and snorted with a smile. "I didn't go to dealing school!" leaving the door open for the eyebrows to attempt another insult. He inhaled for his response. But before he could speak, the dealer beat him to it saying, "That's why I'm such a 'horrible' dealer!" taking the bullets out of the child's gun before he could fire.

The senior Asian woman asked the dealer, "Why you talk to him? Just ignore him!"

The dealer replied to her with the same warmth as before, "He's the most entertainment I've had all night besides you!"

She gave a hearty smoker's guffaw, revealing teeth as crooked as her fingers, eyes smiling with mirth while holding the dealer's arm at the elbow.

The rest of the players enjoyed the verbal boxing match. And they showed it through increasing gratuities to the dealer. White chips of $1 turned to red chips of $5. With every chip the dealer accepted as a tip, he tapped it twice on the edge of the table bank and placed it in his front shirt pocket saying, "Thank you very much!" Every chip was a hot coal on the head of the critic.

The discourse between the dealer and the peevish player continued. No matter what this child said, the dealer countered with a witty, professional retort as though scripted.

Even Katrina took pleasure in his sharp banter. *He would be a good attorney, arguing a case with opposing counsel or making an opening statement to a jury.* She wondered what it would be like to engage with him in a philosophical or ethical debate. But she was *not* prepared for him to make *her* the target of his frivolity.

Once ready, Katrina decided to try her voice through what she believed would be a simple, benign statement. Compelled to pay the big blind of two dollars, she pushed a red chip forward and said, "Three dollars change please."

The dealer looked up from the cards at her with a wide-eyed countenance of astonishment and asked, "Did you just do that math in your head?"

Katrina was taken aback for a second by his patronizing tone. But seeing a twinkle come to the eye of his otherwise sarcastic expression, she realized he was having fun with her. She rolled her eyes at him with a cute smile and replied, "No calculator!"

He grinned as he shuffled. "You should be a dealer!"

The eyebrows spoke up, "You'd be a hell of a lot better than him!"

The dealer gestured toward him while nodding at Katrina as if to express his agreement. She laughed and leaned back in her seat. Then she worried. *Did I laugh a little too loud? I don't care. Maybe it will show that pinché guey that I'm on the dealer's side.* She was starting to feel secure at this new table in a way to which she was unaccustomed in her daily life, perhaps thanks to the dealer.

She thought about him and about how he was the only man at the table who was talking to her but not ingratiating himself. She also took note of the fact that he was not wearing a wedding ring. *But that doesn't really mean anything in Las Vegas.*

Lost in her thoughts, she liked to think about people at their first encounter; wondering if they would be friends, wondering if they would be a significant part of each other's lives. Maybe lovers, maybe not. She remembered when she met most of her best friends and how there was no way she could know at the time how important they would be to her.

Her daydream was interrupted by the feeling of another set of eyes on her. She awoke to see the dealer staring at her with a closed-lip smile. Seeing the two cards face down in front of her, she sat up and asked, "Es my play?"

He replied, "You're pretty, but that's not why I'm looking at you."

"Sorry." She smiled and let out a light, lilty titter while she looked at her cards before folding. As she slid them forward, she examined the dealer's face and took a moment to take in the image. He stared back at her and gave a warm smile with a nice row of white teeth.

A few moments later, a large woman walked up behind the dealer and tapped him on the shoulder to take his place. By coincidence, the hand being played happened to be one in which the eyebrows lost all his chips.

The dealer pushed his chair out from the table and gave the Asian woman a gentle pat on the back while addressing all of the players, "Thank you all! You've been a wonderful audience! May you all end up!"

Both the dealer and the would-be alpha player knew the woman replacing the dealer was not known for her speed. So before the dealer stood, the eyebrows slid a couple of $100 bills in front of the bank and mumbled, "Sell me some chips before you go."

The dealer, not trying very hard to stifle his smirk, froze. He looked at the eyebrows with doe-eyes and false innocence, and said, "I wouldn't want to slow down the game."

The rest of the players erupted in laughter at this statement! The eyebrows appeared to be embarrassed and angry as though he had finally become self-aware.

Trying to be a good sport, the dealer pulled back into the table and quickly exchanged the child's cash for chips saying, "Well, since you have been so entertaining…"

As the dealer slid the chips to the eyebrows, the eyebrows asked, "What's your name?"

The dealer shrugged his shoulders and said, "I forget… Oh! Wait!" He peered down at the badge that prominently displayed his first name on his chest. "drawdE," he said.

"Your name is what?"

"drawdE," he restated. "Oh, no, wait." He took his badge, twisted it on his shirt, and tilted his head so he could see it right-side up. "Edward!" he said with surprise, as though he had just learned his own name. Some of the players laughed. He looked back at the eyebrows. "It says my name is 'Edward'."

"What's your last name?" the player sneered.

"Pokerhands, Edward Pokerhands," said the dealer, eliciting even more laughter. Katrina smiled even though she did not understand the movie reference.

"No, I want your real last name. I'm reporting you to gaming."

"Edward Pokerhands!"

"You are required by law to give me your name upon request!"

Now it was Edward who laughed. "I'm afraid there is no such law."

"He is correct. Es not a law," a voice said. Katrina was surprised to find the voice speaking was her own. But nobody heard her except Edward who gave her a wink.

"Give me your last name!" the player commanded.

Edward took his time as he stood up to his full height, with a weak smile and pitying eyes that never broke contact. He leaned slightly forward while looking down at the child and simply said, "No," before turning and walking away.

Katrina watched him exit the room. He was a handsome guy from the neck up. It was difficult to tell what any of the dealers looked like from the neck down in their baggy, unflattering casino uniforms. She wondered if she would ever see him again. She wouldn't have to wait long.

\*     \*     \*

Katrina had practically forgotten to smoke for several hours due to the distraction and excitement of this new experience. But her craving eventually beckoned her to step away as it was illegal to smoke in a poker room. She decided to take a walk outside into the warm night air of Las Vegas where she happened to find a few employees standing under a dim, amber light, including "Edward Pokerhands".

She didn't want him to see that she was a smoker. She took no pride in her addiction. But when she spotted the cigarette in Edward's hand, she felt it was safe to walk over to the four smoking dealers.

As she approached, Edward saw her out of the corner of his eye, turned his head to her and said, "Hey! I was just talking about you!"

Katrina was surprised but barely broke her stride toward the dealers. "Really?" she asked.

He shook his head. "No, not really," he said with the same close-lipped smile he had at the table. He saw that he had made her feel a little gullible when her face dropped. So he continued, "But I *was* thinking about you."

Her eyes rose back to his as her height was to his shoulders. "Sure," she said with skepticism. She stopped a step from Edward. He and the other dealers adjusted their positions to allow her into the small circle.

"No, really, I was thinking about how you kind of remind me of my poker students," he said. She gazed forward and processed his words for a couple seconds before he followed up by adding, "...and I was thinking that you are pretty."

She looked at him cynically and repeated, "Sure."

"Well, *I* think you are," he threw out as he turned his head back to the middle of the circle, not caring if she agreed. Then he turned back to her, "Would I lie to you?"

She paused to think about his question.

But she didn't get too deep in thought before he interrupted, "Of course I would lie to you! But I'm not!"

This made her laugh with the same lilt she had at the table. Edward liked the sound. He wondered if he could make her do it some more.

Once she recovered, she asked, "I remind you of students?"

"Well, it's your first time playing poker in a casino, right?"

"You know?" she asked with a slight wince. "How you know?"

"Well, for example, there's no need to ask a dealer for change. Dealer's know. And asking for it lets all the other players at the table know that you don't have much experience."

She nodded in thought.

"And the hand you won, it was evident that you did not know you actually won until I pushed the pot to you."

He was right but she had no idea how he knew. *Did I really look that clueless?*

"Ah, sorry," she said as she pondered his words, trying to decide if she should be insulted or grateful for the information. She gave him the benefit of the doubt and chose the latter.

Wanting to deflect the subject of the conversation to him, she said, "*You* know how to be at the table. Why that man was a douchebag?!"

"Yeah," Edward agreed. "He definitely smelled of vinegar, didn't he?"

She shook her head, trying to suppress a giggle, but failing.

"The truth is..." he inhaled, staring into the night with smoky eyes, using silence to build anticipation, "I murdered his father." The whole group got a kick out of Edward's false confession. And again, Katrina wondered if she laughed too much at his absurdity.

"You're funny!" She stood with her left arm crossed in front of her, propping up her right arm at the elbow as she held a cigarette by her cheek, hoping Edward would light it. But he didn't get the hint. Another dealer gave her a light. "Are you scare he will report you?"

"No, they'll never find the body," he returned. "There are a lot of holes in the desert."

"To gaming!" she said through a smile.

"Oh! No," he replied. "Do you know what happens when a dealer is reported to the Nevada Gaming Control Board?"

She shook her head as she took a drag off her cigarette.

"Same thing that happens with all government agencies: nothing at all."

All in attendance had at least a chuckle at the comment. But Edward was listening to the sound of Katrina. "I like the way you laugh."

"I like you to make me laugh," she replied. *Did I just say that?*

They proceeded as though they were all alone and there were not three other dealers standing right there, watching them cheesily flirt with each other. Edward and Katrina had the dealers', and each other's undivided attention. But Katrina focused on her cigarette to give herself relief from Edward's eyes that remained fixed on her.

"I'd like the opportunity to make you laugh some more."

"I like you to make me laugh some more." She realized she was being a coquette. *Where did that come from? Who am I?!* It was an unusual feeling for her, but she figured she was in too deep to stop now.

"How long are you in town?" Edward asked this girl, whom he thought was a tourist.

"I live here."

"What are we going to do?"

"I don't know.  Something exciting!"

"'Something exciting'," he echoed.  "I have a few ideas."

He pulled out his cellphone and asked for her name before handing it to her so she could type in her phone number.  She handed it back to him and he immediately texted: "Edward here!"  At that moment, his phone alarm rang, signaling the end of his break.

"So you know, I don't wait the requisite two or three days to contact someone I just met," he imparted.  "I'll text you later tonight to schedule something."  He clarified, "But it's not a date.  I don't date smokers."  He squared his shoulders to her.  "And I don't kiss smokers either."

"Sure!"  She giggled again and looked down at the cigarette in his hand, noticing for the first time that it was not lit.  He handed it to another dealer, the actual owner thereof, before turning and walking by her toward the door.  Now she had several questions.  Settling on one, she turned to ask, "Wait, you don't smoke…"

As he opened the door to the casino, he cut her off and said in good humor, "It's to keep players from bothering me while I'm on break!"  And he walked inside.

Katrina took a few seconds to reflect.  *So he's insulting, obnoxious, and presumptuous… but very confident… and funny!  He didn't need to smoke a cigarette to look comfortable.  He knew what to do with his hands.  …or what not to do.  How much of this was an act and how much of this is really what he is like?  And why was I acting that way with him?  How was he making me flirt with him?  What if he thinks that's what I'm really like?*

She turned back to the audience of dealers.  They all watched her as they smoked in silence.  Just loud enough for them to hear, she murmured with a pout, "I will never kiss him anyway."

# 4.2

# LABOR WEEKEND, THE THAW

"And besides... it was ice water." Edward awaited her reaction.

Katrina's face went blunt and turned back into Edward's robe. He felt her body go limp in his lap, no longer clinging to him. Her breathing stuttered when she inhaled.

To Edward's surprise, she sprung out of his lap, onto her knees, facing away from him. When she tried to stand up, he grabbed the back of the chain around her neck. Katrina immediately snapped, "NO ME TOQUES!"

Edward froze, still holding her by the collar while she choked herself trying to pull away. She grasped the combination lock in front with both hands and struggled to get to her feet. But Edward held fast. It was then she remembered: "RED!"

Edward released her forthwith and dropped back into the recliner. Katrina caught her forward fall on her hands. She tried to gather any dignity she had left as she rose to her feet, stepped over to the bed, and gathered her clothes. Holding them to her chest in a vain attempt to cover her bare body, she ran to the bathroom before she would burst into tears, trying not to look at him.

Katrina turned on the light and slammed the door behind her in blatant defiance of Edward's order to keep it open. She put her clothes on the counter between the sinks and washed her face, avoiding her image in the mirror. She hoped the voice would help her ground herself. But even her own mind was betraying her, drowning her with questions, mostly in Spanish:

*What the hell is happening to you?!*
*Who does this 'cabrón' think he is?!*
*Who does he think I am?!*
*Why did you think you could trust this man?!*
*Are you just a playing piece in a game to him?!*
*Was this his plan all along?!*
*Did he get you here to mind fuck you?!*
*Did he get you here to really fuck you?!*
*...*
*Is he going to rape you?!*

Then the voice darted back and forth with dissonant points and counterpoints too quickly to examine:

*Is this a game to him?*

*Does he think I am his plaything?*

*He called me his "whore"!*

*Because he told me to!*

*That's not what I call "free will"!*

*FUCK YOU!!!*

                    *Is it supposed to be a game?*

                    *Would he be wrong to think that?*

                    *You called yourself his "whore"!*

                    *And you did it of your own free will!*

                    *Then why did you enjoy it?!*

The internal debate continued as she put on her bra. But it seemed to take on a more consonant, Socratic tone:

*Did he think that was funny?*

                    *Maybe. He did smirk.*

    *But that was such a cruel prank!*
          *What if it was supposed to be funny?*
      *There is nothing funny about*
      *a prank like that at a time like this.*
          *What if it wasn't a prank?*
          *What if it is part of the training?*
      *Is this training that I am failing?*

The sharp tone of the voice was softening as the questions were becoming more introspective. Her breathing was slowing as she pulled her blouse down over her head.

        *What am I not understanding about this?*
          *Why did this make so much sense*
          *only moments ago?*
      *What is different now?*
          *He is as safe as he was before.*
          *Would he really hurt me on purpose?*
      *Why do I feel so hurt?*

Adjusting her blouse, she looked at the closed door and thought about the man on the other side.

*What if he is angry?*
*Will he be willing to talk to me?*
*Can I ask him questions?*
*Will he accept me questioning him?*
*Will I find answers?*
*What if I go out there and he is reasonable*
*and I look like a crazy bitch?*
*What if I am suddenly too reasonable too quickly*
*and I look like a crazy bitch?*

She stepped into her skirt and pulled it to the curve of her butt where she felt a reminder of what drove her to seek refuge in this bathroom in the first place. She took a deep breath before allowing herself to look in the mirror. The pink hue on her otherwise brown behind was punctuated by two horizontal red lines. Her eyes rose to the collar locked around her neck. Her easing pulse began to rise in tempo again, as did the questions:

*What are you going to do?*
*Why did you let him put a chain around your neck?*
*What if he doesn't let you leave?*
*What if you are trapped here?*
*You can't stay here but you can't go back home tonight.*
*Your mother will ask too many questions!*
*Why does the voice in your head sound like your mother?!*

The crescendoing sound of the blood rushing in her head was feeding her panic. The voice took an even darker tone:

*Will I ever see mamá again?*
*What if he keeps me here forever?*
*Do I need to trick him into letting me escape?*
*What if I fail?*
*What if I make him angrier?*
*What if he gets violent... or more violent?*
*Could he severely hurt me?*
*Could he rape me?!*
*Could he kill me?!*

\*           \*           \*

Edward sat in the swiveling recliner facing the door to the bathroom. He was silent but he didn't hear much sound on the other side. He wondered what was going to come out when she finally emerged. He wondered if he should knock and try to talk to her. He wondered if he should force his way in and rescue her from her own panic by holding her in a bearhug until she was calm.

Whatever was about to happen, he knew that this would be a key moment in the trajectory of their relationship... possibly leading to the end thereof.

The sink turned on and off a couple times. And that was the only sound he heard until she touched the doorknob. He put his hands on the arms of the chair and braced for impact.

Katrina opened the door with a blank affect, puffy but dry eyes staring through his feet. Her arms were crossed with shoes in one hand and an overnight bag over a shoulder. This was survival mode.

He asked with the deepest, most calming voice he could muster, "Will you talk to me?"

She sniffed and wiped the bottom of one of her eyes with her thumb before a tear had a chance to form. Referring to the chain, "Take this thing off me and I will talk."

When Edward stood, he saw her inhale through her mouth and shift her weight back to her heels. She was obviously intimidated... by his height? ...by his stature? ...by previous events? But she clenched her jaw in an attempt to hide her fear.

Edward stayed in place and spoke, drawing out each word, "If that is what you want, I will take the chain off of you whether you agree to talk to me or not."

These words fell comfortably on her ears to the point she was questioning her own reaction... or perhaps, overreaction. She didn't know what to think. Katrina wanted to believe him in spite of all the reasons she had been given not to trust anything a man says. And she couldn't think of a reason not to believe the words of *this* particular man. She nodded.

Not wanting to scare her by walking to her, he said, "Come to me."

Her tongue pressed to the roof of her mouth when she almost said *'Yes, Sir'*. She took a few steps until she stood right in front of him, still not ready to look him in the eye.

Edward leaned down, raised his hands to her throat, and began turning the combination lock clockwise. "It's confusing, isn't it?" he began with eyes fixed on the lock. "There are all kinds of conflicting emotions and beliefs. It's terrifying to give up so much control. You have experienced this loss of control before, more than once. And it was traumatic for you." He found the first number on the lock and began turning counterclockwise.

*How does he know this about me? Am I really so damaged?* Katrina took the opportunity to study his face as he focused on the lock.

"But you do not *lose* control in this lifestyle. You *give* control. There is a big difference." He found the second number and began turning clockwise again. "This time, your loss of control is consensual. And it is with someone who cares about you."

His words were taking her deeper into thought as he found the final number. He straightened his posture and was pleased to find her looking at his face. She did not avert her gaze. As their eyes shared the moment, he concluded, "I imagine the mere thought of trusting a man is scarier to you than any of the activities in which we have engaged this evening." And with that statement, he pulled open the shackle.

"Wait," she said as she dropped her shoes and lifted her hands to hold his on the lock. He froze, staring at her. She took a breath and opened her mouth. But she didn't know what to say. Her eyes begged Edward to say something. ... anything. To her relief, he heard her silent plea.

"Here's what we are going to do: I am going to take *my* chain off *your* neck. If you want to walk out the door, I will open it for you. If you want to sit and talk, we will talk. And we can talk about whether or not you want to wear this training collar some more this weekend."

By this time, Edward had somewhat assuaged Katrina of any fear she had of him raping her corpse. She wanted to stay and talk but she was afraid she would look ridiculous if she did. She was also afraid she would look ridiculous if she left.

She lowered her hands to her sides to allow him to remove the chain. The weight being lifted made her feel heavier and the cool air on the back of her bare neck made her feel more exposed.

He placed it on the corner of the bed and started toward the desk. "Water or wine?" But before she could answer, "Let's go with water for now."

"Yes, Sir," she replied out of habit, but with hesitation on the second word.

He spoke as he poured. "Don't call me that for now."

"Okay."

Edward heard the disappointment in her descending pitch.

He invited her to sit on one of the office chairs as he sat on the other. He set his glass of wine on the desk and the glass of ice water next to her. It looked exactly like the glass that was perched upon, and subsequently spilled on her back. For all she knew, it could have been the same glass. The irony was not lost on her.

And that wasn't the only thing she found to be ironic: Before Katrina said the safeword, Edward was in the lead. It was *his* responsibility to decide what would be the subject of conversation. It was *his* responsibility to determine the activities in which she would take part. It was *his* responsibility to fill the agonizing silence and inaction that now grated upon her mind. And a moment like this, one in which the two of them could do nothing but stare at each other, felt so much more comfortable before she employed the safeword. But because of that *damn safeword*, the relief of her obligation to abide by the unwritten rules of social interaction had given way to nothing but the unrelenting pressure to which she had grown accustomed in every other area of her life.

Now, the dolorous expectation to initiate a conversation pressed on her chest, cutting off her speech. It couldn't be just any words that fill the silence. Chitchat in this situation would be unacceptable. She could no longer take comfort in the simplicity of submission. *How do I get back to where I don't have to worry about what to do with my hands without a cigarette? Why haven't I thought about a cigarette for hours?*

As Katrina anguished over these thoughts, Edward was deep in thoughts of his own. He put his lips to his glass but it was his eyes that were drinking. And she looked right back at him, in the face, reminding him of what he already knew; she was no longer under his control. Perhaps she was trying to remind herself of that as well. But he saw through her feigned boldness as her hunching posture made her look like she wanted to shrink into herself.

They sat in silent tedium. Neither wanted to be the first to talk. She did not want to speak because she did not know what to say. He did not want to speak for fear it would only serve the continued establishment of his dominance over the circumstances when he knew they needed to meet on equal footing for the time being. This way, he could be assured he was not just brainwashing this woman into being a mindless automaton. He would be reassured in the mutual pleasure shared between himself and his subject. He would know their desires were aligned. But how was he to ascertain the desires of a woman who did not have the ability to say the word 'no'?

With each passing second, Edward knew he was going to have to be the one to break the silence. He thought about asking an open-ended question that would put the ball in her court; a question that would let her choose the subject of conversation. Or maybe he would give an honest verbal assessment of their situation. Honesty had never failed him in the past. But when he opened his mouth, he surprised himself by saying something that would lay all of his cards on the table:

"I'm going to lay all of my cards on the table. I'm going to try to answer questions that I think you are afraid to ask," he began. "Since you walked through the door, I have had complete control over every step we have taken from the door to these chairs. I was the first to speak. I told you to walk to me. I unlocked a chain around your neck and took it off, even when you tried to stop me. I told you how to address me… or in this case, *not* address me. I invited you to sit. I chose the drink in your hand."

She glanced at the glass.

Edward continued, "I think it is safe to say that I have controlled all of our activities this evening… except for one."

Katrina finally found the will to speak. "My ice water …freakout."

Edward nodded with his lips pressed together. Now was the time for his open-ended question: "Can you explain that to me?"

Katrina stared through his chest to think before returning: "Can *you* explain that to *me*?"

Edward allowed her to deflect his question. With lips still pressed, he shook his head. "No. I can't."

She wasn't sure if he meant he was not able, or he was unwilling to tell her about the events leading up to her "freakout".

He continued, "All I can tell you is that you knew from the night you met me, when you thought we were having a smoke together, very little about me is normal. I think I have further proven this point tonight. I think I scared you in a way that I don't claim to completely understand. And I'm not sure you understand either. But I want to understand. And I hope you will be able to tell me, if not tonight, sometime in the future, exactly what you were thinking and feeling when you 'redded out'."

She repeated the new term in her mind, *redded out*. But it didn't distract her from the fact that he had avoided telling her the purpose of the ice water… *test*, for lack of a better word.

He was right; she did not know why she redded out either. She couldn't explain it. "I don't know," she said. "I know I was 'mind fuck' before and it is like what you do now. Maybe you will help me know someday."

Edward wondered for a moment where she learned the term "mind fuck". But he let the thought pass. "Well," he said. "It's nice to hear you are envisioning a future in which we are still communicating."

"What do you mean?"

"Just a few minutes ago, I thought you were going to walk out of my life, never to be seen again."

"I freak out, Sir," she said with no hesitation on the last word. "I don't know why. I… I feel scare and I freak out. And I want to talk to the man I know. This conversation. You are that man."

"Do you understand that I am the same man you met in the casino? I am the same man you have been dating for a month. You knew the night you met me that I am assertive. I tend to control most situations when acceptable. I was controlling you long before tonight. I open doors for you. I choose our activities when you defer to me, which you do frequently. And now, you are getting to know the depth of my true self far better than almost everybody I know."

Though the word "almost" did not escape her attention, she nodded.

"Does that scare you?" he asked.

"For a minute, it scare me. But I want to know you more."

"What does that mean for tonight? What do you want to do?"

"What do *you* want to do?"

"Nope. Don't deflect. *You* have to tell *me* what *you* want to do."

"I want to stay and train, Sir." She set the overnight bag on the floor.

He slid his wineglass toward her. It had a sip remaining. "Finish that and pour me another glass."

"Yes, Sir." As she stood and turned, the few remaining drops of wine hit her tongue. The flavor was… unexpected. She was facing away from Edward so he couldn't see her eyes squint and her mouth pucker as she forced the vile liquid down her throat. *What was with that wine? Don't offend him. Act like nothing is wrong.*

"Would you like to pour yourself a glass as well?"

"Yes, Sir," she said with reluctance, pouring his wine. *Did he drug me? Do I need to get out of here?*

He took his glass from her and she poured her own. "To what shall we drink?"

"Sir?" she said after filling a tenth of her glass, far less than he had taught her. The pungent odor was already in her nostrils.

"That's all you're going to drink?" he asked.

She said nothing as she put the wine bottle back on the desk and picked up her glass. She tried not to gag at the thought of drinking more of …whatever this was.

"Would you like to drink more wine with me?"

She stood in silence with both hands and eyes on her glass.

"Sit down."

"Yes, Sir."

"Look at me."

"Yes, Sir."

He held his glass just under their shared eyeline. "Do you want to drink this wine?"

She swallowed. "No, Sir."

"What did you say?" he whispered with narrowing eyes.

Her face dropped as she shook her head.

"Did you just say 'no'?"

"Please forgive me, Sir."

"You just said 'no'," he said, astonished.

Her eyes met his again. She watched as a smile grew on his face.

"You just said 'no'!" he repeated like it was a declaration.

"Yes, Sir." Her smile matched his.

"Say it again!"

"'No, Sir'," she mumbled.

"Say it louder!"

"NO, SIR!" she said, laughing out loud.

"I'm so glad you said 'no'! I was afraid you were going to make us drink more of this cooking wine!" he said as he turned the bottle to reveal the label. "It's more vinegar than wine!"

Her eyes burned into Edward in disbelief at the revelation, but her mouth went from agape back to smiling. "You make me drink that, Sir?!"

Edward leaned back and laughed to the ceiling. Katrina couldn't resist joining him. But she did need to drink some water to clear her puckered pallet. *He just got me to say 'no' to something. I can't tell if this boy is a genius or insane!*

Once Edward caught his breath, he said, "I had to know."

"To know what, Sir?"

"If you would be telling the truth if I asked you this question:" He swallowed and asked in a serious tone, "Do you want to stay here with me?"

"Yes, Sir."

And then he asked for good measure, "Do you want to leave?"

She snickered, "No, Sir!"

"She said 'no' again!" he announced. Then his voice sobered once more. "So you understand, if we resume your training, you may say 'no' to my questions, but you may not say 'no' to my orders. Only the safewords will work. Understood?"

"Yes, Sir."

"Tell me again, what do you want to do?"

"I want to stay, Sir."

"You want to stay and do what?"

"I want to stay and train, Sir."

"Stay and train to do what?"

"I want to train to be your submissive, Sir."

"You want to be trained in the submissive arts?"

"Yes, Sir."

"Tell me that."

"I want to be trained in the submissive arts, Sir."

He yelled, "Then why are you still wearing clothes?!"

With her lilty laugh, she jumped up from the chair and began to pull her blouse over her head. But while it was covering her face, Edward stood and put both arms around her so he was hugging her while her arms were wrapped up in her blouse. He waited for her to stop squirming before he spoke through the thin fabric into her ear, "Do you remember what I told you to remember?"

*Did I forget to say "Sir"? No. Did I forget something from my training?* "I don't know, Sir."

"You are in a safe place with someone who cares about you."

"Yes, Sir."

"Say it."

"I am in a safe place with someone who cares about me."

He helped her pull the blouse off her arms and face before looking her in the eye. "You forgot that for a few minutes, didn't you?"

"Yes, Sir," she said with disappointment. "Please forgive me, Sir."

"You are not going to forget that again, are you?"

"No, Sir."

"Good girl. Now give me a hug."

Katrina jumped up and attacked Edward so fast, they both forgot she didn't give the proper verbal response to his order. As she hung from his neck, he pulled her up with his arms around her ribs and her feet off the floor. When she wrapped her legs around him, he put a hand under her butt for support.

Their heads latched over each other's shoulders. She liked his coarse stubble on her neck. He liked her wispy breath on his. The front of his robe was open so they could share the warmth of their skin. Neither wanted to let go.

From this position, Edward playfully squeezed her very tightly with more than half of his strength until she could not breathe. When she wheezed, he released the pressure on her ribcage, set her back on her feet, and listened to the sound of her recovering breath against her giggling. They stood with her hands on his shoulders and his hands on her sides.

"Position one," he ordered.

"Yes, Sir!"

His hands rose between her breasts and unhooked her bra before guiding it back. "Take this off."

"Yes, Sir." She dropped it and resumed position one.

"Hello ladies. I'm glad you could join us." He took a second to look and touch. "I was afraid I would never see my pretty titties again."

"Please forgive me, Sir."

"Listen carefully: Get the training collar and present it to me from position two."

"Yes, Sir." She was not sure exactly what he was telling her to do. She took a few hesitant steps.

"Faster!" Edward demanded as he enjoyed the view of his subject scurrying in nothing but a skirt.

"Yes, Sir!" She put a skip in her step and retrieved the collar from the corner of the bed before returning. Knowing what "position two" meant, she dropped to her knees. But now she was to "present" the chain to her Dom. Her right hand extended with the chain while her left remained behind her back, eyes up to Edward.

"Not a bad guess," he said. "When you present an object to me, be it a chain, a glass of wine, an implement... anything, you will use both hands with palms open and flat..." He waited for her to bring her left hand to her right. "...and it will be in front of your face..." She lifted her hands to the level of her face. "...and your eyes will stay on the object you are presenting. Understood?"

"Yes, Sir," she replied as she focused on the chain. She felt her mind sliding back into a submissive bearing, almost salivating over her desire to have the collar back around her neck.

"This is another variation on position two called 'position two, presentation'. Once you have assumed this position, you will kiss the object and say, 'Your chain, Sir.' Or whatever you are presenting. Understood?"

"Yes, Sir."

"Do so."

She kissed a link in the middle of the chain and said, "Your collar, Sir." But instead of looking at the collar, she looked up at Edward's face and saw the warmth in his eyes coming from his heart.

Edward decided not to correct her gaze. "What do you want me to do with this?"

"Will you please put it on my neck, Sir?"

"Around *whose neck*?"

"Around *your* neck, Sir?!"

"Ask again."

"Will you please put this collar around your neck, Sir?"

He paused before replying, "With pleasure," taking the chain from her hands.

"Pull my hair up."

"Yes, Sir." She put her hair back into the tie that was around her wrist.

He placed the chain around her neck and bent down to kiss her on the forehead as the shackle closed. The weight of the collar, the scratch of his stubble, the warmth of his lips, and the 'chlich' of the lock soothed her.

Unlike the first time he locked this collar, she was cognizant of her emotional release. And it wasn't as unsettling as before. This time, it was like slipping into a warm bath. All of her cares and responsibilities were melting from her mind. The pressure to make decisions or fulfill social obligations fell like leaves from a tree.

He pulled their original bottle of wine out from behind the computer monitor with two fresh glasses and ordered her to pour. While she did, he unzipped and stripped her of her skirt. She assisted him by doing her shimmy until she was back to wearing nothing but a black thong and the collar. As she prepared the wine, he gave her ass a slap and a grab before walking over and taking a seat in his recliner. She soon followed and presented the wine to him as trained from between his feet, on her knees, with the wineglass on her flat palms, thumbs covering the base, ending with a kiss on the rim. "Your wine, Sir."

As he took the glass, he ordered, "Don't move."

"Yes, Sir."

He enjoyed a sip of the dry fruit. Then he returned the glass to Katrina's steady hands, using her like a table. With a calm, contemplative visage, he reached out and ran the fingers of his left hand along the curve of her right breast.

She adjusted the position of her elbow and stuck her chest out, giving him better access. Passing his thumb over her nipple, he asked deeply, "How does it feel to be my cup holder? ...my cupbearer? ...my wine wench?"

Staring at the glass, she breathily replied, "I feel wonderful, Sir."

"At this moment, you have only one purpose. And that is to serve me by holding my glass."

"Yes, Sir."

"Do you know what it's doing for me just to have you on your knees before me? Just looking at you ...touching you? You are pleasing me."

"It pleases me to please you, Sir." She whispered so her voice would not shake at the revelation of what she was accomplishing. She had never been able to give a man so much pleasure with so little effort, let alone, feel cherished for it.

"That's an excellent answer, my charge. How does it feel to please me just by being here?"

"I feel awesome, Sir." She didn't even second-guess using such a common superlative in this, her second language.

"How does it feel to be my favorite plaything?"

"I feel honored, Sir."

Edward enjoyed fondling his toy a few minutes more as he sipped his wine. They both welcomed the silence. But this time, it would be Katrina who spoke first. "Permission to make a request, Sir?"

"Permission granted."

"Can I please look at your face?"

"Permission granted."

"No, Sir. I mean, can I look at your face frequently."

He pondered her words for a moment, seeking the deeper meaning she likely intended before responding. "Do you know why I have you either focus on an object or stare a mile?"

"No, Sir," she said with her eyes on the wineglass. "Concentration, Sir?"

"Go ahead and look at me while we have this conversation but stay in position."

"Yes, Sir." Her face lifted to meet his.

"It is for the purpose of teaching you a mindset that will help you filter out distractions. No matter what is going on around you, you will be able to focus on a specific task. Sometimes that task is active, like an actual physical activity. Sometimes that task is passive, like the one you are doing right now. But I am trying to help you reach a state where your mind is quiet and you are ready and able to accept new orders." He took another sip before continuing. "Frankly, you could say that I am programming you. ...or 'brainwashing' you, if you will." With a shrug, he said, "Maybe you were right when you said 'mind fuck'. But I like to think my purposes are benevolent. In a way, I am breaking you down and building you back up. And I want your lessons here to be something that you can use to benefit every part of your life whether *I* am present or not."

*Breaking down, building up... Did the ice water have something to do with it?*

"Earlier, you said you wanted to be trained to be *my submissive*. We concluded you want to be trained in the submissive arts. So I ask you, are you more interested in being trained in the art of submission, or are you interested in being my submissive?"

Her eyes dropped to the glass again while she cogitated. She already knew the answer, but she wasn't sure it was what he wanted to hear.

Before she was forced into dropping her submissive mindset by considering the most diplomatic answer, Edward bailed her out: "I will also accept 'all of the above'."

She smiled and said, "All of the above, Sir."

"I'll take it!" he said. "It's a good thing looking at your face is like looking at the sunrise on the ocean. Your eyes make me want to jump in. I like it when you look at me."

She giggled as her gaze endured.

Edward felt a flutter in his chest as he stared down at her. He studied her countenance: every line, every curve, every freckle, every wrinkle. Her doe-eyes implied an innocent but assuredly placed trust, conveying a true confidence in him. And it bolstered his confidence in himself. As long as she believed he could not let her down, he believed it as well. And for the moment, he could ignore the weight of self-doubt seated just above that flutter. It was being replaced by the weight of the responsibility he was taking on as she continually bestowed her gift of submission on him with each passing second. Edward decided at that point, he could never allow himself to fail.

"So here are your new orders: You may look at me when I am in front of you unless otherwise ordered. If I am not in front of you, stare a mile. Understood?"

"Yes, Sir!"

He took the glass from her with his right hand, reached for the collar with his left, and pulled her head onto his stomach. Her hands landed between her breasts, right on Edward's penis. She thought she made it look like an accident, but since she didn't relocate, Edward knew better. As he stroked the cheek of his pet, Katrina stroked him as though she found a pet of her own. Through his pajama pants, she charmed it. She coaxed it. And it soon rose to the occasion.

"Sir? Permission to…" She patted the material over his member. She didn't know the words.

He wryly replied, "Why, whatever do you mean, my charge?"

She snorted and tried again. "Permission to touch the cock, Sir?"

He smiled, "Consider it an order."

"Yes, Sir!"

"Pull these off," he commanded.

"Yes, Sir!" Finally! She was going to see what kind of equipment he was working with.

Once his pants were off, she rested her hands on his thighs and observed the object with which he had been teasing her all night. She was uncertain how she could compare it. In previous experiences, she had never been allowed to analyze one's manhood so intimately. Extending from a well-groomed pubis protruded even toned skin of pinkish white, save the engorged veins. The foreskin was a slightly darker hue with a purple head that had a shine, given how taut the skin was.

She allowed herself to delight in the vision of the treasure she had found, keeping the guilt of her pleasure at bay. But when she realized she was staring, she averted her gaze, blushing through her dark skin.

Noticing this, Edward pointed at it and ordered, "Eyes on the cock."

"Yes, Sir," she said with mouth half agape. She could resume staring at it without shame now that she was given no other choice.

"Watch this," he said. With no help from his hands, no strings, or aid from any other object, he flexed an internal muscle that caused his member to jump up and slap his stomach.

Edward had never heard Katrina laugh louder or harder. She braced his thighs to prevent herself from falling backwards and buried her face in the chair between his knees.

"Have you ever seen that before?!"

Through her laughter, "No, Sir!" She perked up to see Edward make it bounce rhythmically, as if to music. "Is that a trick?"

"I guess. It's my 'dancing dick trick'!"

"Can all men do that?" Edward pinched her SIR nipple. "Sir!"

"I don't really know. I always thought so but I haven't shown this to a girl who has seen anyone else do it. Put my hands on it."

"Yes, Sir."

He flexed again while she held it. Of course, her hands were stronger than his penis. But she could definitely feel it pulse.

Edward ordered, "Explore it. Get to know it."

"Yes, Sir." She lifted it up and down, side to side. She traced the veins with her fingers. She gave the shaft a light squeeze. She familiarized herself with the texture of every part, examining one ball… and then the other… and then just his sack. She held his shaft to her cheek and whispered, "I can feel your heart, Sir!"

He adored her more with each passing moment. Although he was generally modest about the size of his unit, he did like how her small hands and frame gave him an even larger appearance. And the power he felt watching his gorgeous girl on her knees, relishing every aspect of his genitals made him feel like a king as he sipped his wine.

"May I kiss it, Sir?"

"You may kiss it but do not put it in your mouth."

"Yes, Sir." She thought that was an odd order but she didn't question it. She kissed the tip to get a bit of his precum and licked her lips, tasting the mild saltiness. Using her thumbs, she spread more of it over the head.

"Ahh," he sighed. "Atta' girl." Seemingly from nowhere, Edward produced a bottle of personal lubricant with his left hand. "Present my hands."

"Yes, Sir."

He pumped a few squirts into her flat palms. She rubbed her hands together and applied it to every inch, from the head to the base, stroking it up and down with fingers interlocked. But she grazed it with a thumbnail.

"Ow! Careful!"

She froze. "I'm sorry, Sir! … Please forgive me, Sir!"

"It's okay, my charge. I'm going to teach you how to handle this cock," he said with an elevated breathing rate.

Per Edward's orders, Katrina placed her left hand around the shaft at the base, and her right hand above. To help her coordinate, he had her interlock the pinky finger of the top hand with the index finger of the bottom like she was gripping a golf club. She tightened and loosened in accordance with his instruction, stroking slowly, learning how to adjust the top hand so each finger could stimulate the head on both the upstroke and the downstroke. Finally, he perfected her technique by using her nipples to pull her closer, resting her breasts on her forearms, making them bounce in tandem with her hands.

"Stop! Stop! Sto… St… S… s…" he ordered through his escaping breath. Katrina stopped, worried she had done something to hurt him again. She gazed at his face with wide eyes. He slouched back in the chair and looked up at the ceiling. But she was relieved and her confidence was boosted when he said, "You're too good at this. You almost made me cum already ya' whore!"

"Thank you, Sir!" She giggled with a radiant smile.

"Focus on my hands. Remember what you were doing there. That's how you are going to make me cum. But I want it to last longer. I've been waiting all night for this!" His tone lowered as he warned, "I'm going to punish you if you make me cum without permission."

The threat sounded sincere. She wasn't going to test him… this time.

"Play around the head with a palm. Massage the underside with your thumbs." A smile came to his face as he corrected himself, "*My* thumbs!"

She continued with her lilty laugh, paying close attention to his every motion, every short breath, every writhe and groan, repeating moves that produced the most pleasurable effects.

"When I cum, I'm going to cum on you. Where do you want it?"

"Anywhere you want, Sir," she replied as she played.

"Nope. You're not deflecting this one either. Where do you want it?" he said with urgency.

She already knew what she wanted to say. She just had to gather the courage to say, "My mouth… *Your* mouth, Sir."

"Request it." He pumped a couple more squirts of the lube on the head.

"Will you please cum in your mouth, Sir?"

"Ask again and start stroking like you were before."

"Will you please cum in your mouth, Sir?"

"Why do you want me to cum?"

"Because it makes me happy. It pleases me to please you, Sir!"

"Keep stroking and keep talking." She did as ordered but with difficulty thinking of things to say. Edward stood up so she was stroking him right in front of her face. "If you can't think of something to say, just repeat what you are already saying. Or say it in Spanish!"

"I want to please you, Sir! I want it on me… in your mouth, Sir! Please give me your cum, Sir!" She switched between Spanish and English phrases.

She did not stop even as he grabbed her hair and yanked her head back. "Look at me while you stroke it. Keep talking. And whatever you do, do… not… stop… until I say."

"Yes, Sir! Please let me have your cum on your whore, Sir!"

He loved the way she looked up at him while she worked. How his submissive was trying so hard to please him, as though *she* wanted him to orgasm more than *he*.

"That's good!" The launch sequence had reached the end of the countdown. "Tongue out! Don't stop! Make me cum, my whore!" He grabbed another fistful of her hair to steady himself as his knees buckled. They closed their eyes. All systems were 'go'!

The initial amount hit her mouth, right on target. The remaining sugar landed on her upper lip... and on her chin... and on her neck... and between her breasts, stomach, and thighs. Though the majority of the payload landed in unexpected locations, her anticipating tongue was not disappointed.

She continued stroking as ordered until Edward said, once again: "Stop! Stop! Sto... St... S... s..." She withdrew her hands and watched as he dropped back down into the recliner to catch his breath and retrieve his wineglass.

With cum all over her hands and a streak of whitewash down her front, she found herself uncertain what to do. So she leaned forward and held Edward's throbbing member again. But this time, Edward jumped. "Whoa! Careful!"

Katrina paused, wide-eyed. After Edward explained post-orgasmic hypersensitivity to her, she asked, "Is painful, Sir?"

"It's not really 'painful'. It's just really sensitive."

Edward caught a mischievous glint in her eye as she asked coyly, "So is bad if I..." She ran her smooth palm over the tip causing Edward to shout something incoherent and instinctively slap her right cheek with his left hand. Though the slap was loud, it was washed out by Edward's shout and Katrina's laughter. She fell on the floor and he flopped back in the recliner.

The sound of Katrina laughing made Edward laugh. And Edward's infectious laughter made Katrina laugh even more! The harmonious wave grew as one would hear the other, passing the contagion back and forth. It wasn't until both of them were out of breath that the wave finally broke, leaving an indelible high-water mark in their memories.

Edward leaned forward and observed his subject lying on her back, covered in cum. He appreciated how she kept her hands off the floor so as not to get any on the carpet. "Get over here," he growled.

Before she could fully balance back on her knees, he grabbed the collar and drew her face to his. She expected another slap... perhaps a nipple pinch. But he surprised her by planting the kiss on her mouth, for which she had been longing the whole night. They both tasted a bit of his nectar as their tongues danced.

His hand moved from the chain to her ponytail. He pulled her face off of his, stood, and started quickly toward the bathroom. She struggled to keep up as he practically dragged her behind him, walking bent at the waist. He stopped in front of the mirror and yanked her head up to stand her straight. As though he were accusing her, he said, "Look at yourself! See what you did?!"

"Yes, Sir?" She observed streaks of cum from her thighs to her chin, next to a rosy slap mark on her cheek. The roughness with which he was handling her and his yelling made her worry that something was wrong.

But she was relieved when he yelled, "Good work, you sexy cum rag!"

"Thank you, Sir!"
"Do you believe you did a good job?"
"Yes, Sir?"
"You better! The proof is all over you! How does it feel to know you can make your Dom do that?"
"I feel great, Sir!"
His volume dropped as he kissed her ear. "I'm proud of you."
"Thank you, Sir."
Still holding her hair and cupping a breast, "Are you proud?"
"Yes, Sir."
"Say it."
"I am proud, Sir."
"Why are you proud?"
She paused to formulate the full sentence before saying, "I am proud I made my Dom cum, Sir."
"You made your Dom cum hard."
"Yes, Sir. I am proud I made my Dom cum hard, Sir."
"Good girl." He repeated, "I'm so proud of you."
"Thank you, Sir."

He turned and opened the sliding shower door. "Get in there." He gave her another smack on the ass as she complied. His robe hit the floor as he stepped in behind her. When she turned to face him, he clamped on to the SIR nipple like a bulldog.

She yelped, "Yes, Sir!" But Edward thought he heard a cry in her voice.
"Position one!"
"Yes, Sir!"

Edward studied the face of his subject. He was standing in front of her but she wasn't looking in his face as she had previously requested. She was looking through him, trying to hide tears in the mile-long stare.

Edward's mind went into "puzzle-solving mode". He replayed the last few statements in his mind. It didn't take him long to figure out what was going on. And he cut to it, asking a question, the answer to which he already knew: "When was the last time someone said they are proud of you?"

Just realizing she was holding her breath, she inhaled with a sniffle. "I don't know, Sir."

"Come here," he said as pulled her shoulders and rested his chin on top of her head.

She buried her face in his chest and wrapped her arms around him. And there they stood, naked, holding each other while she bawled and he rubbed her back.

It was all coming out. She didn't have to be strong and guarded with Edward. She could show vulnerability that was not met with contempt. She didn't have to be the unwavering de facto head of her household when she was with him. She didn't have to act like "one of the guys" in order to be accepted here. It was an encounter that would not end in insults and tirades about how she wasn't able to please a man. And for the first time, she could think of herself as a sexual being who was sufficient, good enough to satisfy the most important man in her life. *And we haven't even had sex yet!*

Her bawling subsided to weeping… and then… stuttered breathing… until she loosened her hold on Edward. The viscosity of the cum between them made her feel like she was peeling off of him, though she would have preferred remaining stuck. She resumed position one, sniffling with wet cheeks.

He leaned down and kissed her on both of her puffy eyes before ordering, "The thong."

"Yes, Sir!" Her enthusiasm was renewed. As she took the thong down to her ankles, her forehead bumped Edward's still partially erect penis.

Now that the sensitivity had worn off, he held her down by the ponytail and slapped her left cheek with his cock until it was as red as her right, feeling powerful and reminding her who was in control (not that she was even remotely confused about that point).

Then he pulled her up, standing her straight and demanded, "Position one!"

"Yes, Sir!"

He grabbed the collar and reached behind her to turn on the shower. The daggers of cold water on her back were a shock. Her breathing raced until she was panting with eyes wide and chest heaving. But Edward's hold on her training collar reminded her not to move. She was expected to suffer. *I will withstand the cold because that's what my Dominant wants me to do.*

Edward mercifully held his front to hers to contrast the water. Her nipples pointed into the bottom of his ribcage. His penis turned to the side at her hip. He released the collar and pulled her head forward so she could rest it on his chest as the water gradually warmed.

"Permission to make a request, Sir?"

"Permission granted."

"I need to pee, Sir."

"Good! Just in time for your next lesson!"

*Oh no. He's not into playing with urine, is he?*

"Have you ever peed in the shower?"

"No, Sir?"

"Have you ever wondered what it is like to pee standing up like a man?"

"Maybe… yeah! …Sir!" she said with a lilt at the embarrassing admission.

"Now is your chance! It's not like we are going to make a mess. We are in a shower! Here's what you are going to do: You will start peeing right here when I give the order. And when I tell you to stop, you will stop. Understood?"

"Yes, Sir," she replied, a little nervous that he wouldn't let her completely drain.

He positioned his hand. She automatically opened her legs as trained. He ordered, "Start peeing!" … … … But she couldn't. After a few seconds, he peered down toward the drain and saw clear running water.

"It is difficult, Sir. I don't know how like this." Something about the combination of standing straight up and having Edward's hand down there rendered her unable to perform her task.

"Okay, assume any position you need to try." She uncrossed her arms and put them on his shoulders, bending down a little. "Close your eyes. Think about what you need to think about. Picture what you need to picture."

She imagined herself sitting on a toilet… without a man's hand on her vagina. And before they knew it… Edward felt warmth in his hand. She opened her eyes and smiled, seeing Edward smiling back. "Okay, ready?" She nodded. He looked deep into her eyes and sent an order straight between her legs. "Stop peeing." And she stopped. "Good girl!"

"Thank you, Sir!"

"Ready to start again?"

"Yes, Sir."

"Go!" She obeyed. "Stop!"

After Edward removed his hand, they repeated the process a couple more times before he allowed her to finish.

"Good girl! Now you can say you have peed standing up!"

"I will tell everybody I know, Sir!" she replied. Edward got a kick out of that. His humor was rubbing off on her, so to speak.

"From now on, wherever you pee, you will start and stop your stream no less than three times. Do it more if you want."

"Yes, Sir."

"You know how I can make my dick dance?"

"Yes, Sir."

"I use some of the same muscles you use to start and stop your stream. You are going to start exercising those muscles as well. It makes orgasms and orgasm control way better."

"Yes, Sir."

"In fact, I am exercising those muscles right now."

*What does he mean by…* Katrina looked down and saw that Edward was peeing on her leg at that moment. She didn't feel it because it was as warm as the running water of the shower. "Thanks, Sir!" she said sarcastically. Edward laughed.

"Watch this!" he said as his penis rose to direct his stream to her stomach.

She noticed the cum that was once sticking to her body seemed to fall right off of her. She leaned down to clean as much of herself as she could before Edward ran out. *So urine is good for cleaning off semen. This is kind of weird. I have to ask:*

"Do you like to do this, Sir?"

"I've been known to pee several times a day."

"Peeing on people."

He grabbed the SIR nipple.

"Peeing on people, Sir!"

"Eh, I'm not into 'water sports' as they are called. I don't get much out of peeing on people. But I'll do it if it's something you like."

"No, Sir. I don't think it is something I like. …except to clean cum, Sir!"

From there, he used the handheld shower head to wash her. He ordered her to hold the safety bars while he sat on the bench at the end of the tub. "Have you ever used a shower head to masturbate?"

"No, Sir."

"Would you like to try?"

"Not tonight. I'm tired, Sir."

"That's fine. Water is a bad vaginal lubricant anyway."

"How do you know these things, Sir? About urine and cum and lubricant?"

"I just made it up."

He continued washing her head to toe and wasn't shy about any part. She did the same for him. If there could have been more of a bonding experience for them that night, that was it.

Both were exhausted. And for Edward, that meant one thing: "It's time to learn 'sleeping positions'!"

Katrina thought he was joking… at first.

\*            \*            \*

Edward exited the bathroom after brushing his teeth.

Katrina remained to brush her teeth, dry her hair, rub in lotion from head to toe, put on perfume, and a clean thong.

Before leaving the bathroom, she took a final gaze in the mirror. Nothing *looked* different but something had changed. She saw the same face and body she always saw. But it was different this time for reasons she could not ascertain. All she knew was, the image looking back did not bother her as much as usual. She decided not to wrap a towel around herself. *He will just make me take it off anyway.*

She exited the bathroom to find Edward lying in bed on his stomach, wearing only boxers, reading a large book by the light of a single lamp in the otherwise dark room. As she approached, "What are you reading, Sir?"

"'The Book of Job'," he replied. Without raising his head, he pointed his finger next to himself in a silent order to lie next to him.

She fulfilled his order, lying on her back. A familiar phrase associated with the title character came to mind. "Como, *'the patience of Job'*, Sir?"

"That's the one. But the book is not really about patience."

"No, Sir?"

His eyes rose from the book to a dark corner of the room to search for a thoughtful reply. "If you learn from Job's example of exercising patience …if that's what you glean from it, that's fine. There's nothing wrong with that."

"What is the book about?" she asked.

He looked her in the eye and answered with authority. "It's about the sovereignty of God. It's about the fact that God *is God* and he has the power and ability to do whatever he wants."

The parallels between this explanation and the activities in which she was taking part with Edward were not lost on Katrina. *Does he think he is a god or something? Does he think I'm supposed to worship him like he is a god? Have I been treating him like God? Is this idolatry?*

Edward interrupted her thoughts. "You haven't read 'Job'?"

Although she was familiar with the story, she couldn't remember actually reading the whole book. "I don't remember. Please read to me, Sir?" she requested as she rolled onto her side toward him.

Edward gave her a synopsis before reading parts of the last few chapters. He read God's rhetorical responses to Job about how He laid the foundations of the earth, questions about the motion of the constellations, questions about patterns of weather, and questions about the psychology of animals both living and extinct. Most were questions that no man would ever be able to answer.

Katrina's fingertips and nails glided up and down his bare back and arm. It occurred to her that Edward had trained her to do this from their first date. But she loved touching him. And the cadence of Edward's voice and the pattern she traced on his back was lulling her into a sleepless hypnotic state. Goosebumps rose on his arm under her hand.

She interrupted his reading. "Tienes frío?"

"No, I'm fine."

"Pero tienes piel de gallina."

"You are kind of tickling me and it's giving me goosebumps." She withdrew her hand and held it to her chest. "Don't stop. It feels great." Before he started reading again, he added, "If *you're* cold, get your skin touching mine."

Even though she wasn't cold, Katrina pulled closer so half of her body was lying on him. She continued exploring every detail of his skin, every line, every curve, every freckle, every wrinkle. The pleasure it brought him only seemed to enhance her own as she listened to him read. Edward's deep, mellow voice reading the ancient scripture, the traveling of her fingers, and her newfound ability to be naked with this man and feel no shame simultaneously brought about a combination of excitement and tranquility that she had never experienced before.

The final verses reminded her of something she learned in law school. "How old is this book, Sir?"

Edward turned to the beginning. "It says 'Job' was written around 2000 BC. Over four-thousand years ago. Why?"

"I like how Job put his daughters in his will with his sons, Sir."

"Is that weird?"

Katrina recalled a section in one of her law school books regarding the history of wills and trusts. "It was unusual, Sir. If Job's daughters married outside of their tribe, their property would transfer out of Job's family."

Edward hypothesized, "Maybe he was so rich, it didn't matter."

Katrina thought before responding. "Or maybe he really loved his daughters, Sir."

She felt the warmth of his stare on her face as he said, "I like your theory more."

# 3

# COURTING

A new cellphone sat on the counter by the sink playing the music of Michael Jackson. A cigarette burned in an ashtray on the open windowsill of the bathroom. Katrina was determined to make it her last one for the night before she stepped into the shower in an attempt to wash away the smell of smoke. But she was washing away more than smoke. She was washing away the stress of the day.

In the shower, she didn't have to think about school or work. She didn't have to listen to the unrelenting internal voice reminding her to worry. And the music drowned out the sound of her mother yelling from the next room. A shower was a daily refuge for Katrina. It gave her an opportunity to accomplish something without expending energy. Such methods of escape in her life were few.

With her exit came an unwelcome but familiar tensity that crept into her chest and slithered to the rest of her body and mind. The peace she was savoring was escaping with the steam on the mirror before her. She stared at the blurred image and looked away with dismay before her reflection could come into focus. Her mother's nagging voice, the vision of her rapid-puberty induced stretch marks, even her own thoughts betrayed her as the soothing water evaporated. *With stretch marks like these, you'd think my boobs would be bigger. And my ass... wait... Do white guys like big asses or little asses?*

She had made a commitment. Though she didn't feel like going through with it, she was intent on sticking to the plan. She stood naked in the mirror applying her makeup in preparation for Edward's imminent arrival.

Something felt different about seeing him for the second time. When she met him at the casino, it was a surprise. She was in a strange environment trying something new. She was playing a character; one who was sharp, flirty, and carefree. The nature of the experience was void of expectations. It didn't afford time to think about how she was perceived or what Edward thought of her. Though it had only been a few days since that first night, she had now spent plenty of time thinking about how to present herself; plenty of time worrying about what he would think once he realized she was not the lust-for-lifer that suggested she wanted to do "something exciting" on their first outing.
…

Edward walked up the two steps of the porch. He paused and listened to a shrill but muffled voice from inside cut through the sound of a passing car stereo. It was a woman rapidly yelling, probably in Spanish but it was difficult to tell.

Katrina heard the firm knock on her door. She couldn't believe Edward had the audacity to show up on time! *Oh no! Edward is at the door. I forgot, white people show up on time, even for social events! Can he hear my crazy mother shouting? I don't have my shoes on yet... or my clothes!*

After knocking, Edward heard the voice get a little quieter but it hardly broke cadence.

He had a feeling he would be waiting at the door for at least a minute... maybe ten. This gave him the opportunity to turn around and take in the ambiance.

The neighbors in the adjoining duplex were grilling in the rock garden front yard by the glow of out-of-season Christmas decorations. One man was picking a guitar. There was a pair of congas but nobody was playing them. Edward gave them an acknowledging nod, but they tried to act like they weren't watching him. Kids across the street were playing among cars. He thought they were a bit young to be out that late. But he knew he was in a different culture.

When Katrina finally opened the door, she stepped out immediately, doing her best to not look exasperated. The woman inside shouted something else in Spanish. Katrina turned back to give a quiet, calm reply before SLAMming the door, and then turned to meet Edward's stare with a smile. "Ready?"

"Absolutely!" He took her hand and placed it in the bend of his elbow as they turned to walk to his car. But before they stepped off the porch, she released him to act like she was fishing for something in her purse.

"I didn't know you come to the door," she said as she walked a step behind him. She was feeling eyes on them to which Edward paid no mind. The only thing to which Edward paid attention was Katrina, though he couldn't get a good look until he opened the passenger door for her. Her little black dress did not disappoint him.

...

The first mile down the road was silent. Edward believed he knew what was on Katrina's mind. So he said it: "That's an exuberant roommate you have there!"

"Yes, my mother. She's in town for a week. Mamá is... *exuberant*," she echoed, employing his word, trying not to let on that this was the first time she had ever used it. She understood what he meant by context.

Edward could sense the weight in her voice. He tried changing the subject. "What's your father like?"

Katrina hesitated before answering. "I don't know."

The silence ensued for another mile until they reached a stoplight. Edward's tone warmed when he took his eyes off the road to ask, "Are you okay?"

She felt his lowered timbre and eye contact convey his sincere concern. She looked at him and attempted to reply with equal warmth, "I am better."

"We don't have to talk about it if you don't want to. But I'm not good at small talk."

*Wait. Does he think something is wrong? How does he know? Am I not being fun? Be fun, Katrina!* "I mean, I am great! I want to do something exciting!"

This made Edward smile. His staring ended when the light on their faces changed from red to green, and he turned back to the road. "'Something exciting', huh?! I have just the thing," he said. "Do you want to know what it is or shall I surprise you?"

"Surprise me!" *That's it. Now he will think I like spontaneity!*

"Was that Spanish your mother was speaking?"

"Yes, she try to learn English but I think she stop."

"I've been trying to learn Spanish."

"How is Spanish to you?"

"Mm. I don't know. I don't think I will ever be as good at Spanish as I am at English."

"That's like English to me."

"But you speak so well," he complimented. "Though I hope you will never lose that sexy accent."

"Thank you." She wasn't sure how to feel about him finding the accent she struggled to shed "sexy". "I hear words I don't understand. I try to remember to learn later."

"Well, feel free to ask me if I introduce any new words to you."

"Thank you." She was glad to have the opportunity to admit her linguistic vulnerability before she embarrassed herself. "It is easy to understand you."

"You are easy to understand as well."

"I think I will be good at English when I think English."

"What do you mean?"

"When the thoughts in my head are English? Not Spanish, I will know I'm good at English."

"You have thoughts in Spanish?"

Katrina thought this was an odd inquiry. She sounded like she was asking a question with her reply. "Yes?"

"I don't think I understand."

"I'm sorry."

"It's okay. You don't need to apologize."

Katrina worried the misunderstanding was because of her. But she decided to try again. "You know when you think, you think English?"

Edward was confused. "No. Not really."

"When you think something, you don't think with words?"

"No. Do you?"

"I do what?"

"Do you think about things with words? …or a voice in your head?"

"Yes?"

"And it's in Spanish?"

"Yes. Frequently."

"Hm."

"You don't think English?"

"I don't really think about things in words."

"You do. You don't know."

Edward returned skeptically, "I'm not so sure."

"How do you think?"

"I'm not sure how to explain how my mind conceptualizes things. I guess you could say I think in concepts."

"Like pictures?"

"Kind of. I sometimes see pictures in my mind. But that's not really how my brain functions. This is something I'm going to think about and maybe I'll be able to explain to you later."

Katrina had no idea the extent to which he would actually be thinking about that. She thought it was odd how he didn't listen to music or the radio while he drove. But she did like how his focus on the road gave her a reprieve from his staring as they conversed.

"So you have lived in Las Vegas for three years and you just visited a poker room for the first time?"

"Yes?"

"What inspired this maiden voyage?"

Katrina didn't understand.

Edward clarified, "What made you want to play poker for the first time?"

"I have to learn for my work... for my bosses."

"Why is that?"

"To play in my office game. My boss say I need to know when people are lying and poker can help me learn," she said, roughly quoting Shannon.

"Well, he's right about that."

"She," Katrina corrected.

"Oh, 'she'... Do you think you learned anything?"

"I learn I don't know about... reading people... and is easy to be reading me," she said with disappointment.

"I hope you were not discouraged."

"A little. I think I maybe stop."

"You might stop? That's a bad idea."

"Why?"

"You had the same difficult experience most people have when they first start playing poker. That's normal. Besides, it sounds like you have an opportunity to know your coworkers better."

"Maybe. I'm already know my coworkers better. Maybe it help my career."

"What kind of work do you have to do in which you need to know when people are lying? FBI? Mafia?"

"No, attorney," she said through a smile. "I'm a clerk now but is my last year of law school."

"Oh! That's fascinating! I love attorneys!" Edward spoke so spiritedly Katrina couldn't tell if he was being serious or not. "You want to be an attorney for the mafia?!"

"Yes!" she replied sarcastically. "I want to be mob attorney."

"Well, you picked the right city for it! A mob attorney here can retire and become mayor!" he joked, referring to the former mayor of the city.

"I meet him," she said.

"Really?"

"Yes. I shake his hand. But I don't think he remembers."

"I don't know," he said. "You are more memorable than you think."

She dwelt on his last statement for a few seconds before she decided he meant it as a compliment. "Thank you." A moment passed before she asked him, "What do you do? Only poker?"

"I also *play* poker. And I teach poker. And I teach poker dealing. That's all I do. I play, deal, and teach poker. Nothing else."

She wasn't sure if he was kidding or not. "That's all?"

"No. But my casino friends, colleagues, and players think that's all I do. I have more than one life. But my lives rarely converge."

"What other lives?"

"I have a music life. I also like to write. And I do some… life coaching. I used to be a counselor. And I'm fairly active in my church. My poker people don't know about my music life. My music friends don't know about my poker life. Almost nobody knows about my writing life. And I try to let my church life show in all parts of my life but I don't always succeed."

"Do you hide your lives…" She didn't know how to finish the sentence. But Edward knew what she was trying to ask.

"Not on purpose. That's just how it is. But I do have a few friends here in town who know about all of my lives. And now… you are one of them."

She contemplated the new things she was learning about this man. The Spanish voice in her mind helped her take stock: *He has more than one career. He is a church guy. Mamá will like that. He plays poker. Mamá will not like that. He considers me a friend now. That's nice. But are we on a date or are we just a couple of friends getting to know each other? Maybe both? He said he doesn't date smokers. I wonder where we are going.*

"Where are we going?"

"You want me to spoil the surprise?"

"Yes, tell me!"

"The gun range, dinner, and whatever you want after that," he replied. But Katrina didn't hear a single word after "gun range".

"Wait, you say 'gun range'?"

"Yeah," he said. "Have you ever fired a gun before?"

"No. I do not." She answered with a detached, lowered monotone as her eyes sank through the dashboard.

Edward tried to conjure some enthusiasm as he pulled into the parking lot. "I'm excited for you! You get to have this experience for the first time!"

*Snap out of it, Katrina! Be fun!* "I can't wait!"

They stepped out and faced each other in front of the car. Edward was holding a case, seemingly from nowhere, in his left hand. He thought he saw some anxiety on her face, but it was difficult to tell since she avoided eye contact. "Are you okay?"

"Yes, I'm fine," she lied. "Let's shoot a gun!"

"We will be very safe. And almost as important as safety, it will be fun."

Katrina had never heard the word "fun" associated with guns before. She was terrified for reasons Edward could not ascertain. He thought she might be worried because she had never had the thrilling experience of controlling an explosion in her bare hands. But it ran deeper for reasons Katrina could not articulate.

He took her arm in his and led her through the door of the 24-hour gun shop/range. Katrina didn't remember talking to the clerk, nor Edward purchasing ammunition and targets. She didn't remember putting on eye and ear protection. She didn't remember him leading her to their lane, preparing the targets, or watching him load a handgun. She was distant, going through the motions.

Just before Edward proceeded, he looked over his left shoulder and winked at her through the safety glasses. She mustered a weak smile in return before the sound of gunfire awoke her from the fog with a jolt.

Edward discharged the full capacity of the magazine into the target, one shot after another with methodical purpose before setting the gun down on the tall bench in front of him. He turned to look at Katrina. She was no longer standing next to him, but behind him, with her back pressed against the wall with a flat affect. He stepped over to her. "Are you okay?"

*No.* "Of course!" Katrina's eyes lifted from the gun to meet Edward's. She grinned as if it were a dumb question.

"Want to try?"

*No.* "Yes! Let me try!" she said, with a little too much exuberance. *Be fun!*

Edward offered his hand. She took it, leaned off the wall, and stepped to the bench. The amalgamation of polymer and steel was alien to her in one way and horrifically familiar in another. She tried not to dwell on the resulting images flashing in her mind as her eyes affixed to the object. She felt self-conscious about her behavior. *Am I crazy to be this way? What if he thinks I am crazy? I don't care if this man thinks I'm crazy! ... Yes I do.*

Edward released her hand and picked up the gun. "Check this out: The entire time I show you this gun, I am going to keep it pointed downrange, that way. Whether a gun is loaded or unloaded, you always want to point downrange. Okay?" Katrina nodded. "I'm taking the magazine out of the gun. It's the part that holds the bullets."

Using his index finger, he explained, "This part is called the 'slide'. As you can see, it is 'locked back'. This is an obvious sign this gun is not ready to fire. And you can see there is no ammunition in it." Always keeping it pointed downrange, he held the top of the gun to his eye, looked down the ejection port, through the magazine well, at Katrina, demonstrating the gun was not loaded. He greeted, "Hello!" This got a fleeting smile from her.

"Are you ready to hold it?" She nodded. "Are you right-handed or left-handed?" She held up her right hand.

Edward showed her exactly where to put her hands on the grip, where to place *and not place* each finger, how to align the front and back sights, how to pay attention to her breathing, and how the trigger should feel. He had her pull the trigger of the unloaded gun to get used to it. The speed with which Edward was teaching distracted her from her fear. He touched it as casually as a toy, though he made certain it was always pointed in a safe direction.

Finally, he asked, "Are you ready to take a shot?" He didn't notice Katrina's lack of response as he loaded a single cartridge into the magazine and the magazine into the gun. He unlocked the slide and warned as he handed her the gun, "This gun is loaded and ready to fire. When you pull this trigger, it will fire."

Edward's last statement hit Katrina like a truck. The tool of death she held in her hands was no longer a toy, but a remote control that could turn off a living being, as she had seen before. She struggled to focus on the target with welling tears obscuring her vision.

Edward didn't notice her tears as he focused on the gun itself. "When you are ready, look through the sights, put your finger on the trigger, and slowly…"

BANG!!!

Katrina's right hand dropped with the gun onto the bench. Edward's initial excitement turned to concern when she placed both hands under her safety glasses to cover her face. He put his arm on her back and leaned toward her enough to make contact with her shoulder in case she needed him for support, physical or emotional. But she stood still, sobbing into her hands.

Edward thought he was helping her defeat a simple fear of firing a gun. But his obtuse nature finally grasped the fact that Katrina's trepidation was greater and rooted more deeply than a fear of shooting for the first time. He didn't know what to say. But he didn't feel the need to say anything at all. Through the light brushing of his hand on her back, all he wanted her to know was that he was there.

After a few moments, Katrina spoke into her hands. "I'm sorry. You think I am crazy."

Edward didn't know if it was a question or a statement. He grinned. "You don't need to worry about what I am thinking."

Katrina tried to control her stuttered breathing. He waited for her breath to find a steady pace and her eyes to glance at him before asking, "Do you want to try again?"

She did not respond.

He tried another question. "Are you ready to get out of here?"

She nodded.

Katrina thought she had ruined the night by crying. Edward thought he had ruined the night by somehow pushing her to tears. She gave an embarrassed chuckle as she looked at her smeared makeup in the vanity mirror on the passenger visor of Edward's car. She asked for tissues but all Edward could offer was a collection of napkins, both wet and dry, in the glove compartment from fast-food restaurants. "These are what I use to fix *my* makeup!"

That elicited at least a brief smile as she fished through her purse for her eyeliner, trying not to let him see her cigarettes. Edward didn't think she looked bad at all. But with regard to aesthetics, Katrina was her own worst critic. Still unsatisfied with her appearance, she decided to use the moist towelettes to take as much makeup off as possible. Then she looked at him, "Now you know."

"Now I know what?"

"Now you know me without makeup. I am very dark."

Edward didn't know if she intended the deep double meaning of what she had imparted. But now that she mentioned it, her skin tone was a shade darker without makeup. "I find dark skin very attractive. And yours is no exception."

"I don't like my skin," she disclosed as her eyes dropped back to the dashboard.

"Look at me," he ordered.

She did so.

"I don't care if you don't like your skin," he said. "I like it. And I think you are beautiful."

Katrina was struck by the intensity of his declaration. She looked away before her eyes could start tearing again. "Thank you for not being angry."

"Why would I be angry?"

"For crying."

"Hey," he said to get her eyes again. "You don't have to thank me for not getting angry at you. You can cry with me. I can handle it."

"Thank you." She wanted to say more but she didn't have enough confidence in her English to try.

Edward thought that was a weird reason to thank him. But he moved on. "Let's get some dinner." He turned off the dome light and put the car in gear.

She took a breath and looked at him, "You want to go to dinner with me?"

Katrina was surprised at Edward's reply. "Definitely! How about we start this whole night over from the beginning?"

"But, I'm not fun."

Edward didn't understand what she meant. "Just be yourself!"

"I don't know what you mean."

"It means to relax and be your normal self."

"I know… But…" She didn't know how to say what she meant. "I don't know me… I don't know how to say."

Edward wasn't sure if they were having linguistic difficulty, or if she meant she did not know herself.

"Maybe we can find out together," he suggested. "Where do you want to eat?"

"I don't know."

"What kind of food do you feel like?"

Katrina had heard this question before. She thought it was funny the first time. She knew what he meant but she seized the opportunity for some levity. "I don't feel like I am food!" she said with a smile.

It took a second for Edward to understand the joke. But once he did, he said with animation, "Well you look delicious!" That got them both laughing.

"I don't know what food."

"That's okay. Would you like me to choose?"

"Yes, please."

"Do you like Italian food?"

"Yes!"

"Let's find out if Katrina likes The Alighieri!"

\*           \*           \*

Within a few miles, the night started to turn around as Katrina became conversational again. Edward was impressed at how she was counterattacking her anxiety.

She liked the way he was treating her. She liked how he handled the craziness of her emotional outburst. She liked the way he led her on his arm, opened the door to the restaurant for her, and pulled her chair out. She liked how he stopped to pray for their meal before eating. But most of all, she liked that Edward was a rich conversationalist. She could tell he was a good listener even though she would rarely allow her eyes to meet his. *If only he would stop staring at me so much!*

He managed to make her feel comfortable enough to ask about his vocabulary. Her adoption of this second language had turned her into a bit of a linguaphile.

With some other people, she had been made to feel stupid when she heard an English word she did not understand. But Edward didn't make her feel that way when she asked him to tell her more about the word he used earlier in the evening: "conceptualize". She also commented on the fact that she learned the word "magazine" wasn't just for periodicals.

He told her a story of how one of his poker players accused him of making a mistake when he was counting some money. But when the Surveillance Department reviewed the video of his activity, he said he was "*exonerated*" when they found no fault on his part. She was excited to hear this word and talk about the moment she learned it in law school: "exonerate". And she complimented him on his proper use of this word she found so interesting.

"Thank you," Edward said graciously. Though he didn't think of it as such an unusual word, he knew she wasn't trying to be condescending. After taking another bite of his salmon, he pointed to the salt shaker. "Will you please *exonerate* the salt to me?"

Katrina lowered her fork to her plate. With the most eye contact she had made the entire night, she glared and grinned at the same time. "Oye, cabrón." Edward's head tilted to the ceiling as he leaned back in his seat. He wheezed and then spilled over with laughter. Katrina knew he was making fun of her. She tried to act like she was not amused. But she found Edward's laughter to be too infectious to resist laughing herself.

Upon his recovery, he looked at the appetizer. "You haven't touched the calamari."

"I don't like calamari."

Edward was confused. "When I asked if you wanted calamari, you said 'yes'."

*Oh no! I forgot to eat it!* "I'll eat it," she said as she reached her fork toward the dish.

"No, wait."

She froze, looking at him.

"Please don't eat it if you don't like it. I'm not angry. I'm curious," he began. "Why did you say 'yes' when I asked if I should order calamari if you don't like it?"

"I'm sorry. I don't know." Her eyes and head tilted down.

In mere seconds, Edward replayed every word of the evening back in his head. He was developing a hypothesis that he wanted to test.

"Will you please tell me? I would really like to know," he requested with sensitivity. He thought he already knew the answer. But he wanted to hear it from her.

Katrina placed her fork on her plate. "I..." She thought about her words. "I think you wanted me to eat calamari."

"Not if you don't like it."

Katrina tried another explanation that was closer to the truth. "I don't like to say 'no'."

"Hmm." Edward subtly nodded and sat upright. The events of the night began making more sense. Though he believed his expression conveyed understanding, his stare made Katrina feel like she was being analyzed.

She felt ashamed. *I shouldn't have said that. Now he is really going to think I'm crazy.*

"Will you tell me about that, why you don't like to say 'no'?"

Katrina shifted uncomfortably in her seat.

"Let me rephrase so it's not a 'yes or no' question," he said with a grin that Katrina returned. "I would like to know why you have difficulty saying 'no'. It's up to you whether or not you would like to tell me."

"I am scare," she admitted. "I am scare to say 'no' because I don't want to... hurt someone?"

"You don't want to *disappoint* someone?"

"Yes. 'Disappoint someone.'"

"Have people had bad reactions to you saying 'no' in the past?"

"Yes?"

"Like your mother?"

Her eyes dropped for a second and she shifted again. "Yes."

"Is it okay if I keep asking you questions?" Realizing he was still asking 'yes or no' questions, he made a revision to his speech. "I mean... I'm going to keep asking questions. I hope you will tell me if you want me to stop."

"Okay."

"You thanked me for not getting angry at you for crying. Does your mother get angry at you for crying?"

"Not my mother," she said. "My husband."

"You're married?" he asked with a hard blink.

"He die."

"I'm sorry to hear that." He said with a depth to his voice. "You are awfully young to be a widow."

"Can we stop talking?"

"Of course." His gaze broke and he spoke to the plate before him. "Like I said, I'm not good at small talk. But thank you for telling me so much."

"You're welcome." *That was a weird thing for him to thank me for.* Now that he was no longer staring at her, she watched him as he ate. But she could tell by his focused eyes he was deep in reflection. *He thinks I meant I don't want to talk at all.* "I don't mean to stop talking. I want to talk about another thing."

"I'll try not to obsess about it," he said with a smile.

"'Obsess'?"

"To think a lot about something. I'm going to think a lot about this conversation. I tend to obsess about things. It's how my brain processes."

"Without words?"

"Without words!"

They shared another chuckle as they continued eating.

"I wonder if you would let me help you learn to say 'no'."

Katrina looked at him.

"That is not a question. I just wonder if you would let me help you."

"How?"

"I want to ask you a question. And I want you to say 'no'."

"Okay," she said with a grin.

"Would you like some calamari?"

"No!" she said, bursting into laughter.

"There! You're cured!" Edward exclaimed as his laughter joined hers.

\*     \*     \*

Once they were finished with dinner, it was too late for a show. And Edward was astounded to find that although Katrina had lived in Las Vegas for three years, she had never toured most of the city. So they decided to take a walk down Fremont.

They started by having their picture taken with the $1,000,000 cash display at Lester's Casino. He liked the way she pressed into his side. So he turned and picked her up in his arms, literally sweeping her off her feet for another picture.

After tipping the photographer, Edward led Katrina on his arm to show her more sights. He walked her through the "Poker Hall of Fame" and "Hall of Poker Champions", telling her stories of the members to whom he had dealt or against whom he had competed. He knew the histories of the members from the modern day players to the posthumously entered inductees like "Wild Bill" Hickok and Sir Edmond Hoyle.

They walked through the cold air-curtain to the heat of Fremont Street itself, though the "roof" and lack of vehicles gave the sense they were still inside. She stopped in her tracks to look straight up, causing Edward to gently bump into her. They stood with her back to his front and with his hands on her shoulders as they watched a music video on the movie screen/canopy that spanned over the street and down more blocks than could be seen. Edward remained vigilant of pickpockets. But he mostly watched Katrina as the images of the video and zipliners danced in her eyes. Her face was like that of a child seeing snow for the first time. And her unvarnished skin changed colors to reflect the overarching cathedral of light.

After the music video, they passed by two girls dressed half like police officers with toy handcuffs, badges, and hats, and half *undressed* like strippers in their fishnet stockings, short black shorts, and undersized uniform shirts. Their shirts were unbuttoned to reveal nothing but sheriff badge/star-shaped stickers on their nipples. They offered to take their picture with the couple for a gratuity. "No, thank you ladies," Edward returned. "But it is nice to be seeing more of a police presence downtown."

As the couple walked down the busy street, Katrina looked back at the two models and thought about the new experience. She had never been with a man that did not embarrass her in front of girls whom she believed were sexier than her, which was pretty much every girl. Edward kept moving through the throng, eyes forward with Katrina in tow.

They arrived at the sparkling entrance of The West End Hotel where Edward recited the movies in which it was featured. Katrina had seen none of them. "We should make a list of movies to watch together," he said, looking up to the red neon sign. "You can't live here without at least seeing *Casino*. You'll like it. It's a chick flick."

He looked back to find Katrina was texting something on her phone. He fought his annoyance at the fact that she was ignoring him. But then she asked, "*Casino, Back to the Future II, Diamonds Are Forever*… and what?"

"*The Grand*," he restated, pleased to find she was typing the movie titles into a note on her phone.

At the Bay Gate casino, he showed her the antique slot machines on a long, tall pedestal and told her about how the earliest casinos didn't even put chairs in front of the machines. He led her by the ladies working in the table games pit and shouted through the music, "That movie, *Casino* features the guy who hired the first female dealers on The Strip."

Katrina studied the scantily clad girls taking turns dealing cards and dancing on small stages. "And look how much progress we have made," she dryly replied. Suffice it to say, Edward thought that was hilarious!

They walked next door to the Gold Rock to view the shark tank and the poker room, but started with the actual nugget of gold. Katrina read the sign under the display of the "Hand of Faith" nugget.

"What is that like," Katrina said, more as a statement than a question. She peered through the glass at the great mass of gold. "You live with your family in a trailer home and find a million dollars in the dirt."

"What would you do if you suddenly had a million dollars?" He took her hand and resumed the tour.

"I don't know," she said, then repeated, "I don't know." She was disappointed she didn't have a good answer for him. A part of her was afraid to think about it. "What do *you* do with that money?"

"Eh. There are other things I need to do before I'll have time to spend money like that."

"What do you mean?"

"There are things I need to accomplish. And I don't need money to do it."

"Like what?" she asked as they strolled across the hotel lobby.

"Like my work; all the projects I have going on. I have my first contract to write music for a video game. I want to write scores for movies someday too."

"With one-million dollars, you will not have to work."

"Yes I would. I don't work because I need money." He pushed a door open and led her along the edge of the glassy water of the swimming pool. "Even if I were a billionaire, I would have to work. I deal poker once a week because I like doing it."

"Why?"

"You could say, I have the 'Curse of Adam'. I was created to work."

"Adán? Adam? Like 'Adam and Eve'?"

"Yep. I am doomed to work the ground like Adam. I have to pursue a purpose. I have to be productive. I have to create. No amount of money will change that."

*He really understands himself. What is that like?*

"Do you ever work with any of these guys?" Edward asked.

As Katrina awoke from her contemplation of Edward's words, she realized he had led her to the shark tank. "Tiburones!"

"Yep! The 'attorney' tank!"

"Yes! I know. Sharks and attorneys!" She was proud to know what she thought was an obscure cultural joke.

"Do you know any of them?"

"Yes!" She pointed into the aquarium. "There is my professor! And there is my boss!"

"Tell me about your boss. What is she like?"

"She is very…" She tapped her head with her finger. "…inteligente?"

"'Intelligent'."

"Yes. She is my mentor. She is 'intelligent'."

"Do you like her?"

"Frequently. She is a shark."

Edward was coming to understand that when she used the word "frequently", she probably meant "usually".

…

The tour of Fremont continued. Street performers like instrumentalists, dancers, models, movie and cartoon characters, contortionists, and magicians, to name a few, occupied designated areas every twenty yards or so. Vendors hawked unique clothing and jewelry. Each block had a stage where bands were performing and energizing the crowds between semi-hourly music videos on the high ceiling above.

Katrina stopped them to watch one of the bands perform an uptempo version of a folk song she remembered from her childhood, "Cielito Lindo". As the music played, she looked up at Edward's face from the side. He looked like he was thinking about something. They resumed their journey at the conclusion of the song.

"What do you think about that band?" Katrina asked.

"They are very talented."

"Can you play on that stage?"

"I have before."

"En verdad? Really?!"

"Yeah," he said, a little surprised that she was surprised.

"You must be talent too."

With a tilt of his head, "Eh, I'm not bad. But I learned the hard way that talent doesn't get you very far. That band up there is more talented than half of the most famous musicians in the world."

"Why are they not famous?"

"If I knew, *I* would be famous!"

"Why do you play music?"

"You mean, 'why am I a musician'?"

"Yes."

"I believe music is the language of God. I believe He used music to create the universe. I've been trying to learn that language all my life. In terms of adopting it as a career, I think it fits my personality. I practically gave my childhood to practice so I could live like a kid the rest of my life! I guess that's where I get my gift for delayed gratification."

…

The couple stopped to watch Dyno Staats, a well-known local magician. Edward volunteered a $20 bill for a trick when requested. After Edward signed it, Dyno made it disappear and then reappear later in the middle of a lemon, signature and all. When he offered it back, Edward waved it off saying, "It's yours!" The dozen people who had gathered applauded Edward's generosity. He turned to them and announced, "I hope you all realize you are witnessing a true master of his craft. Please, everybody tip this man!"

As they walked away, Edward informed Katrina of his personal motto for the town. "A.B.T." he said. "Always be tipping! It's very important in Las Vegas."

Katrina wanted to stop to listen to Clyde W. perform a Michael Jackson song on the steel pan drums. He was an elderly man from Trinidad and Tobago with a long white beard through which a smile was always on display. Edward tried to give her a few dollars to tip him. But she insisted on tipping with her own money. "Good girl," Edward encouraged when she returned to his arm.

*"Good girl"? Isn't that what English speakers say to dogs? Why does that not bother me?* She held his elbow to the side of her breast. Whether it was intentional or subconscious, he wasn't going to complain.

"Some of the people here are on par with the best performers in the world," he explained. "But they are doomed to toil in obscurity for tips on the street."

"Is that good money?"

"Sometimes. I hear it can be good. I've never been a street musician. When I'm not making money playing music, I make money playing poker and vice versa."

"It is your job to 'play'!"

"To 'play'?"

"You say 'play music' and 'play poker'."

"You could say that."

"Those words are different in Spanish. You *'toca* música' y *'juega* poker'."

"That's interesting. Do they mean different things?"

"A little. 'Toca' is more professional, more serious."

"I *toco* música y *juego* poker."

"Perfecto!" she said. "How you know to conjugate verbs?"

Edward shrugged. "I guess I have a talent for conjugation."

…

They were greeted at Cargo Park by the giant dancing mechanical mantis, a curious sight to behold. Katrina stepped to the fence to read a sign about the history of the monstrosity. But before she could finish, the antennae of the beast exploded into two columns of flame shooting into the night sky. She would have fallen to the ground had Edward not caught her. He laughed maniacally at her shock as he pulled her over to a bench for them to sit. With her hand over her heart, she laughed with Edward as she caught her breath. On that bench, they watched the mantis as it shot flames and rocked back and forth to the rhythm of pop music. They felt the heat of the fire from almost fifty feet away!

After the song ended, they were still looking to the sky. Edward pointed out a constellation, a few named stars, and a couple planets. *This guy knows something about everything!*

"How do you know this, about stars?" she asked as they entered the park.

"I made it up!"

"You lie? You say you don't lie!"

"I didn't make it up. It's just… sometimes I think I come off like a know-it-all when I catch myself lecturing outside of a classroom. So I joke that I 'made it up'! I didn't lie."

"You say you lie the night we meet."

"About what?"

"About you think I am pretty."

"That was a joke. I mean, I was joking about *lying* to you. I *do* think you're pretty. That is definitely not a lie."

"Thank you." She noticed how it was easier to talk to him walking side-by-side rather than face-to-face. "I do not lie to you too."

"I appreciate that but you have already lied to me."

"When? … Yes! The gun range. But when?"

"I don't tell people when I know they are lying to me."

"Why not?"

"Because it will make them better at lying to me."

"Please tell me. When do I lie? I don't know."

"Is your mother really in town just for the week?"

Her chin dropped a half inch. "No. We live together."

"Thank you for telling me the truth."

"How you know?"

"I'm not going to tell you. There's a poker lesson for you; If someone lies to you, you don't tell them."

"Why not?"

"You let them keep lying. It will help you understand them better so you can take their money. If you tell them you know they are lying, it will make them better at lying to you. Do you want to be better at lying to me?"

"No."

"Good. Cause I won't teach you how to lie. …except at the poker table!"

"Okay."

"Life is easier when you don't lie. I understand the temptation to lie. From my poker experience, I know how fun it can be to lie! I know how it can make some things easier in the short term. But it makes life easier in the long term to tell the truth."

At the other end of the park, they played checkers on an oversized board with giant pieces. They learned in the middle of the game that they had grown up playing by different rules. So after a brief, lighthearted argument, they compromised. They took back a few moves before continuing to play by Katrina's rules… but Edward still won.

…

Walking back to the western end of Fremont, Katrina saw things she had not observed on their way east. A version of the neon cowboy town mascot, "Vegas Vic" welcomed them on every block as the lights of each establishment became brighter and brighter; bright enough to make them forget it was the middle of the night.

As they walked into the El Hernan Casino, Edward asked, "Do you know what 'El Hernan' means in English?"

The answer to the question was so obvious to Katrina, she doubted herself. "I don't know."

"It means, '*The* Hernan'!" he enunciated as though he were sharing a piece of Earth-shattering knowledge with her.

"I know that!" she said as she pulled on his arm, laughing.

They played the old-fashioned coin-operated slot machines. It was Katrina's first time. They put a quarter in just to say they did. But they won three dollars and immediately cashed out.

Exiting the building, Edward said, "Now if you *never* play another slot machine for your entire life, you can say you are 'up on slots'!"

They played a few hands of video poker on the 6/9 machines at The Quad Kings, losing twenty dollars but getting free drinks (tipping the cocktail waitress, of course).

"Do you always win when you play poker?"

"No. I lost last night."

"You lose money?"

"Yes, sometimes."

"Como? How?"

"No single thing happened. It was a combination." Edward watched the ground before them as they walked. "I got unlucky a few times and I made a couple mistakes."

"You make mistakes?"

"Yes. … Why is that strange to you?"

"My husband like to gamble. But he never tell me when he lose. He lie. My mother too."

"I told you, life is easier when you don't lie. But it might be more accurate to say, 'life is easier when you live in such a way that you don't have to lie'."

*He just told me that he lost money gambling. I've never heard a gambling addict admit a loss. Maybe he is not an addict. Am I starting to believe him? Maybe he really does not lie. He is certainly passionate about the truth.*

…

They ended their Fremont experience where it began by picking up two copies of their $1,000,000 souvenir photos from Lester's. As Edward was lifting Katrina in the photo, the skilled photographer captured their images before they were ready, rendering their smiles all the more genuine. Edward could almost hear her lilty laughter coming from the photo.

Edward led Katrina on his arm through the parking garage and opened the passenger door for her. After he settled into the driver's seat and pulled out onto the road, she placed her arm back in his at the elbow. He placed his right hand above her knee and she placed her right on top of his.

"Talk about that guy," she said.

"What guy?"

"That guy at the poker table. The douchebag."

Edward chuckled. "Oh yeah! What do you want to know?"

"Why he was angry? Not because you kill his father!"

"I really have no idea why he was angry. Maybe an inferiority complex? I think he wanted to try to somehow control the table."

"But you control the table."

"That's correct. That's my job," he said. "Don't get me wrong. I don't care if someone wants to control the conversation or control the pace of the game. But I don't allow people to be rude to me or other players."

"How you do that? Control the table?"

"I've been doing this a long time. Not just in poker. I control classrooms. I control music ensembles and bands when I play drums. I tend to control most situations when I think it's appropriate. I learned how to be assertive at an early age."

Katrina thought about the events of the evening. "You control everything tonight with me."

"I let you make up new rules to checkers!" he pointed out, reigniting the playful argument.

"Those are the rules!" she insisted. "I do not make them up!"

Edward returned to the subject. "I tried to give you choices but you wanted me to decide everything."

"I'm sorry."

"You don't have to apologize for that. I know a lot of girls who find it relaxing to let a man make decisions."

'...*a lot of girls...*' *Nevermind.* "I like it with you," she said as she leaned a little closer. "I frequently don't like it. But I like it with you."

"Do other people try to control you?"

"Other people control me. But they should not control me."

"Is that something you want to change?"

"Yes?"

"What is it that you want to change?"

"I want to control."

"What do you want to control?"

"I want to control me. ...my life."

"That sounds like it might be a good goal, for you to learn."

Katrina sat in thought, not speaking. *I wonder if he knows what I mean. I know I have to let some people control me. But I shouldn't allow others to do so. Maybe we can talk about it more when my English is better.*

"Are there any other goals you might have?"

"I don't know."

"Think about it. That might be a good way for us to get to know Katrina."

Katrina leaned back in the seat. She was slipping deeper into introspection until she shuddered from uncovering an intrusive thought. *Don't think about that, Katrina. Now is not the time. It will make you cry again.* But that only made it worse. *I wish I could listen to music. Why doesn't he listen to music when he drives? Wait! That's it! Maybe I can get him to turn on the radio. ...or at least continue the conversation so I don't think about that day!*

"Why do you not listen to music when you drive?"

"That's a good question. ... There is probably more than one reason," Edward began. "Right now, I have a hot chick sitting in my passenger seat and I wouldn't be able to listen to her or pay attention if music was playing."

He pulled his hand up her thigh. Her fingertips started gliding up and down his arm to his delight. He said, "You can do that to any part of my body as long as you want." At that, she explored both sides of his arm from his hand to his short sleeve.

"You can't talk and hear music?"

"Not well."

"Why not?"

"I don't think I listen to music the same way as most people. I concentrate on it. I analyze it to understand what the composer is trying to tell me."

"Does it make you drive dangerous?"

"I don't think so. I enjoy driving. And when I drive, I like to clear my mind. ...think about nothing."

"What do you mean?"

"About what?"

"You think about *nothing*?"

"Sometimes. ...frequently."

"How do you think about nothing?"

"I don't know. I think I just reflect on my day, resolve any issues that bother me. And soon I'm not thinking about anything but the road ahead. I guess my mind is at peace."

"Yes, but... You have to think about *something*."

"I am thinking about this conversation right now, but I actually *can* think about nothing. Most men can do that."

Edward didn't get Katrina's hint she wanted him to turn on the radio. But she had forgotten why she wanted him to turn it on in the first place.

"I have to listen to music all the time."

"Why?"

"It help me. I study better."

"It doesn't distract you?"

"It distract to not have music."

"How?"

"I think of other things when I don't have music."

"Like what?"

Katrina bristled at the question. Now she was being reminded of what she didn't want to think about. "I don't know," she murmured. "What does music make you think?

"Why do you do that?"

"What?"

"You change the subject when we talk about the way you think."

Katrina said nothing. She knew she had that tendency.

"I can't make you talk about it. But you did say you want to understand yourself better. And it's like we get close to learning something about you and then we hit this wall. And you don't want to talk about it. Do you notice that?"

"Yes. I do that."

"Don't tell me what it is, but do you know what you are trying to avoid talking about?"

"It is a lot of things. But I don't like to think about it."

"Why not?"

"I don't know," she said with the slightest bit of annoyance.

"I think that sounds like something you should explore," he persisted. "I would do it with you if you would allow."

"Como? How?"

"I wonder what would happen if you spent some time *not* listening to music and not doing anything to distract yourself. I wonder what things your mind would conjure. Maybe silence would help you understand yourself better. It might be scary. But that would be a brave thing to do."

Edward's last words repeated in Katrina's mind. She wanted to be brave. And a part of her wanted to be brave specifically for this man. She thought about how this would be a good time to talk about it. Edward's eyes on the road would mean she would not have to endure his staring as she spoke. "I will tell you something that scare me."

"I would like that."

"I don't feel like what I am."

"What do you mean?"

"I am a clerk for a big law firm. But I am not supposed to be."

"Why not?"

"You know you must have a degree to take the LSAT to go to law school."

"Yes."

"I went to college for a degree in Spanish."

"Yes."

"I already know Spanish before college. Is like I ...engañada." She used her phone to find the right word. "Is like I cheated."

"And now you don't feel like you should have the degree?"

"The degree, the law school, the law firm."

"How is getting into the firm cheating?"

"I think they want a Latina for some clients. ...to speak Spanish."

"I understand. That bothers you because you think it's cheating?"

"Yes."

"I don't think it's cheating at all. You are Hispanic and Spanish is your first language. I think you are exploiting an advantage you had from birth. I don't see a problem with that."

Katrina wasn't convinced. "I don't know."

"Seriously. You didn't cheat on anything. It was a smart move. Everybody has an advantage of one kind or another in life. We all exploit those advantages. That's what you did. I don't think there's anything wrong with that."

Katrina still wasn't comfortable with herself. But Edward did have her thinking about it in a different way.

She leaned on him. "Is like my first time to see Las Vegas tonight."

"Watching you experience it made me feel the same way." He gave her thigh a light squeeze and ran his thumb over her smooth kneecap saying, "I like touching you."

"I like touching you," she echoed.

The rest of the ride to Katrina's home was as silent as the ride from her home. But it wasn't awkward. It was feeling like a "date". It no longer bothered her that the radio wasn't playing as she continued to caress Edward's arm.

He opened his door and the dome light illuminated. She awoke as from a dream and looked out the window to find they were in front of her house with her neighbors still in the yard.

She sat up and asked, "Wait, what do you do?"

"I'm walking you to your door."

"No. No!" she yelped. "Is okay!" She grabbed her purse off the floor and was out of the car before Edward could finish his sentence.

"It's not a problem. Just let me walk you to…"

SLAM!!!

# 4.3

# LABOR WEEKEND, END

Yawning, Edward closed the large book with a thump and placed it in the top drawer of the nightstand. He rolled over to face Katrina. "Are you ready for the most intense, hardcore sleeping ever?!"

Katrina was learning to sense the sarcasm in his voice. She replied reticently, "I think so, Sir. Do I wear this collar while we sleep?"

"Is that a serious question?"

"No, Sir."

"I don't 'juega'. I 'toco'."

The lamp turned off as though by his will alone. Her eyes could not penetrate the darkness. But she could feel his arm extend across her hips and she could hear his voice.

"The most important thing to do right now is sleep well. The positions are not nearly as formal as the positions you learned earlier tonight. I'm just going to hold you however I want. And you may move however you wish to make yourself as comfortable as possible."

And with that, he began to position her like a doll. They started by facing each other though her head was below his chin; Edward on his right side and Katrina on her left. He tucked his right arm under her head like a pillow and pulled her closer with his left so the front of their bodies pressed together. With his left foot, he pulled her right knee between his thighs and rested his leg over her hip. Her right arm naturally rested over his side, under his left. Her left arm moved at the elbow, uncertain where her hand should go. "On my cock," he ordered, reading her mind.

"Yes, Sir." She reached down into his boxers to find his member, soft but a handful. He pulled her even closer. She buried her face in his chest. Edward tipped his head down and felt her damp hair on his face as he kissed the crown of her head. They both squeezed as though their bodies could melt into one.

Drifting in and out of consciousness, the next position in which Katrina found herself was similar to before. But she was on her right side with Edward's body cradling hers, right arm still under her head, legs intertwined, and his left hand cupping her right breast with her nipple delicately tweaked in the joint of his thumb.

All positions assumed that night followed a theme of constant and abundant contact. Each position made Katrina feel protected and safe inside a cocoon of Edward. She listened to the rhythm of his breathing as his air warmed her ear; in and out with a soft snort at the beginning of each inhale. The pace of her own breathing was in time with his as she faded back into sleephood.

At one point, she awoke with nothing holding her but the chill in the air and the chain around her neck. She turned to find Edward on his left side with his back to her. *Am I allowed to touch him? Would he mind if I hold him?*

She hesitantly placed her right hand on his side. Though he may not have been conscious, his left hand grabbed her wrist and pulled her closer, welcoming her advance. She laid into him, conjuring more than enough warmth to remain in hibernation.

With predawn light seeping through the edges of the curtains, Katrina awoke on her back with Edward's right shoulder over her left. She held his arm like a teddy bear with his hand just below the middle of her waist. Though his fingers twitched, she could tell by his breathing he was asleep. But right on schedule came a negative thought, straight to her head like the first cigarette of the day. *What if he wakes up and feels the stubble above my twat?*

She stared up at the ceiling and saw the bar suspended from it. *What is that for? Are we going to do something with it soon?*

As her mind became more unsettled, doubt and mistrust also stirred. She mentally replayed conversations from the night before. She thought about the word Edward used: "goosebumps". Given the context, she understood the meaning. She thought it was interesting how the phrase, "piel de gallina", or "skin of chicken", translates to another form of poultry to make "goosebumps". *But wait a minute... How did he know what I meant when I said "piel de gallina"? Didn't I say that in Spanish? Is that such a common phrase that an English speaker would understand it? Or does this guy know more Spanish than he is saying?*

She turned to see the side of Edward's face in peaceful dormancy. But her past experiences filled her with dread. Although she was acutely aware that she had never been given a reason to fear for her safety with this man, she was accustomed to waking up next to a virtual stranger who had a new personality every morning that only grew worse with each day. *Will Edward be the same caring, affectionate man he was yesterday?* She felt a little ridiculous for thinking that way. But old habits...

Any attempt to fall back asleep would be in vain. *I don't want to wake Edward but I need music to sleep. ... How did I sleep last night without it? ... How did I go the whole night without smoking?*

\* \* \*

Edward awoke to find himself alone in his bed with a thin slice of sunlight crossing the room. His bleary eyes slowly brought into focus a few black strands of hair on the pillow and sheet where Katrina's head once lay. He knew she was somewhere in the house... unless she decided to leave with a foot and a half of decorative traffic control chain locked around her neck. Sounds came from the kitchen... uncommon sounds... like someone was... cooking?!

He walked across the house to observe a blurry figure bending over the stove, wearing one of his white undershirts that was almost long enough to cover her thonged butt.

She heard him step around the corner and turned to see a man with furrowed brow and eyes squinting from the light. He didn't look happy. But she couldn't tell for sure. "Good morning!" she greeted, trying to control her breathing while attempting to quell a potential storm. "Breakfast will be ready soon... Sir!"

He started to creep over behind her back, wrapped his arms around her, grabbing a breast, and leaned down on her until his mouth was behind her ear. "How did I get so lucky to have such a fine, hot bitch making me breakfast?"

Though he could not see it, Katrina smiled and once again, felt foolish for thinking Edward would be abusive; with the exception of a welcome smack on her sore seat.

"When I smack my fine ass, what do you say?" Edward asked as he ran a finger across the SIR nipple.

"Thank you, Sir!" Katrina replied.

Edward smacked her one more time as a test. She responded appropriately. He kissed her behind her ear and turned to the refrigerator, saying, "Breakfast! Good initiative, my charge. How did you know I like food?"

"Lucky guess, Sir," she snickered. She watched Edward as he poured himself a cup of water from the refrigerator dispenser. This reminded her to ask about his unique choice in refrigerator decorations. "My refrigerator has pictures my cousins drew, Sir. Did you do all of those?"

"Most of them." Edward looked at the shooting practice targets on the refrigerator. He opened the door to give Katrina a better view. "Each of these is from a different gun."

Edward gave a brief description of each one, talking about the type of gun, the caliber, and the distance. Many of the holes strayed from bullseye. But he didn't mind showing them since he was so far away from the target when he fired.

"What about that one, Sir?" She directed to a target with almost no markings on it.

"Come. Look closer."

"Yes, Sir." She placed the wooden spoon on a saucer on the counter.

When she stepped over and bent down to see, Edward did not waste the opportunity to place his free hand on her backside. She observed a target that was completely clear except for a single hole, dead center in the bullseye. Next to the hole, in Edward's cursive was written: "Katrina, first date, 9mm."

"I do that, Sir?"

"You did that," Edward said with pride as he patted. "Is it as terrifying as you remember?"

"I don't know, Sir," she replied, though her mind was not completely present. She stood up straight, still looking down at her target, uncertain how to feel about it. She didn't want to think about the gun range. But the experience rendered a result that her Dominant felt was worthy of a place on his refrigerator.

Edward kissed her on the temple and asked, "What are you making?"

"Huevos rancheros, Sir."

"Excellent!" he said as he carried his water to the dining table. "I don't think I've had huevos rancheros in the United States."

"Where did you eat them before, Sir?" She stepped back and picked up the wooden spoon.

"I'm sure I've had them in Mexico, at least. Or maybe it was a Mexican restaurant in the U.S." He sat down at the table and turned toward the kitchen to watch his girl. The sight of his submissive to his eyes was as refreshing as the water to his wine-stained tongue.

Katrina felt Edward's stare. It did not bother her as much as before. In fact, she was starting to like it. And Edward allowing her to keep the shirt on gave her a chance to tease him a bit. Although he seemed to be a "breast man", she took the opportunity to show off what she considered her most prized ass-et.

The shirt rose to show her thong as she reached up to a high shelf. With her back to Edward, she bent at the waist to a low cabinet. Edward watched as she searched through each drawer before he finally realized she wasn't just putting on a show for him; she was actually looking for something.

"What are you looking for?"

"I can't find your…" She held a knife and made a slicing motion at her waist.

"Cutting board?" he asked.

"Sí, 'cutting board'."

Edward winced, "Perhaps it's best you know these things about me now…"

Katrina looked at him and surmised,

"You do not have a cutting board, Sir."

"I do not have a cutting board. I bought everything you requested!"

"Yes, Sir. But I thought you have a cutting board!"

"When it comes to the culinary arts and my kitchen complement, it's best to keep your expectations low."

"Yes, Sir!" she laughed.

"Where did you get that shirt?"

"From the hamper, Sir."

"I think it might be dirty. Does it smell?"

"A little. I like it. It smell like you, Sir."

This warmed Edward's heart. He was not accustomed to hearing romantic statements from a woman. He had always thought of such declarations to be the man's job in a relationship. But he took no less pleasure in Katrina's words.

He enjoyed watching his budding submissive as she prepared breakfast. He liked how her thong framed her cheeks when she reached up to a cabinet or leaned over the counter. He liked how the marks from the night before had taken an ebon shade across her butt. He liked how her dark nipples could be seen through his thin undershirt. And of course, the collar and what it represented…

After plating, Katrina walked to the table and set two plates of food on two placemats.

"Is that the way you present something to me?" Edward asked.

"Ah, no, Sir! Please forgive me, Sir!" She quickly took Edward's plate, dropped to her knees in position two, kissed the edge, and held it in front of her, presenting it to Edward. "Your breakfast, Sir."

"Good girl. *Now* put it on the table."

"Yes, Sir." She did as ordered.

"Show me position four, facing that way," Edward said as he pointed to his left.

"Yes, Sir." She kept her knees on the floor, turned to her right, and put her hands on the floor as well.

"Fingers together."

"Yes, Sir."

Edward pulled her closer so her left shoulder was touching his left knee and her left hip was touching his right knee. He picked up the plate and felt the bottom to make sure it was not hot enough to be dangerous.

"Do you see that electrical outlet at the end of the counter?"

"Yes, Sir." It was a few feet away in front of her face.

"Focus on that and do not move a muscle."

"Yes, Sir."

Edward set the plate down gently on Katrina's back between the bottom of her ribs and her tailbone. He prayed for a blessing on the meal, including: "Please bless this food, bless the hands that made it, and bless the girl to whom those hands are attached…"

At her blessing in Edward's prayer, Katrina held back a smile as she continued to stare at the outlet. She found the warmth of the plate soothing as he enjoyed his breakfast. He occasionally paused to compliment her cooking and share a bite with her.

This activity, or inactivity, afforded Katrina time to contemplate her new role in this relationship. She was appreciating the elementary nature of the expectations being placed upon her. Remaining still and responding to Edward in conversation were her only duties in her position as a table. And in spite of the simplicity of her assignment, or perhaps *because* of the simplicity, she felt like she was gaining value.

She felt cherished. She was finding importance through objectification. She found meaning in being rendered a piece of furniture for the use of her Dominant. Through external subjugation, she was finding internal freedom.

Edward was cognizant of Katrina's plate cooling on the neighboring placemat. So he replaced his plate on the table and said, "You may eat your breakfast with me."

"Thank you, Sir."

But Katrina did not want to leave her position at Edward's feet. She was basking in the ecstasy of her submission. So she turned toward the table, pulled her chair closer, placed the plate on the chair, and began eating while sitting on her feet between Edward's knees.

"I think you are developing a natural talent for pleasing me," Edward said as he ran his fingers on the back of her neck, between her ponytail and the collar.

"It pleases me to please you, Sir."

Katrina was no stranger to being objectified. But her objectification had never made her feel so connected to the one who was using her. She was starting to think of Edward's feet as *home*.

"I wish I can eat at your feet everywhere we go, Sir."

"That would be fine," he quipped. "We'll get a table with plenty of space on the floor next time we go to an oyster bar or a steakhouse."

Katrina laughed her lilty titter. She was certain of his sarcasm this time. She put down her fork, rested her head on his thigh, and said, "I mean, I wish we can be like this outside of your house, Sir."

"I know what you mean, my charge. And you are going to be my submissive wherever we go." He stroked her cheek and ear. "As for overt displays of affection in this lifestyle, it is unfortunate we can't be like this everywhere. King Solomon had the same problem. He wrote about two lovers not being able to fulfill their desire to touch in public. But there are places we can go where expressions of this lifestyle are acceptable. I think my friend is hostessing a 'Kinky Karaoke' night in a club sometime next month."

"'Kinky Karaoke'? I can't sing, Sir."

"Good! You'll fit right in!"

"Can we go dancing too, Sir?"

"I don't know how to dance."

"I can teach you, Sir," she offered, not knowing what a huge undertaking it may be.

"I don't know," Edward said, with a glassy stare. "When I was young… I watched my parents die in a tragic dancing accident. Fire consumed the entire ballroom."

Katrina lifted her head, "En verdad?"

Edward looked down at her tenderly and shook his head. "No, my charge. My parents are alive and well. They did not die in a dancing accident." He almost couldn't get the words out before he started laughing.

Katrina buried her face in his lap as she laughed with him. *Just when I thought I was starting to understand his humor!* "But you sound so serious, Sir!"

Edward was not excited about the prospect of learning to dance. But if it would make this Latina happy, it was something he may have to try.

…

Once Edward and Katrina finished their meal, he decided to take advantage of the opportunity to teach his submissive another position, starting with a review. "While you are down there, show me position two."

"Yes, Sir." Katrina slid into the position on her knees, arms crossed behind, with the shirt hanging off the front of her breasts.

"Position two, inspection."

"Yes, Sir." Katrina raised her hands and clasped her fingers behind her head. Edward touched her elbows, reminding her to pull them back as she counterbalanced by pushing her chest out.

Edward sat back in his chair to take in the experience of playing puppet master to such a beautiful and malleable marionette. The shade and shape of her nipples could be seen even more clearly through the thin fabric of Edward's shirt. He reached over to his cup and took another sip of water as his eyes drank in the glorious image before him. He leaned forward and carefully poured some water into his left palm and wet the front of his white undershirt at Katrina's breasts, causing her nipples to protrude even further. He took the opportunity to brush his knuckles up and down her right nipple and gave a tiny tweak.

Katrina fought her instincts to pull away at the overwhelming sensation. Instead, she consciously decided to do the opposite in accordance with her training. Her breathing deepened as she attempted to push her right nipple out even further.

"You like interesting words," he said. "Do you know what the word 'proprioception' means?"

"No, Sir."

"'Proprioception' has to do with your awareness of the position of my body..." He touched her on the hip to clarify. "...*this* body and the location of each part."

"Yes, Sir."

"When I tell you to 'practice your proprioception', you will think about the position my body is in. From the floor up, focus on where my feet are, where my knees are, where my hips are, where my shoulders are, where my head is, and where my breasts are. I am about to order you to go back to position two. Nothing on my body will move except my arms. Understood?"

"Yes, Sir."

"Practice your proprioception."

"Yes, Sir." Katrina did exactly as ordered, feeling her feet and knees in the carpet, her hips directly above, her shoulders and head slightly back with the curvature of her spine so her breasts could be displayed more prominently.

"Position two."

"Yes, Sir." She slowly brought her arms back down from behind her head and crossed them behind her back without so much as twitching another part of her body.

Edward said warmly, "That's my good girl."

Katrina replied, barely louder than a whisper, "Thank you, Sir."

He rested his hands on her hips and kissed her cheek. She remained as still as possible and denied her own urge to curl up into his lap and be held like a child.

"Take the plates back into the kitchen, and return here to this precise position," Edward ordered.

Katrina started to stand when Edward reached out to grab the SIR nipple, reminding her to say, "Yes, Sir!" She took the plates in hand and turned toward the kitchen.

"Move faster," Edward demanded with a smack on her butt causing Katrina to put a skip in her step.

"Yes, Sir!" But she didn't need to be spanked to speed up. Her return to Edward's feet was incentive enough. She settled once again into position two in front of him.

"As you can see, I don't have a cane, crop, whip, or paddle," he said with open palms. "And I don't feel like slapping you or pinching my SIR nipple right now. So if you make a mistake or ignore an order, I will have no recourse. I won't punish you. So you may need to find another motivation besides the threat of pain. You may be doing this for me, but I want you to do it for yourself as well. Do you understand?"

"I think so, Sir."

"Do you think you can find motivation from within… without an external source?"

"I think so, Sir," Katrina repeated.

But Edward could see in her wandering eyes, she looked a bit lost.

*Does he not like disciplining me? Is he not going to do it anymore?*

Edward was reading her mind. "Don't worry, I'm going to give you all the pain, pleasure, and motivation you can stand. But right now, you are going to search for motivation without physical pain from me."

Finding this reassuring, Katrina said, "Yes, Sir."

"Show me position one."

"Yes, Sir."

"Position two."

"Yes, Sir."

"Position four!"

"Yes, Sir!"

"Position one, inspection! Move faster."

"Yes, Sir!"

"Position two, inspection!"

"Yes, Sir!"

"Position two, resting!"

"Yes, Sir!"

"Position two, resting, inspection!"

"Yes, Sir!"

Edward paused to take the shirt off of his submissive and enjoy a groping. She pushed into his hands as he pushed into her breasts before ordering, "Position one, inspection!"

"Yes, Sir!"

"I took the shirt off because I like the way my tits bounce when you jump up to position one."

"Thank you, Sir!" Katrina said through faster breathing. She loved feeling so attractive to this man.

"Position two, resting!"

"Yes, Sir!"

"Position one, inspection!"

"Yes, Sir!"

This time, when Katrina jumped to position, she made her breasts jump as high as she could. The extra links of chain hanging down from the lock almost hit her in the face.

"Position four!"

"Yes, Sir!"

"Position three!"

"Yes…" Katrina froze in position four. "You have not teach me that position, Sir!"

"I haven't?" Edward replied with feigned confusion.

"No, Sir."

"Do you think you are ready?"

"Yes, Sir."

"I think you're ready," he said as he knelt beside her.

"Yes, Sir."

"From my hips down, there is no difference between position four and position three. My hips and legs stay right there," he said as he ran his hand from her butt to her left foot. "From here, you will put my thumbs together on the floor…" She did as guided. "…and you will reach forward with your hands until your face is on the floor."

Katrina obeyed, reaching her hands forward, lowering her face to the carpet.

When Edward saw her hips move forward in the direction of her hands, he took a position between her feet, and pulled her by the hips until they bumped into his crotch. Then, as he did when he taught her position four, he put his right hand at the small of her back and his left hand under at her pubic bone. He pushed down with his right and pulled back with his left. She was willing clay being sculpted in his hands.

"What is this?" he asked as he squeezed one of her cheeks with his right hand.

She stifled a chuckle before speaking into the carpet, "That is your *fine ass*, Sir!"

"Atta' girl! You remembered!"

"Thank you, Sir!"

"This is where I want my hips in position three," he explained. He lightly patted the warm, humid spot between her legs through the thong. "This gives me all the access I want back here. Understood?"

"Yes, Sir," she replied breathlessly into the floor as she concentrated on keeping herself open and exposed for the pleasure of her Dominant.

Edward stood to take his place back in the chair before concluding, "This is position three, also known as 'worship position'."

"Yes, Sir." *"Worship"? Like he is a god? Is that wrong? Maybe this is idolatry after all. If this is wrong, why does it feel so good?*

Edward took a moment to marvel at the sight of this woman bowing before him. He leaned on the edge of his seat to run his hand from the thong at her tailbone to the collar around her neck. He thought about the price of the trust this girl was placing in him. He thought about the responsibility he was taking on as this woman pledged her submission with every obeyed command. Though the undertaking was heavy, the weight of this burden made him feel like he could fly.

"Position four."

"Yes, Sir." She lifted onto her hands, looking up at Edward.

He took her chin in his left hand and brushed some loose strands of hair back from her face with his right. He leaned down until their noses were almost touching and cupped her left breast as it hung down from her chest. Slowly and articulately, he said, "You make any chair on which I sit feel like a throne when you bow before me."

Katrina spoke at an equally intentional pace, "I do not bow to a throne if you are not sitting on it, my King."

This being the most romantic statement a woman had ever said to Edward, he found he had been rendered speechless, perhaps for the first time in his life. He knew no words would suffice as a response. So he planted a kiss on her lips as deep and passionate as the words of their hearts.

Upon the withdrawal of his lips, Katrina requested, "Permission to move, Sir."

Edward sat up. "Permission granted."

Katrina moved forward and laid her head on Edward's thigh where he stroked the cheek of his pet girl. She was basking in the glow of submission, taking comfort in her lack of control.

As her breath warmed his crotch, she found his flag to be flying at half-mast. So she nuzzled it with her nose and gave it a little kiss through his underwear, inspiring it to full staff as Edward looked on. "Permission to touch, Sir."

"Permission granted."

She lifted her head and used both hands to push back one leg of his boxers and pull out his member. She studied it as she had the night before, spreading a drop of precum to wet the tip with an index finger before putting that finger in her mouth for a taste.

Looking up at him, "Permission to..." She didn't know the words. She pointed at her open mouth. "With my mouth... your mouth, Sir?"

"Permission to suck my cock?"

"Permission to suck your cock, Sir? You make me cum two times. I make you come one. I give you another one."

"We're not going to keep score of our orgasms, my charge. That's a game you can't win. If you are as multiply orgasmic as I suspect, I'll never be able to have as many as you. You're going to make me cum whenever I want. And I'm going to make you cum whenever *I* want."

"Yes, Sir."

"Go into the bedroom and fetch the cane. The one I used on my fine ass."

"Yes, Sir."

Since he had not specified how to get the cane, Katrina made the decision on her own so Edward could enjoy the shape her thong gave her butt as she crawled out of the room. She returned a moment later, carrying the cane at the middle with her teeth and resumed her position between Edward's knees, looking up at him. He took the rod in his left hand, holding it like a drumstick.

"Hands on my cock," he ordered. "They will stay there and not move until I say otherwise."

"Yes, Sir."

With his right hand, he presented some kind of belt with a ring in the middle: a ring gag. Katrina wasn't given time to observe the object before Edward was placing the ring behind her front teeth in her open mouth and buckling it behind her head. He tilted her head back by her chin to inspect it. Her eyes were open as wide as her jaw. But her hands held fast with fingers interlocked around Edward's member as ordered.

Though she wasn't sure exactly what was happening, she took comfort in the relaxed smile on Edward's face. She used her tongue to explore the foreign object that rendered the closure of her mouth an impossibility.

"What are the safewords?" he asked.

"'Ed' an 'ello', hir." *Why is he reminding me of the safewords? It doesn't matter. I'm not going to use them.*

"Good. Now if you can't talk and you want to employ a 'safe-signal', you will pat me on the hip. Understood?" He demonstrated by rapping on her shoulder with his fingertips.

"Esh, hir."

"Are you ready to learn how to suck my cock?"

"Esh, hir."

"You are going to learn to treasure and care for this cock as though it is your own."

"Esh, hir."

"Look at it."

"Esh, hir."

She took pleasure in the sight of his manhood. And being ordered to look at it made her feel less shy about enjoying the vision as another bead of precum formed on the tip.

"Do not let a drop get away. Lick that off."

"Esh, hir."

She extended her tongue through the ring to lick off the drop. It was then she became cognizant of the spit that had formed in her lower jaw as some of it spilled over her bottom lip. The ring gag rendered her unable to close her mouth or swallow to stop it. She released her left hand from Edward's member to wipe her chin. But before she could, Edward grabbed her wrist.

"Nope. You're gonna drool. I don't care."

"Esh, hir," she said. She tucked her chin down, feeling self-conscious in her complete disallowance to exercise control over her own mouth. *How much humiliation is enough? He doesn't let me wear clothes, he keeps me chained, he has me worship at his feet, he has me crawl like an animal... Well, maybe I chose to crawl. But now I can't even wipe the spit off his chin, much less hold it in his mouth! Why am I having so much fun?*

"Keep licking that cock."

"Esh, hir."

"Lick all around, up and down. Explore it with my tongue. And if you are going to drool, drool on my dick."

"Esh, hir." *That's it! I'll use his cock to wipe the spit!* But that only made more of a mess on her chin... and his penis.

"My charge, is my brown skin blushing?"

He lifted her face by her wet chin and smiled at her. She looked up at him and gave an embarrassed chuckle as she smiled back at him around the ring.

"Don't move."

"Esh, hir."

He took a moment to pose her precisely the way he wanted, ring gag holding her jaw open with a drool-covered chin, both hands holding his full erection right between her breasts that were supported on her forearms, making her nipples look up at him. Her eyes went from wide to relaxed as he stared, conveying a growing trust that showed her submission was not merely physical.

Edward leaned back into the chair and beheld his artwork. He gave an approving nod as his mouth held agape before taking a breath and swallowing.

She started to tilt her head back in an attempt to swallow her spit. "I said, 'don't move'," he repeated as he tapped her right thigh with the cane.

"Esh, hir!"

"From where you are right now, you're going to drool. I want some drops or a string of drool from my mouth to my dick."

"Esh, hir." She tilted her head forward, still looking up into his eyes. But she glanced down just enough to make sure she was on target. Indeed, a few droplets became a stream trickling from her chin, landing on his tip.

"Mm hmm. ... Yeah," he murmured to himself. "What I'm looking at right now... This is the sexiest thing I have ever seen in my entire life."

"Ank oo, hir," she said, unexpectedly causing a gush to roll over her lip, down her chin, and right onto the contents of her hands.

"I stand corrected. *This* is the sexiest thing I have ever seen!"

The corners of her lips turned up, at least as much as they could with the ring gag. "Ank oo, hir!"

He put his right elbow on the table. Leaning his head on his knuckles, he asked analytically, "How does it feel to be the sexiest thing ever?"

"Ood, hir." *He really means it! I can feel his heartbeat in my hands through his cock!*

He took another moment to burn the image into his mind before saying, "I never want to forget what I am seeing right now."

Katrina considered her response. But she decided on silence.

Edward awoke himself from his daydream. "Get back to work."

"Esh, hir." She bowed back down, resuming her lingual expedition. But she wasn't satisfied to just let her tongue do the traveling. So as she explored the head, she gradually pulled her tongue in so he would break the plane of her lips and then the ring gag. She felt his legs spread wider as he sighed. Since he expressed no objection, she gently pushed down onto him, but could not fit him very far through the ring.

*Why is this infernal ring in my mouth? Is it for me or for him? Is he afraid I will bite him? Is it to keep me from giving him too much pleasure? Is it to keep me from getting too much pleasure?*

Having limited ability to use her mouth, she employed a swallowing motion with her throat and tongue in an attempt to make more contact with his head.

"Whoa!" he said.

She lifted off of him, failing to suck her spit back in as she looked up with raised eyebrows.

"No, I'm fine. That was... I liked that. Get back on it!"

With a chuckle she turned back down. But not before she instinctively used a hand to wipe her chin.

"Wait," he lifted her head by her hair at her crown. "I thought I told you, you're gonna drool."

"Esh, hir."

He laid her head on his right thigh and slid the cane from her right thigh back to her right cheek. Holding her head down, he ordered, "Get those hands and tongue on my cock."

"Esh, hir." She held on and began licking again.

For every word, he smacked her ass with the cane. "You. Will. Not. Wipe. My. Chin. ... You. Will. Drool!"

She started to jump at the pain and almost let go with her right hand to stop the strokes. But the combination of his hand pinning her head to his thigh and her own willpower forced her to settle. The pain was not as intense as the marks she received the night before. But it would definitely serve its corrective purpose. "Esh, hir! Eese oriv ee, hir!"

He lifted her head up again and kissed her on the forehead. "Are you my good girl?"

"Esh, hir."

He kissed her again. "You *are* my good girl."

"Ank oo, hir."

"Say it."

"I an or ood irl, hir."

"Yes you are. Now get back to work on that cock."

"Esh, hir." She obediently went down on him until his tip was inside the ring again, where she continued the swallowing motion that pleased him before.

"Atta' girl!" he encouraged, as he gave her a few light taps with the rod. "Good girl!"

She may have attempted a verbal response. But it was impossible to tell. Edward wasn't going to complain.

"Careful!" He yanked her off of him by her ponytail. "You know not to make me cum without permission and you almost got me there already!"

*And I can't even use half my mouth!*

She pointed at the strap on one of her cheeks looking up at him with begging eyes.

"You want me to take this off?"

"Esh eese, hir."

He reached his hand down from her ponytail to the buckle of the belt before taking the ring out of her mouth. "Exercise my jaw very slowly."

"Yes, Sir. Thank you, Sir." She slowly opened and closed her jaw and used her tongue to wet the roof of her mouth and her upper lip, careful to deny the urge to touch her chin.

Edward reached to his glass of water on the table and put it to her bottom lip. "Drink."

"Yes, Sir."

"I want to see something," he said as she drank. "Show me how far you can take me in." He set the glass back on the table.

"Yes, Sir." She cleared her throat and took a deep breath. And then she practically dove onto him until he felt the back of her throat... and then some.

Edward was astonished. But he retained his composure and said sardonically, "Oh, now you're just showing off!"

With that came a coughing guffaw from Katrina as she pulled up off him, trying not to touch him with her teeth. Then she laid her head on his thigh where they were both overtaken with laughter.

"Do you know that I adore you?"

She wasn't sure what to say other than, "Yes, Sir?"

"After that delicious breakfast you made me, I feel like it's my turn to feed you."

"Yes, Sir," she said with giddiness.

"What would you like?"

"Your cock, Sir?"

"Ask again."

"May I have your cock, Sir?" Before he could respond, she said, "May I have your cum, Sir?"

"You want my cum, you little cum slut?!"

"Yes, Sir!"

"Ask me again."

"Please, Sir. May I have your cum?"

"Alright. I'm going to let you go freestyle on that cock. No coaching from me. You're going to make it cum with your mouth however you want."

"Yes, Sir."

"You're not going to stop until I say. Understood?"

"Yes, Sir."

"It's probably not going to take very long," he said with a fading smile. "Get to work!"

"Yes, Sir!"

At that, she took the hair tie off her ponytail, pulled back all the loose strands that had fallen out, and retightened the tie. She put her right hand around his shaft and her left hand under his balls like she was on a mission. She took the head into her mouth, where she was able to enjoy free range of motion, unencumbered by the ring gag. Now she was able to pull her lips over her teeth and roll out her tongue like a red carpet, giving her dignitary a proper welcome for the first time.

She took him on a tour of her oral palace, from side to side, before closing her lips around the shaft and sucking until her cheeks, tongue, and throat all closed around her guest. Her head started bobbing up and down, intensifying the suction as she lifted. Then she switched to only sucking on the ascent and adding pressure on the descent, all the while keeping as much of her mouth in contact as possible. She studied his reactions, maintaining eye contact until his eyes rolled back in his head. From there, she took him even deeper and began swallowing with every thrust.

When she noticed Edward's hands gripping the armrests and his ankles curling around the legs of the chair, she knew she was doing something right. "Good... girl!" With every exhale, he grunted from deep within, inspiring his submissive to increase her speed up and down. She added her right hand to the continuing motion as she lightly rubbed his scrotum with her left.

"That's my good girl!" he praised. "That's my good little cock sucker!" He took the cane in his hand and began tapping it on her ass again. It wasn't hard like a punishment. The pain encouraged her to keep going. He repeated, "That's my good little cock sucker!"

*I'm his 'good little cock sucker'!*

"Get that cum, you whore!" he gruffed. "Don't stop! Get it!"

She knew he was about to explode when his knees straightened and his talking turned to a wheeze, and then a groan. She felt his nectar fill and slide down her throat. And then she felt it happen again on the next thrust… and the next…

"Don't stop, but slow down."

She obeyed, slowly sliding up and down on him until he finally forced her head back down onto his right thigh while he was still in her mouth. He rested his hand on her head and brushed her cheek with his thumb while he caught his breath. He leaned forward and again gave her a stroke on the ass with each word, "That's. My. Good. Little. Cock. Sucker!"

She pressed her head into his thigh as she fought to remain still and not bite down on the precious prize in her mouth. But her own adrenaline helped her manage the pain. "Ank oo, hir!" she said between breaths.

He set the cane down, lifted her head with both hands, and looked into her eyes. "You are my good little cock sucker."

"Yes, Sir."

"What are you?"

"I am your good little cock sucker, Sir."

Tears were rolling down her cheeks. He wiped one away with his thumb.

"Good girl," he whispered.

"Thank you, Sir."

"Did you enjoy your breakfast?" he asked with more life.

"Yes, Sir! Thank you, Sir," she mustered as she recovered.

"Thank me for what?"

"Thank you for breakfast, Sir."

"Say it again. Make it sluttier."

"Thank you for cumming in your whore's mouth, Sir?"

"Is that a question?"

"No, Sir! Thank you for cumming in your slut, whore's mouth, Sir!"

"You're welcome, my charge." He leaned down and kissed her lips, tasting a bit of himself. And then he kissed her forehead where he tasted the sweat of her effort. "That was truly impressive."

"It pleases me to please you, Sir."

"Where did you learn to do that?"

Katrina felt compression in her chest as her face went blunt. Edward's face did the same as he focused on her. Her presence became a distance. He knew he struck a nerve.

"Can I tell you later, Sir?"

Edward nodded. "I'll allow it for now. But we may have found your next wall."

\*         \*         \*

From there, the morning proceeded into the afternoon in the most romantic way possible: with a poker lesson. After all, honing her poker skill was one of Katrina's personal goals, with which Edward agreed to help.

Katrina watched as Edward lifted the dining top off his table to reveal a poker table. She thought it was interesting, but Edward acted as though she was amazed: "Take it easy, honey. Don't get too excited at how awesome this table is!"

"Yes, Sir!" she said, chuckling.

He leaned under the table to flip a switch, turning the lights on around the rail. Now Katrina actually did look at least a little impressed as she watched the lights lazily change from one color to another. They reminded her of the lights around the pond by her office building.

Edward sat in the dealer's box and began preparing the feast, rainbowing the cards and counting out chips. He directed her to the chair across the table from him. She sat and slumped into the rail. "Sit upright so I can see my pretty titties."

"Yes, Sir."

"What game shall we play? Strip poker?"

"I'm already naked, Sir!"

"Vincerò! I win!"

Katrina gave her lilty giggle.

"I love the way you laugh!" Edward shouted. "It's the cutest thing ever!"

That only made her laugh more as she hid her face in her arms. "Thank you, Sir!"

"The truth is, you might not be wearing clothes, but you are not naked ... yet."

Katrina wasn't sure what he meant. But Edward continued before she could think about it.

"For what shall we play? I don't want to play for money on your first lesson. And you don't have any clothes."

"I can wear clothes, Sir."

He shook his head as he shuffled the cards. "Do you really think I am going to allow you to wear clothes in my house?" he asked rhetorically. "It's like you don't know me at all."

"I'm learning, Sir." she said, smiling. "But you are right. There are things I don't know about you. I want to know."

"There are things I want to know about you too."

"What do you want to know, Sir?"

"I want to know how you just gave me the best blowjob of my life. But I won't order you to tell me yet."

Katrina was conflicted. She doubted he was telling the truth when he said she gave him *the best blowjob of his life*. But she was glad she was able to please her Dominant so well. She wasn't ready to reveal why she was so good at it. So she shifted the subject back by repeating, "I want to know you too, Sir."

"Alright. That's what we can play for: questions and answers."

"Sir?"

"We will play for chips, hand by hand. When I win a hand, I will ask a question and you must answer honestly. If you win, you will ask a question and I will answer honestly. What do you think?"

"Okay, Sir," she said. But she didn't seem very enthusiastic about it.

"Don't worry. I am going to try to teach you how to beat me so you'll be asking more questions." The lesson began. "Remember when you said you were winning at the casino for a while and then you started to lose?"

"Yes, Sir."

"It's because the other players learned your style and how to beat you. We are going to start by learning about different strategies and how and when to change them."

Edward dealt the first hand, told his student the strategy he was pursuing, gave her a word of advice on how to win the hand, and lost. Katrina started with one of the lighter questions on her mind.

"How do you know things, Sir?"

"What do you mean?"

"How do you know things? How do you know about the sound of a car horn changing, and the numbers of the roads, and the stars, and the clouds behind an airplane, and how urine cleans cum? You don't like to read. How do you know?"

Edward sat in silence across the table. He couldn't reach the SIR nipple. So he ordered, "Pinch my SIR nipple as hard as you think you should."

"Yes, Sir." She did so with lips pressed together, squinting but never breaking eye contact.

Edward gave his usual answer. "I make it all up!"

Katrina looked at him, unamused.

"For the changing sound of a passing car horn or train whistle, I learned about the Doppler effect in my third grade physics class. For the interstate highway numeric system, I learned that in Driver's Ed. I've studied stars and the psychology and theology behind them for years. My buddy has a great telescope. For the vapor trails behind an airplane... I don't remember where I learned that. Maybe studying meteorology. But I learn most things from 'Star Trek', 'Jeopardy!', and documentaries. As for urine and semen," he shrugged his shoulders. "Experience!" He concluded, "To quote my favorite 'Star Trek' character: 'I remember every fact I am exposed to, sir.'"

Katrina wouldn't get the reference. But she didn't hear him say anything after "experience".

"You have a lot of experience peeing on girls with cum on them, Sir?"

"Next hand!" he said as he shuffled. "Now keep in mind, just because the advice I gave you worked on the first hand, doesn't mean it will work on this hand. I might change my strategy." Using his advice, she won again.

"You have a lot of experience peeing on girls with cum on them, Sir?"

"Yeah," he said. "That and masturbating in the shower."

"Do you do that a lot, Sir?"

"Masturbate? I don't know if I do it 'a lot'."

"Do you pee on girls a lot, Sir?"

He thought about it. "I'm not sure how to answer that. What constitutes 'a lot'? I suppose most guys have never peed on a girl in their lives. So compared to most, I guess I have done it 'a lot'."

"How many submissives do you have, Sir?" She tried to sound casual, though she feared asking the question as much as she feared the answer.

"Next hand!"

Edward won. It was his turn to ask a question. But he didn't start off lightly.

"Once again, I have to compliment you on giving me such an *incredible* blowjob. I have to know, how are you so good at sucking dick?"

Katrina swallowed and looked down at the table.

"Look at me."

"Yes, Sir."

"You are with someone who cares about you. We are going to keep each other's secrets forever, no matter what. And whatever you tell me will not change the way I think of you as long as you tell me the truth."

"Yes, Sir." She looked back down at the table so she could concentrate. "I had to, Sir."

Edward remained silent.

"I had to be good at it with my husband."

"What's wrong with that?" he asked. "That sounds like a righteous reason to be good at it."

"It was good in the start," she began. "But then I do it so he will not be angry."

"So he would not be angry at you for not sucking him?"

Katrina was being failed by both her words and emotions. She didn't know how to explain it in English. But she wasn't sure she wanted him to understand the whole truth.

"He was always angry. And he was mean to me. I suck him so he will not be mean."

"So it was kind of like a survival mechanism for you."

She nodded though she wasn't exactly sure what a "survival mechanism" was. "He got more and more angry. I had to be good and better."

"You got good at it so he wouldn't hurt you."

She sniffled and nodded. "And for the marriage."

"How long did that work?" He knew it wasn't a sustainable dynamic.

"It did not work. In a year, he can not get hard."

"Did he blame you for that?"

Katrina broke down into tears. Edward stood and walked around the table to her and grabbed the chain around her neck. "Come with me."

"Yes, Sir," she mumbled as she walked, head down, arms crossed behind her back.

He led her to the couch and laid her across his lap where he held her. "You know, it's not your fault he couldn't get it up," he reassured.

"I know, Sir," she said. "He drink too much."

"I'm sure that had something to do with it."

"No, Sir," she said. She rolled toward him. "I don't know how to say." But she tried again. "He will not stop drinking for me. I was not good."

Edward considered her words. He knew there was something she was attempting to convey that he was not understanding. But maybe he understood now. "Are you trying to say you don't think you were good enough for him to quit drinking?"

She buried her face in his shirt, sobbing. "Not good enough for him to be good."

That made the connection for Edward. He didn't say anything. He didn't need to say anything. He just held her tighter and began slowly rocking back and forth as he rubbed her back, feeling the welts he had produced. She laid with her eyes closed as she wept.

Once her tears subsided, he said, "I could sit here and try to use reason. I could tell you all the ways it wasn't your fault. He was a grown man with no purpose or direction in his life. He married a girl half his age that he hardly knew. You were sixteen. You couldn't have helped him. You are right; you were not enough for him to change. But nobody *could* have been enough. I know it is of little consolation. But his problems had nothing to do with you. And you need to forgive yourself for not being able to save him."

She nodded as her wet eyes opened. "I know, Sir."

Edward knew her immediate response meant she understood his words but would not be convinced for a long time if ever. So he steered in a different direction.

"If there is one good thing we can draw from your pain, it's the fact that you have the most incredible cock sucking skills I have ever had the privilege of experiencing." That elicited a weak smile from his submissive. And the repetition of his praise for her skill was starting to get through to her. "If you continue to see me in this capacity, and I hope you will, we are going to work on changing your motivations for sucking me."

"What do you mean, Sir?"

"You won't have to suck me for fear."

"We already have changed, Sir."

"What do you mean?"

*More words in English.* Her mind was getting tired of thinking of these new concepts in this foreign language. And she was never certain if she was getting her point across. But she persevered. "When I suck you... I am not afraid."

Edward knew that statement was much deeper than the words themselves. He leaned down and lifted her head to kiss her temple before staring another moment. She used the sleeve of his shirt to wipe her eyes.

"Next hand!" she said as she rolled onto her back on his lap. They both had forgotten that they were playing poker. And neither of them were interested in continuing the game. So she asked her question there. "How many submissives do you have, Sir?"

"Now, just you," he said as he rested his hand on her breast.

"How many do you have before, Sir?"

"In my whole life?"

"Yes, Sir."

"I really don't know," he said with regret. "The dynamics of such relationships are so diverse, I don't know which women could be considered 'submissives' and which were just deeper friendships. Some girls wanted full immersion into the lifestyle, and some just wanted a taste. I may have had a dozen at one time."

*A dozen at a time?! I don't like that. But it does explain a lot. I guess that's why he is so good at this.* "Why only me now? What happened, Sir?"

"All of my submissive died in a girlfriend accident."

She snorted at the joke. Edward didn't expect her to get the subtle humor.

"'Girlfriend accident', Sir?"

"I stopped working with my submissives for her. Most of them didn't take it well. And to be honest, neither did I. I felt guilty, like I had abandoned pets in the wilderness."

Very little about that last statement made sense to Katrina. But she wanted to get to the heart of the matter. "Are you going to have more submissives, Sir?"

"I don't feel like rebuilding my 'collection'. I don't think so," he replied. "Why? Do you want me to?"

"No, Sir." Once again, she wasn't sure if he was joking or not.

"Do you want to be my sole submissive?"

"Yes, Sir."

"Okay. If you're going to be my only submissive, that will be a big job for you. You know I don't 'juego', solo 'toco'. Do you think you can handle it?"

*I don't know.* "Yes, Sir. I can."

"Good girl. I'm sure you can."

"Thank you, Sir."

Katrina thought about another question that had been on her mind since she stepped foot in his house. She wanted to know about the picture frames at the ends of his couch and on his entertainment center. Though he had several things in his living room that didn't match the rest of his furnishings, the decorative picture frames didn't seem like something he bought for himself. "Next hand! Who give you the frames, Sir?"

"A friend. I haven't talked to her in years."

Katrina noted the gender of the giver. But she didn't have time to think about it before Edward asked, "Do you like that one?" He pointed to one of the pictures at the end of the couch.

Katrina had been so preoccupied by the frames that she hadn't noticed the pictures themselves. She sat up to see the "Lester's $1,000,000" souvenir photo of the two of them from their first date… in the picture frame that another girl gave him. She surprised herself at how much this did not bother her. *At least he thinks about me enough to display our picture in his home.*

"Next hand!" Edward announced. But before he could ask another question, the dryer buzzed. He had not even noticed it was running. "Are you doing the…" He stopped himself from completing the stupid question. He knew *he* wasn't doing any laundry. "I love your initiative, my charge. You might be able to handle me after all!"

"Thank you, Sir."

"Go get the laundry and fold it here on the coffee table."

"Yes, Sir!"

…

She wished she could fold the laundry in the nude in her home. But she would probably be wearing more clothes than usual around her house to keep her mother from seeing the marks on her body. There would be too many questions that she would not know how to answer.

But for the time being, she could enjoy the sensation of the warm fabrics of Edward's clothes on her bare skin. And the feeling of Edward's eyes on her naked body made her wish she could do her own laundry in his home. The thought of her clothes being shuffled with his in the washer brought her pleasure.

She took the folded laundry to his closet. As she put the shirts with the shirts and the underwear with the underwear, she noticed the clothes that were already in the linen closet were folded differently from the way she had done it. This was to be expected, being the first time she had washed his clothes. But some types of clothing were folded or hung in more than one way. She did not want to think about why.

# ACT 2

# Chapter 8.0

# THE TURKEY CLUB, "NO" POWER

Katrina's high heels stepped out the passenger door onto the pavement of the sparsely occupied parking lot. Though she cast a long shadow in the setting sun, she could not hide her timidity as she stood with her right hand at her side and her left hand crossing her body to hold her elbow. With her chin low, her eyes darted about the industrial park, studying the building she was about to enter, until Edward came into view.

"Position one," he ordered.

"Yes, Sir."

Her arms crossed behind her back, her chin rose, and her cleavage went on display through the plunging neckline of the blouse he chose. It was as though she grew an inch on Edward's order alone.

"Eyes forward."

"Yes, Sir." Her stare penetrated his chest.

He saw her flexing every muscle in her face. "Drop my eyebrows."

"Yes, Sir."

He was going to tell her to relax her pressed lips next but the tension seemed to fall off her face naturally, from the smoothing wrinkles in her forehead to unclenching jaw.

"Concentrate on where every part of my body is right now, proprioception. Feel where my chin is. Feel where my chest is. For the rest of the night, this is how you will carry my body. It makes you look like you actually have some confidence. Do you feel confident?"

"I... don't know, Sir."

"Look at me."

"Yes, Sir." She established eye contact.

"It's okay to say 'no' to me as long as you tell me the truth."

"No, Sir. I don't feel confident," she said as her chest deflated. Her chin dropped a millimeter when she opened her mouth to inhale.

Edward put his index finger under her chin and lifted her face to meet his. "I know you don't feel confident yet. I know you feel nervous. But you are going to fool everyone here into thinking your are a strong, self-assured woman. Only you and I will know how you secretly feel. You are going to 'fake it 'till you make it'. Understood?"

"Yes, Sir."

"And if there is a problem of any kind, what are you going to do?"

"I will say our safeword and talk to you privately, Sir."

"That's my good girl."

The couple approached the entrance to "The Turkey Club" with her left hand in his right elbow. Once they reached the front of the short line, He dropped his right arm to reach for his wallet. As trained, she put a finger in one of his belt loops.

Edward loved the power she gave him to lead. And Katrina loved the release that came with following. But this was a new experience, for them to be able to display their dynamic in public. He tilted his head toward her and said, so only she could hear, "I feel like I am wearing you, like a piece of fine jewelry. I love it."

Katrina looked up and replied, "I love it too, Sir!"

She reached into her handbag to fetch her ID. And though it was a bit difficult, she did so without taking her finger out of Edward's belt loop on her own initiative.

She was actively searching for ways to show submission with every motion and thought. Words from Edward's training replayed in her mind. He talked about the importance of having her obedience in this club and how it could reflect poorly on both of them if she failed to submit. And if it should come to pass that *he* failed to lead or did something that embarrassed her, she should take the first private moment to discuss it with him, with an emphasis on the word "private".

Although she was nervous about this experience that she saw as some kind of test, she reassured herself with the memory of Edward's final words before they got out of the car: "You will be magnificent. I wouldn't bring you here if I didn't think you could handle it. I'm just excited to be here with you."

Edward was pulling cash out of his wallet to pay the cover charge as he greeted the hostess through a hole in the window. "Hello, Jennifer! There is a discount for couples, right?"

"That's right!" she replied with an exaggerated smile. But Jennifer's smile was betrayed by her eyes. Edward could see she was trying to remember who he was and how he knew her name without a name tag. She had never seen him out of his security uniform before.

At that moment, the guard on duty stepped to the window, put his hand on Edward's shoulder, and asked Jennifer, "Is there a discount for former employees?"

Edward turned to the guard. "Mark! Good to see you!"

"Hey, Edward! Long time!"

With a nod, Jennifer waved the couple through.

Mark and Edward stepped aside with Katrina in tow to share a handshake. Edward introduced them. "Mark, Katrina. Katrina, Mark."

"Pleased to meet you!" Katrina said as she shook Mark's hand. She focused on maintaining eye contact with a grip that was firm, *but "not too firm"* as trained.

"The pleasure is mine," Mark replied with formality and a subtle glance from cleavage to eyes.

*Do all men do that? I've never kept my eyes up long enough to know.*

"So what brings you out here on this night of nights?" Mark asked Edward.

"An invitation from a friend. She's the DJ... or the KJ of 'Kinky Karaoke' tonight for her first time. I'm here to provide moral support."

"Well I can't think of a better person to provide support of a moral nature in a place like this."

"Thank you. That's nice of you to say."

It was early in the evening and Edward wanted to show Katrina around before it got crowded. As he led her, she focused on walking in lock step with him. He gave no such order to do so. But in spite of his much longer stride, it gave her another opportunity to show submission, or at least keep herself distracted.

Edward started the tour by showing Katrina the sign over the door: "The Dungeon Studios". If the goals at the ends were any indication, this large room with a high ceiling used to be a basketball court. Each 'studio' section was marked by velvet ropes surrounding rugs and carpets of varying types, though all coordinated to a cohesive effect. Each section had an apparatus of some type. Benches, tables, crosses, saddles, sawhorses, and suspension points were all available for use.

One piece looked like a human-sized birdcage. Another looked like an old gynecology table. And there was a bar hanging from the high ceiling that reminded Katrina of the bar in Edward's master bedroom. She didn't know the exact purpose of each piece, but she did notice one thing they all had in common; there were metal or leather restraining cuffs and belts on each item.

Only one studio was occupied at that time. Two planks of wood leaned securely against the wall to form a large 'X'. And on the X was a woman facing the wall with her arms and legs splayed. With the exception of leather cuffs on her ankles, wrists, and neck, she was nude. Her bare feet stood on pads just above the floor through holes at the bottom of the planks. She held handles at the top just above clips that fastened the cuffs. Even from a distance, Katrina could see her knuckles were white.

Behind her was a shirtless man in jeans and cowboy boots, presumably her Dom, or at least *a* Dom, using some kind of cane with a whip on the end. He flung it left and right, left and right, contacting the woman's skin with each stroke. Though the motion seemed lazy and hypnotic like the pendulum of a clock, the snapping sound of each pelt and the woman's resultant twitches and vocalizations conveyed pain between the two. And when he moved to the most sensitive flesh of her thighs, the woman pushed up on her toes and tilted her head back until a wince could be seen.

Her muscles flexed wherever the whip was targeted as she pressed her body deeper into the wood. At one point, she even kicked her right leg back at the knee in a reaction to a well-placed mark. It was this point at which Katrina realized the woman's right ankle had come loose from the X. But the man continued unabated.

Throughout the club were signs that read: "The safewords are 'Yellow' and 'Red'. No exceptions. Failure to respect the safewords may result in ejection from The Turkey Club." But in spite of these signs and the woman's obvious pain, the only sounds from her was the snapping of the whip on her skin and her staccato whimpers and yelps.

Each lash inspired her to hold the handles tighter as Katrina did likewise to Edward's arm with both hands. While she was watching this scene, Edward was watching her nestle the side of her head into his shoulder.

The man conducted himself as though he was producing a work of art. Each motion of the whip was effortless as he aimed for unmarked regions on her body, covering her evenly with razor thin lines. His tender combination of cruelty and care formed a wordless poem on her skin.

A few voyeurs had gathered behind the velvet rope, well outside the range of the Dom's implement. Some gawked with discomfort at the activity they were witnessing. But most looked upon the couple with intrigue. In accordance with the apparent etiquette of the room, all remained silent, leaving only the sound of the couple and the distant music of the Main Hall to fill the air.

Finally, the Dom stopped and placed the whip on a nearby table next to a host of implements. By this woman's multicolored back, buttocks, and legs, Katrina concluded, this particular whip was not the first this woman had experienced that night.

The man sampled from a water bottle as he walked over to his canvas. He pushed his body behind his submissive and held the bottle in front of her.

Katrina was surprised to find the woman's left wrist was also not fastened to the plank when she released the handle and took the bottle for a deep drink. And when the woman turned around for a lusty kiss, it was clear not one point of her body was restrained by anything but the power of her own mind, and that of her Dom.

Though they spoke in hushed tones, it was like they were the only people in the room. He said something inaudible that made them both laugh as he escorted his painting to a nearby mirror so she could observe his work.

She looked over her shoulder with awe and touched some of the deeper colors that were coming to the surface of her back. She said something while pointing to the right cheek of her butt. He nodded at her reflection before grabbing her by the front of the collar. She dutifully placed her arms behind her back to be led.

The woman assumed her previous position on the X while the man walked to the table to retrieve an implement. He returned to her with a much longer whip coiled in his hand and unwound it over her shoulder. As he started to walk backwards, she rested her cheek on it, savoring the burn as it slithered away.

The man stopped a few paces from the velvet rope when the whip fell to the ground. In his first acknowledgment of the railbirds, his deep voice said, "Y'all are gonna wanna stand back fer this."

The crowd members stepped away from the rope and took places near the wall behind them. The man said to his subject, "Point to where ya want it."

Again, she pointed to the right cheek of her butt before replacing her hand on the X.

"Okay, here it comes in three…" The man drew a circle with his hand over his head. "…two…" The whip flowed through the air as though it were an extension of his own arm. "…ONE!"

At that second, the woman's body tensed and jumped just before she heard a sound like a firecracker well above her head. This was obviously an intentional miss by the adept man. The woman laughed maniacally in anxious relief, causing the voyeurs to do the same, including Katrina.

*That was funny! Did he just play a prank on her?*
*Was the ice water supposed to be funny?*

"See now, if I'd a' hit ya, I would'a hit yer leg 'cause ya moved! Ya gotta stay still. That's an order."

"Yes, Master!"

"Alright. It's fer real this time. Are ya ready?"

"Yes, Master!"

"Three…" And with that, the painter struck his canvas right on target, eliciting something between screaming and laughter from his surprised subject.

The appreciative audience gave golf claps at the precision of the mark.

The man wrapped the whip over his broad shoulders, walked to his woman, and massaged her sore cheek in his hand. He kept her there for a few minutes. Then he led her to a mat on the floor by the mirror, where he sat holding, watering, and whispering to his work of art.

As his back was to the audience, most of the members concluded the show was over and moved on. But seeing this activity from the outside for the first time sparked curiosities in Katrina.

*Why were they doing what they were doing? Why did she let him whip her like that if she could have stopped it? Why does that man like doing that? Why do I let Edward do things like that to me? Why do I like it? Why do I want more?*

She quietly asked Edward, "Can I ask them some questions, Sir?"

Edward replied with an equally low volume so as not to disturb the couple. "Definitely not during their aftercare. And as long as this rope is up, we aren't even supposed to approach them. You may get a chance to talk to them later. But for now, I can try to answer any questions you have."

After hearing this word for the first time, Katrina decided to ask about it first. "Okay. What is 'aftercare', Sir?" Edward led her out of the room on his arm so they could speak at a conversational volume. She resumed her attempt to match her stride with his, noticing how he always stepped off with his left foot first.

"You know how I hold you and we sometimes talk at the end of our sessions?"

"Yes, Sir."

"These activities can be really exhausting and emotionally confusing for a submissive, especially if she is in the beginning of a relationship and she doesn't have much experience in this lifestyle. So it is good to have a period of time after a session to hold a submissive, talk to her, maybe get some sugar or chocolate in her, and reassure her that she's not just being taken advantage of. This can make the potential subdrop less dramatic."

He led her past the private rooms toward the Main Hall.

"What is 'subdrop', Sir?"

"Remember after our first weekend at my place, I told you about how you might have some unpredictable feelings after you left?"

"Yes, Sir."

"Sometimes an experience like that can result in sadness or even a deep depression. A sub is essentially coming off of a natural hormonal high, like a drug. It can give her an emotional hangover. That's called 'subdrop'. And one of the ways to help keep a sub from dropping too far, or sometimes avoid the subdrop altogether is to have aftercare. We have had lots of aftercare."

"We have, Sir?"

"Yeah. You know how we take a shower together or I hold you in bed? Sometimes we talk?"

"Yes, Sir."

"That's aftercare. Some people believe it to be more important than the activities that precede it. Wouldn't you agree that it's a bonding experience?"

"Certainly, Sir."

"You are pretty fortunate with subdrop."

"What do you mean, Sir?"

The volume of their conversation was getting louder as they approached the music in the Hall.

"Remember how I called and texted you after your first few times to check on you?"

"Yes, Sir. You asked how I feel. I was fine. I did not know what you want me to say."

"I always want you to tell me the truth no matter what. You know how I obsess about things sometimes..."

Katrina interrupted, "All the time, Sir!"

"Yeah," Edward said with a smile. "But I was trying to make sure you weren't experiencing any depression or subdrop. I think you were okay for the most part."

"I feel a little 'apedreado' that week, Sir."

"Does that mean you felt 'high'?"

"Yes, Sir. I felt high."

"That makes you a lucky submissive."

"I am a lucky submissive for many reasons, Sir."

That stopped Edward at the double-door entrance to the Main Hall where he gave Katrina a kiss on the forehead.

"This must be her!" a young female voice said.

Edward and Katrina turned to see a girl in her early 20s with red hair wearing short black shorts and a red tank top that was so tight around her small breasts, her nipple piercings could be seen. Philena, the Karaoke Jockey stepped up to hug Edward.

"Philena 'The Quee-na'!" he said as he hugged her with his unoccupied left arm. "Indeed, this is the girl. Katrina, Philena. Phile...na, Kat...rina."

They all chuckled at the tongue twisting introduction.

Katrina felt the tiniest bit of jealousy at Edward's familiarity with this girl. But she decided to tuck it away and try to equal the energy by offering her hand to Philena. "Pleased to meet you!"

But Philena said, "No! I'm a hugger!" as she attacked Katrina with an embrace while she was still holding Edward's arm.

With his arm caught between the two girls, he started to pull out of the breast sandwich. But then he thought it best to just ride it out. Katrina retook her position on his arm after the hug.

"Thank you for helping me get this gig, Edward. And thank you both for coming," Philena said. "It's my first time here and I hardly know anybody."

"All I did was give your number to a friend. You did the rest," said Edward. This was the first time Katrina heard anything about Edward helping Philena get the job.

Philena asked, "Can I count on you to stay in the rotation?"

"Whatever you need! I'm in!"

Philena turned to Katrina, "Can I put you on the list too?"

Katrina shook her head with an embarrassed smile. "Ah, I can't sing."

"You have to sing at least one song! That's the rule. If it's your first time, you have to sing, like *Fight Club*!"

"Maybe," Katrina replied, not knowing the reference.

"Great! Have Edward put you on the list once you pick a song."

"Okay."

"I have to run get ready. I'll see you on stage!" And Philena scampered off as quickly as she approached.

Edward and Katrina stepped into the Main Hall. It was the same size as the room with the dungeon studios but filled with tables, pods of couches, and a bar. In the front of the room was a two-foot stage with two stripper poles and an archway holding up chains that formed a spiderweb. To the side of the stage was a DJ/sound booth where Philena was hooking up equipment.

The many questions Katrina had gave way to two new questions on the forefront of her mind. What she really wanted to know was how Edward knew Philena. But so she wouldn't sound jealous, she started by asking, "What is *Fight Club*, Sir?"

"It's a movie. A chick flick. Put it on the list of shows we need to watch."

"Yes, Sir." She wrote the title into the note file they shared on their cellphones as ordered with her left elbow locked in Edward's right. Attempting to look as casual as possible, she continued looking at her phone while asking, "How do you know Philena, Sir?"

Edward was leading her to the bar as he answered, "We met working for the same talent agency. She was the lead vocalist of one of my bands. We've been friends ever since. What would you like to drink?"

They ordered a bottle of wine and two glasses from the bar and took them to one of the pods of furniture. The particular pod they chose had three black leather extended couches and a square coffee table with a wood top and many decorative iron legs around it, making it look more like a cage.

Edward set the bottle on the table next to several small sheets of paper and golf pencils. Their couch afforded a good view of the stage but was far enough for them to hear each other. He grabbed a piece of paper and a pencil and asked, "What song would you like to sing?"

"Do I have to sing, Sir?"

He tried to stir some enthusiasm in her. "You heard the rules! If it's your first time at 'fight club', you have to fight!"

"You have to *fight* in a 'chick flick' called *Fight Club*, Sir? Qué romántico!"

Edward acted like he was trying to stifle his laughter by pressing his lips together while staring at her. "It has… romance in it. Some sex scenes…" This made Katrina smile while rolling her eyes. He asked, "What if we sing a duet? I'll be up there with you."

It was becoming clear that Edward was not going to give up unless she tried a different tack. Katrina asked, "Sir, is the rule to sing, Philena's rule or your rule?"

Of course, there was a big difference in the source of the encouragement to sing: One was the pressure of a young karaoke jockey trying to promote fun and participation. The other was an order from her Dom that could not be disobeyed. Edward thought he understood what she was asking. But he asked her anyway. "Why do you ask?"

"You told me you were going to help me learn to say 'no', Sir." She could tell by the look on Edward's face as his head lifted, he was getting it. And he realized this could be a big moment in their relationship.

Edward considered the factors at play in the situation. On one hand, he could encourage Katrina, or even order her to do something that made her uncomfortable, pushing her limits and expanding her horizons through exposure therapy. On the other hand, this could be an opportunity for her to practice denying somebody. She could practice saying "no".

There would be many opportunities for him to help her push her limits. But chances for her to accomplish her goal of learning to stand up for herself and say "no" were not as plentiful.

All this cogitation took place in three or four seconds in Edward's head before he answered Katrina's original question. "The rule is from Philena. It is not my rule."

"How serious is the rule, Sir?"

"It's not really serious. She was mostly joking. And you may say 'no' if you do not want to sing. Nobody will be offended."

"Permission to go say 'no' to Philena, Sir," Katrina requested.

"Permission granted," he replied before watching her walk to the KJ booth, in her miniskirt.

He didn't think it was necessary for Katrina to go to Philena just to tell her she wasn't going to sing. Perhaps she wanted to try saying the actual word "no". Or perhaps she thought it was the polite thing to do. So he didn't question it.

The fact that she asked for this permission, though expected, still touched Edward. It was like she was using his strength to defeat a fear. It didn't bother him that he did not know why it was so difficult for her. He figured it was one of those things about this woman he would never understand but would accept.

Upon Katrina's return to the couch, Edward asked, "How did that feel?"

Katrina was a bit detached, "I don't know, Sir." She pushed in to lean on Edward. But the negative words in her head were leaking into her consciousness.

Edward saw her in a glassy stare. He could see that she needed to be interrupted from whatever her mind was doing. So he asked, "What are you thinking?"

Katrina's jaw clenched as she swallowed. *Not now you baby! You and Edward have been looking forward to this night. Don't ruin it by crying here in front of all these people!* She tried to separate the emotion from her next words. "I'm afraid I am disappointing you, Sir."

"Look at me." Edward turned his body so his shoulders and face were square to her. Katrina did the same with her face close to his in an attempt to hide her welling tears from the others in the room. "I am not disappointed in you. In fact, I am quite enamored with you. I have the feeling you might have what it takes to make me a better Dominant."

This last statement distracted Katrina from her tears. "How, Sir?" It had not occurred to her that she was helping Edward with… anything.

"You realized an opportunity to work on a personal goal that I failed see. I like how you brought it to my attention." He leaned closer to add, "…in your lawyerly way."

"Thank you, Sir," she replied with a sense of self-satisfaction. *So I can get through to him by talking like a lawyer! I need to learn how to do that on purpose!*

"Are you going to sign up for any songs, Sir?"

"Philena has a file on her computer for her regulars. I have a bunch of songs on there."

*So he has sung enough for Philena to consider him a "regular". Is there something he is not telling me about their relationship? Am I being stupid for feeling jealous? He's not really doing anything wrong.*

\*     \*     \*

Given other people in the club were almost naked, some leading each other around on leashes, and engaging in acts just short of a live sex show, Katrina felt a little more comfortable in the cleavage baring blouse and form-fitting miniskirt Edward had selected for her. As one of the more modestly dressed women, she was able to enjoy showing affection to her man in a crowded place where expressions of their lifestyle were the norm. She didn't mind his wandering hands on her body in spite of the company of two more couples and one silent young man in their pod of couches.

With his unresting eyes and awkward fidgeting, Katrina surmised it was this young man's first time here as well. *At least I'm not the only one who is out of place. He's barely old enough to be here.*

Edward was having a discussion with the couple at the other end of the couch that he already knew. The irony of their relationship was that "London", the native Nevadan, was visiting her namesake English city for the first time where she met her husband.

"Woodrow" was from Portsmouth, England and was in London (the city) on business where his attention was caught by the bright eyes and smile of London (the woman) against her black skin atop a stature that stood a good ten centimeters above his own; not to mention the fact that she had ample bosoms and matching bum, much of which were on display this evening in her white lingerie. A chain of white gold around her neck completed the ensemble.

Woodrow liked to wear suits with no tie, which is pretty much all he wore to both social gatherings and his private mental health practice where he worked as a psychologist.

The two couples mirrored each other on the couch with the gentlemen at the ends and the ladies laying back on them with their feet up, touching legs. As they talked, Edward ran the fingertips of his right hand up and down between Katrina's breasts, occasionally straying to arouse a nipple under her blouse.

He was listening to Woodrow as he talked about… whatever Woodrow was talking about, until both he and London looked up over Edward's head, causing Edward and Katrina to look up behind the couch as well. Two girls had approached and were politely waiting for a break in the conversation. But their appearance had derailed Woodrow's train of thought.

The senior of the two, probably in her early 50s, wore red and black lingerie with a corset and a translucent robe. Her brazier was like a shelf on which she proudly laid and displayed her breasts. The junior, probably in her 20s, wore a schoolgirl uniform with a plaid skirt, stockings, and a very thin, unbuttoned shirt with black strips of bondage tape almost covering her areolae. Both wore collars in the color of their respective ensembles.

"Please pardon the interruption," the senior began. She looked down at Edward and leaned so as not to have her view obstructed by her copious bust. "Edward, I presume?"

"At your service," he replied with equal formality. "My submissive, Katrina." He lifted his right hand from Katrina's chest and offered it to the ladies. Katrina started to sit up but Edward gave a light tug on the back of her hair with his left hand so she knew not to move. As the girls shook his hand, he said, "Pardon me for not standing."

"Of course!" the senior replied. "I can understand your desire to stay close to such a beautiful girl," she said as she looked at Katrina.

Katrina smiled at the woman in acknowledgment of the compliment as she also shook hands with the two.

"Philena tells us you know the male accompaniment to many duets and might be willing to sing with us."

"Probably." His hand dropped to hold the back of Katrina's on her stomach. "What would you like to sing?"

"Do you know the song, 'Paradise by the Dashboard Lights'?"

"You've come to the right guy!"

"A boy as young as you knows that song?!"

"I'm not as young as you think, but I am definitely an old soul. I'll sing it with you."

The older turned to the younger who asked, "Do you know 'Love Shack'?"

Edward looked at her with confusion. "I understand the difficulty of finding someone who knows 'Paradise', but a girl like you can't get one of the guys to sing 'Love Shack' with you?"

"I don't know," she said, crossing her wrists and ducking her head into her shoulder. "They're all shy."

Edward shook his head with a grin and pointed a finger at her. "No, *you're* shy!" Then he waved his finger around the crowd. "There is a guy here somewhere who would love to sing with you." And then he saw the young man still sitting on the far couch. "Hey man!"

The young man's wide eyes grew even wider.

"Will you sing 'Love Shack' with this girl?"

He sat upright, shocked to be addressed. "I… I don't sing."

"Perfect! Neither does Fred Schneider!"

Everybody old enough to know the song chuckled at that statement.

Edward's eyes bounced between the boy and girl. And theirs to each other, both blushing.

Then Edward said, as though he were making a threat, "If you don't sing with her, I will."

The boy stood up and walked away with the girls after they thanked Edward.

Woodrow turned his head back from the girls and asked, "Uh, what was I saying, mate?" London burst into laughter and kissed him under his bearded chin. She enjoyed the view as well, but not quite as long as her husband.

*How does that not bother London the way Woodrow was ogling those girls?*

"You were theorizing that a sadomasochistic relationship led to the invention of adhesive bandages," Edward replied.

"Only you, Edward," London said with a smile.

"What?"

"Only you would talk your way out of singing with a hot girl like that!"

"Nah, she's just a kid. I got the hot one right here!" he said as he groped Katrina's breast under her blouse.

London's eyes dropped from Edward's to Katrina's where they exchanged mischievous smiles.

…

Dane sat with his girl, Dana on the couch to the left. She leaned on him but her eyes were up toward the ceiling with boredom. They were both wearing a lot of black leather… or at least Dane was, in his vest, pants and boots. Dana was in some kind of underwear/bikini that caused her many dark tattoos to pop off of her pale white skin, the most prominent of which stated "We The People" on her décolletage. A thin leather collar around her neck adorned her scanty vesture.

Though the conversation between the men was deep, Katrina still felt connected to Edward when he rested his hand on any part of her he pleased and adjusted to give her access to the part of his arm he wanted her to caress. Nobody else was paying attention to her in this crowed room, and that suited her just fine.

She wasn't obligated to do anything but be there with Edward, reciprocate his affections, and do whatever he told her to do. She paid close attention to her Dominant, feeling every motion, listening to the inflection in every word, watching his eyes when she could see them. She learned that he tended to stare at whoever was talking regardless of gender or attractiveness.

He seemed unfazed at the parade of flesh before them. But she also knew he was a poker player. And he could be impossible to read when he wanted.

The conversation suffered in Edward's sporadic absence when he was called to accompany someone in a karaoke duet. Katrina was prepared for the possibility that he would be singing with other people. But she wasn't prepared for how she would feel about it.

She watched Edward as he performed a few times with girls, and a couple times with guys. He played his role well in each song, never doing anything inappropriate that would embarrass Katrina. But she couldn't deny her jealousy.

After one of the songs, she asked him, "When you sing, do you read words on the screen, Sir?"

"I might glance at them from time to time but I don't really need them. I have a lot of songs memorized."

"Are there songs you don't know, Sir?"

"No, I know the lyrics to every song!" he joked. "The truth is, I don't consider myself to be a great instrumental musician. But I do claim to have a gift for memorizing lyrics. Any requests?"

"Are you going to sing any songs alone, Sir?"

"Probably. I think I'm on the list to sing one soon."

Katrina took her last drink from her glass and saw the empty wine bottle on the coffee table. "Permission to get another bottle of wine, Sir?"

"I'm switching to water. But you may get whatever you want."

"Yes, Sir."

*That's different. He's going to stop drinking? On his own? Without incident? I didn't know a guy could do that.*

She looked to the other two couples as she leaned to the edge of her seat. "Can I get more drinks for you?"

Nobody answered her directly. London and Dana both stirred to talk to their respective Dominants.

Katrina was afraid she had committed an offense. She turned back to Edward. "Do I say something wrong, Sir?"

"No, you're fine," he replied. "Some Doms only let their own subs get their drinks. And some subs don't want other subs getting drinks for their Doms. It's different for everyone. But you did nothing wrong by asking. It was considerate of you."

"Let's all get drinks, ladies," London suggested. "But first, the loo."

Once the ladies were out of earshot, Dane saw the affection in Edward's eyes as he watched his shapely submissive walk away. "You have that one trained pretty good!"

"She's taken to it. I'm quite proud of her."

"What makes you such a good Dom, Edward?"

"Katrina."

\*　　　　　　　　　　　\*　　　　　　　　　　　\*

After performing their necessaries, the three ladies converged in front of the mirror to wash their hands and touch up their makeup, hair, and clothing with Katrina standing in the middle.

To Katrina's left, Dana said, "You and Edward haven't been together long, have you?" It was more of a statement than a question.

"Cómo sabes? ...I mean, how you know?"

"I can tell these things," Dana said as she adjusted the strap of leather around her neck so the charm was in front, just above her "We The People" tattoo.

London interjected, "Oh, don't be catty, Dana. They just met." She looked at Katrina in the mirror as she adjusted her own collar of white gold. "She's saying that because you don't have a collar yet. It's obvious, Edward likes you. I'm sure you'll earn one soon."

Katrina was downcast, viewing the reflection of her own bare neck.

"Oh, don't worry, honey! Edward is very methodical. He doesn't give out collars like candy... like some Doms. He puts a lot of thought into it," London reassured. "Massa and I were married for years before we learned about collaring."

"I still can't believe Woodrow makes you call him that," Dana said.

"It was my idea!" London returned.

"All of this is new for me," Katrina said.

"If you have any questions, we might be able to answer," offered London.

Katrina resumed washing her hands. "I want to know about 'position three'."

London and Dana looked at each other to see if the other knew what Katrina was talking about. They both shook their heads.

"I don't know," Dana said to London.

"'Position three'?" London asked Katrina.

"Yes?" Katrina said, looking back and forth at both of them. "The positions? ... The six positions and variations?"

"Oh!" London said. "If you're talking about 'position training', that can be different for every Dom, every couple. Massa only has three positions for me: 'oral', 'anal', and 'genital'."

"I never got that far with Edward," Dana volunteered as she touched up her eyeliner.

Katrina looked at Dana with questioning eyes. London looked at Dana with contempt.

"What?!" Dana asked with feigned innocence. "I'm just saying, he never taught *me* any positions!"

Katrina and London didn't know what to say, but for different reasons.

Dana turned back to the mirror to reapply her black lipstick before muttering, "It's like he didn't want to touch me just because I couldn't recite the goddamn Preamble."

"The Preamble to the Constitution?!" London laughed out loud. "You know, the first three words *are* tattooed on your tits! And Edward wouldn't stand for a tattoo that didn't mean something to its owner."

"Oh, is that what it is?" Dana replied with a sneer as she turned toward the door. Standing behind Katrina, she said to London, "I'm sure *she* knows the Preamble!" Bruises on her butt were prominently displayed on both sides of her leather thong as she walked away.

London shouted after her, "I don't remember Dane spanking you like *that* before he talked to Edward, ya brat!"

Dana continued her way out, ignoring London.

"It's always the people with the least experience who think they know how these relationships should be," London murmured, half to herself, half to Katrina. She turned back to see Katrina with arms crossed in front, hunched forward with her head down.

She was retreating into her own mind. *How many of these women has Edward been with? Don't cry!*

"Oh honey, don't worry about her. Last year, Dane asked Edward to give her submission training and Edward figured out early on that it was *Dane* who needed *Dominance* training. Something had to have gone wrong in the communication to make Dana feel so rejected." She turned to give herself one last look in the mirror, propping her sizable breasts up in her brassiere in a way that made it both supportive and revealing. "Or maybe it's because Edward doesn't fuck shallow bitches!"

*She doesn't know? At least I know one thing about my Dominant that other people don't know. He doesn't fuck any "bitches" regardless of depth. But how does London know these things about Dane and Dana?* "How do you know these things about Dane and Dana?"

"I mostly know about Dane because he talks about it and gives Edward the credit. But I don't know all the details about Dana."

*Maybe Sir did not go very far with Dana. She doesn't even stop and start her flow when she pees.*

London turned to walk out of the bathroom with Katrina following. "Massa is a psychologist and Edward is a counselor, or used to be a counselor. So they don't talk much about their clients by name because, you know, confidentiality. But they do say what they can when they're shooting stars."

"'Shooting stars'?"

"Yeah, Massa has a telescope." She talked louder over the music as they stepped back into the Main Hall. "Massa and Edward like to gaze at stars on the shooting range behind our house. I like it because Edward asks Woodrow questions I would never think to ask. I learn more about them both every time they talk. We'll invite you next time."

…

As Katrina and London walked back to their men with beverages in hand, they saw they were still in conversation. But now, Dane seemed more animated, perhaps even upset. Dana had already rejoined him and sat up in silence. Edward was leaning forward, listening with a furrowed brow. Katrina thought they were having an argument.

When Edward saw them approaching, he said to Dane, "Hold on. I want Katrina to hear this story."

*Oh no! Did Dana say something?*

Given the environment, Katrina decided to try something she never thought she would do outside of Edward's home: Before all in the area, she placed her wine bottle on the coffee table, assumed position two, presentation, and gave his water bottle a kiss before saying, "Your water, Sir."

Edward's eyebrows unraveled as his visage transformed from one of dismay to one of immense pride in his submissive. He took the bottle and kissed her temple as she settled at his side.

He turned back to Dane and said, "Alright, can you tell this story from the beginning?" And quipped with raised fist, "But this time, with feeling!"

"Sure!" Dane began with a guffaw, though he intended to temper his expression in the presence of their women. "I'm going to tell you exactly what happened and what was said between me and this girl I work with. And then I'm going to tell you what *she says* she heard."

Katrina nodded as he was mostly looking at her. But he had the attention of the few people who had gathered in their square of couches.

Dane began: "My coworker comes into the office on crutches and one of those boot… cast things on her foot. And as she's hobbling by my desk, I joked and asked, 'Football injury?'

"She's like, 'Yeah! A football injury!' She said it ironically. I asked if she would be ready for the game on Sunday. She said she would probably be on the bench this week.

"I said… And this is exactly what I said. I said, 'Oh man! Get well soon. You are on my fantasy team!' You know, talking about fantasy football. And she smiled and limped away.

"That afternoon, I get called in to Human Resources to talk to the rep. The rep asks me what I said to my coworker about her broken foot… or I guess it was a sprained ankle. I told the same story I'm telling you now… You know, football injury, fantasy team, and so on. And the HR rep tells me that the girl thought I said that she was '*my fantasy*' or something like that. I said, 'No! No. I said she was on my *fantasy team*. My fantasy football team.' And I said that she wasn't offended anyway. 'She smiled at me after I said it. No harm done.'

"And do you know what the HR rep said to me? She said, 'It's not about the *intention* of your words, it's about how your words were *perceived*. That's what the issue is.' And that's why she filed a complaint against me.

"I couldn't believe it! It's not about my intention? It's about how I was perceived? Does that make any sense to you?" he asked Katrina.

Those listening to the story turned from Dane to Katrina. All the attention made her self-conscious. She didn't realize she was leaning forward to hear through the music, using Edward's knee as an armrest. Her posture straightened as she tried to ignore the spotlight that had been cast upon her. "Why do you ask me?"

"Edward says you're a lawyer," Dane replied.

"She's in law school," Edward corrected. He turned to Katrina and said, "I thought you might find it interesting since you're clerking for an employment firm. Maybe you would have some advice."

"I can't give legal advice before I am an attorney," she said.

It was this kind of moment in which Katrina wished she knew how to flip a switch in her brain and let her developing legal mind take over at will. She wanted to give some useful input into the conversation. But she felt like she was letting Edward down by not reciting some 'magic lawyer spell' that would help fix this man's problem. *I wish I had asked Edward not to tell anyone what I do.*

"What are you going to do?" Edward asked Dane.

"I don't know. What do you think I should do?"

"File a counterclaim," a voice said from nowhere. Katrina was shocked to realize that voice was her own. She looked around at the eyes. Once again, the attention was on her.

"A counterclaim?" Dane asked. "For what? She didn't do any more harm to me than I did to her!"

Katrina stared through the coffee table in front of the couch. As she was learning in school, she used his point to make her own: "I know. That's the point." Her eyes rose from the table to Dane as she leaned further forward, once again resting her elbow on Edward's knee while his hand was at the small of her back. She forgot about the eyes on her as she continued, "She smiled at you."

Dane nodded.

"And you felt *threatened* and *belittled* when she smiled at you."

Dane was confused. He was about to speak, cocking his head to start shaking it when Katrina held her hand up, palm flat toward him. She got Dane to freeze before he could say something stupid.

"When she smiled at you, you felt like she was harassing you. And you are going to file a counterclaim. Because after all..." Katrina's open hand turned to a pointed finger. "...it's not about her *intention*. It's about how you *perceived* it."

Both Dane's and Edward's faces lit up. Most in the small audience nodded with raised eyebrows and smiles.

It was then that Katrina realized she was on a stage. She was at the counsel's table of a courtroom making a statement to a jury. Or maybe she was framing an argument to advise a potential client... which would be illegal since she was not an attorney. So as she leaned back next to Edward, she concluded, "Of course, that is not legal advice. That is just my opinion. I'm only a law student."

She tucked herself in behind Edward's arm and rested her head to his shoulder, trying not to look like all the attention was making her shy. She could use him as a refuge when she felt this way.

Once the audience members moved on to be engrossed in their respective conversations, Edward tilted his head down and Katrina looked up at him. He said so only she could hear, "You are one impressive little girl, you know that? Muy impresionante!"

She smiled, "Thank you, Sir," before hugging his arm and pressing into his shoulder. *Maybe it's okay if people know what I do. I want to cry now. But I won't.*

When Katrina leaned toward the coffee table for her wine, Dana leaned toward her at the same time and said, "I bet you really do know the Preamble."

Katrina didn't say anything. She just shrugged and nodded. The two girls giggled like it was a slumber party.

Though she didn't know how or why they were getting along now, it made London smile.

# 5.0

# DENIAL

Featuring the entrancing music of "Portishead"
and the classical music of Louise Farrenc:
Symphony No. 3 in G Minor, Op. 36: IV. Finale (Allegro)
Symphony No. 3 in G Minor, Op. 36: I. Adagio - Allegro

From the ceiling hung the bar. From the bar hung the D-rings. From the D-rings hung the suspension cuffs. From the suspension cuffs hung Katrina. The handles on the D-rings and the spread blocks under her feet were the only objects she could reach, molding her body into an "X"; adorned only with the training collar around her neck.

A silicone ball was held in her teeth by a belt that buckled behind her head. Her tongue and lips capitulated to the foreign object, taking shape around it, wetting it in her inability to swallow. The mere presence of the gag hindered, or perhaps accentuated, her mellifluous vocalizations; rendering her the prima donna of an opera, reviving a dead language.

She lifted herself off the blocks in a vain attempt to avoid the single-tail whip Edward wielded behind her. He watched as the pelting inspired every muscle in her backside to flex, adding depth to the dimples in the small of her back and cheeks.

Realizing the futility of her efforts, Katrina's arms eventually lowered her body, replacing her spread feet on the blocks, surrendering to the will of the whip.

Edward, ever the helpful Dominant, stepped over and kicked the block out from under her left foot. Her attempts to say "no" through the gag only sounded like "oh". She protested his progress by pushing both feet into the block on the right to no avail as he kicked that one away as well. The battle ended with her dangling; pointed toes searching empty space. She turned her head to see Edward out of the corner of her eye and said... something.

"I can't understand you because there's a ball gag in my mouth," he retorted.

At this, Katrina both huffed and laughed, causing a trickle to start down her chin.

Edward resumed his work, this time, with a flogger in each hand. He brandished his implements like a ninja to the steady rhythm of music that was as alien to her as it was entrancing. Every time it would reach a climactic boom, he would firmly swing one of the floggers in such a way that only the tips nipped at her butt, giving her a sting that made her sway forward and backward while her feet danced in the air.

The floggers fanned her neck with short gusts of wind, blowing her ponytail over her shoulder. The frequency of the gusts increased to a breeze until it felt like he had four arms driving floggers down her back, making her skin feel like it was glowing. The intensity of the strokes ebbed and flowed with that of the music, pulling her into hypnosis.

Once the composition reached its denouement, Katrina awoke and tried to say… something else. But Edward whimsically reminded her, "Oh! I forgot to tell you, I can't understand you because you have a gag in my mouth."

He draped the floggers over his shoulders and walked in front of her. Being suspended, her eyes were level with his. "What are the safewords?"

"'Ed' an 'ellow', hir."

"And you will say them over and over, loudly if necessary."

"Esh, hir."

"Are my arms getting tired?"

"Mm," she replied with a tilt of her head to express a small amount of fatigue.

"What are you going to do about that?" He reached up and felt for warmth in her fingers to make sure blood was circulating.

As he did, she surprised him by swinging forward and wrapping her legs around his waist, just above his boxers. She pulled him forward a step and locked her feet behind his back. Then she clamped down and used him as leverage to take some of the strain off of her arms.

"Impresionante! That's one way to handle that!" he said as he transferred the floggers from his shoulders to hers.

He reached forward for yet another unabashed groping of her breasts, pushing into her chest, causing her legs to clutch him even tighter. But when he pinched her nipples, she squealed and unhooked her ankles, trying to swing away from him. She immediately regretted her decision to let go of him when he did not let go of her. "Where do you think you're going?"

She caught him in her legs again and whipped her head back, attempting to crush him in her agony. He switched to giving a soothing massage where he was once giving pain, using the trickle dripping onto her décolletage to wet her nipples, standing them even more erect. He moved his hands to support her butt, giving her arms respite to adjust her grip.

His eyes drank her in as strands of hair were falling out of her ponytail, sweat was accumulating on her forehead, and her breasts heaved as she struggled to breathe through the gag without spitting. Now the drool was streaming down her chest. "Look at you. You can't even hold the spit in my mouth," he taunted.

She leaned her head back and tried to swallow what was under her tongue. But the act was pointless as the stream of dribble was already turning to a deluge down her chin and between her breasts. She was powerless to remedy her ignominy through the control of such an elementary function. When she tilted her head forward, Edward kissed her top lip, and then her wet bottom lip as it curled around the gag.

"You are not coming down until you have another orgasm."

"Esh, hir!" she replied in acceptance that she would be suffering even more indignity.

Edward's right hand went from her butt to the humidity between her legs, carefully penetrating her with a finger. His left reached to her right nipple and gave a lighter pinch than before. But it was enough to cause her to clench around the finger inside her so tightly his knuckle cracked. The contact with his digit was enhanced as it slid in and out. He paused to push another finger into her warmth, then pulled both away to explore the outer area, rubbing and patting, allowing her lust to subside.

It was this point at which Katrina became cognizant of the classical music that was playing. She noticed Edward was controlling her arousal in accordance with the symphony orchestra's ebbs and flows; or in some cases, the soaring and crashing.

The maestro skillfully conducted her pleasure along with the rise of the strings before withdrawing and toying with her breasts when the instrumentation dropped to a softer statement from the woodwinds. Upon the strings' reestablishment of their dominance over the motif, his fingers reestablished their position inside her as the music climbed.

Once her whimpering was as loud as the orchestra, Edward looked through her eyes. "Are you ready?"

"Mmmm! Esh, hir!"

"When do you want to cum?"

He couldn't understand her mumbling as the music was rising.

"You will cum in ten seconds. You will count... starting... now!"

"Esh, hir! ... En, hir! ... Ing, hir! ... Eh, hir! ..."

But the music dove back down to the woodwinds.

"Nope!" Edward stopped her countdown and withdrew his fingers. "I changed my mind," he said as he slapped her labia in rhythm with a punctuation from the timpani.

Now she knew better than to release him from the grasp of her legs while he had his fingers on a nipple. Besides, the musical journey was taking him back to wiggling his thumb on her clitoris with the woodwind melody. She was pleased to find that the pattern of peaks and valleys did not fail as his fingers reentered along with the strings. As he repeatedly thrust into her, she lifted and dropped herself at tempo, riding him like a stallion.

She tried to say something but it came out as moaning through the gag. Edward reminded her in an aristocratic tone, "I'm afraid I can't understand you because you have, ...what can only be described as... 'a gag in my mouth'." But the pitch of her voice rose as she kept trying.

She pulled him closer with her legs and felt the warmth of his bare chest against hers, his erect member tapping her butt through his boxers every time she dropped down. Try though she might, it was just beyond the reach of her sheath, teasing her with every motion, compounding her desire.

Though Edward kept her on the edge, she dared not orgasm without his permission.

"Now you are going to cum for me in ten seconds," he demanded.

"Esh, hir!" *Is this it? Is he finally going to allow me?!*

As she counted down, her hips gyrated even more forcefully, causing him to reach up with his left hand and grab the bar for his own balance. He would not stop the action of his right hand for the sake of her pleasure. Her legs constricted around him like pythons. He pushed against the bar and pulled back to give his hand enough space to conduct, laying her supine in midair. She fell mute as her eyes closed and her head dropped back; ponytail cascading down along with the falls of the floggers on her shoulders.

It was this point at which Edward found himself as blissfully trapped as his subject. With her legs locked around him and his newfound inability to move his fingers in the tightening stronghold where angels fear to tread, he froze with her. Where time once moved in a line, in this instant, he was discovering breadth and depth in a new definition of lucidity.

Every muscle in their bodies held tension in the silence. Her arching back beckoned him to view her glistening breasts holding fast atop a chest that refused to relinquish the air that filled it. She was as unconscious of her breath as he was of the music that once guided his rhythm.

He wasn't certain she made it all the way through the countdown. But when her legs released him, he lost his position as well, dropping to his knees; leaving him with a wet spot on the front of his boxers and two pruney fingers.

A shadow cast across his face as he looked up at the silhouette of his angel, swinging back and forth between himself and the light that gave her a halo. He took her dangling feet in hand and gave a kiss on the top of each before pulling one of the blocks back over for her to stand. She placed one foot on the other and relieved her shoulders. Her posture hunched over with her arms up and her head hanging, eyes closed, panting.

He arose, pulled the floggers off her shoulders, and hung them at the ends of the bar; then embraced her though she could not do the same.

Once her eyes reopened, he took the ball gag by the belt at her cheeks with both hands and lifted until she peered through her loose hair.

"I'm going to say something to you. You will remain silent. You will not give a verbal response."

She nodded.

Edward looked deeply into her eyes with his hands still holding the straps. He inhaled and said, "I love you."

Katrina's eyelashes fluttered with hard blinks at Edward's declaration. This was the first time either of them had uttered those "three little words" to the other.

He continued to study her twinkling eyes for a few seconds. She remained silent as ordered. Finally, he pulled her face down by the belt and held her forehead to his mouth, breathing in the scent of her hair and tasting the salt of her sweat on his lips. At the conclusion of his indulgence, he lifted her face again to meet her eyes.

"I'm going to take this gag out of my mouth. Remember 'the procedure'."

His hands traced along the belt to the buckle behind her head. He loosened it but he did not release it. Without taking his eyes from hers, he reminded, "Fight the urge to close my jaw and swallow."

At that, he released the belt and pulled the gag out of her mouth. A gush of drool spilled over her lip and down her chin. But her jaw remained static in accordance with "the procedure".

"That's my good girl," he praised, a little louder than a whisper. He studied her face, analyzing the red lines across her cheeks from the belt. Though his eyes traveled from cheek to cheek, hers remained fixed upon his as she held her mouth agape. "Relax my jaw and close it way slower than you think you should."

She did exactly as told, taking almost a minute to close as Edward looked on. Once her teeth met, so did her lips. She took a soothing swallow, wetting the dry roof of her mouth with the pool under her tongue.

Edward gave a peck on her wet chin. "Good girl," he said. "Now, almost as slowly, open and then close my jaw again. Over and over. Exercise it." He repeated, "...slowly." He unconsciously demonstrated with his own jaw as he watched hers.

As she worked her jaw, Edward felt her fingers again, still warm. Loosening the cuff on her left wrist, he said, "On top of my head." Once her hand was free, she placed it on her head as slowly as she moved her jaw. After doing the same with her right hand, he helped her down off the block, returning her to earth. "Shoulders."

Her hands slid down the sides of her head and rested on her shoulders as instructed, though she doubted the necessity of the glacial pace. Whether her body weight was held by her feet or the cuffs around her wrists, her jaw and youthful joints were not severely taxed by the activities in which they were plunged. But she obeyed, nonetheless.

He spent a moment staring at her. She was becoming so accustomed that it no longer bothered her. She liked being the primary focus of his attention.

"Hips."

The procedure continued.

"Relax my arms. Slowly roll my shoulders."

As she did so, Edward reached forward and pinched the SIR nipple. "That was an order."

She winced at the pain but ignored the instinct to stop him, squeezing her arms into her sides. "But Sir! You say not to talk!"

Edward freed the nipple. "You're right! I did!" He leaned over to her breast and lifted it in his hand. "I'm sorry, Victoria. I forgot my own order." And he gave the nipple a wet kiss between his lips.

She giggled her lilty titter at that. "Thank you for the pain, Sir."

He rose to give a similar kiss on Katrina's lips. "You're welcome, my charge. Does Victoria forgive me?"

"She's 'Victoria' now, Sir? I think your other breast was 'Victoria'."

"No, that's 'Elizabeth'. ...I think. All names are subject to change."

"Why do you give those names, Sir?"

"That's between me, Victoria, Elizabeth, and Priscilla," he replied. "Does Victoria forgive me?"

"Victoria forgive you, Sir."

"Will my charge forgive me?"

"Your charge forgive you, Sir."

He kissed her again.

"Permission to ask a question, Sir."

"Permission granted."

"Why do you have me move my jaw and arms slow when we finish, Sir?"

"Well, my charge, should it come to pass that you want to continue doing this into your senior years, it's good to establish these habits while you are still young."

"Why, Sir?"

"If you are an old lady who has had my arms suspended above my head, you may find my heart doesn't pump blood up there as well as it does now. So if you drop my arms and let all that cold blood flow to my heart and head, you could pass out and fall. ...or worse." He concluded, "And if we are still acquainted in our senior years, I will definitely be doing things like this to you."

He saw a smile flash before she tried to hide it by pressing her lips. She looked up at him and transferred her weight to one foot, dropping her stance an inch. Edward gave her the kiss her body language requested.

*How did he know I wanted him to kiss me?*

When he grabbed the chain around her neck, she crossed her arms behind her back and followed him as trained. He laid down on the bed and draped her over him like a blanket before the lights dimmed.

With her head on his chest, she rode the steady swells of his breathing, listening to his heartbeat. His fingertips lazily traced the welts he had produced up and down her back. The excess blood under her skin accentuated the sensation of his touch.

It was this time, after their sessions, that she relished, almost more than the sessions themselves. The aftercare afforded her the opportunity to think and reflect on her man and the experiences they shared. And these thoughts chased away all of the worries of day-to-day life that imposed upon her.

However, this time, there was a dark cloud on her peaceful horizon. She wanted to talk to Edward about it but didn't know how to broach the subject. So she started with a lighter topic.

"Permission to ask another question, Sir."

"Permission granted."

"Why did you not want me to talk when you said you love me, Sir?"

"Because I wanted to tell you that I love you, and I didn't want you to feel like you had to tell me that you love me too, just because I said it. And besides, it is with the deepest regret that I must inform you, you had a gag in my mouth."

"What if I do love you too, Sir?"

"I already know. But tell me later."

"Did you understand what I said when I had the gag in your mouth, Sir?"

"Yeah, you said, 'I love lasagna.'"

"Yes, Sir. That was it," she said, employing the sarcasm she was learning from him. "I love lasagna."

"I think I know what you said. Maybe not everything. Because if you will recall, you were suffering from a condition commonly referred to as 'gag-in-mouth' disease."

"I was requesting something, Sir."
"To cum?"
"That too, Sir."
"What were you requesting?"

Katrina wasn't sure how to ask. *If there is anything I am learning from this man, it is how to be brave. How to keep my own thoughts from intimidating me. I know I can talk to him. I'll just ask:*

"Why won't you fuck me, Sir?"

The pace of Edward's breathing hit a speed bump. He cleared his throat before speaking. "I don't know if you would believe me if I told you."

*What does that mean?* "You let me suck but you don't let me fuck. Is there something wrong with me, Sir?"

"No," Edward replied with certainty. "I can confidently say that the reason I won't have intercourse is not because of any problem with you."

"Will you please tell me, Sir?"

"I'll tell you but you are under strict orders to keep it a secret."

"Who will I tell, Sir?"

"Don't ask me that," he scolded. "That's irrelevant. Secrets are not secrets simply because there is no one to tell."

"Yes, Sir. Please forgive me, Sir."

"I forgive you."

Katrina's head lifted to rest on her chin at Edward's sternum.

"The reason I won't have intercourse with you… is because…" He announced, matter-of-factly, "I am a virgin."

Katrina was not amused. "Serious, Sir. Please tell me," she pleaded.

"I'm telling you the truth. I'm a virgin," he said with conviction.

Katrina lifted her head to look at his dimly lit face.

"I'm a virgin," he repeated. "I can't get anybody to sleep with me."

"I can't tell if you are making fun of me, Sir."

Edward took on a more somber tone. "Okay, that last part was a joke. But I'm telling you the truth when I say my cock has never been inside a pussy."

Katrina tilted her head in disbelief, even though she knew he was telling the truth. Now she had so many questions she didn't know what to ask. "How… Why…"

"I don't want to do that until I'm married," he volunteered.

Katrina laid her head back down and took a moment to let Edward's revelation sink in before saying, "You are the most amazing man, Sir."

"Thank you, my charge."

She twisted her right leg around his. "Why do you want it secret, Sir?"

He took another breath before explaining. "Here's the thing: Remaining a virgin through your teens is good. Remaining a virgin through your 20s, even better. But something strange happens when you get to your late twenties or thirties. People start to look at you like there's something wrong; like it's something you should be ashamed of. Most girls wouldn't have a conversation with me if they knew there was no chance I'd be having sex with them."

"They are jealous. I think it is something wonderful, Sir."

"Thank you, my charge. I think you're pretty wonderful too."

She thought about what Edward might think of her, given what she told him about all the men to whom her deceased husband had sold her. "You must *really* think I'm a whore, Sir," she said as she buried her face in his chest.

"Hey," he said as he gave a tug on her hair to lift her head for her eyes. "You are *my* private whore, remember?"

"Yes, Sir."

"Say it."

"I am *your* private whore, Sir."

"Will you help me stay a virgin before marriage, my whore?"

"Yes, Sir. As long as you need, Sir."

"Will you join me in my goal to not have sex before marriage?"

"Yes, Sir," she said, equaling his conviction.

"Will you let me help you with that goal?"

"Yes, Sir."

"You realize we are taking responsibility for each other's sexuality. That's no small undertaking. And it can be far more difficult for a woman than a man."

"I understand, Sir."

"Good girl."

"Thank you, Sir." She turned her face down to kiss a spot on his chest and then laid her head on it.

"So you believe me when I say there is nothing wrong with *you*, right?"

"There is much wrong with me, Sir."

"I mean, there is nothing wrong with you that keeps me from wanting to stick my cock in you."

"Yes, Sir."

"In fact, my cock really wants to experience that kung fu grip you've got down there!"

"'Kung fu grip', Sir?"

"Yeah, when I finger you, it's like a Chinese finger trap. I'm afraid if I stick my dick in, I won't get it back!"

Katrina spoke through her laughter. "Is that bad, Sir?!"

"Nah. I'd just be stuck in you forever. That doesn't sound so bad. People would have to get used to us walking around together with me wearing you on my cock. We'd be the talk of your whole law firm!"

Though she knew Edward was joking, Katrina pictured the scenario in her mind. Her lilty laughter swelled with every absurd statement he made. It was like a song to his ears even as it waned.

He caressed her face and hair like she was the pet they both believed her to be. He rested his hand on her cheek and traced her eyebrow with his thumb from the outside, in, against the grain. Her head quivered like she was shaking off a fly. Edward did it again.

"I don't like that, Sir."

"I just hung you from the ceiling and tortured you for an hour, and you can't stand it when I ruffle my eyebrow?" he asked with a chuckle.

"Do what pleases you, Sir."

He kissed her on the crown of her head and ran his thumb *with* the grain of her eyebrow.

"Don't fall asleep before you make me cum," he said as he tapped her on the cheek.

"Yes, Sir," she said drowsily. "May I have your cum now, Sir?"

"How do you want to get it?"

"However you wish, Sir."

"Nope. You are going to choose this time. You are going to make that cock cum. How are you going to do it?"

"Permission to suck your cock, Sir?"

"Eh, maybe. I'm thinking about it."

Her face glided down his body, tracing her journey with kisses and licks, loose strands of hair in her wake.

At the first sensation of wet warmth on the tip, Edward stopped her. "Hey! What are you doing?"

She lifted her head and replied, "Sucking your cock, Sir?"

"I didn't give you permission to suck my cock!"

"May I please suck your cock, Sir?"

"I'm... still thinking about it."

"Please, Sir?" She gave it a lick from the root and kissed his frenulum with open lips. She begged with her fingertips holding it and her palms together. "Pleeeeease, Sir?" She hid her face behind it, looking at him with an eye on each side. "Pleeeeeeeeeease, Sir?"

He seized her right hand with his left and kissed her knuckles.

She found it touching the way he would hold her hand while she was going down on him. The physical contact, the way his hands and legs moved, the pace of his breathing, and his pulse told her all she needed to know to please her Dominant. And though she delighted in the objectification she experienced on a regular basis with Edward, the act had never made her feel more connected to a man.

He pressed her hand to his heart and replied with feigned reluctance, "Oh... alright. Fine. Suck that cock, you whore."

"Thank you, Sir."

"No, thank me while you're sucking!"

"Esh, hir. ...ank oo, hir."

This time, Edward understood her words, in spite of the fact that she had contracted, what he would later diagnose as, an acute case of rapid onset "dick-in-mouth syndrome".

# 5.1

# DENIAL

"Do you think oral sex is 'sex', Sir?" she asked as she laid on top of him.

"Truth be told, I do. I do believe oral sex to be 'sex'."

"Why will you not put your cock in me but you will let me suck it, Sir?"

Edward's eyes opened to stare through the darkness until he could see the ceiling. "That's an even bigger secret."

"A bigger secret than you are a virgin, Sir?"

"Believe it or not!"

"I promise to keep your secrets, Sir."

"Maybe another time."

"Please tell me now, Sir."

Edward inhaled deeply and thought about his words. He knew he could trust her. But this was a very big secret for him. "I'm going to tell you something I have never told anyone before. It will be our secret forever. Understood?"

"Yes, Sir."

He thought about how he wanted to tell her: Facing her over a table? Turning on a light and lying here in bed? Or perhaps it would be easier to tell the story to the darkness of the room and listen to his own voice bounce off the walls. And then there was the matter of how she would react. Would it change the way she thought of him? Would it make him look weak to her? Would it change how she feels about him?

"Well, I have to tell someone sooner or later. … You've put so much trust in me. I want to trust you too," he said in a detached, almost disembodied voice.

Katrina wasn't sure if he was talking to her or to himself. But she remained silent and attentive.

"When I first moved to Vegas, I went out on a date with a girl I met years earlier in Grand Cayman. She was born and raised in Vegas. We had stayed in touch from time to time online. But this was the first time I saw her since we met.

"I was not yet acclimated to the Vegas culture, so it was a little unexpected that she asked me if I wanted to go to a topless show with her. Being a Midwestern boy, I didn't think taking a girl to a topless show was very classy. But this was Vegas, she invited me, she already had free tickets, and she knew I liked breasts!"

*How did she know he likes breasts? Nevermind.*

"We went to the show and then dinner afterward. I thought it was weird how she brought up that she was not going to be having sex with me. She said it two or three times throughout the evening. And each time she did, I just said, 'I know.' I could tell she didn't expect an answer like that. It was like she was half surprised and half offended. Looking back on it, maybe that was some kind of a pickup line for her to bring up the subject. I don't know."

Katrina balanced her head on her chin to see Edward's face as he continued. Even in the darkness, she could see in his eyes that he was essentially reliving the events in his mind as he told the story.

"Anyway, we get back to the low budget weekly hotel where I was staying when I first moved here. I parked right next to her car and was walking over to open her driver's side door. But *she* started walking toward my building. We had been having good conversations all evening and neither of us wanted the date to end, so I invited her up. I reminded her of her assertion that we were not going to have sex. And this time, *she* said, 'I know!'

"So we are talking and we are cuddling a bit. And we are both getting tired. I invited her to spend the night. She accepted. I let her wear one of my shirts and I was wearing boxers. And then I thought it was weird when *she* asked *me* if we were really not going to have sex. I said, 'No.' She asked if I wanted a blowjob. I politely declined. But I think she was really offended. I doubt she had ever been turned down for a blowjob before. I was satisfied to just hold her while we slept."

As Edward stared into the darkness, his left hand raised as though he was picturing himself holding this girl while recalling the story. Katrina could sense this third person in the bed with them.

"I remember I was having a dream... an erotic dream, because I was hard as a rock. And it was like a wet dream that I used to have when I was a teenager. I was confused because I felt myself cumming. But in my dream or sleep or half unconsciousness, I couldn't tell if I was really cumming or if I was peeing. So I reached down to my cock. But I couldn't find my cock! I couldn't tell what I was feeling. The confusion was enough to finally wake me up.

"I open my eyes and I'm looking around this strange room that I didn't recognize at first because I had only lived there a couple weeks. I've got something going on with my cock that I can't understand. I'm reaching and I lean up to see this girl, down there, sucking me off. I grab her by her hair and rip her off me as I'm cumming. She starts yelling... I don't remember what either of us said. But she got dressed and left."

Edward took a breath before continuing slowly, "And that was the first time anyone had gone down on me. ... She will never know that she was my first."

He concluded at a more conversational pace, "So to answer your question, that was an experience I wanted to save for marriage. But it was not to be. So now if I have a special girl in my life whom I feel is worthy of sucking me..." Edward's arm gave Katrina a squeeze. "...I allow her if she so desires."

Katrina contemplated Edward's story. Then she broke her silence with the only thought on her mind: "You were raped."

Edward's gaze turned down from the ceiling to Katrina. "No I wasn't."

"Yes you were."

"How so?"

Katrina's legal mind was kicking in as she mentally prepared a list of factors in the story that constituted sexual assault. "So I understand," she began. "She asked you for permission to suck your cock, correct?"

"Correct."

"You said, 'No', correct?"

Edward replied with reticence, "Correct." He wasn't sure he liked where the conversation was going.

"And then she sucked your cock anyway, correct?"

"Well, yeah. But it wasn't *rape*." He was getting agitated. "I wasn't even awake."

Katrina continued with sensitivity in her voice. "You were asleep when this happened."

"That's right."

"Because you were asleep, you were not able to give consent after you said 'no' when you were awake. But she did it anyway. That is rape, Edward."

His body went limp under her as his gaze returned to the ceiling and her head returned to his chest. His heart rate was elevated and his breathing was choppy. She could feel his brain processing.

They laid in the darkness of the room for a few moments before Edward calmly stated, "I don't see it that way."

Katrina's arms tightened at his sides in her attempt to make him feel the love she had for him. Perhaps it also served as an anchor to keep him grounded while his mind wandered. She knew this would be replacing her as the subject of his obsession, at least for a time …maybe for a long time. *Did I make a mistake using the 'r' word? Did I hurt him? How much pain does he feel about this? Did I make it worse?*

She wondered how this event would manifest itself. Would he revisit the subject with her in the future? Would he talk it out? Would he take it out on his drumset? Or would it come out unexpectedly with a vicious punch to the stomach while they walked down the aisle of a grocery store, as she had experienced with someone else?

She didn't know how to leave the subject for the night. So she ended by whispering the most important thing on her mind: "Te amo también."

# 8.1

# THE TURKEY CLUB, CONTINUED

With Philena's guitar strapped over his shoulder, Edward stepped to the microphone while tuning.

In the front were tables of about a dozen true karaoke enthusiasts who shouted, whistled, and clapped for him before he even made it to the stage.

Though they bore the mantle of "cheerleader" for each performer, Edward understood they weren't really applauding for him personally since they didn't actually know him. But they did enjoy the duets he sang and were looking forward to hearing him in his first solo performance of the night.

After graciously accepting the support of these strangers, Edward looked over the sea of faces to find his favorite, that of Katrina. She sat up straight, watching him.

"I wrote this song for my sub, Katrina. She's the one in the back, blushing through her caramel skin!" Some heads turned to see if they could find her. "Wave at us, my charge!"

Katrina waved at the audience with a shy smile. But she felt like she was about to pass out from the attention before she heard him say, "Good girl."

London turned to Katrina and asked, "Did you know he was going to do this?"

She shook her head.

Before playing the first chord of the song, he murmured into the microphone, "Te amo, I love you."

From there, he proceeded with the following lyrics:

## So She Knows/Asi Que Ella Sabe

VERSE 1
casta llano hay no fácil para mi,
y ni inglés tampoco,
pero quando palabras hay no suficiente,
dos lenguas hay más claro,

CHORUS
digo "i love you" porque ella la gusta,
digo "te amo" así que ella sabe,
digo "i love you" porque es bueno a decir lo,
digo "te amo" porque lo hago,
te amo, i love you,

VERSE 2
she taught me the meaning of "love",
and "cheese" and "walk" and "blue",
though we may run out of words to say,
i will never run out on you,

FINAL CHORUS
i say "i love you" because she likes to hear it,
i say "te amo" so she knows,
i say "i love you" because it's good for me to say it,
i say "te amo" because i do,

i say "i love you" because she likes to hear it,
i say "te amo" so she knows,
i say "i love you" because it's good for me to say it,
i say "i love you" because i do,

te amo, i love you,

te amo, i love you.

Katrina's vision blurred as tears welled at Edward's public declaration of his love for her, in two languages, no less.

Now the entire crowd applauded almost as much as the fanatics in the front. London shouted over the applause, "He's good!"

"He is!" Katrina agreed. "Now is the first time I hear him sing!"

As Edward did at the end of each of his performances, he stepped over to the KJ booth, placed a bill in a bucket, and admonished the crowd to "Always be tipping!"

After returning Philena's guitar and microphone to her, he started back to the couch, but Philena stopped him. "Wait, Edward. Don't go anywhere." She handed the microphone back to him.

"Okay, another duet?"

She winked at Edward and announced, "Next to the stage, let's give it up for Edward's girl... Ka-tri-na!"

The crowd applauded again though they didn't know Katrina any more than they knew Edward. She felt a sinking in her chest when she heard Philena say her name.

Edward was confused. He looked back and read Katrina's nerves on her face, spacey eyes, lips tight at the corners. If his submissive's wishes were not being respected, it was his duty to intervene. He turned back to Philena.

"Katrina said she wasn't going to sing," he said, with a hint of Domly assertiveness.

Ever receptive, Philena returned, "I know! She told me 'no' earlier but she changed her mind." She held up a sheet of paper for Edward to see, Katrina signed herself up.

Astonished, Edward conceded, "Apologies, I stand corrected."

Katrina managed to rise from the couch before she froze. She had planned on surprising her Dom. But her heart started racing to the edge of panic. *What do I do now? What if I can't do it? What if I embarrass myself? What if I make Edward ashamed of me? What if...*

"Excellent!" Edward's voice broke her from her line of negative thinking. "I was not expecting this. Here comes my girl, Katrina!" The cheers and clapping were reignited.

The sound of her own name from Edward's lips began to melt her catatonia.

London asked, "Has he ever heard you sing before?"

Without looking back, Katrina simply replied, "No." And with that, she forced one foot forward to begin a climb to the front of the room. Her heart was pounding hard enough to feel the pulse in her neck. But she was determined to beat this anxiety... this terror. And it was too late to stop now.

Edward could see the apprehension in her gait as though she was walking on a rope bridge in her high heels. And it was compounded by the natural waning of applause as more and more eyes were on her. So he started talking into the microphone with whatever came to his mouth: "You know, it's like the more I drink, the harder it is to make it to the stage before the applause stops..." His stream-of-consciousness monologue elicited enough laughter from the crowd to shake some of her tension.

She didn't hear his words, just his voice. She had already decided what she was going to do. And the sound of Edward made each step easier as she walked down the aisle.

On her way, she saw an empty chair and grabbed it without breaking her smoothing stride. Edward was intrigued.

She set the chair in front of the fanatics, stepped up to Edward on the stage, took the microphone from his hand, and requested, "Will you please sit, Sir?"

"As you wish, my charge." He stepped down.

Katrina turned and walked to the chain spiderweb. And with her back to the audience, she nodded at Philena.

In stark contrast to the rhythmic guitar strumming in Edward's song, the distorted power chords of an electric guitar blasted the introduction of Katrina's selection. Through her form-fitting miniskirt, her butt jerked left and right with each chord change.

With the entrance of her voice, Katrina spun around to see Edward pinned to the chair, eyes locked on her with mouth agape. His undivided attention assured her she was off to a good start. With the beginning of each measure, she took a small step toward the front of the stage, pushing the emotion of her performance forward with every line.

Edward was not familiar with the song. But if there was any doubt about the message or intention of the composition, it was made abundantly clear in the lines of the chorus, when Katrina sang: "Hit me like a man, love me like a woman!"

On the second verse, Katrina stepped off the stage and made her way to Edward. Without a stutter in her singing, she sat on his knee for one line, she slid up to rub her butt against his crotch for another. Then she stood between his legs and buried his face in her cleavage. From there, she lowered to her haunches and found she was providing him with more than enough inspiration for his personal growth.

Edward was overwhelmed with bliss at this multi sensory experience. His head bobbed to the music as he patted Katrina on the thigh with every backbeat. He felt a rush from the realization that every step she took, every word she sang, and every move she made was for his pleasure. It was her declaration to him and to all who were present that her purpose was to please her Dominant. And he was getting high on the power his blossoming submissive was giving him.

For the final chorus, Katrina pushed Edward's legs together and pulled her skirt up to straddle his lap. And with the repetition of the final line, "Love me like a woman," she slid back to his knees. With her face in front of his, she repeated, "Love me like a woman." She backed off of his knees and rested on her own. Leaning on his legs like an altar, and looking up into his eyes, she sang with a begging cry, "Love me like a woman."

Their ears popped at the silence before the stunned crowd exploded, reminding the couple they were not alone. But they didn't care.

Edward reached forward and lifted Katrina until she was straddling his lap again. They unleashed a kiss on each other that raised the volume of the spectators even higher. But they only heard the sound of their own hearts beating at the tempo of the song as they melted into an embrace.

She locked her chin over his shoulder with her closed eyes and hair covering her face. When he put both hands under her butt and stood up, she wrapped her legs around him so he could carry her away. To where? She did not care as long as it was with her Dominant.

\*     \*     \*

By this time of night, The Dungeon Studios were almost as loud as the Main Hall. Edward walked through the door, carrying Katrina. And given the noise level, they were able to talk at a normal volume without disturbing anybody. He sat in a chair between two studios with Katrina straddling his lap again.

"Where in the world did that come from?!" he asked, still stunned by Katrina's performance.

Katrina shrugged shyly, "I just wanted you to like it, Sir."

"Are you kidding?! That was incredible! I loved every minute!"

She giggled with the lilt Edward loved to hear. "Were you surprised, Sir?"

"If I wake up tomorrow with my head sewn to the carpet, I won't be more surprised than I am now."

Katrina thought that was an odd thing for him to say but it did make her laugh.

Edward was still breathing heavily with his heart racing. "I know you planned that. You *had* to practice that. That was too good!"

Still feeling bashful, "Yes, Sir. I practiced it when you told me we are coming here. When we come here, I get scare and didn't want to do it. But I changed my mind."

"Thank you for changing your mind. You're so amazing." He sighed to slow down his heart. "Did you plan it with Philena?"

"No, I gave her the paper while you were singing with the other girls. She said I will go after you sing. And when she said my name... I don't remember until now."

"How do you feel?"

"Magnifico, Sir!"

"Me too. I love you."

With her head on his shoulder, she asked, "Why do you love me, Sir?"

"Hm?"

"Nevermind."

This was new for Katrina. In spite of all her efforts through all her years of life, she never felt like she had ever been able to please a man as much as she had pleased Edward that night. And it made her eyes tear once again, but for joy.

He adjusted his erect member so she could sit across his lap. She lifted her head and scanned the room.

Many of the various pieces of furniture were occupied at this time. A cacophony of voices, whip cracks, paddle smacks, cries, and laughter among other sounds bounced around the cavernous room. But nobody appeared to be having actual sex as far as Katrina could see.

The studio next to them featured a ring the size of a steering wheel hanging down by a chain from the ceiling. Katrina turned to see another couple entering that studio.

They looked to be about the same age as each other, both older than Edward. The man was much taller than the woman. He was wearing black pants with a black, long-sleeve shirt. She was wearing a pair of slippers and a blanket over her shoulders that did little to hide her naked front. But she made no attempt to cover herself.

They were both fit for the most part. He was not skinny. But he wore his weight well. Although she had a few extra pounds, she was top-heavy and unashamed. One very red nipple could be seen peeking out from the blanket. It was apparent by the pink streaks of her skin and wet eyes that she had been worked over to tears.

The man stopped her just inside the border of the open studio to pull the velvet rope across like a "Do Not Disturb" sign. He turned to walk his woman with his right hand on the back of her neck and a gym bag in his left. He guided her under the ring and snapped his fingers, pointing down. With that gesture, she knew what to do. She lowered to her knees and sat on her feet, leaning over with her face to the floor.

The man set down the gym bag, unzipped it, and fished through supplies. The first thing he retrieved was a rope.

He walked to his woman and pulled the blanket off of her with his free hand revealing a possible reason she did not try to cover herself before: Handcuffs with leather padding restrained her arms.

The pink streaked skin on her back matched the streaks on her front. Katrina recognized the streaks from her own experience. *He probably used a flogger like the ones Edward uses on me.*

The woman's butt was an even deeper color of pink with red and blackening punctuations. The two had been busy.

The man took a knee, and tied the middle of the rope around the chain of her handcuffs. Then he stood to thread the ends of the rope through the ring above. He pulled the rope through the ring until there was no slack from the handcuffs, to the ring, to his hands. But he did not stop there.

The woman's hands were slowly raised behind her back causing her to put her face even closer to the ground. The position of her arms rendered her unable to sit up. But she could lift herself on her knees as her arms rose. Her breasts hung down from her chest along with her head. And as the man continued to pull the rope, she was finally forced to stand on her feet.

The man lowered her hands until they rested at her butt. Then he threaded the ends of the rope through the original knot at the chain of the handcuffs, creating another knot.

She stood with her back to the man, facing a few feet to the side of Edward and Katrina. They could see on her face that she was a million miles away as tears were already starting to trickle. She was probably not cognizant of their presence nor that of the few voyeurs who had gathered at the velvet rope.

Without warning, the man began with a single-tail whip on her thighs. The initial contact awoke her from her subspace daydream. When she jumped, her breasts seemed to jump even higher.

For a moment, she attempted to block the lashes with her hands. Once she learned she could not lower her hands any further, she high-stepped, lifting a knee, one at a time. So the man simply whipped the leg that remained on the ground. When she started moving away, the man followed without missing a note.

Now the woman was finding that each step away from the ring only raised her hands higher, exposing the tender flesh of her buttocks and back for the man to target. Her natural reaction caused her to step to the limit of the rope, lifting her arms until she was bent over on her feet. Her hanging breasts swung and bounced about, accentuating every pain-inspired motion she made.

The man was leading a dance. She would take a few steps to her left if the man was concentrating on her right side. Then she would step back to her right when the man switched to her left. If he hit one leg, she would try to block it with the other. So he would simply target the most convenient leg. If she bent a knee behind her back, he would sting the bottom of her foot before moving back to her bottom. And once she could bear no more pain on her butt, she stepped back toward the man so the rope would afford her the ability to stand upright and cover her ailing bottom with her hands, sending the whip back to her thighs. Such was the dance of this couple. And for a time, it seemed like the silent song would never end.

Though there was no music, the woman's whimpers and cries had crescendoed to a volume that some voyeurs found disturbing. And were it not for the first couple she observed earlier in the evening, Katrina might have been among the disturbed. But she looked upon the scene with enthrallment and arousal. She did not notice her knees slowly parting as she watched.

Through the whipping, the woman had trekked as close to Katrina and Edward as the rope would allow. And by this time, her cries had grown to screams.

The man stayed his hand as suddenly as he had begun and approached his submissive. She stood bent over, hands suspended behind her back, breasts and head hanging down, on one foot with one leg wrapped around the other. Her crying was getting softer as he untied the rope from her cuffs and guided her arms to her back. He grabbed her by the hair with his left hand and lifted her head, causing her to stand up straight and stumble back into him. He steadied his sub with his arms around her, his right hand holding her by a breast.

He whispered in her ear. Nobody could hear what he was saying. But all could hear her responses: "No, Master. ... "Yes, Master. ... Yes, Master! ... No! Please, Master. Don't stop!"

And with his first intelligible words, he declared, "I will never stop!"

With his left hand, he reached down between her legs with a small vibrating toy wrapped around a finger and began touching her in such a way that caused her to struggle to stay on her feet. She tried to bend over but he held her up by her breast. In a short amount of time, she started pleading, "Please, Master."

"Please what?" his gruff voice replied.
"Please, may I cum?"
"No."
"Please, Master? Please, may I cum, Master?"

"No!" he repeated as his hand continued.

Her pleading persisted and grew to begging. And still, she was denied. Until finally, with a panicked voice as though her apotheosis were an unstoppable oncoming train, she screamed, "PLEASE, MASTER? PLEASE, LET ME CUM, MASTER!"

"CUM!" he demanded as he dropped her breast and placed his right hand over her mouth, pinching her nose, holding her breath. Her knees buckled before going limp. The man returned his right arm around her chest and controlled their slow descent to the floor. But he never stopped what his left hand was doing between her legs. And she started begging to cum again.

It was difficult to tell how many times she orgasmed. It could have been several short ones… or a couple long ones, perhaps a combination. But one thing was clear as she laid on the floor, a weeping mass of tears and multicolored skin: This woman was *exhausted*.

Her Master unlocked one of the cuffs and directed her hands in front of her. He lifted her head to rest against his chest. He reached over for the blanket she originally wore into the studio and wrapped her in it as she curled into a ball between her Master's legs.

Katrina sat in awe of what she had witnessed. Her dry eyes were transfixed on the couple. She felt relief when she blinked. And it made her wonder if she had stopped blinking the entire time she was watching. Spit covered her parched tongue when she closed her mouth. She realized she hadn't swallowed the whole time either. And with the depth of her breathing, she wondered if she had held her breath as well. By the unconscious spreading of her legs and Edward's hand rubbing her through her thong panties, her loins were stirred, to say the least. And under her thigh she could tell Edward felt the same way.

The questions that Katrina had earlier in the evening were dwindling and giving way to an inexplicable understanding. The appeal of complete immersion into this lifestyle was growing stronger with every event she witnessed. She was feeling empowered, as though she was gaining the ability to conquer fears and change things in her life that she did not like. In a search for the next high, she turned inward to the depths of her own psyche. *Where is the next mountain for me to climb? Where is the next wall to break? What is the next challenge?*

"Sir? Will you please take me shooting again?"

# 9

# HOLES IN THE DESERT

There are a lot of holes in the desert. And a lot of problems are buried in those holes. The time had come for Katrina to bury a problem of her own.

"Would you like to talk about what it was that scared you so much the first time we did this?" Edward asked as he turned off the highway and onto a gravel road.

Katrina's mind froze. And then she bluntly forced the words out of her mouth before she could feel their gravity. "My husband kill himself with a gun," she murmured as she stared out the passenger window.

Hearing the detachment in her voice, he decided to forgo disciplining her for her lapse in verbal decorum for the time being.

"That might have something to do with it," he drolled. "Are you afraid something like that will happen again?"

"It happens frequently. Like the shooting."

Nobody who lived in Las Vegas would question which "shooting" to which she was referring.

Edward was uncertain if she was attempting to redirect the conversation away from her personal experience. But he allowed it. "Is *that* what you would like to talk about?"

"I don't know, Sir."

"Do you know what all mass shooters have in common?"

"No, Sir."

"They are all *weak men*. And there is nothing more dangerous in this world than a weak man."

"Do you mean my husband was a weak man?"

"I don't know," he replied. "You would know better than me. I'm just glad he was strong enough to only shoot himself." His voice, gruff with disgust.

Katrina thought upon his words. *He's angry with my dead husband and they never even met. Do I really make Edward pay so much for what that bastard did to me?*

"I didn't know about your husband at the time. But I knew something was bothering you."

"Why did you have me do it if you knew it bothered me?" she asked the window.

"Because it sounded like a fear that I might have been able to help you conquer," he replied. "Maybe it was just what I wanted to hear, but you convinced me that you were excited about it."

"I was not, Sir. I was scare."

"I know that now. Thank you for telling me the truth."

"You're welcome, Sir."

"When I asked you if you wanted to do it, I didn't understand your inability to say 'no'. But you have made great strides in that area since."

She turned from the window to face him. "With your help, Sir."

Edward didn't speak. He took his right hand off the wheel and placed it on her bare thigh. She understood that physical touch was his method of responding with more emotional weight than affirming words. She wrapped her left arm around his right and leaned into him.

It had been two weeks since Katrina asked Edward to take her shooting again. And in those weeks, devising a way to help her was his primary obsession. "What do you need from me to help you do this?"

She thought about the question for a moment to no avail. "I don't know. ... I don't know the answer."

"There are two ways we can go about it," he started, as he held her hand on her lap. "We can get things set up for you, the target, the gun. I'll make sure everything is safe. And then I can let you proceed on your own under my watch. Or... We can completely adhere to protocol. You will do nothing unless I order you. And we will work through it like any of our normal exercises." He waited for an answer before adding, "Or we could do something in between. Whatever you think has the potential to be the most therapeutic." He looked at her out the corner of his sunglasses. Even though she was also wearing sunglasses, he knew she was thinking as the gravel road turned to a dust trail.

*The thought of slipping into submission and doing nothing but what his voice tells me is appealing. But will that really help me get over this?*

"Will you tell me what to do at the start?"

"We'll start there. And then maybe I'll lengthen your leash as we go. How does that sound?"

"Good."

It was time to tighten the leash. "Good, what?"

"Good, Sir." She came to realize her lapses. "Please forgive me, Sir."

He squeezed her thigh. But he could hear in her voice, she wasn't fully present with him.

He pulled the car off the trail and parked about 40 yards away from a giant pile of sandy gravel: one of several that dotted an otherwise flat landscape. They might as well have been on the moon for all the desolation of the setting.

"Are you ready?"

"Yes, Sir," she replied with tension in her voice.

"Perhaps this will help you," he said as he pulled the chain and lock from the pocket behind her seat.

"Yes, Sir!" Katrina smiled and exhaled with relief as she stared at the collar like... well, like Edward stares at her. Without being ordered, she automatically pulled her hair back and leaned toward him as an invitation, not that he needed one. Once it was secure around her neck, Edward tested it with a yank toward himself for a kiss.

He relinquished the collar and reached behind his own seat to retrieve a box. He set it in between the two of them and opened it to reveal… things that Katrina did not recognize, *gun things*.

"Watch carefully," he said as he pulled out an empty magazine and a box of ammunition.

"Yes, Sir."

He started by loading a few bullets into the magazine. And then he pulled out some kind of… *thing* that made it easier for him to finish loading. Katrina looked on as ordered. Then, by the small holes in the back of the magazine, he showed her that it was loaded to capacity. He pulled out another empty magazine and handed it to her along with… *the loading thing* and ordered her to do the same.

She complied, loading the magazine as Edward had demonstrated. She felt how the magazine offered more and more resistance with each cartridge to the point she was using arm strength and her bare knee. But she didn't think of it as loading bullets into a magazine. She thought of it as carrying out the orders of her Dominant. This distracted her from the dread of the oncoming storm on the horizon. And it distracted her from… whatever Edward was doing next to her.

"Is this good, Sir?" she asked, upon completion of her task.

Edward took the magazine and analyzed it. "That's very good."

"Thank you, Sir."

He set it down and handed her another empty magazine. "Do it again."

"Yes, Sir."

They both worked on their respective projects but Edward completed his first. So he affectionately watched his submissive struggle to load the last few cartridges against the tightening magazine. She felt his stare.

"This is hard, Sir."

"This is not the first hard thing you've handled."

"True, Sir!"

She handed the loaded magazine back to Edward for inspection. After his approval, he placed the magazine back in the box and closed it. Then he handed her something else.

"Do you know what that is?"

"It's a… 'muelle', Sir. I don't know in English."

"It's a 'spring'."

"Como 'primavera', Sir?"

"Same word, different meaning. We have the season of *spring*, 'when kings go off to war'. And we have this thing, also called a 'spring'."

"Yes, Sir."

He handed her a bar of metal. It had grease on it that left black marks on her hands. A similar conversation ensued. That's how she learned what a "guide rod" was.

With the third piece, he asked again, "Do you know what this is?"

By this time she had figured out what these things were. "It's a part of a gun, Sir?"

"That's correct. That part is called the 'slide'."

Even though her hands were full of gun parts, he handed her another as it grew comical. And then he finally showed her the most recognizable part of a gun. He had her put all of the parts down on top of the box and wipe her hands off with a towel before he handed her the grip, which included the trigger assembly.

Though the gun was not in functioning condition, obvious even to a layman, she still pointed the grip safely toward the dashboard. He had her pull the trigger after reminding her how to hold it. She seemed comfortable. Far more than her first experience. But Edward continued the lesson at the same slow pace.

"Look at all these parts."

"Yes, Sir."

"Have you ever used any tools like a hammer or a screwdriver?"

She wasn't sure what a "screwdriver" was but she knew what a "hammer" was. "Yes, Sir."

"All of these are just parts of a tool. Watch."

"Yes, Sir."

And with that, he turned the slide upside down and placed the barrel. Then he slid the spring onto the guide rod and ran the guide rod from the front of the slide to a notch on the barrel. Then he took the grip from Katrina and slid the slide onto the rails thereof. He locked the release on the side of the grip and racked the slide a few times before he revealed the gun in its completion to her. Her face went from the gun to his with a grin, and then back to the gun.

"Would you like…"

Katrina took the gun from his hand before he could finish the sentence. Edward could see her eyes behind her sunglasses. She was in awe of the exquisite craftsmanship of the tool. Or perhaps she was in awe of Edward's skill with the firearm. He showed her how to cycle it and how to get a feel for the trigger function and line up the sights. It was difficult for her to rack the slide, but she was determined.

"If we get you one of your own, we will get a smaller caliber that will be easier for you to use."

"Can we shoot it now, Sir?"

He turned off the engine and exited the car giving Katrina a burst of the hot desert air. He walked around the back and opened her door.

"Stand up."

"Yes, Sir." She obeyed, standing before him, still holding the gun aimed to the ground in her right hand.

"I like the way you got up and kept the gun pointed in a safe direction and my finger off the trigger even though it is not loaded."

"Thank you, Sir! I remember some of the first lesson."

"Good. Don't move."

"Yes, Sir."

She was wearing a baggy white shirt with the collar and arms cut out so it only covered one shoulder at a time. He pulled the holster off his belt and leaned down to tuck the right side of her shirt into her short denim shorts. He placed the holster on her belt by her right hand. "Put the gun in the holster."

"Yes, Sir." She learned that she would need to use some force to get the gun in and out. Edward had her repeat the process for practice.

"Think you got it?"

"I think so, Sir."

"Position one."

"Yes, Sir." She crossed her arms behind her back and faced forward.

Katrina didn't see where it came from, but Edward attached the end of a 6-foot chain leash to the chain collar around her neck. *He was serious about a leash!* The leather handle on the opposite end was just the right size for Edward to put around his left wrist comfortably. While his chain around her neck always felt like a warm hug to her, the leash only accentuated the connection to her Dominant.

"Get the magazines out of the box."

"Yes, Sir."

As she turned around and bent over at the waist to retrieve the magazines, Edward did not waste the opportunity to grab the curve of a cheek that had slipped out from under her shorts, ending with a smack.

"Thank you, Sir!"

"What is this?" he asked as he rubbed his hand on her backside.

"That is your 'fine ass', Sir!"

As he admired her fundament, he thought he was waiting for her to get all of the magazines. "Do you have them?"

"Yes, Sir. I'm enjoying you touching your fine ass!"

"Good girl! Get over here," he said with a tug on her leash.

"Yes, Sir!"

He deposited two of the magazines in the magazine holster on his belt and the third in the gun on *her* belt. He led her on the leash to the back of the car where they put on sunscreen and put in earplugs. She observed a few more foreign objects in the trunk including a 2x4 piece of wood, a long locked case, and some big metal parts.

He handed her a rectangular steel plate that was almost as big as her small torso. Its weight made it difficult for her to carry. And since the smoldering trunk had heated it, she couldn't hold it to her body. But she was feeling tougher by the minute and was going to obey every order from her Dominant. He pulled out the 2x4 and an even bigger piece of steel.

As he led her to the sand and gravel berm, never more than 6 feet behind him, she saw the spent brass and shotgun shells littering the desert floor, becoming more abundant with every step. She set the edge of the plate on the ground and watched Edward as he set the 2x4 on the stand and then placed the plate on top.

She saw the rectangular plate she had been carrying had a square to form the head and abdomen of a human being. This conjured a flash of the same image that she allowed to haunt her dreams for years. She swallowed as she started to feel her heart beat. But she was awakened by a tug on her leash.

She snapped around to catch up with her Dominant who seemed to be ignoring the fact that her neck was chained to his wrist. Once he had marked approximately 15 feet from the target, he turned around to face her and pulled the leash until her nose was almost in his chest.

"Position one."

"Yes, Sir."

"Don't think. Just do what my voice tells you to do."

"Yes, Sir."

"Turn around and face the target."

"Yes, Sir." She did so, remaining in position one. He stepped up to her right.

"Watch carefully. I'm going to take a few shots and I'm going to tell you what I'm thinking while I do it. We will get into tactical shooting later. Right now, I just want you to relax and connect with this target... and have fun." He reminded her how to hold the gun, how to control her breath, how to align the sights, and how to allow the trigger to "surprise" her. And with that, he took a breath, squeezed, and... BANG!

Katrina jumped at the sound. But she did not break from her ordered position. BANG! BANG! BANG!

Edward blasted through the magazine, looking at her every two or three shots to observe and distract her with a tip about the technique he was utilizing.

Katrina noticed how she went from jumping with each shot to a slight flinch, until she was just blinking with each controlled explosion from the tool in the hands of her Dominant. Her eyes traced from the gun, to Edward's hand, to his wrist, to the grip of the leash around it, to the rattling leash itself, to the collar around her neck. She took comfort in seeing him control this toy in his hands as much as he was controlling her. She was cognizant of her deepening awareness. She even started to hear the loud "TING" of the plate with every bullet driven into it, producing more of a "BANGTING".

Finally, Edward stopped, took his finger off the trigger, turned to her, and placed the gun in the holster on her belt.

"It's your turn."

"Yes, Sir!" she said, forcing a little more volume than usual.

Edward stepped behind her and pulled the leash back over her left shoulder. He leaned forward and kissed her right ear.

"Remember, you will do everything my voice tells you."

"Yes, Sir."

"You will not give another verbal response until after you have fired your first shot."

She nodded.

"My feet are already in a good position from position one. So relax my arms at my sides."

She did so, uncrossing her arms from behind her back. He placed his hands on the sides of her ribcage. Though his lips were by her ear, he spoke directly to her mind:

"Without touching the trigger, draw that tool from the holster with my right hand.

"Point it toward the target.

"Bring my left hand to the grip.

"Align the sights.

"Put my finger on the trigger.

"Take a deep breath.

"Exhale.

"Pull the trigger slowly until it surprises you."

BANGTING!

The sand in front of the target stirred in a straight line on the plane of the plate as shattered lead scattered.

Katrina immediately spun and wrapped her arms around Edward's neck and locked her lips with his like he was the last meal on Earth. They were laughing and kissing at the same time until they stopped by holding each other's faces at the cheeks, foreheads and sunglasses pressed together.

"Was that good for you too?!" Edward asked.

"I want more!" she said. "…Sir!"

"Get it, girl!"

She turned and unholstered the gun again. Though she was a bit more reckless with her breath control, she lined up the sights and pulled the trigger. … But nothing happened. She turned the gun to its side to find the slide was locked back.

"I gave it to you with only one bullet. I had to see what you would do with it after your first shot. And you did great! You took your finger off the trigger and kept it pointed at the target or the ground until you holstered. I'm proud of you!"

"You're proud of me, Sir?" she asked as she turned back to him, careful to keep the gun pointed downrange.

"I'm *very* proud of you, my charge. You know that. I've told you before."

She holstered the firearm again. But she didn't say anything.

"Hey," he said as he twitched the leash.

She looked up at him.

"Who is proud of you?"

"You are proud of me, Sir."

"That's right." He kissed her on the forehead, pulled out a fresh magazine, and handed it to her. "Get to work."

"Yes, Sir!"

She blasted her way through half of it before Edward stepped her back to 20 feet. He lectured her a bit on how she would eventually need to learn to lift her shirt off of a concealed gun before she draws. But she solved the problem by taking her shirt off entirely, revealing a black string bikini top.

"Will you please hold my shirt, Sir?"

"I think I like your solution more," Edward said as he took it from her.

"Thank you, Sir!"

She finished the magazine before they stepped back to 30 feet. Then they took turns firing the third magazine at 40 feet, and then 50 feet. He used his phone to video her before returning to the car.

They stood at the trunk, reloaded the magazines, and drank some water.

"Do you need some more sunscreen?"

"No, Sir. I don't burn."

"I wish I could say the same."

"What's in that big box, Sir?" she asked, referring to the case in the trunk.

"That's my sporting rifle."

"How many guns do you have, Sir?"

Edward paused to think. "I'm not sure."

"Can I see it, Sir?"

"Yes, you *may*." He opened the case. The sight was as foreign to her as the handgun on her hip once was.

Edward watched her face as she gazed upon it. He lifted it out and wrapped the sling over her shoulder, pulling the leash through, keeping his warrior submissive under his control. "This might be the sexiest thing I've seen all day," he said, taking a picture.

"Thank you, Sir. *May* I shoot it?"

"Yes, you may. But first…"

He ordered her to put another layer of sunscreen on the back of his neck and legs as he drank water. When she was finished, he leaned over to put the bottle back in the trunk… right next to her bikini top. He looked up to see his favorite nipples looking right back at him with the sling between them, supporting the rifle below and Katrina's mischievous grin above.

"Why, Miss Gomez, you're trying to seduce me!"

She looked down at her exposed breasts as though she were surprised. "Ay! How did that happen, Sir?!"

She started to lean to retrieve her top but Edward pushed her back and slammed the trunk. "Position one!"

"Yes, Sir!"

He reached into his pocket and pulled out his keys to unlock the cable gun lock on the rifle. After pulling it out of the magazine well, he turned to open the trunk when a better idea occurred to him. He looked at Katrina with a smirk. "I think you've graduated to a more appropriate training collar."

He locked the black cable around her neck, transferred the leash to it, and took the chain off. He stood straight up with his hands on his hips to inspect her from head, to tits, to toes before saying, "I would like to revise my previous statement, your honor; Now *this*, is the sexiest thing I've seen all day."

"Sustained, Sir!"

He took another picture of his blooming submissive and acted like his phone was on fire: too hot to handle as a result of the image he had captured, much to her amusement.

They proceeded as before with a lesson on how to use the rifle. But with the scope, they started at 50 feet and worked backward from there. They began by shooting together, she with the rifle and he with the pistol. The further back they moved from the target, the more time between the "BANG" and the "TING". And they could hear that the ballistics of the rifle were traveling far faster than that of the handgun.

Once Edward's pistol was no longer a match for Katrina on the rifle, he added extra challenges for her, like attempting to make the plate sing while he smacked her ass or grabbed her tits. She didn't hit every shot. Sometimes she put another hole in the berm, making the dust dance. But that wasn't all that was dancing.

As she leaned to absorb the recoil, her breasts hung down and jiggled with each shot, to Edward's delight. At the end of a magazine, she turned to find him videoing her performance. She held the gun to the side and shook her bust side to side before bursting into laughter.

"Yeah, baby!"

"What are you going to do with this video, Sir?!" she asked into the lens.

"I'm going to watch it on repeat while you play with my cock!" And he pulled on the leash to plant a kiss on her over the rifle at her midriff.

"I'm going to play with your gun, Sir?!" she asked with her hand on the front of his jeans.

"You're going to play with *my* gun, while I clean *these* guns."

"Yes, Sir!"

\*     \*     \*

They stepped into Edward's favorite gun shop for cleaning supplies. They browsed to give Katrina some ideas for when she was ready for her first gun.

"Oh, what a lovely necklace!" a woman said to Katrina.

"Thank you! He just give it to me," she said as she put her arm in Edward's. She relished showing her submission in such a public place, even if most of the people in the shop did not understand the subtext.

Edward turned to the clerk. "I think I'm going to need a new cable lock."

The staff was all too happy to assist the little minx. It was clear she was not wearing anything under her loose fitting shirt as she leaned down on the handgun showcase. Edward grabbed the back of her shirt in his hand to keep the front of it from revealing too much, grinning at the clerk.

…

As they pulled out of the parking lot, Katrina asked, "May I please wear this collar to the club next time, Sir?"

"*If* we go back to the club," he replied with a raised eyebrow. "Are you going to be good if we go back?"

"Yes, Sir! I promise I will be a good girl for you, Sir. Can we please go back? Please? Pleeeease?" she begged.

"We can go back," he relented.

"May I please wear my new collar there, Sir?"

"That's *my* collar you are wearing."

"May I please wear *your* collar there, Sir?" She clasped her fingers together. "Pleeease?"

"Consider it an order," he said, trying not to let on that she was the most adorable thing he had ever seen.

"Thank you, Sir!" she said as she pushed up in her seat to kiss him on the cheek and hold his arm. "I wish I could wear it to work."

"Why can't you?"

"I can't wear it to work, Sir!" she said laughing. She knew he was joking.

"You will if I refuse to take it off of you!"

She laughed some more. But he did not. *He is joking, right?* She stared at the side of his face as he drove, searching for any sign of humor.

Finally, the corner of his lip turned up. "Maybe you'll get a collar that you *can* wear to work."

"Yes please, Sir!"

Edward loved the mood Katrina was in. He was getting high on her euphoria. It was like she was a shooting star and he was along for the ride. "Tell me, was this day as scary as you thought it would be?"

"No, Sir. I had my Dom with me."

Edward's heart skipped as he breathed a deep satisfying breath. "I think you are the most romantic girl I have ever met."

"I love you, Sir. Te amo, Señor."

"Te amo, también. I love you too."

With her Dominant at her side, that was the day Katrina buried one of her biggest fears in the desert.

# 8.2

# TURKEY CLUB, JEALOUSLY INSANE

Woodrow, London, and Edward stood by the exit of The Turkey Club, finishing a conversation while waiting for Katrina.

"No. Not me. That's him right there," Mark said to a young lady at the edge of the lobby. "Edward!" he called out. "This is…" Before Mark could make a formal introduction, the girl attacked Edward with a hug, causing him to spill water from his bottle just before he could drink. She might have knocked him over had he not been standing with his back to a wall.

Edward looked down at cat ears atop blonde hair dyed black as she buried the side of her face in his shirt. He looked up from her head at a wide-eyed London and Woodrow. They were as surprised as Edward was confused. He put his free hand on the girl's back. "What's the matter sweetheart?"

"This is Kayti," Mark said as he caught up. "She's acquainted with… you know. She wanted to meet the security officer involved."

"Kayti?" Edward looked back down at the cat ears.

She pulled her face off of him to reveal blue eyes through horn-rimmed glasses on a chubby cheeked face with whiskers painted out from the tip of her nose.

"Nice to meet you, 'Kayti Cat'. Is there something I can do for you?"

"Uh… Jimmy is my owner.?" Her statements ascended on the last word as though everything she said was a question.

"Jimmy, yeah. How's he doing?"

"He's alive because of you.?" She dropped her hands and took a half step back from Edward showing a skintight black latex bodysuit with a v-neck to a pierced belly button. In one hand was the end of a leash that was attached to a stainless steel diamond encrusted collar around her neck. "You saved my owner's life.?" She lifted the leash grip to nibble the leather with her teeth.

"I don't know about that," Edward said. "He was trying to keep the peace. He was saving himself and I helped."

"Uh… That's not what he says.?" She saw through Edward's modesty. "He says he owes you, big time." She took the grip of her leash and slowly ran it along his forearm, from elbow to the hand that held the water bottle. Her statements stopped sounding like questions. "And when my owner is in debt, *I* am in debt. Sooo…" With both hands, she daintily placed the grip over Edward's wrist. "So he sent me to thank you."

Edward forced his eyes to stay on hers in spite of the display. He knew she was probably not accustomed to being rejected. His next words had the potential to hurt this girl. So he spoke as sensitively as he could. "I would be a fortunate man. And please believe me, I am *quite* flattered. But I don't share my toys and I don't play with the toys of other men."

At Edward's denial of the offer, she gave a pout, only looking *a little* dejected which was about as much for which he could hope. He delicately tucked the grip under her costume near her collar and added, "Maybe if my submissive would like a pet…"

Kayti's eyes lit up. "That girl that gave you the lap dance? That would be cray! She's totes adorbs! I'm jelly!"

"Thank you. I agree… I think." He made it very clear: "I'm in love with her."

Edward knew Katrina would never go for taking in a pet, which was fine with him. But his 'pet suggestion' and declaration of love for his submissive eased the blow to Kayti's young ego.

"Look. The fact is, there were three guys giving Jimmy a hard time. I don't know why. Jimmy was trying to deescalate the situation. He was being peaceful and he saved himself by keeping a cool head and asking for help."

"Jimmy said there were only *two* guys."

"Actually, I think there were closer to ten guys. No, a dozen! All ninjas!"

Kayti smiled.

"And of course, Jimmy could fend off an attack from *eleven* ninjas. But not twelve. That's when I stepped in to help with that last guy who *almost* got the drop on Jimmy."

"You put that guy in the hospital?"

Edward's humor and expression sobered. "I think Metro took him to the hospital on the way to jail."

"And you got fired for that?"

"No…" Edward hem-hawed. "Not exactly." He paused before saying, "I was probably going to get fired soon anyway. I was on my way out."

"Thank you again," she said as she gave Edward another hug. "Tell me if you change your mind? Please change your mind?"

"I'll let you know, sweetheart. It's nice to meet you, Kayti Cat."

Woodrow and London watched Kayti as she departed. The back of her costume matched the front with a 'V' and a cat tail below her tailbone. London turned to Edward who was observing the smudge of Katy's cat whiskers on his shirt.

"That was the most adorable thing I have ever seen!" Then she mocked, "It was 'totes adorbs'!"

"Yeah, she's cute," Edward said as he brushed his shirt with his hand.

"No! Not her. You!"

"What do you mean?" He looked at London.

"Every guy in this club… and half the girls, want to fuck the shit out of her. And you treat her like she's your daughter!"

Edward shrugged. "I'm allergic to cats."

He lifted the bottle to his lips. But before he could take a drink, a slap across his cheek sent it flying, shooting water in his face and across the lobby, grabbing the attention of all around. Through the water in his eyes, he saw an upset Katrina push him with both hands into the wall.

He was stunned. "My charge?"

She wound up for another slap that Edward caught by her wrist.

"No! Katrina!" London stepped forward with Woodrow just behind. She was about to seize Katrina's shoulders when Katrina yanked her arm back from Edward and briskly walked out the door, leaving him wiping water off his face.

"Katrina!" London yelled.

"No!" Edward stopped London. "I'll, uh… I gotta' go."

Edward rushed out and scanned the parking lot. He didn't see Katrina. She wasn't on her way to the car. She was nowhere in sight. He didn't know how he lost her so quickly.

He reminded himself to think logically, like he was playing a video game; pulling his phone out to track *her* phone.

"There are always security jobs," Mark said as he was walking back to the door from the parking lot.

"Mark! Did you see Katrina come out here?"

"I didn't see her on *that* side of the lot. But I was escorting someone to her car."

"It's okay," Edward said, fooling Mark into thinking he was calm. "Her location will show up on my phone in a minute."

"You know, you could easily get the job back. You just have to leave the gun in your car."

"I appreciate it, Mark. But it's been a long time. And I don't really want the job."

Finally, Katrina's location pinged on his phone. She was on the far side of his car. As he walked away from Mark, "Please be careful, my friend. There's no such thing as 'unarmed security'."

*     *     *

Edward found Katrina in the dimly lit parking lot, sitting on the back bumper of his car. She was leaning over her knees with her face in her arms, sobbing. He stepped next to her and put his hand on the back of her bare neck. There was silence except for the text chime of her phone. She didn't move.

"Let's get in the car," he murmured.

She didn't move.

"Come on, my charge. Get in the car."

And still, she did not move.

Edward bent down at his waist to put his mouth by her ear and softly said, "I am your Dominant, you are my submissive, and I love you, te amo. I will only give you this order one more time:" And then he crunched, "Get in the fuckin' car."

He kept his hand on the back of her neck as she sniffled and stood to walk with her head down to the passenger door. Edward opened and closed it as usual.

He took his place in the driver's seat. By the dashboard lights, he saw his submissive in the same position, leaned over, head in arms. He reached over and pulled her up by her hair. She put up a weak fight to resist him. But she stopped when she realized he was only putting her safety belt on.

Neither of them spoke. There was no sound but that of the road. But to Katrina, the silence was deafening. There was nothing to distract her from her anger. Nothing to distract her from her pain. Nothing to distract her from her fear of what was about to happen. *How could he do that to me? All night I say nothing while he sings karaoke with other girls. I talk myself out of being jealous. I put it out of my mind. And then I catch him holding someone else in front of all those people?!*

The unwelcome thoughts crescendoed until they were screaming. Then her hand surprised her when it snapped forward and turned the radio on to full volume. She didn't know what song was playing. But it didn't help. *Is he going to punish me for turning on his radio? He never said I wasn't allowed or it was against the rules. Am I going to be punished for anything?*

She peeked out the corner of her eye to see if he would react. But Edward drove on, unaffected.

Katrina's phone chimed again. Though the radio was too loud to hear it, she did feel it vibrate. Grateful for something that might succeed in distracting her, she pulled it out to see London had texted her... more than once.

Once Katrina had finished reading and responding to London's lengthy text messages, she sheepishly reached toward the radio and turned it off. Silence ruled again.

*I'm so stupid!* She thought carefully about her words. *Now what do I say?* Another text from London chimed on her phone that answered her question.

"Massa?" she said with eyes at her feet.

"Mm?" Edward wasn't sure he heard her right.

"Your stupid cunt whore of a submissive humbly begs your forgiveness, Massa."

"Did you just call me 'Massa'?"

"Yes, Massa? I think it means 'Master'."

"Yeah, that's an archaic term that wouldn't be appropriate for us."

"I hear London call Woodrow that. And I read what London text to me, Sir."

"Woodrow and London have a unique dynamic that is fine for them."

"Is because we are not married?"

Edward waited.

"Is because we are not married, *Sir*?"

"London has an Antebellum fetish. I'll explain the historical significance later. But it's not right for us."

"Dana did not like it too, Sir," she said, trying to use the conversation to show that she was ready to behave.

"It's not for anyone else to like or dislike Woodrow and London's fetishes. As long as it's consensual, it's not our place to judge their dynamic. There's no universal protocol."

"Can I call you 'Master'?"

"No. Nobody is going to call me 'Master' until they are my slave."

Katrina was confused on several levels now. She knew she wasn't a "slave" per se. But her experiences this evening and the events to which she bore witness made the thought of slavery sound appealing for the first time in her life. *He doesn't consider me his "slave". Is that good or bad? If this isn't slavery, what is it?*

"Did London tell you to say that apology?"

"Most of it, Sir. I add 'whore'."

"What else did London say?"

"She say that girl was thanking you and you were good, Sir."

"Why did you need London to tell you that? Why couldn't you talk to me instead of humiliating me in front of all those people?"

Katrina didn't know what else to say. So she tried this: "Your stupid cunt whore of a *slave* humbly begs your forgiveness, *Master*."

Edward shook his head. "I'm not going to have a slave until I'm at least engaged."

Katrina didn't know if that would apply to her, though she hoped it would someday. He wasn't closing any doors with that statement. She rested on: "Will you please forgive me, Sir?"

"I forgive you, my charge," he said. "But we haven't fixed this yet."

"Yes, Sir. Thank you, Sir. I accept any punishment you believe I deserve," she said, employing another line that London had texted her. *I'm not his "slave" but at least I'm still his "charge". What does he mean when he calls me "charge"?* "What do you mean when you call me 'charge', Sir?"

"Look it up," he said. "There are a dozen definitions and almost every one applies."

"You save that girl's life, Sir?"

"No. She thinks I saved her owner's life."

"You save*d his* life, Sir?"

"I don't know," he said with botheration. "Some people say I did but we'll never know if that's true."

"Why not, Sir? What happened?"

"Somebody was attacking her boyfriend and I stopped him. That's all," he said curtly, hoping she would drop it.

"Why don't you like to talk about it? You saved his life, Sir!"

"Whether or not I actually saved a life that night, I don't like talking about it."

"Why not, Sir?"

"Because it doesn't feel good to beat a man unconscious," he gruffed. And then he murmured, "...no matter how much he deserves it."

Katrina's empathetic reading talent was off. She was mistaking Edward's annoyance for modesty. And after destroying the mood, she thought she could cheer him up by getting him to talk about his heroics to no avail. *Why does he love me?*

"Why do you love me, Sir?"

"What?"

"Why do you love me, Sir?"

"Why do you keep asking me that? What do you mean?"

She didn't know what to say.

"Why did Adam love Eve?"

Katrina remained silent. She felt like she was failing at every level. And hazarding a guess at an answer to Edward's question would only result in another failure. There was a canyon dividing the car in two. All she wanted was for her Dominant to touch her. She remembered she had permission to touch him whenever she wanted. But did that still apply in the light of her outburst? *What if I try to hold his arm? What if he doesn't want to touch me? What if... Oh, there he is!*

Katrina was rescued from her thoughts by Edward's hand resting on her thigh as though he read her mind. It was that moment at which her desire to be as good as she could for her Dominant was renewed. *Be a good submissive for Sir.* She wrapped both arms around his and stroked his forearm, as was becoming their custom.

But that was not the only custom they were developing. Walking into the house behind him, the second she broke the plane of his front door, she started stripping her clothes off. Though she tried to do it even faster than usual this time, it would never be fast enough for her to be completely naked before Edward turned around and shouted, "What the hell are you doing wearing clothes!" She giggled as she relieved herself of her last few stitches.

She ran past Edward in the hall on their way to the master bedroom so that when he turned on the light, he would see his nude submissive under the suspension bar, on her knees, in position two, presenting the collar and lock. The mere 'chlich' of the shackle closing, securing the chain around her neck was music to her submissive heart. "Thank you, Sir."

"Position one," he ordered, as he lifted her by the collar.

"Yes, Sir!" she said, jumping to her feet. *Be good for my Dominant.*

She stared forward a mile, ignoring… whatever Edward was doing behind her. There was typing on his computer keyboard. At one point, she thought she heard a bell ring. But she let her cognizance of the sounds flow out the back of her mind as trained.

She relaxed her arms behind her when Edward uncrossed them and tied her wrists together. He took the ends of the rope and strung them through the loop in the center of the bar and pulled until her hands were lifted to the middle of her back, causing her to lean forward. But she kept her head level and her eyes on the horizon.

She recognized her situation from the one she witnessed earlier that night at The Turkey Club. Although the beginning of the activity would bear resemblance to that event, little else would be the same.

Edward stepped in front of his submissive with more foreign objects. "Stand upright."

"Yes, Sir." She stretched her arms up behind her as she straightened her posture.

"Watch this."

"Yes, Sir."

He unbuttoned his shirt and exposed his right peck. He took some kind of clamp and locked it onto his nipple. His gritted teeth gave a 'hiss' as he sucked air through them. "I'm glad I'm not you," he said as he took the clamp off and rubbed the pain out. "Eyes forward."

"Yes, Sir." She wasn't sure what the object was or what Edward did to himself. But she knew she was about to experience it.

He bent down and held her left breast to his mouth where he wet and sucked the nipple, tweaking and arousing it with his tongue, and then blowing cool air until it stood erect.

Katrina inhaled at the arousal that echoed from her breast to her clitoris. And then she drew an even deeper breath at a sharp pinch, the likes of which she had not experienced before.

It was not the familiar pinch of Edward's fingers. It was something new. When he moved to her right breast, the pain remained in her left nipple. She wanted to know what was causing it, but she resisted the urge to look. *Don't look down. Be good for Sir.*

Edward did the same with her right breast, arousing the nipple to a point and placing a clamp. Then he lifted two tiny sleigh bells in front of Katrina's face and shook them to make them jingle. She knew them more from the sound than her vision as she did not allow her eyes to waver from the distance. He hung the bells from the clamp of each nipple, adding the slightest but noticeable weight to both. "You may look."

Katrina peered down at her breasts to see two clamps locked to her areolas, forcing her nipples to remain at attention. The clamps were connected by a thin chain that hung down to her belly. Where the chain connected to the clamps, two sleigh bells dangled.

Katrina was breathing, mouth open at the sight and sensation. It had broken her mile-long stare and pulled her back into her body. She was struck at how the bite of the clamp on her left nipple subsided when the right one was connected. And now the sharpness of the pain was growing dull as it seemed to distribute a burning across her chest.

Edward reached down to the middle of the chain and lifted it with his index finger. Katrina's eyes followed as he made a "come-here" gesture, causing the bells to ring and gather the pain back into her nipples. She winced and bent toward his finger, relieving the strain on her arms. But it was only a second before he raised the chain further, restoring her to her upright position with a whimper. She took a small step forward but it only stretched her arms higher behind her. Her head dropped back with eyes squeezing out tears as she lifted to her toes. She thrusted her breasts out for some relief. Her shallow and rapid panting caused her chest to drop and pull against the chain when she exhaled, so she tried holding her breath. But the relief was only temporary. Edward needed only twitch to ring the bells and restore the tension.

Without a word, he had made his point. He held Katrina's world at the tip of his finger. If there was ever a doubt about his control, it was never clearer.

With no warning, he dropped the light chain and took a step back. Katrina exhaled and opened her eyes. She returned to stand flat-footed on the floor as she caught her breath.

Edward stood staring at the breasts he had decorated like a Christmas tree. He shook his head and said, "Mm. That looks painful." He reiterated, "I'm really glad I'm not you."

Katrina almost smiled at the comment but pressed her lips together. She knew he wasn't trying to be funny.

"Make the bells ring."

"Yes, Sir." She turned side to side for a second, making her breasts shiver just enough for the bells to give a twinkle.

"I said, 'make the bells ring'."

"Yes, Sir." She did the same a couple seconds longer and louder. And with the increase in volume came an increase in the ache. She stomped her left foot into the floor at the pain.

Edward walked behind her, beyond her field of vision. Then she felt the dowel rod with which she was familiar slide up from the back of her knees to her butt and begin a light rapping. Although his voice was stern before, the addition of the rod accentuated the order as he repeated, "Make the bells ring."

"Yes, Sir!" She went from shivering to jiggling her breasts, enough to ring the bells continuously. As the rapping on her butt intensified, the pain seemed to drain out of her nipples and gather at the target of the rod.

Once he had balanced the pain between her chest and fundament, he stayed his hand and said, "Don't stop."

"Yes, Sir!"

"Louder!" he demanded. "Up and down!"

"Yes, Sir!" she cried, jumping from her ankles to bounce her breasts. But then a thought occurred to her that was even more uncomfortable than her nipples. *What if something jiggles that I don't want to jiggle? What if my tummy or...*

WHACK! The rod marked her butt. "Thank you, Sir!"

"I said, 'Don't stop!'"

"Yes, Sir!" She didn't realize she stopped.

WHACK! "Thank you, Sir!"

"As loud as before!"

"Yes, Sir!" Her attention had shifted from self-consciousness about unwanted jiggling to the motivation of pain. And she used that ever rising pain in her nipples to inspire herself to continue ringing.

Edward walked back around in front of her, pulled her posture up by her hair, and stared into her face. "What the hell was that at the club?"

"Please forgive me, Sir!"

WHACK! "Thank you, Sir!" She was given a mark on the outside of her left thigh. Again, she didn't notice she had stopped the jingling. She resumed.

"What happened?" Edward asked as he crossed his arms. His voice was calm and measured in contrast to the panic of Katrina's whimpering words.

"It was that girl! I was jealous, Sir!"

"And how did you react?"

"I slap you. Your stupid cunt whore of a submissive humbly begs your forgiveness, Sir!"

"You didn't just slap me. You slapped me in front of my friends. ...in front of a dozen people. Did you think your behavior was acceptable?"

"No, Sir!"

"You humiliated me. You humiliated *us*!"

"Please forgive me, Sir!"

Edward began pacing back and forth. Katrina kept jingling but she bent over as far as the ropes elevating her hands would allow, hanging her breasts, clamps, bells, and chain forward; trading one type of pain for another.

Watching his submissive hunched over, ringing bells, Edward said, "Let me help you with that, you sexy 'Quasimodo'."

He walked behind her and started on another project.

WHACK! Katrina jumpstarted the bells. "Thank you, Sir!"

Then he stepped back in front of her. "You may stop."

"Thank you, Sir."

"Position one."

"Yes, Sir." She assumed the position as well as she could in spite of her bound wrists.

Two long lengths of twine hung from his neck. He tied the end of one into the clamp on her left nipple where the chain and bell connected before doing the same on her right. Then he took the loose ends of the twine and threaded them through the loop of the suspension bar above.

Standing in front of his submissive, he held the ends, one in each hand and demonstrated the effect each string had on her respective nipple. First, he made the bell on her left nipple ring, causing her to lift that side of her body as she whimpered. Then he did the same to her right nipple, leading her the opposite direction. And when he did thusly to both nipples at the same time, she was once again coerced to her toes as she writhed.

She had experienced the clamps hanging down and hanging forward. And now, they were lifting up, giving her nipples the full tour of torment.

He watched his submissive dance for him as he twitched the twine. "See how these work?" he asked, teaching his student.

"Yes, Sir!" she cried.

He walked behind her and lifted her bound hands with his shoulder so there was the smallest bit of slack in the rope. He tied the ends of the strings into her fingers and ordered, "Wiggle my fingers."

"Yes, Sir." She did so, twinkling the bells.

He unexpectedly pulled his shoulder out causing her hands to drop and yank the clamps. She was left to choose between straining to keep her hands raised, or lowering them and lifting her breasts.

As Edward walked back in front of her, he said, "There you go! Now it's up to you which way you pull on my nipples to ring."

"Thank you, Sir."

"You're welcome, my charge."

"Sir?" She locked eyes with him and whispered with a sincerity that expressed true gratitude at the favor he was granting her. "Thank you, Sir."

He lifted her chin and kissed her deeply. Then he pressed his forehead to hers and said, "You're welcome, my charge. Who loves you?"

"You love me, Sir."

"Damn right, I love you. Te amo."

"Te amo tambien. I love you too, Sir."

"I know."

WHACK! "Thank you, Sir!" The ringing and the pain were both reignited.

Edward resumed the lecture and his pacing. "I'd like to pose a hypothetical, 'counselor'."

Katrina decided to forego the reminder that she was not yet an attorney. "Yes, Sir?" she said between breaths.

"What if London wasn't there to *exonerate* me?" They grinned at each other at Edward's conversational use of their safeword, though Katrina's smile was through a locked jaw. "What if she didn't say anything? And you still thought I was trying to pick up another girl, or whatever you thought I was doing?"

"I don't know, Sir. I was angry. I was jealous."

Edward was crestfallen as he turned away to sit in the recliner. "Why couldn't you talk to me?"

Katrina didn't know what to say. She did let the jingling subside but did not stop.

"Why couldn't you tell me what was bothering you instead of humiliating both of us in front of all those people? All the things you've told me. All the things we've talked about. I thought I made it very clear that you can talk to me about anything. Did I do something to make you feel like you can't tell me when something's wrong?"

Katrina's head dropped and she began weeping. *The only man who has ever made me feel safe to talk about my deepest darkness thinks he failed me. I let...*

WHACK! Katrina was startled to see Edward through her tears standing right in front of her. She started jingling again.

He leaned down and put his forehead to hers and said, "Te amo, I love you. I'm going to get you through this. You cry all you need but you are going to keep those bells ringing."

"Yes, Sir," she whispered, grateful for the reaffirmation of their connection.

"You know, you're allowed to tell me how you feel. I mean, you are under orders to tell me when something bothers you."

"I know, Sir," she said through the sound of the bells. "Please forgive your stupid cunt whore submissive, Sir!"

"Next question:" Edward stepped back and moved on. "What if I actually was doing something wrong? Did you handle it properly?"

Her eyes squeezed shut as she searched for a position that allowed her to hold her arms up without bending over too far. All the while, not allowing the ringing to stop; not for fear of another stroke of the rod, but for a desire to obey her Dominant. *Be great for Sir!*

"I make a big mistake, Sir. Please forgive me, Sir!"

"What are you going to do if something like this happens again?"

"I will do anything you say, Sir! What do you want me to do?"

"I want you to do what I ordered you to do; what I *trained* you to do! If you feel like throwing another tantrum like that, you will wait and talk about it with me *privately*!"

"Yes, Sir!"

WHACK! He gave her another mark even though the bells had not stopped. "Thank you, Sir!"

"Stop ringing."

"Yes, Sir!" she said with relief, though she had to keep her hands raised to keep from pulling the strings.

Then he used her hair to turn her head. Her body followed to face the computer. The screensaver scrolled text. "Can you read that?"

"Yes, Sir."

"Read it to me."

She blinked the water out of her eyes and read word-by-word as the text scrolled. "'I will have faith in my Dominant's fidelity to me.'"

"Do you know what that means?"

"Yes, Sir."

Then he turned her head to look at him. "It really hurts me that you think that I would cheat on you. We made an agreement. It's like you don't believe in me."

She saw the pain in his eyes through the tears in her own. "Please forgive your stupid cunt whore of a submissive, Sir."

He held her head to his chest with no regard for the strings to the nipple clamps, "I forgive you, my charge."

"Thank you, Sir."

"I forgive you, but we're not finished. Look at the screen."

"Yes, Sir."

"Read it again."

"Yes, Sir. 'I will have faith in my Dominant's fidelity to me.'"

"Don't stop. You're going to add this line to your mantra."

"Yes, Sir. 'I will have faith in my Dominant's fidelity to me.'" She repeated the sentence over and over while Edward started... doing something else behind her. There was a 'snip' before the upward tension on the clamps went slack, returning the downward pain. Though it caused a stutter, she fought to keep it from interrupting her repetition of the line.

She continued chanting, ignoring the rope that was tied around each ankle; ignoring her feet being lifted off the floor; ignoring her inversion with a foot at each end of the bar. Upside down, she could no longer see the screen. Nevertheless, she persisted: "'I will have faith in my Dominant's fidelity to me.'"

As the blood rushed to her head, she looked through the chain from her nipples hanging in her face to see Edward's feet in the carpet. But the rope suspending her hands behind her back kept her from viewing him from the knees up.

He helped himself to a feel of the smooth skin between her legs that were now splayed before him. He patted the area with his hand, lightly at first and then more firmly. He slapped her there causing an interruption to her words and a ring of the bells. She tried to close her legs, but the best she could do was bend her knees, lifting herself higher and spreading herself wider. She found her attempt to resist only made her more vulnerable, and more amorous. He slapped her again, "Don't stop!"

"Yes, Sir! 'I will have faith in my Dominant's fidelity to me!'"

He watched as his slapping turned her lips red. He parted her petals and took delight in the sight of the pretty pink against her reddening brown skin. He stuck a finger into her warmth and found ample lubrication to spread to her clitoris, causing her to relax her legs as well as the rest of her body.

Her repetition of the line became quieter and breathier. But she was returned to her task with another slap!

"*Do not stop!*"

"Yes, Sir! 'I will have faith in my Dominant's fidelity to me!'"

Edward went back to work on Katrina, in and around, with both hands: one on her clitoris, one much deeper. She felt the pressure of the blood in her head rise along with the pleasure between her legs.

"'I will have faith in my Dominant's fidelity to me!'" And then she stopped to ask, "Sir? May I please cum, Sir?"

"Cum!" he ordered to Katrina's surprise.

She usually had to ask at least two or three times. But she wasn't going to waste the rare opportunity for immediate gratification. Her legs shook causing the bells to ring. As the first orgasm subsided, between breaths, she said, "Thank you for letting your pussy cum for you, Sir. May I please cum again?"

"Cum again, slut!"

"Thank you, Sir!" She had another one, even more powerful than the first. She bent her knees, raising her body again. But Edward hooked a finger over her pubic bone and pulled her right back down like he was slamming a garage door. She adhered to protocol, thanking her Dominant and requesting a third orgasm.

He graciously granted it a third time and then a fourth. After her fifth, she thanked him and did not ask for another. But Edward did not stop working on his subject. "Cum again, ya' whore!" he commanded.

"Yes, Sir!" She went on with her sixth orgasm and thanked him accordingly.

"Cum again!"

"Yes, Sir!" And after her seventh, she thanked him but had a different request: "Sir! May I please stop cumming?!"

He took the twine connected to her nipples in his teeth. "No. Cum again," he said as he gnashed. "Do not stop!"

"Yes, Sir!" She was already halfway through her eighth. "Sir? Sir! Please! May I stop cumming?!"

"Nope! Cum again!" He jerked his head with the strings in his teeth, ringing the bells.

Katrina felt as though her vagina and all within would fall out were she not upside down. But she came again as ordered, defenseless against wave after wave; a ninth time, a tenth time, and finally an eleventh.

Edward ended with another slap to her labia and released the strings, but she hardly reacted. He laid down on the floor under her as her subtle swinging came to a halt and she opened her eyes. They rested, face-to-face, catching their breath, staring at each other like the stars of a night sky.

"How do you feel?"

"Like you cut me in two, Sir."

Edward laughed at her answer and leaned up for a kiss. "Is it safe to say we have resolved our issue?"

Katrina's eyes glanced away before she said, "Yes, Sir."

Edward squinted. "No, we haven't. What is it, my charge?"

"Sir…" *I know what I want to say but how do I say it like a lawyer? I can establish foundation by…*

"I order you to tell me what you are thinking immediately."

"Will you please not sing with other girls, Sir?"

"Yes."

Katrina flinched as though she had been slapped in the face with a feather. "Sir?"

"Yes," he repeated.

"Nada más? You will not sing with other girls, Sir?"

"Not if it bothers you that much."

This time, Edward allowed her to slip back into her thoughts as her eyes fell through him.

*All I had to do was ask? If it's not that important to him, should it be that important to me.*

Once she returned, she said, "Maybe it does not bother me so much, Sir."

"We'll talk about this some more. But in the meantime, you are going to have to learn some songs that *we* can sing together."

"Yes, Sir!"

After another kiss, he stood and freed her from her inverted position one leg at a time, slowly turning her upright as her blood redistributed. Her arms were detached from the bar as well but he kept her wrists bound. He helped her down and ordered, "Position two."

"Yes, Sir." As she assumed the resting variation of position two, sitting on her feet, she saw Edward was down to nothing but his unbuttoned shirt as his fully erect member pointed directly at her. She felt the juices in her mouth as though she were looking at a ripe piece of fruit. She unabashedly took in the vision with no shame for her lust to satisfy her Dominant. *Be magnificent for Master!*

With the rod in his left hand, Edward bent over to kiss his submissive on the forehead and took the middle of the chain in his right. He pulled her up out of resting position. She panted at the pain but the ringing of the bells was just as loud.

When he dropped the chain, she held position two on her knees, looking up at him, head tilted back with her mouth open, wordlessly beckoning Edward to put something in.

He rested his balls on her chin and his member on her face, right between her eyes and asked, "What is the lesson you are learning tonight?"

"'I will have faith in my Dominant's fidelity to me.'"

"Good girl."

"Thank you, Sir."

"What else are you learning?"

"To talk to you, Sir. …when something is wrong."

"And not do what?"

"Not embarrass you, Sir?"

"Not embarrass *us*."

"Not embarrass *us*, Sir."

Edward kept the conversation going just to feel her breath on his sack.

"You will not throw another temper tantrum ever again."

"No, Sir."

"Say it."

"I will not throw another temper tantrum, Sir."

"Good girl."

"Thank you, Sir."

"What do you want to do now?"

"May I please suck your cock, Sir?"

"Mm." He shrugged. "I don't know. Maybe."

"Pleeeeease, may I suck your cock, Sir?" she begged with pleading eyes.

"Get to work on that cock."

She knew not to thank him until her mouth was full. "Ank oo, hir!"

Edward relished the initial wet warmth of Katrina chasing his dragon. Though it seemed like he couldn't get any harder, he felt like he grew another inch when Katrina sucked and closed her throat around him. As she bobbed, he began tapping her ass with the rod in rhythm. He leaned down to grab the chain of the clamps and made the bells ring.

Katrina paused her motion and whined, pressing Edward to the roof of her mouth with her tongue at the pain in her nipples. But she dutifully kept her watering eyes on his.

"Don't. Stop!" he ordered with two firm lashes.

"Esh, hir!" She resumed.

He continued to ring the bells with his right hand while marking her ass with his left. "You're doing an excellent job, my little cock toy," he said through labored breaths. "Use the pain. Use the pain to focus on getting the cum out of that cock!"

She squealed with every stroke, but she was determined to win her prize. *Get my Master's cum!*

"The sooner you get your cum, the sooner the pain stops. So get it, bitch!"

The pain inspired her to take her performance to a level she had never attempted before. And she knew she was doing something right when she felt in her nipples that Edward had dropped the chain. He reached his right hand up to hold the suspension bar for balance.

"Good. Girl!" he said as he gave her a stroke of the rod with each word. "Get. That. Cum! Get. That…" He dropped the rod and reached his left hand up to join his right on the bar.

Katrina felt his hot nectar fill her mouth and swallowed as much as she could. She felt some of it in her sinuses and some of it slid down her chin along with her drool. But she persevered, undaunted by the discomfort for the pleasure of her Dominant. *Be a magnificent slave for my Master!*

"Slow down!" he said.

"Esh, hir." She slowed down but she knew not to stop until Edward gave the order.

He released his left hand from the bar and yanked her off of him by her hair. He looked down and smiled at his submissive and laughed as he caught his breath, causing her to do the same as cum and drool ran down her neck.

"You are magical!"

"Thank you, Sir!"

"I think you made me cum around the mountain!" They both cracked up at the statement. He looked at the cum on his member and ordered, "Clean my cock off."

"Yes, Sir!" She obeyed, licking every inch of him until it was glistening with nothing but her spit.

He bent over and tasted a bit of his own flavor on her lips. As they kissed, he reached down and unhooked the nipple clamps without warning, causing Katrina to scream into Edward's mouth at yet another way to have her nipples tortured.

"Please, Sir! Put them back on!"

"That's not going to help, my charge. It will only hurt worse. And keeping them on much longer could be dangerous."

She moaned as she pressed her lips into his again while he massaged the pain out of her breasts.

"I'm so glad I'm not you!"

"I love to be me, Sir."

Edward's eyes warmed even more as he gazed upon his submissive. But Katrina could tell that a troublesome thought was occurring to him as his eyebrows furrowed and his smile dimmed. He stood upright, still looking down at her and asked, "I've been punishing you for humiliating us in public. But since you are a pain slut, I can't help wondering if I have been reinforcing your bad behavior. Have I been rewarding you by punishing you?"

"No, Sir. I will never throw a temper tantrum again. Please believe me, Sir."

"Okay," he said, though not completely convinced. "Time will tell." He helped her to her feet by the training collar and reached down to feel she was soaked. "How's my pussy?" he asked as he lightly patted it.

"Your pussy came around the mountain too, Sir!" It was still very sensitive down there. But she resisted the urge to close her legs and weakened knees on his hand.

"Does she need anything else?"

"No, Sir! I think you broke your pussy!"

"How many times?" he laughed.

"I don't know, Sir. I didn't know what happened."

"I think I counted eleven."

"Thank you for giving your pussy eleven orgasms, Sir."

"No, those were *my* orgasms. My pussy gave *me* eleven orgasms."

She corrected herself. "Thank you for allowing your whore cunt to cum eleven times *for you*, Sir!"

"You are welcome, my charge." He raised his hands to put his palms over her ailing nipples and winced when he saw her wince. "I'm so glad I'm not you."

"I'm glad you are not me too, Sir." She leaned into him as though she was using her breasts to feel his hands. "You make me like to be me."

# 10.1

# MEN ARE TALKING

"Venus is rising," Woodrow said.

"Indeed." The wandering star peeking over the eastern horizon inspired Edward to wax poetic:

"As continents drift and shape the globe and form the land and sea,
and as our own sun turns the night to day,
as stars burn bright and planets knit their patterns 'round the light,
i was weaved together the same way."

Woodrow heard Edward recite the verse before. But he had never asked about it. "What's that from?"

"A song I wrote a long time ago."

"You'll have to show it to me."

"I will. I just showed it to Katrina the other day."

"Did she like it?"

"She said she did."

"Did you believe 'er?"

"Yes. I showed her a bunch of my songs. About three or four in, she asked me, 'Why are you not famous?' I asked her why I would be famous. She said, 'Because your music is amazing!' That felt good."

"Then what did you say?"

"I said, 'Thank you but when was the last time you heard a famous person perform 'amazing' music?!"

Woodrow snorted, trying not to laugh too loud. "I think you can trust that she likes your music, mate. I'd take that as a compliment."

"I do. It's nice to have a girl believe in you."

"Too true. Just now learning that, are you?"

"Yeah, can you believe it? I'm in my thirties and I still don't know everything there is to know about women."

"It's not like all you've done before is teach and train your subs. I'm sure *you've* learned a thing or two."

"Of course I've learned. I learn when I teach. I like the training part. It helps people. And it appeals to my intellectual vanity."

"What kind of things do you teach your subs that help them?"

"It all starts with training in the submissive arts. It's like a foundation for a therapy boot camp. A lot of the usual goals have to do with areas of personal growth and individual responsibility."

"Like what?"

"Like dealing with trauma, confidence, concentration, posture, boundaries, emotion management, weight loss and fitness, trust... pain tolerance, orgasm control... personal finance... phobia control..."

"I wasted all that money on a degree when I could have immersed myself in the D/s lifestyle!"

"Yeah, Doctor! You could have dropped out of college like me and gone straight to training patients in the submissive arts!"

"I'll grant, it is an innovative form of therapy."

"May I refer my old clients to you? I've retired."

"I only perform that kind of therapy on one woman. But out of curiosity, what kind of phobic behavior have you helped with?"

"The most interesting phobias I've helped with... I had a sub who was afraid of escalators and moving sidewalks. Another was afraid of driving on steep mountains. I taught another to swim; she was afraid of water. Katrina was terrified of guns. But now she likes them. ...or at least isn't afraid of them. That's important to me."

"Why?"

"I made it clear to her that when a man loves a woman, he makes sure she can defend herself when he's not around. And getting comfortable with the use and disuse of guns shows she loves me enough to defend the woman I love. 'Love always protects...'"

"You Americans and your guns!" the Tory mocked, the fact that they were sitting in his backyard shooting range, notwithstanding. "What else are you working on with Katrina?"

"Well, ...I'm only telling you because she gave me permission: Specifically to her, she has a kind of impostor syndrome issue. She thinks she's advancing in her career for reasons besides her talent and hard work. We work on her confidence with that. That's also helping her learn to deal with confrontation. She also wanted to quit smoking. Mission accomplished. And she wanted to get better at poker. She's made strides in all areas."

"What happens when you don't know what to teach next?"

"What do you mean?"

"What will you do when she's got nothing else to work on?"

"I guess I'll have to *learn* that when we get there! And I doubt I'll ever be done working on me and my never ending quest to earn her submission."

"What are *you* learning? How are *you* growing?"

"I'm trying to change things I don't like about myself."

"Like what?"

"I know I can be a pretty selfish person. I used to take people for granted. I used to throw away relationships when they had a few small problems instead of working on them."

"What kind of problems?"

"Trust is a big deal to me. I've thrown away girls the second they do something to betray my trust."

"What kind of trust? Trust not to cheat on you?"

"I wouldn't talk to a girl if I thought she could cheat on me. I mean trusting her not to embarrass me in public. Trusting her to keep my private life private."

"Is that something you're learning from Katrina?"

"I think so. No need to rehash what happened at the club. But there was a time when I would have ended the relationship right then and there."

"How was this time different?"

"I wanted to try fixing the problem rather than throwing away another relationship. We talked it out like two grown adults. ...one of whom was hanging from the ceiling by her ankles."

"Do you trust 'er now?"

"I think I do. She knows things about me that nobody else will ever know. And the trust she places in me makes me want to be better. If you knew half the crap she's been through, you'd wonder how she's even remotely functional in this world. She pushes my limits more than anyone I've ever known."

"How's that?"

"Well, I've never really considered myself to be a sadist. I only like to use pain to help a submissive reach her goals. But we've learned that this one's a real pain slut. And I find myself getting turned on by giving her pain. I'll be working on her and look down to see I'm hard as a rock!"

"To be young!" returned the elder Englishman. "Enjoy these days while it's easy, mate."

"Does this mean I'm a sadist after all?" Edward asked.

"I suppose that's a philosophical question."

"How so?"

"Is it the act of causing physical pain that turns you on? Or is it Katrina's reactions that you enjoy?"

"That's a great question. What is it that a sadist really likes: *causing* the pain, or the *effect* of the pain?"

"Exactly."

"I'm just trying to get more comfortable with it though."

"More comfortable with being a sadist?"

"Yeah, if that's what I am. Katrina needs to feel a lot of pain. ...*a lot of pain.*"

"That must be extreme if it's difficult for *you*. You've given subs pain before."

"I know I'm helping her work out some deep-seated trauma in a controlled environment. We've talked a lot about that. And while I'm trying to help her find what she's looking for, I'm also trying to check in with her without pulling her out of her headspace."

"How do you 'check in' with 'er?"

"If things are going far, I'll tell her to remind me our safeword so she knows she can use it. But then it either pulls her off her journey, or she's too deep in subspace to remember the word or respond, and I stop things because I'm on the cusp of drawing blood!"

"And you're not ready to take it as far as she needs it."

"Yeah! It's like, I start to feel like a psycho for torturing her like that. But all she wants is more."

"Do you feel like a psycho for torturing 'er or do you feel like a psycho for *enjoying* it?"

"Damn." The suggestion cast Edward into cogitation. "This is why you're a good therapist."

"Cheers."

Their eyes returned to the sky as they sipped Woodrow's homemade mead. Edward laid his head back and watched Orion pursue the Seven Sisters before breaking the silence.

"What attracted London to a Pompey like you? It's not just because you're white."

"I don't think it's that she likes *white skin*, per se, as much as she likes the contrast in our colors. She likes it when we interlock fingers. We look like a backgammon board. And the sight of my white wang in 'er black biscuit makes 'er randy!"

"So you exploited an advantage with which you were born to get your wife."

"You could say that."

"Katrina has trouble with that."

"With what?"

"She thinks she's advancing in her career just because she's Latina and can speak Spanish."

"What's wrong with that?"

"I don't know. I can see her point but I don't think it should bother her. I think she brings a lot more to the table than she realizes. It's another thing we're working on."

"I don't know if London would have been *as* attracted to me at first if I weren't white. Though she is an Anglophile. I was ready to take 'er any way I could get 'er!"

Edward laughed. "You got lucky with her!"

"Too true, mate!"

"Even if being white did help you attract your wife, I don't see a problem with that."

"Nor do I. And in the same way, I think Katrina should be proud to know two languages and should use them to 'er advantage. Even though technology helps communication, the skill is in demand. I'd be chuffed to be bilingual!"

"That's what I try to tell her! But it goes beyond her career. When I tell her I love her, she thinks it's just because I like Latinas and I'm using her to learn Spanish. And it doesn't help that I'm fascinated by her profession. You'd think the legal field would be a common interest that would help us connect. But to her, it's just another reason I love her that she thinks has nothing to do with her. And then *I* get insulted when she questions my love!"

"Are your racial differences ever a problem for the two of you?"

"Not really. At least not in terms of skin color, just cultural differences. She doesn't like me walking her to her door because of what her neighbors will think of her dating a white guy. But I think being white is the only thing her mother *likes* about me!"

"There were some racial things that made me uncomfortable with London that I had to get past."

"Such as?"

"We've talked about London's fetish."

"Yeah, her Antebellum America fetish."

"It's not that precisely. We've concluded she doesn't fetishize or romanticize the Antebellum era itself. She thought she did but she was trying to relate 'er desire to explore the slave/master archetypes with me. And she loves to be called the n-word during playtime."

"Why is that?"

"I think summink about the forbiddenness of the word gets 'er off. At first, I didn't want to do it because I thought it was demeaning to 'er; like she weren't being respec'ful of 'erself. But then I realized that *I* weren't being respec'ful of *her* by not honouring 'er request. It was like I didn't think she could take the degradation. So I got over my discomfort to please my wife. And the first time I called 'er that word while we're havin' a bang, she said it was the best orgasm she'd had hitherto!"

"You got over your discomfort to please your wife."

"London's asked me to do much more unsettling things than call 'er a slur. She likes to show off whip marks as much as the other masochist subs at the club. But it's not easy doing what I got to do to mark such dark skin. The 'n-word story' is a smaller example of larger challenges I've had as a Dom. It's those challenges that remind me, submission may be a gift, but so is dominance."

"I forget that sometimes too."

"Tell me, would you call Katrina a racial slur if she asked?"

Edward shrugged. "If she asked… I see what you mean. It would be disrespectful if I didn't."

"And it would be disrespec'ful of you to withhold pain when she's asking for it. Talk to 'er about not having safewords and take it a little further each time. You may have to get out of your own head and make 'er bleed."

# 10.0

# CIELITO LINDO

"Edward doesn't like lettuce on his turkey club," London told Katrina as they prepared snacks for their men. "And he'll probably want more mead."

"You know Sir more than me," she said, face down to the sandwich.

"Oh honey! I told you. Don't feel bad about it! We've known Edward for years!"

Katrina nodded but still felt a bit dejected.

"You told him what I told you to tell him, right?"

"I told him it's okay for him to tell you and Woodrow personal things about me."

"Fabulous! So now that he knows that, here's what we are going to do: When we go outside, we are not going to say a word. Not. One. Word. Not to each other. Not to Massa or Edward. And when you snuggle with Edward, don't move a muscle. Just stay still and quiet. Snuggle close under the blanket because it will get cold!"

"Will they think that's weird? Not talking?"

"They're used to it with me. We'll find out if it works with you there."

"What will we do? What will happen?"

"If this works, the boys will forget we are there, and they will talk, Dom to Dom."

"And they will talk about personal things? Two men?"

"Massa is a psychologist. Edward was a counselor." Imitating her husband's Portsmouth/English accent, she said, "They both fancy themselves philosophers. Ours are not normal men."

Katrina was still skeptical but she figured it couldn't hurt to try. "Are we being deceptive?"

"I don't think so. It's not like they don't know we're there! They just... *forget* we're there."

"What if Sir talks to me?"

"You do whatever he tells you to do. But you won't be able to talk back."

"Why not?"

\*         \*         \*

When the girls walked onto the porch of the backyard observatory/ shooting range, they could tell the swish of the sliding door stopped the conversation of their men. Katrina lost track of London in the darkness. Though she presumably went to Woodrow's chaise lounge if not Woodrow himself. Katrina could see the figure of one of the men standing at the telescope by the dim red glow of the controller. But she wasn't certain it was Edward until he spoke.

"Is that my charge?"

Katrina did not reply. She carefully made her way in the darkness around the lounge chair toward her man where she dropped to her knees and presented the snack plate and a glass. He could see the plate by the light of the controller, but not much else. "Thank you, my charge. Put it on the table by the chair and come back to me."

Again, she gave no verbal response as she carried out the order. Edward thought this was a tad askew. But he looked back into the telescope.

Once Katrina returned to his side, he lifted his head from the eyepiece. "Would you like to see Jupiter? I'm seeing four moons right now." He waited for her to respond. But she said nothing. He was looking at her but could not see her face. He did not feel it was an appropriate time to discipline his submissive in the presence of their host and hostess. So he asked at a low volume, "You okay?"

Katrina's hand searched for, and found his. She guided his fingers to her lips where Edward felt the smooth, familiar texture of bondage tape holding something like an adult-sized pacifier in her mouth. He continued the tactile inspection of his submissive to find she was wearing nothing but a thick blanket and panties.

"I don't know what game you girls are up to but it doesn't anger me one bit," he murmured. "But you will still adhere to verbal protocol even when muzzled."

She did her best to reply through her sealed lips: "Mm hm."

He pointed over the telescope tube to an object that appeared to be the brightest star in the sky. "That's Jupiter. Look at it through here," he said as he pulled her in front of him and directed her to the eyepiece.

"Mm hm."

Through the lens, Katrina saw a bright, light gray circle with two reddish-orange bands across it. Four much tinier points of light formed a perfect line that crossed the great planet, three on one side, one on the other. She squeezed Edward's hand as he held his body to hers.

He spoke into her ear. "You are looking at the largest planet in our solar system. It's because of that planet, Earth was able to form the way it did. If it weren't for Jupiter, we wouldn't be here," he said. "Well, Jupiter and Saturn. I'll show you Saturn next."

*How does he know these things? I'm going to have to remember a lot of questions for later.*

Edward turned to the darkness where Woodrow's lounge chair was. "London, would you like to see Jupiter before I go to Saturn?"

"She's occupied at the moment, mate," Woodrow returned.

"Atta' girl," Edward encouraged. "It'll be there when you're done."

Edward turned and kissed the back of Katrina's neck, giving her goosebumps and erect nipples as she stared at the heavenly wonder. She let out a little lilt that sounded more like a whimper through her sealed lips. She lifted her head, leaned back into her man, and wrapped both of his arms around her. She pulled one of his hands under the blanket and placed it to cup one of her breasts. She stared at Jupiter with her naked eyes.

"That one right by Jupiter, that's Saturn. Would you like to go to Saturn?"

"Mm hm," she said with a nod.

He picked up the controller with his unoccupied hand and typed on the keypad with his thumb. The telescope made a winding sound that lowered in pitch as it homed in on its target. Once it was silent, he ordered position two, on her knees, so he could look over her and adjust the manual focus on the planet. Then he pulled Katrina back up to him and said, "Take a look."

"Mm hm."

Katrina gasped through her nose at the sight she beheld. She had seen pictures of the great planet before. But they could not do justice to her vision.

"This is a great night," Edward began. "You can't always see the shadow behind the planet on the disks. But tonight, you can see that, plus a little bit of the separation on the outer ring."

From there, Edward took her on a journey of his favorite sights, periodically changing eyepieces and filters for the best views.

He showed her the constellation Orion and the Orion Nebula, first with the naked eye. The nebula was like a sword on Orion's belt. Then, through the telescope, he showed her the colorful gas of the nebula itself along with the four brightest stars of Orion's Trapezium. "I can actually tell you the names of all four of those stars," he boasted. "They are Orionis A, Orionis B, Orionis C, and... aaaaand." He shrugged off, "Eh, I forget the fourth one."

Katrina giggled and snorted through her nose at Edward's absurd humor.

"Remember when I read to you from the Book of Job?"

"Mm hm."

"Orion is mentioned in that book along with the Pleiades and the Bear."

He showed her all three along with the surface detail of the quarter moon and more of his favorite nebulas, constellations, clusters, and galaxies. When he showed her the Sombrero galaxy, he softly sang the chorus of "Cielito Lindo". She could only hum along as he gently rocked her side to side on her feet in rhythm.

Katrina's favorite destination was the Owl Cluster. She couldn't see it at first. It looked like just a bunch of stars to her. But when Edward told her to think of the two brightest stars as the eyes, it revealed itself. It was like the owl looked right back at Katrina and spread her wings across the diameter of the field of vision, flying away and taking Katrina's breath with her.

After some time, the two took to their chaise lounge where Katrina spread her own wings over her man with the blanket atop. He held her tightly to share their warmth. She remembered to stay as silent and still as possible.

Edward looked at the tiny sliver of the crescent moon and smiled back like they were old friends. "You know what I don't understand?" he asked rhetorically, given the muted status of his submissive. "There are people who see these things I am showing you right now. They see the brilliance of these lights and shapes in our sky. They see the effects of the invisible forces of gravity. They see the behavior of these celestial beings; the patterns in the randomness;

the order in the entropy. We know exactly where all these planets and stars were a thousand years ago and we can predict exactly where they are going to be a thousand years from now. It's all set like clockwork. But what I don't understand is how anyone can see all of this and still doubt the existence of God."

Katrina's eyes began to tear. She wasn't sure if it was the splendor in the sights she was seeing for the first time, the affection and warmth her man was sharing with her, or the passion Edward was expressing in his appreciation of creation. Since no response could be appropriate, she was grateful to be unable to speak. All she could do was hold him tighter and silently love him more in her own *cielito lindo*.

"Venus is rising."

# 12.0

# ISSUE AT BAR

Katrina stood before the judge with Shannon by her side. Edward, Alison, and Katrina's mother looked on from the gallery.

"Miss Katrina Gomez, raise your right hand and repeat after me." The judge looked down at his personal copy of *Conventions of the Constitution* wherein he had handwritten the Nevada Oath of Attorney. He adjusted his spectacles and began, "I, state your name…"

"I, Katrina Gomez…"

"…do solemnly swear…"

"…do solemnly swear…"

"…that I…"

"…that I will support the Constitution and government of the United States and of the State of Nevada…"

The judge looked up from the venerable book in disbelief that he was being interrupted in his own courtroom. It was evident he was not pleased, to say the least.

Katrina realized she may have made a mistake. But she was in too deep to stop now. "…I will maintain the respect due to courts of justice and judicial officers; I will support, abide by, and follow the Rules of Professional Conduct as are now or may hereafter be adopted by the Supreme Court…"

By this time, Katrina's heartbeat was louder in her ears than her own voice. The judge glanced at Shannon as he leaned back in his chair. Shannon held still with a pokerface as though she were carved in marble.

Katrina concluded, "…and I will faithfully and honestly discharge the duties of an attorney at law to the best of my knowledge and ability." She returned her right hand to clasp it with her left in front. The courtroom was silent but Katrina couldn't tell with the sound of blood rushing in her ears.

Shannon murmured without moving her lips, "I told you, you didn't have to recite it from memory."

Katrina maintained a bold face, though her thoughts rendered her expression a bluff. *Did I just bring my legal career to a crashing halt before it even starts?* She was pulled from her mind by a loud, flinch-inducing "THUMP".

The judge had closed the large book with a sound that resounded from the bench and echoed through the courtroom. Katrina was fully present.

"Miss Gomez."

"Yes, your honor?" she said with a hint of timidity.

"Is it your intention to spend your career interrupting presiding judges in a misguided attempt to impress them?"

She swallowed. "Not anymore, your honor."

The stone face of the judge melted into a grin of amusement. His lips tightened at the corners to stifle a laugh before projecting his voice to the rest of the court.

"Then it is my honor to present Miss Katrina Gomez, Attorney at Law."

"Thank you, your honor!"

Shannon followed the judge to his chambers after a brief hug with Katrina. But the small remaining audience clapped as smiles, hugs, and kisses abounded.

\*     \*     \*

Katrina pulled out of the parking garage of the Regional Justice Center.

"What's it like to be an attorney?!" Alison asked from the passenger seat.

"I've only been an attorney for thirty minutes! I don't feel like an attorney yet."

"Does this mean Shannon and the other associates are not your bosses anymore?"

"Technically, yes. They are not my bosses anymore. But I'll still take their advice. And Shannon is still my mentor."

"Ugh. I wish I could have a different boss!"

"I know. I can be a real slave driver."

"No! Not you!" Alison said with a laugh. "I wish you were my only boss."

"Shannon can be… difficult. But she's very intelligent. I've learned a lot from her."

"Now that you're an attorney, do you think you could talk Shannon into getting a new assistant so I can work for just you?"

"Maybe. Send me your resume and references and I'll think about it."

"References?! You're my only reference!" Both ladies were laughing over this.

"I'll talk to the associates and see what I can do. But don't get your hope up. Shannon likes you. She may try to keep you."

"Shannon likes me?"

Katrina nodded.

"No she doesn't."

"Yes, she does. She says nice things."

"Jesus. She has a funny way of showing it. She doesn't ever say anything nice to me."

"With Shannon... If she's not saying anything mean to you, you are probably doing well."

"I don't know how you have been working so closely with her."

"She's not my only boss."

"That'd be great if I could choose my own boss."

"You can always choose your own boss."

\*     \*     \*

Katrina and Alison entered the restaurant and approached the table where Edward was waiting alone. Katrina was disappointed but not surprised at her mother's absence. When Edward stood, she kissed him and slid into the booth. "Mamá didn't want to come?"

"She asked me to take her home."

TG was one of the couple's favorite restaurants. Katrina introduced it to Edward as the gathering place of people in the Las Vegas legal community. Free copies of "LV Law" magazine were available in the lobby. This, in combination with an assortment of fine alcohol beverages, prompted Edward to nickname the restaurant, "The 'Bar' Association". The enclosed booths and lighting made it feel like it was nighttime at all hours. And they afforded enough privacy for deep conversation, the only kind in which Edward was interested.

"Okay. What about Sarah Connor?" Alison asked Edward from across the table.

"What about her?"

"She's a strong female character who didn't have a man." She caught herself. "She didn't have a man from *Terminator 2* on."

"Yeah, but..." Edward gave a wince. "Her biggest character arc was in the first *Terminator* movie in which she was inspired and taught to fight by her love interest."

"But she didn't even kill her first terminator until after he was dead."

"You make an interesting point. But it's hard to argue that he wasn't a major factor in Sarah's 'badassery'. Do you think she could have killed that terminator without his influence?" he asked rhetorically. "Compare her character at the beginning and end of the film. And then she went on to be an Oedipal single mother to her son." Edward held up his unoccupied right hand. "...perhaps with some justification given the circumstances."

Alison didn't want to admit she didn't know what "Oedipal" meant. She looked at Katrina sitting next to Edward.

"Don't look at me! I've never seen the movies." She turned to Edward. "She became 'edible'?"

"'Oedipal', not 'edible'. She was an 'Oedipal mother'. I'll explain when we watch them." He turned back to Alison. "I'm still catching her up on the classics."

"Okay. You're a poker player. What about Molly Bloom?"

"I love Molly Bloom!" Edward declared. "What about her?"

"Welcome to TG! My name is 'Brendon', I'll be your server this afternoon. Can I get you anything to drink besides water?"

"Hello, Brendon! I am Edward. This is Katrina and Alison. We'll be your diners this afternoon..."

After the drink order, Brendon asked if they would like an appetizer. Edward asked Katrina, "Are you in the mood for some calamari?"

"No! No calamari!" she emphatically returned as they leaned into each other in laughter.

Brendon and Alison glanced at each other and shared a puzzled smile, knowing they were on the outside of an inside joke. He departed with the ladies' order of two wedge salads and Edward's order of a cup of the (highly recommended) New England Clam Chowder.

"What was the 'case at bar'?" Edward asked.

"Molly Bloom," Katrina answered.

"Thank you!" He turned to Alison. "You were saying?"

"Molly Bloom is a strong female character with no man for a love interest! And she's a real person! 'Molly's Game' is a biopic!"

Edward winced again and inhaled. "How do I put this?" He chose his words carefully. "Like Sarah Connor, I think Molly Bloom is a good, strong female role model for both boys and girls. And it is true that she does not have a love interest ...*in the movie*." Edward reached for his glass of water.

Alison knew he had more to say. "But?"

Edward lifted the glass to his lips. Just before he took a drink, he muttered, "Just don't read her book."

Alison was dispirited. "Okay. What's in the book?"

Edward set his glass down and said, "In the book, she has, not one, but two boyfriends. ...not at the same time. I'll grant you, I'm not sure the boyfriends were completely integral to the building of her poker empire. But she did make them sound like they were supportive."

"I thought you didn't read," Katrina said.

"Audiobook," Edward returned.

"Okay," Alison sighed. "I'll find some more examples."

"I don't think we are looking at this the same way. You see a woman's dependence on a man as a sign of weakness; like independence in and of itself makes someone strong; like Molly Bloom and Sarah Connor are weaker for having been influenced by men."

Alison didn't have a response. She was being cast into cogitation. So he continued.

"Nobody makes men think we're weak for having a relationship with a woman. ...or depending on a woman. I depend on Katrina," he volunteered as he clenched his left hand that was on her inner thigh. "I don't think that makes me weak. She makes me feel stronger. In so many ways, I feel like my masculinity is more defined by her than by me."

"I wish Troy talked about me like you two talk about each other."

"Oh? You talk about me?" Edward asked Katrina with delight.

"Sometimes," she replied coyly.

"Try, all the time!" Alison said. "'Sometimes'," she mocked. "She won't shut up about you!"

Edward tilted his head to give Katrina a peck behind her temple, causing her to smile and pull her shoulders in. Alison's heart melted. She was not accustomed to seeing this side of her boss.

"So?" Katrina asked Edward.

"So what?"

"Are you going to ask her?"

Edward glanced at Alison before leaning over to whisper in Katrina's ear. Alison watched as the couple spoke inaudibly before interrupting: "I'll do it!"

The two turned back to her at the same time.

"Do what?" Edward asked.

"You're gonna make me say it?"

The couple was confused.

"May I ask you some personal questions?" Edward asked.

"Okay."

"Why would you want to buy a house with someone who won't marry you?"

Now Alison was confused. She cleared her throat and straightened her posture. Edward turned back to Katrina.

"It's okay," Katrina said to Edward. "She said she was okay with talking about it."

"Forgive me," Edward said to Alison. "I know I can be blunt…"

"No! It's okay!" Alison said. "I was thinking you were going to ask… something totally different."

Edward pressed his lips to hide a grin. Katrina wasn't sure what was going on.

Alison moved the conversation along by answering, "I'm sure we are going to get married. I'm just giving him time."

"How long have you been dating?"

"Three years," she answered in monotone.

"How long have you been living together?"

"Two years."

"Alright." Edward nodded. Both ladies were looking at him. He glanced back and forth between them. He knew they expected him to say something. "No further questions, your honor."

"Overruled 'counselor'!" Katrina said.

"What?"

"What do you think?"

"About what?"

"About Alison and Troy?!"

Alison thought the couple's exchange was humorous. She was finding Edward to be as aloof as Troy.

"I already ham-handedly brought up the subject like a stampeding bull and she hasn't even asked for my opinion," Edward said to Katrina.

"What's your opinion?" Alison asked with a smile. "Give it to me straight, doc!"

Edward's head turned to Alison. "I think Troy sees you as a hole to keep his cock warm."

The smile fell off of her face.

"Alrighty folks, here are your drinks. I've got the soup and salads on the way. Have we made any decisions about the main course?"

After a momentary pause that everyone found awkward, except for Edward, Edward ordered on behalf of the table in accordance with their previously discussed wishes. Brendon departed.

Edward looked at Katrina. "Cock warmer," she reminded.

"Oh yeah! Thank you." He turned back. "Alison, you have given Troy all the power in your relationship and he has no respect for you. It's got to be hard for him to respect you because you don't respect yourself. He's just taking you for an extended test drive. And if things don't work out, he can go test drive another model." He took a drink of water. "Don't get me wrong, I'm not saying Troy is a bad guy. Neither of you may be the 'bad guy'. After all, you are doing the same thing to him by living with him with no commitment. You're test driving him too."

Edward could see on her face she was going deeper and deeper into thought as she stared through the table. But when he saw the tears start to well, he tried to add some sensitivity to his voice.

"Here's the good news: You have allowed this. And you can change it or end it by choice. I'm sure you love each other. But neither of you respect each other. And crazy though it may sound, I think respect is more important than love to a man. You gave away your power and you can get it back simply by learning how to respect yourself, and it will help him respect you."

"I have to go to the bathroom," she said, sliding out of the booth. She tilted her head so her hair would hide part of her face.

"I didn't mean to make you cry," Edward said.

"No, it's okay," she said. "I'm just going to… cry about something else."

Without prompting, Edward stood and let Katrina out of the booth. He was aware of the unwritten rules of women and restrooms. Katrina squeezed his hand as she walked by him.

"Alrighty folks…" Brendon had returned with the soup and salads. He lifted the tray up over his head as the ladies made their way around him. Edward sat back down and went into a stare. Brendon silently placed the food on the table and awoke Edward from his thoughts by asking, "Was it something I said?"

"Yes, Brendon," Edward replied sardonically. "It's all your fault."

"Fresh cracked pepper?"

"Please." As Brendon twisted the mill over the soup, Edward said, "To quote the apostle Paul, 'Fresh cracked pepper covers a multitude of sins.'"

"I think it was Peter who said something like that."

"Yeah... Yeah, I think you're right."

Brendon departed. Edward sat alone, watching his soup get cold.

…

Upon Alison's return, Edward started to slide out of the booth but stopped when he saw Katrina was not with her.

"Where's Katrina?"

"She got caught in a networking conversation in the lobby," she said with her usual happy-go-lucky timbre. "She still likes handing out paper business cards more than digital cards."

"We are old souls," Edward replied. After a few seconds of silence, the air still needed to be cleared: "Listen, I'll just say this and we can drop it if you want." Edward leaned into the table. "I didn't mean to upset you. I'm frustrated, and I think I might have directed some of that frustration toward you. It's just that…" He looked over her head to formulate his words before reestablishing eye contact. "I'm not saying you don't deserve any blame. It's just that men tend to have more control in relationships than women so it bothers me when I see men treat women the way they sometimes do. But that's just my opinion as an openly sexist man."

His admission elicited a chuckle from Alison. "Why does that frustrate you?"

Edward leaned back. His eyebrows furrowed in thought as his eyes returned above her head. "I think I see men exhibit qualities that I used to have... or maybe still have that I don't like. Perhaps it reminds me of things that I don't like about myself."

"Jesus, you're deep."

"Thank you. But only my followers call me 'Jesus'."

Hearing Alison's laughter as she approached the table, Katrina was relieved to see the cloud had lifted. Edward stood to let her in.

"I was giving out business cards," Katrina said. "A thousand new cards arrived last week that say I'm still a 'clerk'."

"I can order new cards for you, Miss Gomez!" Alison volunteered.

"No. Not yet. I don't want to waste the new cards, and my last name is going to be changing in a few months."

"K., you are an attorney at a billion dollar law firm," Alison cajoled. "I think we can afford to get you new cards now, and we will be able to get you new cards when you get married."

"Yeah," Edward said. "You don't want to give away *all* of your 'rookie cards'. They might be worth something someday!" But neither girl got the joke.

Katrina pondered a moment. "You're right. The appearance of professionality is worth the small amount of money."

"Should they say 'Gomez' or 'Henderson'?" Alison asked.

Katrina looked to Edward. He nodded and said, "They can say 'Henderson'."

Both girls smiled at each other with wide eyes. They squeed and did a three-second "happy dance" in their seats that had Edward cracking up.

"Done! I'll put them in the morning order," Alison said while typing on her cellphone. She set it down and picked up a fork.

Edward said, "We're going to ask for a blessing on our food. You are welcome to join us or ignore us. No pressure."

Alison set her fork down. "I would like to join you."

With that, Edward gave a ten-second prayer that included a blessing on Katrina's career and requested wisdom for Alison's future decisions, ending with, "Amen."

"Amen," Brendon repeated. He was waiting silently with a tray of their main courses. Though the diners had yet to touch their soup and salads, they made room to welcome the new dishes.

"So counselor," Edward began. "What else are you going to have on your new business cards? 'Katrina Henderson, *Esquire*'?"

"Mm. Probably not."

"How about, 'Katrina my Quee-na'?"

She smiled but never took her eyes off her plate. "Maybe, if I become a judge."

"How about..."

Alison watched as Edward leaned over and whispered another suggestion in Katrina's ear. Katrina put her napkin over her mouth so her laughter wouldn't make her spit her food across the table. Edward was laughing too, which made Alison laugh even though she didn't hear what he said.

Alison leaned into the table and spoke in a hushed tone. "I have to ask, you two *have* started fucking, right?!"

*What? How does she know... Oh no. I told her. How did I forget?* Katrina's laughter ceased for a split second as she glanced at Edward. She felt her eyes widen but she stopped them as poker had taught. She continued laughing but her tone changed. *This might not be so bad. At least, she didn't say the 'v' word. Please don't say the 'v' word before I can talk to Edward!*

On the other hand, Edward laughed even harder as he set down his fork and put his own napkin over his mouth. He laughed until his eyes were tearing.

*This could be good. Or is he giving a false signal? Is his laughter as fake as mine?*

Edward wiped his eyes as he recovered his breath. "What do you mean?" he asked Alison.

"I mean, you two are obviously in love. Did you start fucking or are you still a virgin?"

*And there it is. Now he knows I told Alison. He's a virgin and I'm fucked!*

"Not forever," Edward replied in stride. "Just until I'm married."

*He just said "until I'm married" instead of "until we're married". Was that on purpose?*

"But how do you know it'll work?" Alison asked Edward.

"How do I know sex will work?"

"Yeah. How do you know it will be good with you two? How do you know if you don't take a 'test drive'?"

"What do you think, concha?" Edward asked Katrina. "Do you think there is a chance we will not be sexually compatible?"

Katrina wryly replied while looking at Alison. "I don't think that will be a problem. I am very much looking forward to being his cock warmer."

Edward pointed a finger at Katrina and leaned into the table. "Candidly, I don't need a test drive to know, I'ma beat the breaks off this car!"

The ladies looked at each other again, smiling. But Alison was not well-versed in poker tells. She didn't know that Katrina's eyes weren't quite matching her lips.

Edward turned to Katrina and added an inside joke, "Que curvas! Y yo sin frenos!"

*I can't tell if this is incredibly good or incredibly bad... or somewhere in between. ... No... it's not somewhere in between.*

"How about a *picture* on your business card?" Edward recommended. "A picture of you dressed like Justicia, Lady Justice? With a sword in one hand and a scale in the other. ...wearing a blindfold and a toga with my breast hanging out?" In light of Alison's company, Edward quickly corrected by mumbling, "*A* breast hanging out?"

He had the ladies laughing at this. Alison heard his slip but thought nothing of it in that moment. The glimpses she was getting into the nature of their relationship didn't seem to fit given the fact she had never encountered a *kinky virgin* before. But she wasn't the type to dwell on a thought for long.

"Lady Justice?!" Katrina returned. "I've been an attorney for an hour now!"

"She said she doesn't feel like an attorney yet," Alison recalled.

Edward looked at Katrina. "You don't feel like an attorney? What are you waiting for?"

"I don't know. I just don't *feel* like an attorney yet."

"What will it take?"

"What do you mean?"

"Did you think getting your degree was going to make you *feel* like an attorney? Did you think being sworn in was going to make you *feel like an attorney*?"

"A little. That's how you become an attorney."

"I'm a musician. I'm a poker player. I'm a teacher. I didn't get a degree in anything. I dropped out of college."

Katrina nodded. She already knew these things.

"My point is, nobody is going to walk up to you, shake you by the shoulders, and tell you that you're an attorney now. You have to tell yourself what you are."

Katrina's nod slowed down from one of acknowledgment to one of contemplation. He had told her things like this before. He hoped she would listen someday. He let the silence work on her.

But Alison interjected, "Jesus, you *are* deep!"

He shook his head. "Please, just call me 'Edward'."

\*         \*         \*

Edward was engaged and affectionate through the rest of lunch. He kept the ladies laughing as he held open the door out the restaurant. He was conversational while escorting them to Katrina's car, walking arm in arm with her. It seemed like all was right as rain. But she wanted confirmation.

When he opened her car door for her, she asked so only he could hear, "Is it still okay for me to put your name on my business cards, Master?"

He smiled and gave her a kiss on the cheek before whispering with a growl in her ear, "Get in the fuckin' car."

Her face lost all expression as she sat. He closed the door.

"Did he say *your* breast was *his* breast?!" Alison asked. "I guess I know who *your* boss is now!" she teased as she watched Edward walk away.

"He's going to kill me," Katrina said in contrast to Alison's enthusiasm.

"Kill you?" Alison's eyes went from Edward's butt to the side of Katrina's face. Her amusement turned to concern.

"Oye. You told him you know he's a virgin," she said, staring at the steering wheel.

"Yeah?"

"I know I didn't tell you not to say anything. It's not your fault. But I'm in deep trouble."

"Because you told me he's a virgin? What's wrong with that?"

"He doesn't want anyone to know."

"Why not?!"

"I don't understand it either but that's irrelevant. I told him I would never tell anyone."

"And you think he's going to kill you for *that*?"

"Not *kill* me. Just really punish me."

"I know he won't literally *kill* you. But what do you mean 'punish you'? Like a child?"

"No. No, nothing like a child," she clarified. "But you're right. He *is* my boss."

"I don't know what you mean. That's not right. He doesn't get to *punish* you!"

"Yes he does! He does anything he wants to me!"

"That's sick, Katrina. You sound like one of those abuse victims, like one of our clients. You need to get away from him if that's what it's like."

"I can't do that. He is the greatest man I have ever known. I love him."

"Katrina, if it's that serious, let me help you. We can get you out of this."

"NO! I don't want out! I... I can't talk about it."

"You can't talk to *me* about it?"

"Oye, look. I can't talk about our relationship. Nobody understands."

"Make me understand, K. If you can't talk about it with me..." Alison threw up her hands.

Katrina thought about her words. "There are types of relationships where one person is the 'Dominant' and the other is the 'submissive'."

"I've heard of that. Is that what you've got with Edward? Is that why he gave you that... 'necklace'?"

"I can't talk about my relationship with Edward. I'm just speaking in generalities."

"Okay," Alison scoffed. "I've heard of those kinds of relationships but I could never live like that, being a slave to a fucking *man*, losing myself."

"It's not what you think. I didn't lose myself. I found myself. It's the most freedom I've ever had."

Shaking her head, Alison looked at Katrina with knitted brows but said nothing. Katrina gave up on keeping some details of her relationship to herself. Alison was figuring it out but she was getting a very wrong impression.

"Look, you know that problem you have, not knowing if you are satisfying Troy?"

"Yeeeaaah," she replied, uncertain if she was being attacked.

"I don't have that problem. I just have to do whatever Edward tells me to do and I know I'll satisfy him."

"That's great for *him* but how does that satisfy *you*?"

"To be able to satisfy my man so much?"

Alison didn't say anything.

"I don't know how to tell you how satisfying it is to please him." She held her hand over her heart and made a loose fist. "It's like... It makes me feel like a woman."

"It makes you feel like a woman to have a man punish you?"

"It makes me feel like a woman to have a man in control."

"To have a man control you?"

"To *give* a man that kind of control. It makes him even more manly... at least to me."

"That's great, but... what does he do to satisfy you?"

"What he does makes no difference to my loyalty to him. I am his. And I do whatever he wants me to do no matter what he does for me. It's not quid pro quo. But that's what makes it so good. He works very hard to satisfy me! He's always trying to earn my submission. And he doesn't do it so I will do things for him. He does it because he loves me. That makes it… so… much…"

When Katrina leaned back in her seat, Alison could see her mind was trailing off with her words.

"Sometimes he makes me tell him what I want. He orders me to tell him how to satisfy me. I used to hate having to think about it. But now… I don't know how to explain it." She pushed her hands forward with her fingers spread. "I can put out what it is that I want without thinking about it. And he makes it happen."

"That must be some good dick," Alison said. And then she snipped, "Oh, wait. He's not dickin' you down at all!"

"It's not like that," Katrina said. "When we walk around… I feel like a queen! I don't have to drive myself anywhere with him. I don't even have to open doors. He leads me everywhere. He's like a GPS; I just turn him on and he tells me where to go!"

This got a faint snort and smile from Alison.

"It's like I can hide in plain sight right next to him if I feel shy. He does all the talking to strangers if I don't want. I feel protected when he's around and I feel strong when he's not. And Alison, the boy is hilarious! You saw how he kept us *both* laughing through most of that lunch!"

"Jesus, Katrina, listen to yourself." Alison shook her head again. "I thought he was a great guy too. But it's like he's brainwashed you!"

"Yes! Yes, that's exactly what it's like! All the crap he's washed out of my brain! All the insecurity! All the stuff I could never talk about because I didn't know about it myself! When something happens that bothers me, I don't have to pack it away and carry it alone and live in fear that it will come pouring out at the worst possible time; like when you used to catch me crying in the bathroom at work. I can control when I cry now. I can talk to him about it. Even when he doesn't talk or do anything, it feels better. I don't have to be afraid of silence anymore, or be afraid of being alone with my thoughts. And I can turn my brain off if I need to. It's like a vacation from my own mind when we're alone. Just to have that masculine energy near me, it's like I go into some kind of meditative state. Even my *mom* relaxes when he's around!" She concluded, "You're exactly right; I'm 'brainwashed' and I've never been happier in all my life!"

"'Masculine energy'? More like 'toxic masculinity'."

"'Toxic', 'intoxicating': All I know is, I need it," she said. "Remember when you met me and I was too shy to talk?"

"Yeah."

"He's got me singing in church or at one of his gigs almost every week. Can you imagine me doing that when we met?!"

Alison didn't respond.

"I'm teaching him how to dance! He says it makes him a better musician. We make each other better."

"And that's why you think *your* tits are *his* tits."

"They *are* his tits! …because I gave them to him. They're like his favorite toys. This whole body is his! And he treats me better than he treats himself. He's got me going to the gym with him. He made me quit smoking. Do you know what that's like, to be the most cherished possession in the world of a real man?!"

"Okay, well, maybe he's not *abusive*," she relented. "But it's still not right that he 'punishes' you, or whatever."

"Alison, if he doesn't punish me, it will be because he's finished with me. He's the most trustworthy man I've ever met. I've broken his trust before. And this was it. This was my last chance. I *pray to God* he will punish me." She started the car and said, half to herself, "I've chosen my boss. I don't know what I'll do if he doesn't choose me."

# ACT 3

# Chapter 12.1

# HURDLING THE BAR

Katrina drove herself and Alison back to the office where she proceeded to accomplish absolutely nothing. It was reminiscent of the way she felt after the night she turned Edward away from her door in chapter 6. She was adrift at sea. And this time, there was no email from him waiting for her at work to guide her to shore, like in chapter 7.

She tried to focus on a transcript she had been reviewing. But she realized it was no use when she caught herself reading the same line a third time. *Why do I want a cigarette?*

She tried texting Edward to see if it would help the distraction subside:
Katrina: Can we talk, Master?
Three torturous minutes later:
Edward: Not yet.
Katrina: Please, Master?
Edward: I'm working.

Edward "working" could mean he was playing or dealing poker, teaching a class, writing lyrics or poetry, conducting a rehearsal, composing or recording music, or practicing an instrument. He was always indulging his "Curse of Adam".

*Take a shower.*

*A shower without him won't help.*

*He needs time and space.*

*I want to fix this.*

*Time... and... space.*

*Fine, I'll give him 'time and space'.*

*...an hour should do.*

Katrina used her cellphone to find his location: his house.
The rumble of drums could be heard from his front door. She entered using the digital key on her phone. *At least he hasn't rescinded my access... yet.*
She peeked through the studio door to make sure he was alone, not giving a private lesson. She observed him at his drumset, shirtless and sweaty in

gym shorts. His muscles were defined in a way that could only result from years of practice in the percussive arts.

Edward was in a hypnotic state as his eyes glided along the sheet music of a bossa nova. The accompanying tracks played from the monitors along with a click track to help him perfect his time. At the end of the song, he stopped, took a long drink of water, and prepared to throw down the next selection: a hard rock tune in uncommon time that opened with a raucous drum solo.

As the song started, he was startled to see his submissive enter the room with her hair pulled back, wearing nothing but her engagement collar. But he didn't stop the groove he was practicing. Though his eyes stayed fixed upon the sheet music, he could see out the corner that she assumed position two, presentation, right in front of the drumset, with the chain and lock resting on her flat palms.

Although she assumed this position on many occasions and for much longer amounts of time, she never felt as much pain in her knees as they sunk deeper into the carpet with each passing moment. But she dared not move.

The bridge of the song settled to the softer rhythmic plucking of a guitar with no drum part. Edward placed his drumsticks on the snare and took another drink of water. He sat upright and stared at his frozen submissive with her eyes on the chain.

Without saying a word, he stood and walked around to the front of his drumset where he took the chain from her hands. She crossed her arms behind her back. He placed the chain around her neck and locked it two or three links tighter than usual. Then he held his fist in front of her face and opened his palm to reveal two foam earplugs. She put them in without a word.

He returned to his throne behind the drumset and lightly tapped the cymbals with accents on the toms, adding color to the soft guitar riff. It held a resolving chord and all instruments faded to silence.

CRASH!!!

Katrina flinched as though she had been shot when the ensemble shattered the silence with a mighty clash of cymbals; the wind from which brushed a few loose strands of hair from the side of her face to her ear. The volume was sustained by the repetition of the same guitar line at ten times the volume with distortion and added drum rolls around the kit that ultimately climaxed in repetition of the opening drum solo and guitar riff with the screaming vocalist adding the cherry to the top of the musical cacophony.

It may have been a coincidence that Katrina walked in during the performance of this particular composition. But the emotion that Edward clearly conveyed through the selection could only be described as "rage".

At the denouement of the piece, Edward replaced his sticks on the snare, stood, and walked briskly by his submissive, grabbing the chain from behind her neck on his way out the studio door. Her eyes widened as she snapped her body around to be transported like a piece of luggage. She stumbled back and forth between crawling and walking with her head down, trying not to be choked, but also trying not to challenge the unwavering gait of her Master as she tumbled down the hall.

Once they arrived in the master bedroom, Edward released the chain. "Position two, eyes down."

"Yes, Master," her strained voice said. He didn't turn on the lights. But there was enough light from the hallway to see shadows, not that there was anything to see on the floor before her.

Edward went into the closet and rolled out, something. ...something big in front of Katrina. But she still couldn't tell what it was. And she wasn't sure she would recognize it even if the lights were on.

A tug on the chain almost lifted her to her feet. But before she could stand upright, she was pulled onto... whatever this thing was. She found herself straddling and then laying face down on what felt like a bench with leather padding.

She started to ask, "What is..."

"Shut up."

The curt order was a thorn prick to her submissive heart from a Dom who was otherwise so receptive to anything she said. But she reminded herself it was *she* who had hurt *him*. And she was coming to understand, her status may be even worse than she initially realized. Uncertain she should reply at all, she whispered, "Yes, Master."

Her head was placed face down on something that cushioned her forehead and cheeks. Her elbows and knees were placed on pads, one by one, on each side of the... thing. Belts were buckled all over her body; a pair over each forearm, a pair over each calf, and one over her back held her secure.

Finally, she saw Edward's feet stop in front of her before turning to the light. The closure of the door left Katrina alone in complete darkness.

She wondered for a moment if he was still in the room. But her question was answered when, through the earplugs, she heard the muffled music in the studio restart before Edward resumed his practice.

She took mental stock of her situation starting with her body. *Proprioception.* She was on her elbows and knees, similar to position four. But she knew she was above the floor on some kind of furniture that was actually rather comfortable. Whatever it was, it was padded and supportive to her appendages and torso, except for her breasts which she could feel hanging down. And with her legs straddling the bench, she was open and exposed from behind.

She tested the restraints to find she had less than an inch to her range of motion from each belt. The only thing she could move was her head. She lifted it to look around. There was nothing to see but a couple of tiny red lights from the computer on the desk. She replaced her head on the cushion. *This is how my Master wants me. This is how he will have me for as long as he wishes. Whatever he feels I deserve, I accept.*

The thought occurred that this might be an opportunity for a nap. But her mind would not stop churning. And it might defeat the purpose of... whatever purpose she was to fulfill, waiting in storage.

As her eyes were deprived of light, her ears were eventually deprived of sound when Edward finished practicing. *Now he will come back for me. Be good for Master.* But she was wrong. He did not return for... an amount of time that was imperceivable. For as her eyes and ears were rendered unnecessary by the silent darkness, her sense of the passage of time was also slipping away. *How long have I been here? An hour? Two? Master will not forget me. Will he?*

Katrina began to weep, fearing the worst. *What is he thinking? What is he going to do? Is he thinking about breaking our engagement? Would he end our relationship?* But she also tried to reach for comfort in logic: *At least he put the chain on me. He wouldn't do that if he intended to break up... Would he?*

Each breath became shorter and more erratic. The earplugs afforded her the ability to hear the sound of her own heartbeat as its tempo crept faster. She attempted one of the meditative exercises she had been taught. But it was no use trying without her Master there to guide her.

…

The door opened. The light turned on. Katrina squeezed her eyes closed at the brightness. She started to squirm but thought it best to remain still. Then her head was lifted by her ponytail. He removed the headrest from the apparatus causing her to hold her head up. She opened her eyes but had to squint as she faced the recliner where Edward took a seat. He looked away after a glance at her welling tears.

He sat on the edge of the recliner and leaned to one side, still shirtless in gym shorts. He was uneasy, like he couldn't remember how to sit in a chair. Then he stood with his crotch just beyond the reach of Katrina's face. With his right hand on his hip, he put his left hand on her back and drummed his fingers as though he were leaning on an inanimate object.

Katrina stared at the drawstrings of his shorts, ready to perform any duty her Master required of her. Her body reacted to his sweat as she breathed him in. She didn't think of the smell as good or bad. She simply thought of it as *the smell of Edward*, which was usually good. But she didn't know how to feel about her Dominant's presence at this moment.

She tried to push forward so she could touch him with her nose, or maybe her tongue in her eagerness to please her Master. But it was no use. He wasn't paying attention to her anyway.

Edward turned toward the bathroom saying, "Not yet," just before closing the door. Never more than now did Katrina wish her introverted man would verbalize his thoughts.

Without the headrest, Katrina let her head dangle down toward the floor. She heard the sound of the sink turning on and off a few times. Then she heard the water of the shower flow for another imperceivable amount of time. *He takes long showers when he's alone too. … … … He's taking a shower… without me.*

Edward exited the bathroom wearing a towel around his waist and continued to ignore her. With her face down, Katrina followed his feet with her eyes until he was behind her, beyond her field of vision. She heard him doing… things. But she didn't know what. Finally, he returned to the recliner and sat, still wearing the towel. She raised her head but kept her eyes down.

Time passed before he calmly asked, "What did you do wrong?"

"I told Alison that you are a virgin, Master."

"More importantly, what did you do?"

She pondered. "I betrayed your trust, Master."

"Why did you do that?"

"It was after we broke up and I was upset, Master. I was depressed because I thought I would never see you again, Master. I honestly forgot that I told her, Master."

More time passed before his next question. His voice was detached, hiding... whatever he was feeling. "When I told you that you were under orders to keep it a secret, do you remember what you asked me?"

Katrina searched her mind. "No, Master."

"You asked me, 'Who would I tell?' ... Do you remember?"

"Yes, Master. I remember now. You said, 'Secrets are not secrets just because there is nobody to tell.'"

"That is correct," he said. "Do you know how many people I told about you and the things that you've told me?"

"Nobody, Master?"

"Nobody," he nodded.

They remained silent for two, maybe three minutes. Katrina knew not to speak until Edward spoke to her. And she was willing to wait forever if that was as long as it took, not that she had a choice. But she did dare to glance at him a time or two. He just sat in the recliner, in a towel, staring into nothingness, until he finally spoke.

"You know, I think I was attracted to you because I thought you could not hurt me. I was stupid."

Katrina was getting her wish: to hear her Master's thoughts. But the words were not easy to accept.

She was afraid of the question on her mind. But she had to speak before she lost her voice. She sniffed and asked, "Are you not attracted to me anymore, Master?" Her oncoming emotions turned the end of the sentence into a squeak. She sniffed again as her face turned redder. She forced the words through her tears, "Why do you love me, Master?"

"Again with that," he said with his face in his palm. "I don't know what you are asking me. I tell you I love you all the time. ...in two languages! I love you like Adam loved Eve! What proof can I give you? I don't know what it is you want me to say! And I don't think you know either!"

He stood with his hands on his hips. "What is it? You don't *feel worthy* of my love or something?" he mocked. "You don't *feel worthy* of our relationship. You don't *feel worthy* of your education. You don't *feel worthy* of your career. You don't *feel worthy* of anything!"

"Are you going to end our relationship, Master?"

"Is that what you want?"

"No, Master!"

Her head dropped, face to the floor as she wept. She heard Edward walking around but she kept her eyes closed. Then her head was yanked up by her ponytail so she faced forward. She was held in that position while Edward... did something. When he returned to the recliner, she found her hair was tied to a point above so she could not lower her head. She had no choice but to face Edward through her tears.

"Look at me," he ordered.

"Yes, Master."

"Ending our engagement would be the easiest thing to do now, wouldn't it?!" he said. "But you're not getting off that easily. That's not how marriage works.

"You don't feel like you deserve me. Maybe you're right. What difference does it make? I know I don't deserve you. But I'm taking your love anyway. And you are going to take mine whether or not you *feel worthy*."

"I accept any punishment you believe I deserve to save our engagement and marriage, Master."

"See, therein lies the problem. For all my experience, I don't know how to punish a pain slut like you without resorting to emotional abuse. And I'm not going to do that."

Katrina said nothing as she cried. Edward stood again and started walking counterclockwise around her.

"If I give you pain, how do I know I'm not rewarding you? How do I know you didn't just do this to provoke me into giving you the pain for which you have been begging and I have been striving to give?"

Katrina made no sound, save her stuttered breathing. Edward continued pacing around her.

"I mean, I take it further and further every session as you request. I try. I try to push my limits. I try so hard to give you the pain you want. Could you trust that I would eventually get you to the level you were seeking without provoking me?"

"Please believe me, Master. I did not try to provoke you. I made a great mistake. I thought I would never see you again," she cried.

"Does that make it right? If I never see you again, does that make it okay for you to defy my orders and share the most intimate details of my life with other people?!"

Katrina's crying turned to bawling.

Edward couldn't bear to look at her face. He stopped walking and sat on the floor behind the bench and leaned back on it between Katrina's bare feet. He mumbled to himself, as much as to his submissive, "What if the real punishment would be to *not* punish you? I'll just let it go as though you were some meaningless jackass at the poker table who was trying to insult me." He thought about it and then said much louder, "Would that work?" He rose to his feet and walked back around in front of her face. He pulled her head up even higher by her hair, looking into her eyes. "Would you rather I *not* punish you?"

"No, Master!" She forced her voice to a shout as she wailed. "Please punish meeeeee! Pleeeeeeease!!!" She begged over and over.

"It won't be the kind of punishment you'll enjoy."

"I accept any punishment you believe I deserve, Master!" she repeated.

"Do you have any idea what you are saying? Can you even fathom my capabilities? Do you have any idea the fucked up shit that goes on inside a man's head?! Are you ready to know?!"

"Please show me, Master! I need to see! My husband wouldn't show me. He wouldn't let me help him. He just killed himself!" She choked: "He forced me to watch!" She struggled to catch her staggered breath through a cackling cry. "He was too scared to show me and he let it kill him! I beg you, Master..." And then she dared yell, "I *order* you, Master! Please, show me!"

"As you wish."

\*        \*        \*

The results of repeated impact, from every tool and implement he owned, from the towel to all of his whips, floggers, paddles, and crops, left her tenderized. With the exception of her lower back where he draped the towel, there was hardly a place on his submissive's back, from her shoulders to her ankles left to conquer.

He walked around to face her. His gaze was not *on* her but *through* her with a flat affect. His penis was just as flaccid as it hung inches from her tear soaked face. Though she was crying, she dutifully opened her mouth in case it was required for service.

For all the torment she was experiencing, she never failed to make herself available in any way possible for the service of her Dominant. But she noticed that in all the activity of the evening, at no point was he aroused. She had never seen her Dominant like this. Not one time did he touch her breasts. He never stopped to feel the bumps of the welts he produced, or trace the lines of his whip marks. Pleasure for either of them was not a consideration.

In his right hand he held up a thin bamboo cane about three feet in length. In his left, a shorter steel rod with a sharp point. "Choose for my feet," he said in a daze; the strength of his exhausted voice dwindling.

She turned her head to the steel rod and mouthed the words, "That one, Master."

He placed the middle of the cane in her mouth where she bit down to hold it.

He started on her left foot by sticking it with the point. Her reflexive attempts to resist the rod only caused her to stab herself. Then Edward held her toes back with his left hand and gave it a hard whack.

"One, Master," she wheezed through the cane.

He stroked her foot in the same way he had with the other implements to her back. On this night, he did not warm up her pain tolerance to a climax. He started at full force, shocking her with every swing. And he sped up to a rapping pace until she could not verbally number the strokes. Her counting, once again, turned to screaming. Her free right foot fluttered up and down at her ankle, toes spreading and curling. Her hands flexed and gripped in fists. She struggled against her bonds, trying to kick away. But her agony-inspired strength was just enough to shake the apparatus on which she was perched, scooting it forward by inches, tightening the rope that connected her hair to the ceiling. What little range of motion her head was afforded was accentuated by the bamboo rod in her teeth. Still, she continued to stir because there was nothing else she could do. And for all of her efforts, the repeated impact on her foot was inexorable.

The sensation gradually turned from a sharp sting to a consuming burn, culminating in a fear greater than the pain itself; it was a fear that the skin was actually being flayed from her foot. The bamboo rod fell from her mouth as her screaming reached a peak, the likes of which neither of them knew she was capable. And still, he was unceasing. *What if he does not stop?*

And then with as little warning as she had for the commencement of her anguish, the strokes came to an unexpected halt. Her screaming turned back to crying.

Edward placed the rod on the towel that was draped over her lower back and returned in front of her. He took a seat, laying back on the recliner. He listened to her crying subside before he spoke. He didn't look at her as he asked with a hoarseness in his voice, "Why couldn't you just tell me what you did?"

She continued to weep, breathing heavily, unable to speak.

"It would have been so much easier to trust you if you would have told me."

"Master?"

Edward looked at her but said nothing.

"There's something more, Master."

Edward shook his head. "I'm… I'm too afraid to ask," he said. He opened his mouth to speak again but could only gasp and swallow. Shaking his head, he tried again, saying, "I'm terrified to ask." He took a deep breath through his nose with mouth closed and jaw clenched. With a failing voice, he asked, "What else did you do?"

Katrina looked at him through the water in her eyes. His right knee shook up and down with anxiety. His face looked as though he was watching an atrocity in slow motion. But she had to tell him. She began, "The n-night my mother saw the mmmarks you gave me…" She paused to watch Edward. He remained frozen except for his knee. "When she was convincing me to ssstop seeing you, she said many horrible things about you. She told me you were a, a fucker who was going to sell me like my husband did, like a prostitute. Then she said…" She paused to try to get control of her breathing. "I could not believe it when she talked about how it was a mistake for her and my father to give me to my husband and… she didn't want to have that happen to me again. It was the first time I ever saw her cry. We were both crying. She never talked about that before."

Edward's knee joined the rest of his body in stillness and woe.

She continued. "When she said she was afraid that I would become pregnant, I told her that we were not having sex. And you were a good man." She started to cry again. "She wouldn't believe me."

Edward inhaled. He knew what she was about to say.

She half mouthed, "…I told her too, Master. But I didn't think about it because she didn't believe me." She continued through her sobbing, "She got into my… I let her back in my head. I told her I wouldn't see you anymore. And…" She inhaled for another confession. "I lied to you, Master. I was the one who told my cousin you would have a gun. Not my mother. I know I shouldn't have done that. I know they could have made you kill them. And I knew what a terrible mistake I made when you talked to me at the door. It wasn't anything you said. It was hearing your voice that night. It was everything I needed."

Edward was in a catatonic state with his eyes looking through her.


"You are the most amazing man I have ever met, Master. You have kept a gift that I desperately wish I could give you. And all I want is for you to be my owner forever. I will never deserve you. But I will try every day for the rest of my life."

Edward wet his eyes with some hard blinks as his head laid back on the recliner.

"Please don't leave me, Master," she squeaked. "I accept any punishment you believe I deserve. Please don't let me go. Pleeeease."

She continued to plead and try to get through to him while he sat static in the recliner. Though it could not be seen from the outside, Edward started to let her tears soak his calloused heart. She stopped talking when he leaned forward and put his face directly in front of hers. He watched as her bawling and begging subsided. There they stayed, studying each other's eyes, until at last, he whispered, "Thank you for telling me the truth."

"You're welcome, Master."

And then he delicately kissed her drenched, disheveled face.

\*     \*     \*

Katrina panted rapidly as Edward lowered her into the shallow ice bath, turning the water a light shade of red. The emotionless, unrelenting cold invaded every inch of her ailing back. She was unable to control her shivering as her skin went numb. Though much of her body was under the surface, her head was supported from behind by Edward's hand.

After a few minutes, "M M, Master," she whispered through her panting.

Edward said nothing. With his right hand still behind her head, his left hand reached over to pull the drain plug and turn on the shower head with lukewarm water. Katrina could feel the sensation raining down on her but it would take time to feel the temperature as Edward gradually raised it.

With the water draining and the ice melting, her body sank to the bottom of the tub where the pain of her punishment was reignited all the way down from her shoulders by her own weight. There was no way to lie that did not hurt. But once her shivering ended and her breath regulated, she made no effort to find a more comfortable position. She remained motionless, staring at… nothing, welcoming the pain she felt she deserved.

Edward reached for the sponge. He used it to wash her front from head to toe. Then he turned her over, once again revealing the results of her penance and his wrath. The shades seemed to grow darker and deeper by the minute. It was a ghastly sight, even to Edward. But he continued to wash her. Though he was gentle, he was undaunted by her panting and whimpers.

Once he was finished, he helped her to her feet and guided her to the mirror. She limped along gingerly, only putting weight on her right foot. She stood at the mirror with Edward behind her; his hands on her shoulders. She leaned back into him in an attempt to borrow his warmth.

"Turn around and look at me."

"Yes, Master." She did so.

He continued to look over her head at his work in the brightest light yet. Katrina had never seen this expression on her man before. His brows were low; jaw clenched like he was looking curiously at a tragedy. He didn't know whether to feel pride or shame. She could sense his pulse and breath rate were elevated. He blinked, looked down into her eyes, and swallowed. "Are you ready to see?"

"Yes, Master."

"Look."

She turned her head over her shoulder and gasped at what she beheld. She was a lattice of razor thin cuts, stripes, and discolored bruises from all manner of instruments, some of which, she had never experienced before.

"It felt like I was bleeding, Master."

"There was some blood."

Their eyes met in the mirror. Still not knowing how to feel about these events, he asked, "Did we go too far?"

"No, Master." She turned her face to his and put her hands on his cheeks. "You have given me something no man has given me before."

"What have I given you?"

"I don't know if there is a word in English for it. But I don't know of a word in Spanish, Master."

Indeed, there is no word that describes the mutual awe they felt for each other, born of the eustress and trauma they had inflicted upon themselves and survived together. But there was no need to define their ever strengthening bond with words. They had reached an understanding that would abide.

"How do you feel?" he asked.

Katrina had to think about it as she observed her image in the mirror once again. She turned back to him before answering. "Cleansed, Master," she replied. "How do you feel, Master?"

Edward took an equal amount of time to think. His expression softened as his mind searched for the word. He licked his lips and swallowed. Now she had seen him as none had seen him before. And she was strong enough to accept him. "I feel... lighter."

He was relieved to find that in spite of what he felt was a loss of control, at least he had the wherewithal to avoid impact to her kidneys. He was pleased to learn that he knew how to lose control responsibly. But he was still concerned. "Will you look at me differently now?"

"Yes, Master," she said. "I have never loved anyone or anything more than I love you now. Te amaré por siempre."

"Te amo también. I love you too." Edward was finding comfort in her giddy demeanor. "Is this what it feels like to share your life with someone?"

"I hope so, Master. It's the first time for me too."

\*     \*     \*

They were both exhausted as they laid in bed, staring at the ceiling, with her arm in his arm and her knee over his knee. But as the predawn light turned shadow to form, neither could sleep. The silence was periodically broken.

...

"Do you forgive me, Master."

"I forgive you, my charge."

...

"Thank you for my punishment, Master."

"You are welcome, my charge."

...

"Are you going to need to go further than that in our play now?"

"I don't think so, Master. But it is nice to know you *can* go that far."

...

"Now you know the kind of man you are about to marry."

"I already knew, Master."

...

"You know... It doesn't bother me anymore."

"I'm glad, Master. But I hope you will let me heal before we do any more."

"No, not that. I mean... It doesn't bother me that Alison and your mom know. ... I don't want you to go around telling anyone else. But... Maybe *I* should let other people know, people who need to know, people who look up to me, if it comes up in conversation."

"That's a beautiful idea, Master," she said. "Why doesn't it bother you now?"

He pondered. "I don't know. Maybe you reminded me of what an accomplishment it's been for me to save myself for so long," he hypothesized. "Or maybe it's because I have a sexy, supportive slave girl who is going to marry me and thoroughly fuck the virginity out of me soon."

Katrina gave that lilty giggle that made Edward's heart flutter.

...

"Have you told anyone about... you know?"

"No, Master. I understand why you ask. I will never tell anybody."

"Good girl."

"Will you talk about it with me, Master?"

"Not yet."

"What if I *order* you to talk about it, Master?" she asked with a hint of playfulness.

Edward rolled onto his side to face his girl. "Do you like the dynamic of our relationship?"

"Yes, Master."

"So do I. If we want to keep it this way, your orders had better be few and far between. Do you understand?"

"Yes, Master. I understand. I was joking."

"I know."

...

"Master, I've been thinking. It was your intention to not have oral sex until you are married."

"Yes."

"What if we don't have oral sex again until we are married, Master?"

"Truth be told, I was thinking the same thing," he said. "We can hold out that long. Good idea."

"Thank you, Master."

"But be ready," he warned. "Once we're married, we're going to be giving each other more head than Easter Island."

# 15

# THE CASE

Katrina stood atop high heels that were fastened to her feet by cuffs around her ankles. A belt adorned each thigh and was connected to matching cuffs around her wrists by nylon straps. The straps were long enough to afford the natural motion of her arms, but not long enough for her to reach up and release the clamps from her nipples. The clamps were connected to small chains that ran up and through the rings on both sides of the bit gag in her mouth, to the leather reins that were held by Edward's right hand.

"Walk," he ordered. "Make a perfect circle around me."

"Esh, hir."

She began walking clockwise around Edward as the coachwhip in his left hand gave a few light strokes of encouragement. The reins kept her from walking outside of the circle. The whip kept her from walking in.

"Let my hands swing freely. Atta' girl."

Though the chain between the clamps and the reins passed through the rings of the bit gag, she dropped her chin in a vain attempt to ease the pull on her nipples. This was met with a snap of the whip to her bottom.

"Nope. Shoulders back! Head up! There you go," he said.

"Esh, hir." *Shoulders back for Sir. Head up for Sir.*

"Now lead me to the mirror in the bedroom. Walk in there like you own the place!"

"Esh, hir."

As she made her way to the master bedroom, he followed behind, reins in hand, ever ready to remind her of any area of her posture that grew lax. She resisted the urge to hunch over as it would only result in an upward pull on her nipples. And a bowing of her head would result in a stream of drool down her chin and a sting from the whip on her butt. So she walked into the pain with her head held high, chest first.

"Whoa!" he said. He walked by her toward the master bathroom and led her by the reins. "Come here."

"Esh, hir."

Upon their arrival, he stood in front of her to admire her stately stance. Then he faced her toward the mirror, standing behind with his hands on her shoulders. But she fixated on his warm eyes and proud grin, the only reflection of herself she needed to see.

Without warning, he released the clamps, causing her posture to collapse as she whimpered through the gag. She tried to lift her hands to her nipples but they could only raise the length of the straps. When she started to bend over, he yanked her back into him by her ponytail and massaged the pain out of her breasts himself. She closed her eyes and laid her head on his chest like she was lying down while standing.

His hands went from her breasts to the back of her head where he unbuckled the gag and withdrew it from her mouth. She exercised her jaw while he rebuilt her posture with his hands: from hips, to shoulders, to chin.

"Look at my gorgeous girl in the mirror."

"Yes, Sir."

"Do you see what I see?" They shared her image. He reached around between her legs to pet his pet, just the way she liked, feeling the results of her pleasure and humiliation. He murmured in her ear, "Look at you. Now you're walking with confidence. That's my elegant palomino pony." He kissed her neck and said, "You look like a woman who belongs wherever she is."

"Thank you, Sir." *Be Sir's confident and elegant palomino. Look like you belong wherever you are.*

\*       \*       \*

Shannon walked into Arnold's open office door with a newspaper in hand. She dropped it before him on his desk and pointed at the picture on the front page. It was a man's professional headshot with shoulder to the camera and head turned to display a white face, jet-black hair, and a bright smile.

"This is Nathaniel Alighieri, CEO of Alighieri Resorts."

"I know who Nathan Alighieri is," Arnold said drolly, looking up from his chair.

"He's coming in this afternoon with his wife. They are shopping for a firm to get them through this sexual harassment and racial discrimination complaint from a former employee. A college friend of mine who works for Alighieri recommended us. I want this one, Arnold."

"Go get it."

There were three firm knocks on the open door. But Katrina didn't wait for an invitation. She walked into the office of the founding partner with her shoulders back and head up.

"Good morning, Katrina," Arnold greeted.

"Good morning, Arnold," she said, stopping next to Shannon.

He turned back to Shannon. "How you wanna kick it?"

"We're gonna kick it root down. Katrina is going to ride shotgun with me on the intake…"

Katrina stood by, watching two of the most respected legal minds in the business discuss strategy. They had worked together long enough to develop their own shorthand expressions. She understood what it meant to "ride shotgun". But she would have to research what it meant to "kick it root down".

She kept in mind that there was once a time when these two masters of litigation had as little experience as she. And she was on the same path as they. That is why she was worthy to be among these giants in their field. All that separated them from her was experience. Standing with her pad computer in her left arm like The Statue of Liberty, she looked like she belonged where she was, almost to the point of believing it herself.

"I'm essentially going to interview him twice," Shannon explained. "Once in front of his wife, once alone with him. We'll see how full of shit he is… or hopefully, is not." Shannon turned to Katrina, "When I'm ready, I'll suggest you take Deborah for a coffee or to see the fish tank. Whatever. Just keep her entertained."

Katrina nodded, trying to act like she knew exactly what to do. *Master would know how to keep someone entertained.*

"Do you think you might want a man to talk to him with you?" Arnold asked.

"Maybe, but not yet. I want to assess his capacity for political correctness."

"Do you think he'll want to settle or fight?"

"If this article is any indication, he'll fight."

\*   \*   \*

"Mr. and Mrs. Alighieri, it's a pleasure to meet you!" Shannon greeted with an extended hand. "I am Shannon Smith, my colleague, Katrina Gomez."

Katrina decided not to correct Shannon when she forgot to introduce her by her new married name.

"Please, call me 'Nate'!" he said with the same bright smile she recognized from the picture in the paper. But now he had teeth that were a little too perfect to be real. And instead of black hair, it was white as snow. His eyelids relaxed when he turned to introduce: "My beautiful wife, Deborah."

Deborah had black colored hair with very tan skin, and unapologetically fake breasts that were slightly disproportionate to her thin frame, in Vegas tradition. But she was dressed modestly in a knee-length skirt with matching jacket and heels.

Out of habit, Katrina concentrated on eye contact with a firm, *but "not too firm"* grip as she shook hands with the septuagenarians. When they shook, Katrina noticed how Nathan didn't sneak a glance at her chest like most men do. *I wonder what that says about a man.*

Shannon invited the group to retreat to a small conference room. Alison opened the door and offered beverages. Deborah preferred to prepare her own coffee and that of her husband.

Nathan sat directly across the table from Shannon. Deborah sat to Nathan's right and Katrina sat to Shannon's left. Once everybody had been watered and 'coffeed' in accordance with their wishes, Nathan started, "I'm sure you know why we're here."

"We do know why you are here," Shannon replied. "And I'm guessing we're not the first firm you've talked to today."

"What makes you guess that?" Nathan asked.

"You are diligent and thorough. You want to look at a few options before you make a decision. And you strike me as the kind of man who wouldn't wait until the afternoon to start tackling this problem."

"I like an astute attorney. Where do we begin?"

"First, I would like to know why you are looking for a new attorney to handle this with the stable you have at Alighieri Resorts."

"Actually, it was one of those attorneys who recommended me to you. I asked for three recommendations and you were one of them."

"I'll have to thank Robert for his reference."

"Robert and all of my attorneys are very good at what they do. But I don't need corporate attorneys right now. And I want to keep this as private as possible. Though today's headline will make that difficult."

"Were you impressed with any of the attorneys you met today?"

"Actually, we were. I hope you don't feel like I am wasting your time but one of the firms we met with this morning has us leaning toward settling." Nathan held out his hand. "Not that I am admitting guilt of any type. But we did the math. It would cost me more to fight than to settle."

"How is that?" Shannon asked. "Is there any truth to the allegations?"

"None whatsoever," he said with conviction. "The time I would waste on a trial would force me to neglect my business. The story in the media would have me guilty until proven innocent which would drive my stock price down. The board, my shareholders... It would be easier for everyone if I settle privately and get past this. I'll lose more money fighting."

Katrina knew this was not what Shannon wanted to hear. Shannon wanted this case. And she wanted to see it through a trial if necessary. But there was no conflict of interest for Katrina. She found a congruence between the best interest of a potential client and that of her mentor.

"Michael Jackson," Katrina said as she stared at the table.

"Pardon me?" Nathan asked as all three heads turned toward her.

Katrina sat up in her chair. Once again, 'thinking out loud' would push her to voice her opinion.

"I was just thinking about how you are making the same mistake Michael Jackson made by settling. He figured a settlement for the first complainant would save him money. And in that particular time, in that particular situation, he was right. But after he settled the first time, more and more complaints were filed. And it didn't matter how many times the legal system exonerated him, or if complainants recanted their stories once they became adults. The media convicted him for the rest of his life."

"And then there are the ethics of the situation," Shannon began. "You know this is a spurious allegation. You are right. Your accuser is wrong. You have the means and opportunity to fight. Fighting is the right thing to do."

Nathan turned to his wife. Her raised eyebrows suggested her belief that the pair of attorneys had a point.

Shannon kept the ball rolling. "With regard to privacy, are there any other potential complainants that may come forward?"

"Quite the opposite. Just this morning I've had a dozen or so of my closest female colleagues email and text me messages of support and volunteering to be character references. I didn't ask anyone to do that." As Nathan was speaking, his wife pulled a laptop computer out of her bag and set it on the table in front of her. "We can forward these to you if you want. I didn't talk to her very frequently but I do have several pieces of correspondence between myself and Angelita."

Katrina noticed how he didn't anglicize the name of the complainant. He pronounced it with a 'g' that sounded like a soft 'h'. This was not something she expected from this white grandfatherly figure.

"Please send any documents you have," Shannon said as she slid her business card across the table to Deborah. Katrina did the same with her card as she opened her pad computer. "Tell me about the complainant."

"Her name is 'Angelica Gomez'. But most people call her 'Angela' or 'Angelita'." Nathan turned to Katrina with his smile, "Any relation to you, Mrs. Gomez?" He had observed the ring and tattoo on her finger. It was her only jewelry besides what appeared to be a necklace.

"I don't think so," Katrina said, returning the smile. "'Gomez' is as common as 'Smith' in Hispanic cultures," she said as she looked at Shannon Smith. But I believe you will find Shannon's representation to be anything but 'common'. And please, call me 'Katrina'." She was feeling good about this exchange as Shannon gave a nod of acknowledgment for the compliment.

"I have no doubt, Katrina," Nathan said.

Katrina was stuck at feeling the same warmth from hearing Nathan say her name as Edward.

Shannon tried not to appear anxious to get the conversation back on course. So she waited a beat before asking, "I assume the union is providing representation for her?"

"No, strangely enough. She has retained her own counsel. I'm sure she can afford it for what she used to make working for me. But rumor has it, her mother came across some money some years back. I don't know the details."

Nathan continued to talk about the nature of his relationship with Angelica Gomez. She was hired right out of college to work in the corporate office. He recalled she had a few good ideas about how to restructure some individual departments. But she also had problems dealing with the chain of command. She tried to go over her manager's head on more than one occasion.

As Nathan spoke, Katrina reviewed some of the documents Deborah was sending. She started with the text messages and was impressed to find that most were in Spanish, though elementary at times. She noticed some misunderstandings they had in which they would switch to English for clarity. But Angela's English wasn't much better than Nathan's Spanish. And although his messages seemed friendly, there was one glaring problem that Katrina would have to address. "Nate, do you have the phone numbers of all of your employees in your phone?"

"I do for most of my team that works in the corporate headquarters."

"Have you had text conversations with all of them?"

"Probably a majority of them at one time or another. I find it can be a good way to have a personal conversation with less risk of it getting inappropriate. And if it ever did get inappropriate, there's a written record." He mumbled, "A lot of good it did me."

"Have you ever been accused of anything like this before?"

Nathan leaned back in his seat, staring into space to recall a memory. "I used to be in the habit of giving people a pat on the back while they worked or if they did a good job with something. And sometimes I'd shake hands with both of my hands. Maybe I shook hands too long. I don't know." Nathan's eyes found Katrina's again as he leaned back to the table. "But my HR manager said someone complained about that. So I stopped. I had to break decades-long habits that were once seen as friendly gestures."

"Are there any other examples of this happening?"

"Just this. I've always tried to keep a professional and friendly work environment. It never occurred to me that any of my efforts would be seen in a sexual way. And now this, from a girl younger than my grandchildren!"

At this last statement, Shannon and Katrina glanced at each other. Shannon said, "Nate, I'm sure you are aware that there are men in this world who are attracted to girls, …forty or fifty years their junior."

"Of course I…" Nathan was interrupted by his wife.

"You have to understand something about my husband: He is a good man. And he is an excellent business man. He doesn't think of people in sexual terms like most men." She turned to make eye contact with her husband. "He might be an old codger but he's still very handsome and he has a magnetic personality." Katrina saw the same relaxation in Nathan's eyelids as before as his gaze fell into his wife.

He continued to look at Deborah when she turned back to Katrina and Shannon. "He doesn't see it when a woman is attracted to him. I've watched women flirt with him and their advances go right over his head! In spite of his years of experience, he can be naive about things like that. When he says it never occurred to him that his attempts at creating a friendly work relationship could be construed as a sexual advance, I believe him."

With that, the two of them looked at each other and locked hands under the table. He pulled his handkerchief out of his pocket and consoled her as she dabbed the bottoms of her eyes. It was clear that a day spent being scrutinized by attorneys had taken its toll.

Shannon was thinking this might be the right time to get Deborah out of the room. But before she could signal, Katrina tried to redirect the conversation to reach the problem on her mind. "How long have you been learning Spanish, Nate?"

"I started about three years ago."

"What made you want to learn?"

Nathan rambled a bit about how he regretted not getting better at speaking the native language of his parents: Italian. He had an opportunity to learn Spanish. It was another latin-based language he thought would be useful. "I figured it would be good exercise for my aging brain and it would give me a chance to relate better to my employees. I hire a lot of immigrants." He made it a point to clarify, "…all legal. I usually eat lunch with my office employees. The brown folks sit at their own table so I sometimes sit with them for a Spanish lesson."

"As a practice, let's not refer to people by the color of their skin," Shannon said. "We wouldn't want any such language to end up on a transcript or any other record."

"Even if they refer to themselves that way? They invite me to sit at what they call 'the brown table'."

"I'm afraid so."

"My apologies if I am being offensive," Nathan said as he turned to the only brown person in the room.

"It's not offensive to brown people," Katrina replied. "And they wouldn't care if you *were* trying to offend them. But we want to try to use the most politically correct language when referring to a group so we don't offend overly sensitive white people!"

Nathan snorted with a grin and a nod.

Katrina continued, "So for now, since you were sitting with the Spanish speakers in order to practice Spanish, let's say you ate lunch with the '*hispañohablantes*'."

"That's a good word," Nathan replied. "'Hispañohablantes'."

"So you know, Nate, I think you have noble reasons for learning Spanish…"

Shannon kept her hands off the wheel and let her protege steer the conversation with more questions. She tilted her head to see what was on Katrina's computer. It was mostly Spanish, which might as well have been hieroglyphics. She realized Katrina was tactfully trying to get some specific pieces of information from Nathan. But she was dancing around the difficult questions. Perhaps her method was being hindered by Deborah's presence. So Shannon decided *she* would call a silent audible and be the one to invite Deborah to observe the aquarium in the lobby.

Deborah turned to Nathan who wordlessly encouraged her to leave the room with little more than a glint of his eye. He squeezed her hand and replaced it on her lap before she stood, leaving the computer and her jacket. Nathan stood at the same time as his wife and didn't sit down again until she was through the door.

As Shannon closed the door behind herself, she made eye contact with Katrina. And then her eyes darted to Nathan for a split second, as if to say, 'Reel him in!'

"Nate," Katrina started gently. "I have some questions that I have to ask you that I hope will both help me understand your perspective, and help you understand your situation."

Nathan swallowed and nodded.

"Do you know what an 'amiga especial' is?" She read the phrase from her computer before focusing for signs of deception from the man.

"A 'special friend' if I'm not mistaken."

"Okay, do you know what 'amigos con derechos' are?"

"'Amigos con derechos'," he repeated. "I think the words literally mean 'friends with rights'. But I'm not sure if that's actually what it means."

"That is the literal translation, word-for-word. But do you know what it means?"

He looked at her askance. "Probably not."

"Do you know what 'friends with benefits' are?"

"I think so. People who do sexual things together but are just friends."

"That's right. Do you know what country Angelica is from?"

"Somewhere in South America, I think."

Katrina slid her computer to Nathan and stood to walk to his side of the table. Once she took a seat to his left, she showed him the last text conversation he had with Angelica. "Do you remember this conversation?"

Nathan pulled out his reading glasses and studied it. "Yes I do. I remember being confused about it."

"Let me translate it for you." Katrina pointed to a message from Angelica. "In this message, she is asking you to be 'amigos con derechos' with you: 'friends with benefits'."

Nathan's eyebrows furrowed and his lips held a skeptical grin. Katrina could see this was something he had not previously understood, and still had his doubts. "Are you saying, *she* was trying to initiate a romantic relationship with *me*?"

"It is pretty clear to me."

The grin started to fade from Nathan's face. He didn't like what he was hearing.

Katrina continued by pointing to his text reply. "Here, you tell her that you consider her to be an 'amiga especial'. Exactly what did you mean by that?"

Nathan sat back in his chair before responding. "I wasn't sure what she was asking me. I understood the word 'amigos'. I thought she was trying to say she wanted us to be friends. But I didn't understand the 'benefits' part. I was trying to return what I thought was a friendly sentiment."

"And that's when you told her you consider her to be a 'special friend'."

"That's right," he said. "And then it felt like she was getting angry but I wasn't sure."

"Nate, where I come from, it is totally acceptable to call someone a 'special friend', 'una amiga especial'. But in some latino cultures, an 'amiga especial' would translate to something like 'a prostitute that you refuse to pay'."

Nathan's head slowly turned from Katrina to square with his shoulders, mouth agape. He sat in a state of shock, struggling to breathe. "I think I'm going to be sick."

Katrina looked at the trash can and was about to get it when Nathan leaned forward and pressed his right hand on the table, saying, "She has to know I didn't mean that! I mean... Why would I..." He put his right elbow on the table and his fist to his mouth. His eyes burned into a distant void as his body held rigid. He didn't know what else to say.

"I believe you, Nate. You didn't mean what you said."

Nathan soothed himself by rubbing the knuckle of his index finger back and forth on his lips. He took a breath and asked, "So you are saying that she was expressing interest in a sexual relationship with me, and I called her a 'whore'?"

Katrina said nothing. She just looked at Nathan with pressed lips and sympathetic eyes.

Nathan lifted his head from his hand and took off his glasses. "Is that all this is? Is this complaint based on a misunderstanding by text?"

"No, I think there's more to it here. I'll need time to read the rest. That is, if you want to hire us."

    \*        \*        \*

Shannon and Deborah stood side by side at the 1,500 gallon fish tank that occupied an entire wall of the firm's lobby.

Deborah spoke first: "I suppose it would be cliché to have sharks in the aquarium of a law office."

"Oh, we have plenty of sharks in our office," Shannon replied with a close-lipped smile. "We try not to bare our teeth until all diplomatic solutions have been exhausted."

Deborah smiled in kind, but her eyes never left the water. "I bet diplomacy rarely fails you."

Shannon remained silent as she stared at her own reflection in the glass.

"I'm seeing about fifty species here, probably more," Deborah said. "Each species was no doubt selected for their compatibility with the others."

"I'll take your word for it. You'll find my knowledge of marine biology to be lacking."

"Nathaniel took me to an aquarium on our first date, almost sixty years ago. Neither of us knew anything about fish except how to eat them. His favorite species was the hammerhead shark. He said it made him think of building things." Her vision extended further into the water. "It was just a word association that made him like the hammerhead. It took another date for me to realize his ambition for 'building things'."

Shannon glanced at Deborah but said nothing.

"His father was a good man. But when he died, he left Nathaniel, his mother, and younger siblings destitute. This made Nathaniel a man with drive and determination, but no direction."

"I'm sure you found his ambition appealing."

"I certainly did, even though ambitious men were much more common in those days."

Shannon thought about what it would be like to find such a man for herself. But she put the idea out of her head believing that two people so career-focused would have no time for each other.

"Did you know I like marine life when you… *invited* me to see this aquarium?" Deborah asked as she turned to study Shannon.

Shannon kept a poker face. "We did our due diligence." If Deborah was testing her, she thought her lie passed.

"Mm." Deborah's eyes narrowed as she turned back to the glass. "I know you wanted to get me out of that room so your partner could see what my husband says when I'm not there."

"It's true that sometimes clients- or *potential* clients- need to say things to their attorneys in ways they can't say to their spouses. I was trying to make sure Katrina felt free to ask some questions that she might not want to ask in front of you."

"There's that diplomacy," Deborah replied as she looked at Shannon again. "But I'm willing to bet his story doesn't change regardless of my presence. Do you understand what I am telling you, Ms. Smith?"

Shannon noticed Deborah declined her invitation to call her by her first name. She didn't think it was an accident. The pretense between the two of them was being shed. So she dared to answer, "I think you are trying to say: your husband might be a hammer, but you are the head."

A quizzical smile came to Deborah's lips. She tilted as her eyes rolled to the side. Shannon's words echoed in her head. "I like that," she said. "An apt description for a host of reasons… even if it is just an attempt to patronize me. But the truth is," she returned her eyes to Shannon's before articulating, "Nathaniel and I are to each other whatever we need the other to be. Though I am anything but the head, it's our unity that makes us a shark." And with that, she turned back to the fish.

Now it was Deborah's words that were echoing in Shannon's head.

The attention of both ladies returned to the aquarium. Shannon would be the next to speak: "With what species of marine life do *you* identify?"

Deborah started to open her mouth to reply. But it was a voice from around the corner of the tank that answered. "She's my angel fish!"

Shannon watched a satisfied smile wash over Deborah's face as the ladies continued to look at each other. While Nathan helped his wife put on her jacket, she said, "Some things never change!"

"Tell me, my queen," Nathan began. "Has Shannon been any more successful than me at getting you to like aquariums?"

Shannon's face froze, as did the warmth she felt from Deborah's countenance.

"Not yet," Deborah replied, never breaking eye contact with Shannon.

Nathan said, "She has tolerated my love for aquariums for as long as I've known her."

As Katrina was a few paces behind Nathan, the four of them exchanged departure pleasantries. Nathan promised to let them know whether or not he would make use of their services. But he made it a point to express his belief that regardless of the outcome, he considered the meeting to be "time well spent".

Nathan had their computer bag in his left hand and his wife on his right arm as they walked away. Deborah's heels decrescendoed as she crossed the marble floor until he opened the door for her.

"For what it's worth, his wife believes in him," Shannon said to Katrina as she turned to walk to her office.

"Me too."

*         *         *

"Oye. Listen to me," Katrina said to the group of clerks and paralegals. "Today was the second time this month you didn't have enough coverage for the associates during business hours. If you guys can't coordinate your lunch schedules so you all don't leave the building at the same time, the partners are going to make me do it and I'm just going to have you choose by seniority."

"That works out great for the paralegals!" Randy, the clerk said with dismay. "They've all been here longer than the clerks! And some of us, not me, but some of us have childcare issues to deal with."

"How would you coordinate the schedules, Randy?" Katrina asked.

"I'd start by seeing who has the greatest preference, who needs consideration, and then use seniority as a tiebreaker."

"I like it. You're in charge of the coverage schedules."

Randy's eyebrows raised with pleased surprise. "Yes, ma'am!"

…

Before Katrina walked into her private office, her assistant, Alison said, "That must have been an intense meeting with the Alighieri's."

"Why do you say that?"

"Nobody touched their drinks!"

Katrina stopped with one foot in the door to think about it.

Alison awoke her. "Don't forget to call Shannon."

"Thank you for the reminder. Please finish the witness list before you leave."

"Yes, ma'am!"

...

Katrina sat behind her desk and breathed for a moment in an attempt to let the smoke clear. But she was interrupted by an incoming call from Shannon. *This day is relentless.*

While she was on the call, a blip at the corner of the computer screen informed her of a text message from Alison: "The food delivery boy is here."

With no interruption to her phone conversation, Katrina typed: "Send him in."

He walked into her office with a cooler in hand and locked the door behind him. He turned to close the blinds of the window on the door, giving a sarcastically raised eyebrow to Alison outside. Alison shook her head with a smile and returned her eyes to her computer.

Katrina unbuttoned three buttons on her blouse. But she stayed focused on her phone conversation. "Yes. ... How did you know? ... He can't hear you. I'm talking on my earpiece. ... I'll tell him."

He set the cooler on the desk and walked around it. She raised her hands and interlocked her fingers behind her head. He leaned over the back of her chair and placed his right hand on her chest. With his thumb on the heart-shaped lock of her day collar, he kissed the crown of her head. Then his hand crept over to her left breast for a groping and a light pinch that she felt in her clitoris, even before her nipple, causing her to stutter on a word.

"Okay. ... I'll c-call you back." She squeezed her eyes and lips closed in an attempt to keep her attention on the call, struggling not to laugh. "Yes? ... Okay, will do!" Katrina took the earpiece off to disconnect her call before her laughter spilled over. She returned her hand behind her head. Once she regained her composure, she said, "Shannon dicé 'hola', Amo."

"How did she know I was here?" Edward asked.

"She says when you are here, my accent is more pronounced, I sometimes randomly switch to Spanish, and my voice gets... 'dreamier', whatever that means, Amo," she said as she leaned her chair back into Edward, giving him better access under her bra.

"That's quite observant of her considering she hasn't met me yet," he said as he supported her breast in his palm and lightly flicked her nipple with his thumb.

Katrina closed her eyes and sighed. Edward kissed her crown again before withdrawing his hand, leaving her nipple exposed. She knew not to cover her breast. He walked around to the front of the desk. She divided their meals out of the cooler for a late lunch as he pulled up a chair.

After praying for a blessing, Edward asked his attorney, "Is everything okay, my charge?"

"Yes, Amo?" She looked at him inquisitively.

"You know I don't require you to call me 'Amo' or 'Master' when you are at work. Are you in particular need of some Dominance?"

"I think so, Amo. It's been a stressful day. We had a big case come in and I'm the only one who can handle some of the details. Everybody is counting on me."

"Get over here," he said as he pulled a chair up beside him.

"Yes, Amo."

As she walked around her desk, Edward put her food and drink on the chair. She took her place at his feet and resumed eating, leaning into his knee.

"Was that the 'clerk jerk'?"

"What do you mean, Amo?"

"The guy you put in charge of lunch schedules."

"You saw that, Amo?"

"Yeah."

"You were there the whole time, Amo?"

"At least for the end. I was coming up the steps but I didn't want to interrupt your meeting. Then I followed you here," he said. "Do you have them all call you 'ma'am'?"

"I never told anyone to call me that. Some people started doing that on their own," she said. "I didn't know you were there, Master."

"That's because I'm as stealthy as a jungle cat," he said with his dry humor.

"Es la verdad, Amo!" she affirmed, in the same spirit as Edward. "That was Randy the 'jerk clerk'. But he hasn't been too bad lately."

"I think you handled him well. You delegated your authority and gave him a task that made him feel like he's in control of something. I'm not used to seeing you in charge."

"Maybe I learned it from you, Amo. Because you are in charge of me. ...when I know you are there."

"Well said, my charge."

"Randy can be difficult but he is our most productive clerk. He'll be fine if he doesn't fail law school, Amo."

"He's going to flunk law school?"

"That's the rumor, Amo. I hope it's not true."

"Maybe he's like me, bad at school but good at his profession."

"I have a new client who is like you, Amo."

"He must be pretty awesome," he said, biting into his turkey sandwich.

"He's an old man, like you, Amo!"

"Of course, he is!"

"Actually, he is 77 and his wife isn't much younger. But they are both doing well, Amo."

"Are you allowed to tell me their names?"

Katrina pulled a dollar out of her bra and handed it to Edward who put it in his pocket. This was their understanding that Edward was employed by Katrina as her paralegal and was therefore allowed to learn about her new client without breaking attorney/client privilege. It was the ethical thing to do even though Katrina had more faith in Edward's ability to keep secrets than she did in her own.

"His name is 'Nathaniel Alighieri' and her name is…"

"Deborah Alighieri."

"You know her, Master?"

"We dated in high school."

Katrina grinned and shook her head at Edward.

"Nathan and Deborah of 'Alighieri Resorts'. I've dealt poker to them at charity events. They were nice but they wouldn't remember me." Edward took another bite. "Quite philanthropic… and good tippers. Now they're clients here?"

"Yes! Shannon is lead counsel but Nate is retaining us both."

Edward lowered his sandwich to the desk. "You call him 'Nate'!" he laughed. "And he is *your client*?!"

"I'm co-counsel, Master," Katrina replied. "And until this morning, I was the only person in town who didn't know who they were!"

"We ate at one of their restaurants on our first date; 'The Alighieri'."

Katrina shook her head at her failure to make the connection.

"What happened this morning?"

"Did you hear the news or read the paper, Amo?"

"I've been in rehearsal all day."

"Someone filed a complaint against him for sexual harassment and racial discrimination."

"I see. What's her name… assuming it's a *her*?" He took another bite.

"Angelica Gomez."

"Hm." Edward's eyes fell through the desk in thought as he chewed.

"What, Amo?"

Edward shook his head and pushed the food to the side of his mouth. "No relation to you, I presume?"

"None."

"And you're riding shotgun!"

"That's right!" The repetition of the "shotgun" colloquialism reminded her to ask: "By the way, Amo, what does it mean to 'kick it root down'?"

"'Kick it root down'?" he asked with a chuckle at hearing the urban American expression from the Latina lips of his wife.

"Yes."

"I know it's a line to a 'Beastie Boys' song. I've never really studied the lyrics. I think it's a rallying cry."

"Is it sexual?"

"I don't know."

"There's something you don't know, Amo?!" she asked with exaggerated astonishment.

"I know. Hard to believe. I'm not the genius you thought you married," he said. "Remind me to play the song for you later."

"Yes, Master."

"So how does Nathan Alighieri remind you of me? Is it the way I am constantly sexually harassing my attorney?" He crunched into an apple.

"I just like the way he treats his wife, Amo. He opens doors for her. He stands when she stands. He helped her with her jacket."

Edward asked through a mouthful of apple, "Does he talk wif his mouf full?"

Katrina rolled her eyes. "He also looks at his wife the way you look at me... con ojos dormitorios?"

Edward thought for a second. "Bedroom eyes." Edward found it gratifying to know habits that were like second nature to him meant so much to his bride. But he couldn't pass up the opportunity to tease her. "It's a good thing you are telling me you like it when I do these things. I was about to stop!"

"You know I love the things you do, Master!" she said with concern. "Why would you stop?!"

Edward looked down and locked eyes with Katrina. He lowered the apple to the desk and swallowed before saying, "I will never stop."

Katrina sighed. Once again, Edward was joking and she took him too seriously. *Will I ever learn?!*

"What is Deborah like?" Edward asked.

"She's the perfect helpmate for Nate, Amo. She wouldn't even let Alison prepare coffee for him."

"Do you think they are involved in the lifestyle?"

"She follows orders like they are." She thought about how Nathan ordered Deborah to leave the room. "And he didn't need to say a word. Would you like me to get your breasts enlarged, Master?"

"No. So you know, if I'm called to represent *Nate* in court, I may have to recuse myself since I have worked at one of his resorts. And I'm sure his company is in one of my 401(k) mutual funds, making me a partial owner. I wouldn't want to create a conflict of interest."

She rolled her eyes again and said, "We will have to find a way to proceed without you if you *withdraw*."

She may not have laughed at his humor as much as she once did. But she still found his demeanor energizing.

She watched her man's attention return to his lunch. From her place at his feet, she studied his features: his kind eyes, his emotive lips, his shaggy hair. *What will his eyes look like with deeper wrinkles? Will he always have that sharp jawline? I look forward to seeing him with white hair.* Katrina came to the realization that she had never seen this far into her future before. And she could not recall ever imagining sharing so many years with a man, let alone, a husband, let alone, a Master, an owner she loved as much as Edward. *Is this what it is like to dream? Please God, don't let it end.*
...

At the conclusion of their lunch, Katrina returned behind her desk to repack the cooler with their reusable containers. Edward stood in preparation for his departure, still eating the apple.

"One more thing, Master," Katrina said. "Before I hung up the phone, Shannon told me to '*get fucked*'."

Edward chuckled at the way Katrina used the phrase, but wondered if Shannon had meant the suggestion in the more colloquial fashion.

"Well, if I'm your paralegal, and Shannon is *your* lead… far be it from me to disobey an order from my boss' boss. And I did tell Alison to hold my calls…"

Katrina stood in position one without a verbal order, breast ever exposed. Edward was impressed at how adept she was getting at following orders he didn't know he was about to give.

He walked around to her side of the desk, leaned down to her computer, and searched her music service to purchase a song.

Although the stress of the day had been replaced by the simplicity of submission, she remained still and mentally prepared herself to be thoroughly disabused of any lingering illusion that she was in control of anything during her Master's visit. She was ready for use.

He bent her over the desk and lifted her skirt. He removed her handgun and garter holster, setting them between her computer monitor and her framed copy of the "Lester's $1,000,000" souvenir photo. He pulled her thong to the side to inspect his cock holster.

From the computer speakers came a funky bass line. Four bars later, a drum groove accompanied it. Finally, three voices initiated an opening chorus.

He yanked her head back by her hair and shoved the apple in her teeth. It was this point at which Edward and Katrina proceeded to kick it… *root down.*

# 16

# ACCEPTANCE

"Permission to sit on my cock, Master?" Katrina asked, wearing nothing but one of Edward's shirts and a collar. Edward knew this either meant she was feeling amorous or she had something she wanted to discuss. Perhaps both. There was no denying, *sexual* intercourse was an effective way to get her husband's undivided attention for some *intellectual* intercourse.

"Oh, all right," Edward said with his usual feigned reluctance. He paused the song he was analyzing and laid back on the couch. "Permission granted. But I think Victoria and Elizabeth need to be a part of this conversation."

"Yes, Master!" She unbuttoned the shirt to expose her breasts.

He helped her pull his pants down far enough to clear her throne and sit cross-legged before he could get erect. She placed his flaccid member just inside her entrance so she could feel him grow into her.

"Something on your mind, my queen?"

"I want to know more about worship, Master."

"Worship? You mean like worshiping God or worshiping me… or position three? What do you want to know?"

"All of the above."

"You're asking me about worship? You're the one who is teaching *me* about that."

"What do you mean?"

"Well, I remember, before I met you, playing drums or guitar in church; to be honest, my worship was going stale. It was just another gig. I was enjoying it, but I was more focused on the music than I was on worshiping God. That changed when you started coming to church with me."

"How, Master?" She leaned forward and put her elbows on her knees, hanging her breasts forward as she felt Edward ascending.

"I remember looking out into the audience at you as you worshiped to the music. You were so… transcendent. I don't know how to describe it. But you reminded me why I was up there on the stage. It wasn't to play music but to worship God. Watching you was bringing me back to the heart of worship." He reached up to cup a breast and trace his thumb around her areola. This caused her to clench down on him. He grunted with pleasure. They smiled at each other.

"And there's the way you worship me: when you're on your knees or bowing before me. The trust in your eyes. The faith you have in me. The belief. … You make me feel like I can conquer the world. You're a role model for the way I want to worship God."

And then he said, "Honey, you're gonna have to move. You're crushing your cock! Priscilla is too shallow!" Feeling the same discomfort, she was already adjusting her position.

"Your pussy's not too shallow!" she retorted. "Aquila is too big!"

She uncrossed her legs and straddled him. Then she unbuttoned his shirt and bowed to him on his chest in position three with her hips tilted to keep him inside her. He played with her hair and dug his fingernails into her scalp the way she liked.

"How is this not idolatry, Master?" she asked between kisses on his chest. "…for me to worship you?"

"You're not prioritizing me above *God*, are you?"

"I don't think so, Master. Maybe sometimes. I try not."

Edward decided to employ the Socratic method to explain a concept to his wife: "Does God need us to give Him money?"

"No, Master." She stopped kissing his chest but kept her face down.

"Does God need us to be a part of His plan?"

"No, Master."

"Does God need us to worship Him?"

"No, Master."

"Does God need… anything from us?"

"No, Master."

"No, He doesn't need us for anything. But we need Him," he said. He pulled her hair, lifting her face. "We need to give money back to Him. We need to be a part of His plan. And we need to worship Him. The biggest difference between worshiping God and worshiping me is…" He articulated, "God does not need you to worship Him. *But I need you to worship me.*"

She exhaled a sigh of relief into his chest as she lowered her face again. "Thank you so much, Master," she said in response to the sermon on his mount. "I didn't know if I had been committing idolatry all this time."

"How long has that been bothering you, my charge?" he asked with concern.

"Since you taught me position three, Master."

"You've been worshiping me and feeling guilty about it this whole time?"

"I don't know, Master. I didn't know if it should feel wrong or not."

"Don't you wish you would have talked to me about it back then?!"

"Yes, Master. I should have."

"I'm glad you did."

"Me too, Master." She sat back up with her hands on his pecks, taking him in further. She saw his lust for her in his eyes.

"What a view," he whispered as he gazed upon her magnificence.

"Do you really think of me as a role model, Master?"

"Yeah. In lots of ways. You're the bravest person I know."

She found that puzzling. "What makes me so brave to you, Master?"

"All the things you've been through, all the stuff you've told me. I don't know if I could recover."

"I couldn't have recovered without you, Master."

"You put so much faith in me. I don't think I could be that brave."

"I don't think I could be brave enough to be the head of our marriage, Master."

He wrapped his fingers around one of her hands. "It's your submission that empowers me, my charge."

"Master? You know you can tell me anything too?" As though she had turned off a light, she watched his expression go blank and his eyes push through her. His grip on her hand loosened as he deflated in more ways than one. "We don't have to talk about it right now, Master," she said in an attempt to recover his arousal. "I just want to make sure you know."

Edward took a breath. She could see in his eyes and feel through their most intimate connection, he was returning to her. "I know, my charge. I'll talk about it soon." And he added, "It will be sooner than ever before!" making her smile. "Now make your cock cum, skank! I'm getting hungry and we've got a movie to watch!"

"Yes, Master!" she said as she started rocking her hips and biting her lips. It was against the rules to start a project without finishing it. It didn't take long for her to restore his empire to its previous glory.

She knew exactly what to do. She knew how to change angles for the best contact. She knew what to flex and release inside to maximize their pleasure. She knew what to say to make herself feel and sound like the "slave slut wife" she had become. She knew when to go from rocking back and forth to jumping up and down so her breasts would have the perfect bounce that made her husband cum at the same time as she.

And as the time of their mutual climax approached, he reached up and grabbed her collar with one hand and her breast with the other as an unnecessary but welcome affirmation of his dominance. She wrapped both hands around his steady forearm and used it for leverage to bring them home. As he started bucking up into her, he ordered, "Make that twat cum on that cock, you whore!"

"Yes, Master!"

\*             \*             \*

Katrina was in position four, being used as a tray table while Edward sat on the edge of the couch and ate sushi off the plate on her bare back. With chopsticks, he fed her a bite, and then himself. He continued this pattern until… "Okay, so I had a *nonconsensual sexual experience*."

Katrina stopped chewing. Her eyes widened as she stared at a point on the wall.

"I was raped." He almost choked on the word.

Katrina became even more still than before, if that was possible. She couldn't see his face. But her mind recorded every word, every inflection.

"I didn't realize what happened because it wasn't what I thought rape was like. I thought it was like it is on TV or in movies, but it's not. I wasn't screaming. I wasn't being overpowered. There was no music score to tell me something was wrong or how I should feel. I wasn't even awake when it started.

"I shrugged it off. I told myself, 'You're 29 years old. You're a man. It's no big deal.'

"I did everything wrong after that. I did everything the rape victims I used to counsel did. I blamed myself. I told myself it was my fault for letting someone I didn't know that well sleep at my place. It was my fault for trusting her. It was my fault because I was the man, she was the woman, and I allowed myself to lose control of the situation. But I still didn't think of it as 'rape'."

Katrina was relieved he was finally talking about it, even if he was getting faster and louder as he spoke.

"And then I made it worse. Just like my rape victim clients, I became hyper-sexual. Before it happened, I almost never let my subs or ex-girlfriends touch my cock, let alone suck it. I was intent on only letting one woman do that to me for my whole life. But then, after the first time, I started letting all of my subs suck me. If anybody had earned it, they did. And why shouldn't I allow them? I had been practicing my brand of 'submission therapy' on them for years to help *them* deal with past traumas. Maybe *they* would be able to help *me*. But eventually, old girlfriends… hell, I even let girls that were barely acquaintances latch on, sometimes the day they met me! I became the cliché; I was 'damaged goods'!

"And I did it for the same fucked up reasons all of the rape victims I know did it: Because I wasn't going to let that whore win. I wasn't going to let her be the one and only person who ever had control over my cock besides me. Every girl I let suck me was a finger to that cunt."

Katrina heard the tone of Edward's voice shift to one of contemplation; like he was trying to understand his own reasoning.

"But that wasn't working. I was in control with all the others. Maybe I was trying to reaffirm control… at least in my head. Maybe each one was an attempt to render that first time a more meaningless first link in a chain of meaningless acts. The funny thing is, I fooled myself into thinking it was working!"

Katrina's relief was turning to sorrow as she listened to the words pouring out of her once silent man. She heard his voice start to get angry again.

"There was nobody I could talk to about this. They would have the same reaction I had: blaming me for trusting someone I thought I knew better. And besides, there is not a man on Earth who wants to listen to another guy *complain* about getting his dick sucked!

"And how stupid is it that I'm complaining to *you*?! *You* spent an entire marriage getting raped and prostituted!

"Even the girl who did it doesn't know what she did. I was just another swingin' dick for her to suck!" Through a cynical smile, he appended, "But it wasn't '*rape*'!"

Edward took a moment to reflect on all he had unfolded before calmly concluding, "And now you are the only person besides me who knows about this."

Katrina swallowed and asked, "Permission to move, Master?" pulling Edward back into his body.

He placed the plate and chopsticks on the coffee table right next to her. "Permission granted."

Katrina rose to her knees and placed her hands on his thighs. They looked into each others' faces. Edward saw the tears in her eyes as his own vision blurred.

"Are you crying, Master?"

Edward felt his eyes and observed his wet fingers. "I think I am," he said matter-of-factly with a sniff and a smile.

They stared at each other. Katrina didn't know what to say until her heart voiced her desire: "Permission to hug you, Master?"

Edward didn't speak. He responded by pulling her to him by the collar, wrapping his arms around her, and leaning back into the couch with her head on his chest. She responded in kind with her arms around him. And together, they wept.

"How does it make you feel to know your Master couldn't stop a stupid little bitch from taking advantage of him?"

She spoke into his chest, "It makes me feel like I have a man who is so irresistible that women will commit a crime just to taste him, Master."

That gave him a chuckle through the tears. "I never thought of it that way," he said before kissing the crown of her head. "Do you know what you have done for me?"

"What have I done, Master?"

"In the time I've known you, you have taken something away from me that was ugly and redeemed it for something beautiful."

"You do the same for me every day, Master."

# 17.0

# THE DEPOSITION

It was Edward's hand jiggling Katrina's breast that awoke her. She turned to him but couldn't see in the darkness. "Hmm?"

"Will you please turn your phone off? It's been vibrating."

"Please forgive me, Master," she murmured as she reached for her cellphone on the nightstand. She lifted it to see who had been trying to contact her at this hour.

Edward was getting back to sleep when he was awakened again by Katrina sitting straight up. "Something wrong?"

Katrina didn't reply as she scrolled through her text messages. Finally, she lowered her phone and asked, "Master, what is 'Bell's palsy'?"

"Partial facial paralysis."

"What causes it?"

"Stroke, stress, or brain damage."

Katrina looked up from her phone into the darkness. *How does he know that?* "How do you know that, Master?"

"I just made it up. Why?"

"Shannon has Bell's palsy. She's asking if I can do the deposition tomorrow."

"You mean, today?"

Katrina saw the time. "Today, Master. Permission to go to the gym tonight instead of this morning? I have to go in early."

"Permission granted. We'll go after work," he said. "I'll make you breakfast when you hit the shower."

"You're going to make breakfast, Master?"

"Why not? How often do I get a chance to set *you* up for a good day?"

"You make every day a good day, Master. But you don't know how to cook!"

"I know how to scramble eggs… by watching you!"

"Thank you, Master."

"For this morning, call me 'Chef'! I think it means 'Master' in German anyway."

"Yes, Chef! Will you please fuck me in the shower first, Chef?"

"Yep."

Katrina wasn't ready to get out of bed. She curled into a ball and laid her head on Edward's chest. He pet her while she listened to his deep voice reverberate in his ribcage.

"So this will be your first deposition alone, without a net?"

"Yes, Chef. If I make a mess, Shannon can negotiate for a 'part two'."

"You're qualified. You wrote the outline."

"Yes, but she says she is revising it and sending it back to me. I'm not sure what she is going to want me to ask. I don't know if I can imitate her deposition style, Chef."

"What do you mean?"

"Her style… It's like how you say about some poker players: 'She has one tool in her toolbox and it's a hammer.' That's how she deposes. …and plays poker, come to think of it."

"Maybe this is an opportunity for you to find your own style. You can develop your own strategy," he said through a yawn. "Can you do it?"

"I don't know if I can. But I already said 'yes', Chef. I'm not waiting for someone to tell me I'm an attorney."

Edward grabbed a handful of her hair and kissed her on the crown. "You are going to be magnificent."

…

Those were the words that repeated in her mind as she stared up at the BANK tower of the Howard Hughes Center. She had crossed the threshold of this building many times. But this was the first time she felt like it wanted to devour her. So she reminded herself, *Master says you are going to be magnificent.* She was struck at how a repetition of Edward's words made her believe: "It's all going to be magnificent."

On her way in, she passed by two reporters who were probably there to talk to Nathan Alighieri's legal counsel. She was glad they did not recognize her as such.

Katrina found Nathan and Deborah sitting on a bench in the lobby. They stood and exchanged greetings with handshakes. Although he was a client, Nathan's familiar smile put Katrina's mind at ease. But something was wrong.

"Is everything okay?" Nathan asked with concern.

"Forgive me if Shannon didn't tell you, she won't be able to be here today."

"I know about Shannon. She texted me this morning. I'm asking about *you*. Are *you* okay?" he asked, eyebrows raised.

Katrina thought this was an odd question. She was worried she was showing her anxiety in spite of her attempts at a pokerface of confidence.

"I'm well, thank you," she said with a tilt of the head.

"That's good." Nathan looked like he was searching for more of an answer. But he decided to move on. "Shannon said we didn't need to be here but I couldn't resist."

"No, I'm glad you are here. Are you wanting to watch the deposition?"

"I don't know if I should or not," Nathan replied. "I'll leave it up to you. Were you able to catch up on the case with Shannon?"

"Catch up?" Katrina asked.

"Yes, from the meeting."

"I felt good about all of our meetings," Katrina replied, not certain what he was talking about. But Nathan was equally confused.

"I'm talking about the meeting on Monday, this week. You weren't there. Shannon said you had an emergency."

Now Katrina felt even more clueless about Nathan's assertion. *Did Shannon have another meeting without telling me? I'm sure there is a misunderstanding here. I'll try to cover for Shannon ...without lying.*

"It turns out there wasn't really an emergency at all. Thank you for asking." Katrina could see on Nathan's face he wasn't buying the story.

But Deborah would be the one to cut to the chase: "Did Shannon tell you there was a meeting this week?"

Though it may have been easier to lie, Katrina admitted the truth.

"No. She did not," she said, lips pressed with disappointment. "But I will be deposing from an outline that she revised. Everything will be magnificent." Katrina even managed to impress herself with how confident she sounded. But she was relieved when the attention of the Alighieris was drawn behind her.

Katrina turned around to see Angelica Gomez, her attorney, and a man with whom she was unfamiliar walking by. The attorneys exchanged cordial smiles. Katrina recognized her as one of the more expensive lawyers in town. The man walked with eyes forward. His hand was on Angelita's shoulder like he was guiding her.

But the most interesting person to observe was Angelica herself. The expression on her face wasn't the kind that implied fear or victimhood. At least it was not any fear of Nathan. She maintained eye contact with him. She didn't seem angry or disgusted... perhaps bewilderment? Sorrow? Some kind of pleading? Katrina couldn't give Angelita's visage a name, in English or Spanish.

At the "ding" of the elevator, the plaintiff's party boarded.

Katrina turned back to the Alighieris and said, "I think you should come in with me."

# 18.0

# OFFICE PARTY

"You don't feel that, Amo?" Katrina asked her husband as they crossed the parking lot to her office arm in arm.

"Feel what?" asked Edward.

"Anxious. You don't feel anxiety about going into a party with a bunch of people you have never met?"

He halted them both and looked up at the building before him. It tapered in at the top, giving the illusion of infinite height. With a breath, he took in its ominous grandeur as his vision dropped to focus on the angles and reflection of steel and glass, all the way down to the line of strangers being swallowed through the front doors... and then turned back to his wife.

"No," he said. They continued walking. "I mean, I want to make a good impression for the sake of *your* reputation, since a lot of the people here are in your field. But I can't say it causes me *anxiety*. Why? Do you still get anxious before social events?"

She pondered. "Not as much as I used to, Amo."

Katrina was not accustomed to seeing her office like this. The area in front of the building became a valet parking lane. A brand new sports car, a luxury automobile, and an open-wheel racecar were on display, surrounded by velvet ropes to the right of the main entrance. Though such sights were not common here, Katrina did recognize the group of smokers to the left of the doors as the couple approached.

"Katrina!" a voice greeted. A woman stepped forward with a patch over her right eye.

"Shannon? I didn't expect to see you here so soon!" Katrina's gait turned toward the smokers. Edward obliged. The ladies gave each other a one-arm hug since Shannon was holding a cigarette and Katrina was holding her husband's elbow. She introduced him to the group.

"So you are the one who has been sleeping with my associate," Shannon said out the left side of her mouth.

"What can I say? She won't stop sexually harassing me!" He looked at Katrina. She smiled back. "But she says she's just doing research for her job, getting the perspective of a guilty defendant."

"We do specialize in many various forms of harassment," Shannon replied. "Let me know if you need representation." She put her whole hand over her mouth, pinching her lips together to take a drag from her cigarette.

"Do you think I have a case? I have been considering filing a complaint for 'consensual harassment'."

Shannon nodded and said to Katrina, "He'll fit in just fine."

"Congratulations on becoming a partner," Edward said. "The first female partner of your firm, I understand."

"Yeah," Shannon returned. "There's talk they might even let women vote someday."

"Ahh yes," Edward replied. "The good ole' 19th Amendment, guaranteeing the suffrage of women, and it could be argued, we've all been suffering ever since."

"He's definitely going to fit in," Shannon repeated to Katrina, trying not to laugh. She offered the couple a cigarette in jest.

"No thank you," Katrina replied.

"You know," Edward began. "I've been trying to *start* smoking."

"Is that so?" Shannon asked.

"Well, I've been doing nicotine gum and patches. But I think I should work my way up to vaping before I do the real thing." This caused a bit of laughter among the smokers. "My friends say I should go 'hot turkey' but I want to build up a good addiction before I hit the raw tobacco."

"This from the man who got Katrina to *stop* smoking!" Shannon said.

"That gives her more time to… 'harass' me."

Katrina's eyes ascended into space, shaking her head with a huge smile.

"It gives her more time to smoke your cock," Shannon said nonchalantly with eye fixed on Edward.

"Ahh. You read my subtext," Edward said with a grin.

"Saw that coming, did you?" She took another drag.

Edward shrugged. "Like you said, I'm going to fit in just fine."

Shannon gave half a grin, closed and opened her left eye.

"I can't tell if you are blinking or winking at me," Edward said.

That got a wide-eyed reaction from a couple of the smokers. Katrina went stone-faced. But they were all relieved when Shannon laughed.

"Seriously, how is your condition?" Edward asked with abrupt sincerity.

"Thank you for asking," she started. "The doctor said it could take up to six months to recover. …if I fully recover. But considering the fact that I could hardly talk at all until today, I think I will be fine."

"If you are half the fighter Katrina says you are, I have no doubt you will make a full recovery."

"I'd drink to that… if I had a drink."

"I'm afraid my attorney and I are suffering from the same dearth." He turned to Katrina. "Shall we seek remediation, counselor?"

"We shall!"

\* \* \*

Edward and Katrina turned from the open bar with wineglasses in hand to observe the lobby. With the exception of the area in front of the aquarium, it was lined with sponsor booths on one side and a long silent auction table on the other.

The sponsors included a winery, a tequila dispensary, and a couple of restaurants, all of which offered free samples of their products. A car dealership featured a poster declaring they were responsible for the display cars out front. A slot machine company provided a few machines set for free-play.

Guests were mingling. Old acquaintances were reuniting. Spouses, significant others, friends, clients, and colleagues were introducing each other to their respective spouses, significant others, friends, clients, and colleagues. Whether the guests were dressed for a courtroom or a night on the town, it was easy to see, most of them were older, and most of them had money.

When meeting some of Katrina's male colleagues, Edward could sense their attraction to his wife as their eyes and attention stuck to her a little longer than necessary. But it didn't bother him. He only needed to look at the day collar around her neck and the warmth of her eyes to know she was his. And he liked how they never let her words fall to the ground.

After introducing Edward to the Alighieris, Katrina continued to converse with them as Edward looked on. It was this moment at which Randy approached and introduced himself to Edward. "They call me 'The Jerk Clerk'!"

"So 'they' tell me! What are 'they' going to call you when you become an attorney?"

"I'm already an attorney. But nobody's come up with a clever nickname that rhymes with 'attorney'!"

As for Katrina's female colleagues, he did his best to be his charming self. For once, Edward was the jewelry being worn by his wife. And he was all too proud to fill his role. He felt like a celebrity just for being married to someone that everyone liked so much.

It was evident the sponsor booths were placed with the purpose of funneling people into the law-brary. But before the couple could make their way there, they were greeted by the one face in the crowd Edward knew before this evening:

"If you think it's impressive here, you should see the law-brary!" Alison and Katrina greeted each other with a hug. "Nice to see you as well, Edward."

"And you," Edward replied with a handshake.

"Where's Troy?" Katrina asked.

"He says he's running late," Alison replied with dead eyes and a tone that implied there was more to the story than she wanted to tell.

"That's okay," Katrina said. "Edward's enough man for the both of us!"

"How kind of you to share!" Alison joked as she took Edward's free left arm.

"I'm relieved I won't have to be breaking up any cat fights between the two of you tonight," Edward quipped. "I'm escorting the two hottest girls at the party!" he bragged to himself.

After refilling their drinks, Edward and his girls made their way into the law-brary. To Katrina, the room was almost unrecognizable. The study tables had given way to gaming tables that formed a casino pit. Roulette, blackjack, and craps, among other games were being offered at this charity event. And almost every seat was filled. There were people sitting at poker tables but nobody appeared to be playing. A receptionist at the entrance gave both Edward and Katrina ten complementary gaming chips to "gamble" how they pleased with the option to buy more for cash. Katrina slipped her chips into Edward's pocket, figuring he would have a much better idea of what to do with them.

All three stood at the end of the pit watching the roulette wheel on a table full of players. Alison had relinquished Edward's arm but was still next to him. They talked louder to compete with the music, slot machines, and other guests.

"All right, ladies," Edward began. "If you were to put your entire annual salary on 'red' or 'black', what would you choose?"

"Those are our only choices?" Katrina asked as she studied the table for the first time.

"You can choose something else. Put it on the inside if you want."

Katrina didn't know what that meant. But Alison might have understood.

"Troy always plays the 'red snake'," she said.

"You want to spread your *annual salary* across the 'snake'?" Edward asked.

"No!" Alison said with a shy laugh.

"How does Troy do with that bet?"

"Not well," she admitted.

They watched as the wheel spun counterclockwise and the ball, clockwise. "No more bets," the croupier announced with a wave of the hand.

Finally, the ball settled. A couple of the players were happy with the result. But most of the table was subdued. The croupier placed the marker on 22.

"See!" Edward said. "If one of you would've chosen 'black', you could've taken a year off!" Katrina chuckled and Alison laughed. "Ironically, '22' is my favorite roulette number," he said.

Katrina's cellphone vibrated, prompting her to read a text message.

"Forgive me, Shannon wants to talk in her office, probably about the deposition." She looked at Alison. "Will you please keep my husband out of trouble?"

"I can't promise I'll give him back," she replied as she took his left arm once again.

"Go make that money, sugar mama!" Edward encouraged.

"It shouldn't be long," Katrina said. She lifted on her toes to give him a peck on the cheek before she took her leave to Shannon's office. A few paces away, it was the only office that had any light.

"Katrina is your 'sugar mama'?" Alison asked as they looked upon the gaming pit. "I thought you made more money than her."

"We make precisely the same amount of money, because we share our income."

"I wish I could have that with Troy."

"Why can't you?"

Alison decided to change the subject. "Why is '22' your favorite roulette number? Because it hit?"

"Have you ever seen the movie 'Casablanca'?"

She shook her head.

"It's from before you were born. Watch it. You'll see."

"Before I was born? You're not that much older than me!"

"Old enough to know what 'Casablanca' is."

"I know the movie. I just haven't seen it. It came out in the '50s!"

"The '40s," Edward corrected.

"And you were alive then?"

"I remember the '40s like they were just… four decades before I was born."

This got Alison laughing right proper. She held Edward's arm tighter to steady herself. Edward flexed so the drink in his hand wouldn't spill.

"Troy, I presume!" said a voice from behind. But it only got Alison's attention. She dropped her hands from Edward's arm and clasped her fingers in front. After Edward saw Alison turn, he did the same.

"Oh, no, Mr. Kalish," Alison explained. "This is Edward Henderson, Katrina's husband."

"I'd be a lucky man to be Troy but I'm an even luckier man to be Edward," he said as he offered his hand.

"Edward! The man, the myth, the legend!" Arnold Kalish said as he shook Edward's right hand with his left on Edward's right shoulder.

"Guilty as charged!" Edward returned. "It's nice to finally meet you and put a face to the name, Mr. Kalish."

"Call me 'Arnold'." They dropped hands. "I'm sure you heard your wife scored a big touchdown for us."

"So I'm told," Edward said. "But she gives Shannon the credit for getting the ball down the field."

"She's said something like that to me. But I think she's being modest."

"You may be right, but I'm proud of her either way."

Alison liked hearing Edward talk about his wife.

"I understand you are the one who turned Katrina into a poker player!"

"Eh, she may have read my book."

"Sounds like both of you are modest. I've read your book too. Quite informative!"

"Thank you. I'm glad you liked it."

"I bet you sold a few books after you were on TV for that final table."

"It gave me a boost for the duration of my fifteen minutes!"

"You and Katrina: both modest. Do you still play?"

"Just enough to support my music habit."

"You're a musician too?"

"That's why I came to Vegas. I've worked in entertainment for most of my life. Performance, composition, recording, teaching. …and a little stand-up comedy on the side."

"I'm starting to understand why Katrina finds you so interesting."

"That's ironic considering how fascinating I find her, not to mention her career."

"All those things you do and you find the *practice of law* fascinating?" Arnold said with a skeptical grin.

"Absolutely," Edward said with raised eyebrows. "I'm sure you understand the history of your profession. Scripture uses the word 'law' synonymously with the name of God."

"Honestly, I never thought of it that way." Arnold was a bit stunned. Edward's statement had thrown him into cogitation. "You're so passionate about the law, but you don't pursue it?"

"I pursue it every day."

"I mean, the practice of law as a profession. You do music and poker… and stand-up comedy!"

"I think stand-up comedy is a very important art form, especially these days from a legal standpoint. But I did pursue a career in law."

"Really?"

"Yeah, I had a brief career as a bailiff," Edward said, his tone dry.

"I don't know if I would consider a bailiff to be 'practicing law'." He couldn't tell if Edward was being serious.

"Well, I figured, if an attorney or a judge wasn't able to make it to court, I could fill in for them and get some litigation or judging experience."

"I see," Arnold said with a laugh. "You could practice law and save money on tuition."

"Exactly! As a bailiff, I could be a substitute attorney or judge, and I wouldn't have to beat up anybody who wasn't already in handcuffs!" Arnold and Alison's laughter was now creating a snowball effect as more individuals joined the circle. "I might have been a bailiff to this day but the judge didn't like me."

"Oh no? Why not?" Arnold asked, happy to play McMahon to this Carson.

"I'll try to make a long story short: I was standing… not in the middle of the well of the court but to the side of the well like I've seen on TV. I thought I was fine there but the judge asked me if I thought the *well* of the court was a good place for me to stand. I said to him, 'Your honor, I figured, why stand in a place that is *good* when I could stand in a place that is *well*.'"

Edward had the growing group laughing at that, or at least the litigators. So he kept going: "The judge called me to the bench and told me to save my stand-up comedy for a trial that was not dealing with murder and rape. So the judge killed my legal career *and* my stand-up comedy dreams in the same day. I got fired and I never found out what happened first, the murder or the rape." This earned a collective wince from Edward's audience. But he quickly won them back by saying, "I got to see the *law* but not the *order*!"

"And that was the sum total of your legal experience!" Arnold said as he recovered from laughter.

"Yep! That was it," Edward said. He glanced at the door to Shannon's office and noticed it was now closed.

Thinking about Katrina gave him an emotion that was foreign to him. For the first time in Edward's adult life, he found he was feeling what can only be described as "self-consciousness". But not for himself. He was concerned he was making his wife look like she married a court jester.

Uncertain if he should keep going, he tested the water by saying, "At least, that was the sum total of my legal experience from the *front* of the defendant's table."

231

"Dare I ask?" Arnold prompted. Edward decided to go for a final laugh.

"It was a small problem with the TSA: They found a pair of handcuffs in my carryon luggage at the terminal screening. I tried to explain, 'It's not what it looks like. These handcuffs are just for sex. That's all!'"

At that point, an intrigued Alison couldn't resist asking through the laughter: "And Katrina wouldn't back your story?"

To which Edward returned: "Oh, I had already tied her up and packed her in my checked luggage!"

That was the joke that caused the laughter to reach its peak. But it wasn't so loud that Edward couldn't hear a strange sound from Shannon's office cut through. It was like a loud knock along with the sound of glass breaking. Most people didn't hear it. Edward continued smiling to keep the audience from knowing he was worried about what was transpiring on the other side of the door.

"Pardon me, folks," Edward said. "I'm going to check on that." He handed his wineglass to Alison. "Would you be so kind?"

He walked over to the closed door of the office and listened through the music for a few seconds before he saw Arnold had followed him. "I wonder if there is a way I can go through this door and not make things worse."

"I was wondering the same thing," Arnold replied.

With that, Edward turned the handle. He stepped one foot in and saw broken glass and a bendy straw on the floor. He looked up to see his favorite figure in front of a desk with her back to him. She extended her arm behind her with her hand giving a 'stop' signal. He didn't know what she was talking about but he did hear her clearly put emphasis on the word "exonerate". Though they no longer had safewords, he got the message and closed the door.

"I think they're okay," he told Arnold, before shaking his head and muttering, "Attorneys."

Arnold rolled his eyes. "Tell me about it."

# 17.1

# DEPOSITION DEBRIEFING

Shannon's office was dark, save the glow of her computer screensaver. But it was enough to illuminate the various icons of accolades and accomplishments displayed in a glass showcase behind her desk. Two decades of achievements were summarized by trophies and plaques surrounding a law degree. A framed cover of "LV Law" magazine exhibited a twenty-something Shannon, from a time when she dreamed of being where she now found herself.

She was not looking *at* the showcase, but *through* the showcase. The darkness of her office afforded a view out the windows into the night. The walkway around a pond featured lights changing color in patterns that lazily chased each other. Lights on a fountain in the middle behaved in tandem. She was accustomed to watching the fountain during the day, especially on smoke breaks. But the night lights were only lit for special occasions such as the charity event the firm was hosting this evening.

The volume of the music and chatter outside crescendoed as Katrina opened the door. "Shannon?" she called into the dark room.

When Katrina turned on the lights, Shannon's patched right eye was spared from the shock. But her squinting left eye caught a glimpse of her own reflection in the window. It was in stark contrast to the magazine cover. She took no pleasure in the view of her half paralyzed face. But she was determined to put on a good face for Katrina.

"Katrina! Tell me about the deposishhun," Shannon said as she sat behind her desk. Her impediment reminded her to put more effort into her enunciation. "You scored a big one for Alighieri! All claims dropped! What happened in there?" She took a sip of wine through a bendy straw like a drag off a cigarette.

"I just had a hunch when I saw the deponent show up with her stepfather," Katrina said with one foot toward the open door. "I pursued it."

"Tell me about this 'hunch'."

"We should be able to go over the transcript when it arrives next week," Katrina said. Though she was holding a wineglass, she tried not to look anxious to postpone the conversation to a more appropriate time.

"We received the video today. I've already watched some of it."

"Good!" said Katrina. "Was something wrong?" Leaving the door open on purpose, she took a few steps to stand between the chairs in front of Shannon's desk.

"I was curious about your process in the deposition," Shannon began, looking up at Katrina. "When you asked that the deponent's stepdad leave the room, I thought he was gonna shhhit!" Both ladies chuckled. "I thought you did it to show some teeth," she gritted. "…to show you're the boss of this deposition!" Shannon's half smile faded. Her voice darkened as her left eyebrow lowered. "But then, you took a different tack. You went back to baseline questions. You even used some levity. At one point I thought I was listening to a couple of girls at a sleepover." Katrina understood Shannon was exaggerating. But she couldn't tell if Shannon was disappointed. "I want to know about this 'hunch', that caused you to completely abandon the script I sent you."

It was becoming clear that Katrina was not going to get a continuance. And she was still uncertain where Shannon was going. *Is she disappointed? We got our client out of a potentially lengthy and expensive trial.* She sat down. "You remember, we discussed our theories about where Angelita was getting her funding since the union wouldn't back her."

"Right."

"We knew that her mother won that big settlement, also for sexual harassment and racial discrimination."

"Right," Shannon repeated, a pitch lower.

"We were going to ask if that was where Angelita was getting the money. And we were going to try to determine what kind of influence her mother had on this complaint."

"I remember."

"And then when Angelita's stepfather showed up, I wondered if he had anything to do with it. When I had him leave the room a few questions in, Angelica became a new woman."

"And that's why you ignored my outline?" Shannon asked, derailing Katrina's train of reason.

"I asked every question on your outline. But I had plenty of time for more questions."

Boisterous laughter burst from outside the open office door causing Shannon to look up over Katrina. Katrina, taking the initiative, stood and walked to the door. She placed her left hand on the handle with the wineglass in her right. She looked out to see what was going on.

A small crowd had gathered around Edward. She couldn't hear what he was saying but it must have been entertaining. *How does he do that?* She closed the door quietly, bringing a hush to the room.

"Is something wrong?" Katrina asked as she walked back to the desk.

"I thought we were on the same page," Shannon replied. "From the second you helped me convince Alighieri to fight using… *Michael Jackson* as a cautionary tale," she said, rolling her eye.

"I believed it was in his best interest. I was advising our potential client." Katrina was confused. *What did I do wrong?*

"'*Our* client'? He was never supposed to be '*our* client'!"

"What do you mean?" Katrina asked.

"Why do you think you were on this case? Did you think I needed your help? I only wanted you for the intake, to distract Nate's wife! And then you sprinkled some 'Spanish fly' on him and it made him think he needed both of us! You didn't think you got this case on your own merit, did you?"

Katrina was on her heels, mouth agape in disbelief. *I'm not going to fucking cry.* Shannon continued.

"Oh, is this news to you? Did you think you got this job a year earlier than most associates because you're *good at poker*?" she mocked. "Kalish was sick of losing Hispanic business because we were 'too white'. We needed to fast-track a Latina. ...one who was born speaking Spanish. And it didn't hurt that you were easy on the eyes! How much of *that* did you earn?!" sneered Shannon.

Katrina held fast and swallowed with jaw clenched. Shannon was not finished. She sat back and swiveled her chair away from Katrina, assuming a quieter tone.

"Do you know how we learned about Angelica's mother?" she asked, pronouncing the name with a hard 'g'.

Katrina didn't respond.

"It turns out, she came to us first looking for representation. She didn't hire us. Can you guess why?"

Katrina remained silent at the rhetorical question. Gripping her wineglass in front with both hands, she sat again.

"She hired someone who looked like her... who could speak her language." Shannon turned to Katrina again. "We hired *you* to get clients like *her*! You are not good enough for clients like Alighieri!"

Shannon watched Katrina and waited for her to say something.

"Well forgive me for helping you catch him," Katrina attempted carefully, so her voice wouldn't break.

"Don't flatter yourself," Shannon countered. "We were going to get him with or without you."

"I'm sure you would have," Katrina said. "I have no doubt."

"Don't try to placate me," Shannon returned. "I don't need your reassurance."

"It's unfortunate you're so dismayed with my work and the outcome of this case." She rose to her feet. "But your dissatisfaction has nothing to do with me."

And with that, Katrina turned to walk out. As she reached for the handle, a wineglass flew by her shoulder and shattered on the door. She shielded her eyes with her hand before slowly turning around to face Shannon, aghast. But Shannon was looking back out the windows with her hands on her hips. Katrina walked straight toward Shannon's desk.

"Is this about credit?" she asked. "Nobody is going to forget that you were lead counsel on this!" She set her wineglass on the desk and leaned down with both hands. "You got your picture *and* quote on the front page the week the complaint was filed!"

Just then, Edward opened the door and poked his head inside. Katrina saw his stern expression out the corner of her eye. She held her hand out behind her to stop him and continued, "The only article that mentioned me was the one that *exonerated* Nate. It was buried in the business section and read like a gossip column!"

Edward bowed out, closing the door.

"Because of the way I handled the deposition, I got *our* client out of the charges! But you sound like you wanted to go to trial!"

"YOU'RE FUCKING RIGHT, I WANTED TO GO TO TRIAL!" Shannon screamed as she snapped around and pushed into the desk.

Katrina stood up straight with hands at her sides and took on the wind of Shannon's wrath.

"I would have *dominated* a trial!" She clenched a fist in front of her chest and seethed, "And you took it from me!" She stood straight up and talked with her hands. "You come waltzing into this profession and have everything handed to you. It's no wonder you think this is some kind of game! You haven't bled for this. You haven't sacrificed a family for this. You haven't given up a social life. …or your 20s and 30s." She pressed her knuckles on the desk and articulated, "You have everything. But you deserve *none of it*!" She took a deep breath and straightened her blouse before sitting back down and turning her chair to the dark corner of the room.

"I am such a fool," Katrina said with pitying eyes. "You wanted to use a courtroom as a stage for the whole world to see you." She looked over Shannon's head in thought. "No. That's not right," she said to herself. "Who is it you were really trying to impress?" Shannon's eye darted to Katrina and shot a dagger. "Withdrawn. Forgive me." Katrina moved on before she lost momentum.

"Did you keep me in the poker game to help me network or were you tired of being the only woman? Or were you just looking for a rookie to haze with all of your passive/aggressive verbal jabs? …telling me how well I've done for 'someone from my background'?"

Shannon stared into the darkness and said nothing. The left side of her face was as blunted as her right. But Katrina knew her words were getting through, Shannon's dismissive position notwithstanding.

"And then sabotaging my work, dismissing my ideas with no explanation, informing me of assignments hours before deadlines, the secret meetings with clients. How much more information about Angelica's mother do you have that might have proven useful to me at the deposition?"

Katrina pulled a chair to the front of the desk and sat up to take a conversational posture and tone. "You shortened my outline to two hours of barely relevant questions for a four-hour deposition. I had to keep going. I had to make sure we had as much information as possible." She leaned forward. "I didn't proceed to spite *you*. I did it for *our client* as our ethics dictate."

Shannon swallowed and spoke glumly to the shadows, "You've been practicing law for a year now and you presume to tell me about legal ethics?"

"I learned it from you. You were my teacher. …my mentor. I looked up to you. Maybe that's why I was in denial about what you were doing."

The ladies sat in silence for a moment before Shannon spoke.

"Maybe you're right," she said, motionlessly. "I don't know. I don't even know if I realized what I was doing," Shannon lamented, adding the word, "...allegedly." She turned her chair to look at Katrina. "But I was confident you would 'faithfully and honestly discharge...'"

Katrina joined Shannon as they recited together:
"'...the duties of an attorney at law
"'...the duties of an attorney at law
to the best of your knowledge and ability'."
to the best of my knowledge and ability'."

"You stood by me when I took that oath," Katrina recalled.

"And you still have it memorized." Shannon sighed. "Tell me about your hunch. I won't interrupt."

Katrina leaned back in her chair and crossed one knee over the other before telling the story.

"When I saw Angelita's stepfather at the deposition, I wondered if he had something to do with the suit. Angelita kept looking at him before she would answer my questions. Something he was doing was distracting her. So I asked for his dismissal. When he asked why he had to leave and Deborah could stay, Nate looked at her and she left without a word.

"Once her stepfather was gone, Angelica was a new woman. She was in control of herself. At some points, it was like she was happy to see Nate when my questions recalled fond memories.

"Anyway, the text messages always fell badly on me for reasons I could not ascertain. I finally figured out that there was another voice on Angelica's end texting Nate. I was close to getting her to admit that not all of the texts were her words, when her attorney asked for a break.

"On the break, I suggested to opposing counsel that we may need to depose Angelica's stepfather. Then I casually mentioned the suit that his wife won four years ago. I told her that if he had anything to do with *that* suit, we know he wouldn't have been compelled to testify due to spousal privilege. But of course, there is no such privilege for stepchildren. His testimony would be public record. There would probably be questions about both suits. And there may be some people in his past who would be interested in the transcript.

"Counsel asked if we could extend the break. A half-hour later, she informed me they were dropping the charges.

"Nate and Deborah took me to TG for lunch."

"Hm." Shannon's eye dropped from Katrina's face as she reviewed the story in her head. She nodded in thought for a few seconds before saying, "That's brilliant." Her eye raised back to Katrina. She repeated with sincerity, "That's brilliant."

Katrina gave a close-lipped smile but said nothing.

"Remember how I told you that you have to dominate a deponent?" Katrina nodded.

"I think you've found a method that works better for you, at least in this case. That was brilliant." Then she added, "...for someone of your background," causing them both to laugh.

"I'll be honest with you," Katrina began. "I'm not going to apologize if there is anything about my background or aesthetics that helped me in my life. I'll use all the advantages God gives me whether I deserve it or not. And if you think it's easy to become bilingual, you should try it."

"Bilingual," Shannon snorted. "I just met your husband and I can already tell you've learned a lot of English from him. You sometimes sound more like Edward than yourself!"

"Well, I do frequently hear him speak English!" Katrina said. "He's a good teacher."

"Maybe," Shannon replied. "But you are a good student."

"I don't know about that. I was actually reciting the 'Oath of Attorney' off the plaque behind you," Katrina admitted.

Shannon shrugged and pointed toward her computer. "It's on my screensaver."

# 18.1

# FOR THE KIDS

When Katrina emerged from Shannon's office, she found Edward standing guard outside the door. He was talking to Alison about the musical pitches of slot machines and the dopaminergic effect they have on gamblers.

"Where did you learn that?" Alison asked.

"He makes it up!" Katrina answered as she took his arm.

"Sidebar, your honor." He leaned down to ask *soto voce*, "Is everything okay?"

"It's all going to be magnificent," she said. "We can go whenever you want, Amo."

"I'm fine with leaving if that's what you want. But Arnold asked if I would be one of the 'celebrity bounty players' in the poker tournament. I told him I would give him an answer later."

"Really!" she said with a smile.

"Yeah. I mean, it's a charity event so it won't be for much money but…"

"Let's play!"

The conversation was cut by a high-pitch squeak from Alison. The couple looked to see her as excited as a kid on Christmas as she threw her arms around... Brendon.

"The guy from TG?" Edward asked Katrina.

Katrina shrugged, eyes wide as she watched the two.

Alison composed herself. "This is a nice surprise!"

"'Surprise'?" Brendon said. "I told you I'd be here if I got off work in time."

The girls had a sidebar of their own as the guys talked.

"You didn't tell me you invited him."

"I didn't think he would come. I was getting used to guys disappointing me."

"What if Troy shows up?"

Shaking her head, "Troy is not showing up."

Alison invited Brendon outside for a walk around the pond. They were not seen again for the rest of the night.

\*       \*       \*

Arnold Kalish took to the microphone to speak about the charity organization the event was supporting and the importance of providing advocacy for children in the legal system. He announced that all donations to the kids were tax deductible. As a new benefit, the firm would give paid maternity and paternity leave for employees who adopt a child. And as always, associates doing pro bono work for the agency would receive full billing credit.

He concluded by declaring the imminent start of the poker tournament. He introduced the celebrity bounty players who were wearing red lanyards, including Edward, and explained that knocking them out of the tournament would net them an additional prize of $1,000.

With Edward's table being the closest to where Arnold was standing, he looked at Edward and asked, "Would you do us the honor of getting this tournament started?"

"The honor would be mine!" he said as he rose to his feet.

But before he handed him the microphone, "Edward, let me put you on the spot and ask if you will give us a signed copy of your poker book for the silent auction."

"Of course! I'll include a lesson with the book!"

On the mic, Arnold repeated Edward's willingness to donate a book and his time for the auction so the whole audience could hear, to some applause.

"Mr. Ed, the talking horse, ladies and gentlemen!" he said as he handed off the microphone.

Edward took the microphone and responded, "Thank you! Arnold, the talking pig, ladies and gentlemen!"

Although the majority of the people who got the joke were seniors who lived through the "talking animal era" of television, their laughter spread to the entire crowd for what was said to be the funniest moment of the evening. Arnold had to put his hand on Edward's shoulder to steady himself as he wiped tears. It was about two minutes before the laughter of the crowd diminished to the point at which Edward could give his personal poker blessing: "Dealers, at your leisure. Players, may you all end up!"

…

"This is fun!" Edward told his three remaining opponents and dealer. "You guys make me wish I would have finished law school."

Arnold and Nathan looked at Edward with confusion. Katrina grinned.

"What?" Arnold asked. "Why didn't you finish law school?!"

"Because I never *started* law school," Edward returned, invoking laughter from the surrounding spectators.

Arnold turned to Katrina. "I can't figure out your husband to save my life!"

Nathan slid his cards to the dealer and scooped a small pot. He asked, "Of the twenty bounty players we had in this event, how were you the only one to make it to the final table?"

"Because of all the bounty players, I'm the worst!" Edward quipped. "Everybody overestimated me!"

This got a snort from Nathan. The dealer shuffled and dealt another hand.

"No, seriously," Arnold said. "I know there's a reason for it. How did you do it with the whole field targeting the bounty players?"

Edward relented. "The bounty was my advantage. Since everyone was aiming for me, all I had to do was sit back and wait for really good hands. I could overbet the pot, and with the bounty on my head, I was guaranteed callers."

"Why didn't any of the other bounty players figure that out?" Nathan asked.

"They didn't read your book!" Arnold said. "Is that how you took out Shannon? What did you think of her?"

"Shannon is quite formidable," he complimented. "She's a hammer."

Edward shared a glance with his wife sitting to his right before she peeked down at her cards. She made a raise that Edward, Arnold, and Nathan called, in that order.

"So now that it's down to the four of us, are we being called to order in the matter of Alighieri and Kalish v. Edward and Katrina Henderson?"

"I want Katrina on my side!" Nathan declared.

"So do I!" Arnold said.

"I'm on my husband's side, thank you very much!" Katrina proclaimed. "But at the poker table, we work alone."

"Oh? You two are not colluding to beat me and Arnold?" Nathan asked with a hint of suspicion and a wink to Arnold.

"I'm afraid her affinity for ethical behavior extends beyond her profession to include poker," Edward replied.

"Did you teach her that?" Arnold asked.

"I just taught her poker. She was already well versed in ethics," Edward answered. "I'm all-in." His bet was larger than the amount of the pot. He turned to Katrina. "You're going down, my queen!"

Katrina sucked the corner of her lip and softly mumbled, "Don't tease me, my king."

"Newlyweds," Arnold said, even though they had been married for almost a year.

Nathan didn't hear what Katrina said. But he did hear Arnold say, "Speaking of 'overbet'!" before folding to Edward, prompting Nathan to fold as well.

"I call," a voice said. Katrina was not surprised her instincts caused her to speak another reality into being.

"We have an all-in and a call," the dealer announced, loud enough for the surrounding observers to hear. "Please table your cards."

Edward tabled his hand first to show an Ace and a King.

Katrina tabled her hand to reveal a Queen and a King. With a Queen among the community cards, Katrina won the hand.

Edward slumped back in his chair with his hand over his chest as though he had been shot.

"Looks like the honeymoon's over!" Arthur joked.

"Nonsense!" Edward said as he watched Katrina stack her new chips. "Gentlemen, I don't know if you have a clue how proud I am of my wife!"

"I have a clue," Nathan said as he looked over his shoulder at Deborah, standing a few steps behind him.

Although the loss did not eliminate Edward from the tournament, the meager amount of chips he had left only sustained him for a few more minutes before he succumbed to his demise at the hands of his wife. They gave each other a peck before Edward shook hands with the gentlemen and waved at the applauding audience. He hung his bounty lanyard around Katrina's neck, giving the collar the subtlest tug before joining the railbirds behind her.

"That puts to rest any suspicion about the two of them colluding!" Nathan said to Arnold.

"How do we know Edward wasn't dumping all of his chips to this shark on purpose?" Arnold turned to Katrina. "How did you know you had him beat on that hand with just a pair of queens?!"

Katrina knew he was joking but she volunteered her reasoning: "You asked Edward how he was the only bounty player to make it to the final table. He told you how he made big moves with strong hands. Did you think he was going to keep playing the way he told you he was playing?"

"I'm a fool!" Arnold declared. "He changed his strategy. He made a big move with a weak hand. And you caught him!"

"He didn't change his strategy," Katrina said, shaking her head. "He was lying to you the whole time!"

"Wives know when their husbands are lying," Nathan said.

"Edward only lies at the poker table. I know my man."

…

Deborah made her way around the table and through the crowd to stand next to Edward. They greeted each other with a tap of their wineglasses and stood side by side, watching their spouses and Arnold battle on the felt.

The next victim of Katrina's poker fury was Arnold. As she shook his hand, she smiled and said, "I'm not sorry!"

"Good! You shouldn't be!" he laughed. "You're an excellent poker player and a better attorney."

It was time for a heads up, one-on-one match between Katrina and Nathan. But before they could begin, the two exchanged some words that ended with a handshake and a hug. Then they spoke to Arnold.

Arnold got back on the microphone. "Ladies and gentlemen: Our associate, Katrina Henderson and our esteemed client, Nathan Alighieri have decided they are calling it a draw and giving all of their winnings to the kids!"

# 14, 13, AND 11:

# HONEYMOON, WEDDINGS, PROPOSALS

THE HONEYMOON:
    The couple learned Edward did not need to throw his dice very far to hit Katrina's back wall.

    She laid on the bed with her hips hanging over the edge, ankles tied to the corners, keeping her spread at the pleasure of her owner. Though her arms were not restrained, they did nothing to impede the exploration of her Master's hands as he desired. Hers took advantage of the same freedom, touching as much of him as she could.

    His manhood partially penetrated her as he reached for a handful of her hair. He ventured further until she could yield no more, involuntarily clenching around him. But the pain inside was drawn away with slaps to her thigh, causing her capitulation. He carefully gave her another increment in his search for the delicate balance of sensations that would aid his conquest.

    Her eyes closed and her head thrust back into the blanket, leaving her neck defenseless from his lips. She let out a whimpering moan at the brief pain and profound pleasure as her man discovered a new depth in her. He stayed his position, absorbing her warmth as she eased open inside, accepting her purpose.

    She tensed and stretched with the ebb and flow of the tides of ecstasy until her internal strength compressed once more as though it were attempting to expel him, to which he replied, "No, mi amor. I'm staying right here. It's all yours." And then he growled, "Now cum on *your* cock."

    "Yes, Master," she said breathily. But her womanhood was already flexing around Edward as though it heard the command come directly from him. Her ankles tugged at the ropes, pulling herself closer, causing him to go even deeper. The inability to close her legs or protest his dominance, willfully or otherwise, enhanced her surrender.

    Her arms opened as wide as her legs. Her fingers sank into the blanket, giving herself to him in every possible way. She was accustomed to the thought of belonging to this man. But she had never felt as truly possessed as she did in this moment.

With a few thrusts, their juices intermingled, raising their temperature another degree. And there they remained, frozen by the heat, until Katrina's eyes opened to find Edward's. They stared into each other, wordlessly sharing their astonishment at their newfound inability to discern one soul from the other. They had become one flesh.

Their eye contact abided as he stood and withdrew himself. He observed the breadth of his bride, arms and legs splayed before him, and said, "I feel like I am still inside of you."

"I feel like I am inside of you too, Master."

He released her ankles from the ropes and laid back down with her. They intertwined, making every bit of contact they could find.

"Permission to ask a question, Master."

"Permission granted."

"This body has been yours since our first weekend together. You named your tits "Elizabeth" and "Victoria" and your pussy "Priscilla"."

"Correct."

"But now that we are married…" Her hand gave his member a light squeeze. "…this is *just now* becoming *my cock*, Master?"

"My consort, I have belonged to you since before the first time I told you 'I love you'. You just didn't know it until now. That includes your cock. You can give it a name if you…"

"'Aquila', Master! I name my cock 'Aquila'!"

"Perfect!"

At that, they kissed and held each other tighter.

"Everything feels different now, Master."

"I know what you mean. Is that what sex does?"

"No, Master. I've had sex before. It's never been this good."

"I'm sure it's different with everybody."

"Not just that, Master. *You* are different than before."

"How so?"

"I don't know, Master. You're more… connected with me, emotionally."

"I think I had to stay a little disconnected before. If I was more emotional, I might not have been able to stay a virgin until now."

"How does it feel to not be a virgin anymore, Master?"

"Mmm. I'm still feeling a bit virginal. We may have to make love a few more times to get that out of me. Considering how long I was a virgin, I may need a few hundred, or thousand more times."

"Whenever you want, Master!"

"Oh, I know!"

Katrina snickered. "Permission to make a request, Master."

"Permission granted."

"Will you please… lick Priscilla, Master?"

"That's a good idea. It's time for you to teach me the Queen's Spanish."

What ensued was a conversation between Edward and Katrina's vagina that soon devolved into Edward speaking Latin gibberish with his tongue on her clitoris, teasing and taunting with every call and response. After the king began a speech, Katrina tightened her thighs on his ears to stop him before she suffocated from laughter and screaming at the combination of comedy and cumming.

"Excuse me!" He used a sheet to wipe his chin as he stood. "This is a private conversation between me and Priscilla!"

"Yes, Master!" she wheezed, trying to catch her breath.

He forced her knees open and retied her ankles to the corners of the bed. "What is it you need, my queen?"

"Master, will you please…"

"You know I don't speak English!"

He made her tell him what she wanted, mostly in Spanish. But since she wasn't exactly sure what she wanted herself, she learned along with him as they fumbled through their early lessons.

The jack of all trades was determined to be the master of one vagina. For as promised, between the two of them, there was indeed, more head than Easter Island.

      \*            \*            \*

THE WEDDINGS:
    The bachelor party took place at Woodrow's backyard observatory/ shooting range where the groomsmen tried out the gifts the couple gave them. Each received an old-fashioned single-action revolver with a holster that they were to wear in the wedding. On the left side of the barrel was engraved the words, "Edward and Katrina Henderson", along with the date of the wedding. And on the right side of the barrel: "BLESSED ARE THE PEACEMAKERS".
    The name of each groomsman was etched into the grip of their respective pistol including that of "Flaco", whom Edward had since learned, really was his nickname. Katrina's cousin would be in the wedding at her behest, which was no problem for Edward. He and Flaco had made peace of their own.
    As Flaco opened the wooden box containing his gift, with a laugh, he said, "I thought you say you will never give me a gun!"
    "I was wrong, my friend," Edward returned.
    "Something I want to know about that night we meet," Flaco said. "Did you have a gun or were you bluffing?"
    At this, Edward smiled. He put a hand on Flaco's shoulder and said, "You'll never know!"
    London, as always, was the hostess with the mostess, making sure her home cooked fare was available throughout the evening and into the night. She was not allowed to leave the kitchen, which suited her just fine. Woodrow was happy to provide a steady stream of his homemade wine and mead. Though he and London would be in the bridal party of the wedding, they would be the best man and matron of honor at the collaring ceremony, which took place the night after the wedding.
    Edward's father and Katrina's mother were the best man and matron of honor of the wedding. After a shopping spree with Edward's mother, Katrina quipped that she would have been just as happy to have her be the matron of honor.
    "Your mother is amazing, Master."
    "Thank you, my charge. I'm fond of her myself."
    "I don't know how I am going to live up to her."
    "What do you mean?"
    "I don't know how I am going to be as good of a wife to you as your mother has been a mother to you."
    Edward thought about her statement. "Did she say something to make you feel that way?"
    "No! No, Master. She's so loving and smart and spiritual. She made me feel… I don't know."
    "You can tell me."
    "She made me think about what it would be like if she were *my* mother."
    "You're about to find out. She is about to be one of your mothers!"
    "Yes, Master!"
    "You know you are not competing with her, right? I'm very fortunate to have my parents but I'm choosing you over them, no contest. They wouldn't have it any other way. They love you. If our marriage wasn't going to last, I'm pretty sure you would get them in the divorce!"
    "They think I'm changing you, Master. For the better."

"I believe it. Wait until they see us dance at the reception."

"They say you are more gentle than you used to be. They think it is because of me."

"I'm not sure what they mean," he chuckled. "Did you tell them you have the scars to prove how 'gentle' I am?!"

"I think you're gentle and merciful all the time, Master; even when you discipline me."

\*       \*       \*

They exchanged vows before God and their church body, standing in front of a cross before being declared "husband and wife". The next night, they had a collaring ceremony at the Turkey Club, standing in front of the chain spiderweb, once again, in the presence of God along with the more initiated among their friends, where they declared themselves "Master and slave".

For the second time on that stage, Edward performed "So She Knows/ Asi Que Ella Sabe" on guitar. But this time, Katrina sang with him.

After the song, Edward switched the lock of the collar to one with an engraving: "E & K SOS 7:10". It was in the shape of a heart with a keyhole in the middle. It was silver on one side and gold on the other so it could be worn with other styles of collars.

Katrina recited her lengthy mantra as her vow from memory. Edward looked on with pride as his linguaphile employed words that would send some native speakers in attendance to the dictionary:

"I am the beloved, collard, cherished, enslaved property of my Master, Edward, who claims me as his own. I will gratefully accept his love no matter how unworthy I feel. I will respect and worship him all the days I live. This heart belongs to him as this soul belongs to God. This body is his garden, which I will maintain only for him. All of the pain and pleasure experienced by this body is his. This is his mouth, his pussy, and his ass where his cock will always find refuge.

"Through his use of these holes, I find virtue.
"Through subjugation, I find freedom.
"Through debasement, I find dignity.
"Through my trust, I find security.
"In my vulnerability, I find his acceptance.
"In my thralldom, I find unity.
"In my submission, I am empowered.
"When I am naked, he clothes me in rope and chain.
"I will be a vault for his secrets.
"I will have faith in my Master's fidelity to me.
"As I proudly wear his collar, he protects me from ignominy.
"My purpose is to serve my Master at his bidding.
"With these lips, I shall provide trustworthy counsel for his mind and a haven for his cock.

"I am his consort, his sex toy, his odalisque, his helpmate, his private whore, his cock warmer, his cum rag, his inamorata, his anima, his trusted advisor, his queen, his charge, his WIFE! ...*his*. All I am that is not enumerated in this vow, belongs to him. All of my rights and privileges are granted by my Master alone. And I will faithfully and honestly discharge the duties of the sole bondwoman of my Master to the best of my knowledge, ability, and magnificence.

"I am the beloved, collard, cherished, enslaved property of my Master, Edward, who claims me as his own, in perpetuity."

At the conclusion of her vow, she attached a leash to the collar and presented the grip to him, from her knees.

After the ceremony, they had their initials tattooed on each other's ring fingers by the artist on site. Edward had the addition of a pair of handcuffs with the 'K'. To those who understood the lifestyle, their placement looked like the 'K' was about to wear them. But to those who were unfamiliar, Edward could explain that in Spanish, the words for "wife" and "handcuffs" are the same.

\*       \*       \*

THE PROPOSALS:
Katrina rested upon her knees in position two, looking up at Edward. She recognized the sinister twinkle in his eye as though she were his prey.

"Eyes forward," he ordered.

"Yes, Sir." Though her vision burned through the wall in front of her, her mind projected the image of her Dominant's face as he stalked her. She steadied her breathing to relax her mind.

He walked slowly but intentionally behind her. Though her focus was on the wall, she heard him making preparations. There was the rattle of a chain, the click of clamps, and the sound of unknown objects being adjusted and placed. She directed her awareness of these sounds out the back of her mind. She would allow nothing to break her from meditation as she motionlessly fulfilled her purpose. Even Edward tugging on her ponytail, compelling her to stand and step to her mark did little to pull her from her profundity.

"Position 5, standing," Edward ordered.

"Yes, Sir."

"Hands on the bar," he said, releasing her hair.

"Yes, Sir."

She stood in position with her arms and legs forming an 'X'. Edward guided her hands until the tips of her fingers wrapped around the loops at the ends of the suspension bar. She put her feet closer and stood on her toes to reach. But she kept her vision forward, looking through his chest.

He set a thick blindfold on her forehead and around her ponytail. He bent down at the waist until his face was level with hers. By the power of his mind, he pulled Katrina back into her own body until she was no longer looking through him, but directly into his eyes.

He placed his left hand behind her head and his right at her throat. The couple proceeded to devour each other through a kiss that explored the depths of their mutual desire. Her fingers gripped the bar tighter in an effort to push her naked body into him as much as he was pushing into her. But there was no use in trying to match his force.

At the conclusion of their wordless discourse, Katrina opened her eyes to find Edward had recovered his previous position, face-to-face. They took a moment to share the air through their heavier breathing as they peered into each other's souls. Her eyes closed when he pulled down the blindfold.

In the darkness, she stared at the image of his face etched into her mind. It was this image that would now be the icon of her worship as she continued to fulfill her purpose.

Rope was wrapped around her wrists and across her palms. First the right, then the left. Then rope was wrapped around her ankles and under her arches. First the right, then the left. And finally, belts were wrapped around her waist and each thigh. First the right, then the left.

Though there was pressure on multiple parts of her body, her attention was dormant within her own mind. She had nothing but the ground under her feet and the bar in her fingers to keep her cognizant of which way was up.

And there she stood, exposed and defenseless in her submission at the will of her Dominant. Anything he desired was his for the taking, no permission necessary. And the pleasure she took in being the subject of his lust gave her a bliss unequaled to any experience in her life, imagined or otherwise.

A quick but acute pinch to her right nipple sent a shooting pain down that manifested in pleasure between her thighs. She inhaled sharply at the sensation before licking her lips and closing her mouth again. But her accelerating heart was making it difficult to control her breathing.

A hand at her throat increased her burden. She couldn't tell if it was pushing her from the front or pulling her from behind. She struggled to hold fast as her Dominant added pressure to her windpipe. Her attempt to remain in position was in vain.

Her fingers slid out of the loops of the bar but the ropes around her wrists and hands did not stop her as she expected. Falling backwards, she broke from position and gave in to instinct and attempted to pull her arms behind her back to catch herself. But when the ropes around her wrists tightened, the ropes around her ankles lifted her feet off the floor.

With the terror of free falling and no way to catch herself, a shriek escaped her mouth and bounced around the room. She flailed about in mid-air before holding her breath and stiffening her appendages in preparation for the impact of the fast approaching ground.

A second passed, affording her the impression that she was falling further than she thought, compounding her fear. And then another second …and another; her panic gave way to the understanding that she was not falling, but was suspended. All the ropes were equally tensioned.

She sighed in relief as she tried to retain control of her breathing. But her body held rigid with her arms extended in front and her knees bent. Only the weight of her head pulling back gave her any indication of where she might find the floor.

"Oy, cabrón!" she exclaimed before adding, "Sir!" in an attempt to correct her lapse in comportment. Edward was winning yet another match between himself and her self-control.

The sound of his stifled snicker caused her to give a short wheezing laugh before she pressed her lips together, with corners upturned. But she was given help regaining her composure with another pinch, only this time, it was to her left nipple and it was sustained. She writhed in pain until she pulled on the rope with her left hand. When she did this, she found the rope around her left ankle compelled her to straighten her knee. Her nipple was released.

Testing the ropes, she learned her hands were connected to their respective feet with the bindings around her hips and thighs being comprised of elastic cords and belts. But she would not be given much more time to explore her circumstances before Edward's hands would commence with a vicious tickling.

He started under her arms. She screamed with laughter that inspired Edward's as he continued mercilessly. She pulled her arms in, which pulled her legs up, causing blood to rush to her head, indicating her inversion. Then the tickling was behind her knees, forcing her to bend them and pull her arms forward. One hand stayed behind her left knee as the other found the left side of her ribcage. An attempt to protect one part of her body only exposed another to the torturous tickling. She felt herself rolling and diving in a pointless effort to defend against the intruding hands that she welcomed to touch anywhere they pleased.

A smack like a firecracker rang out, burning her butt, abruptly ending the tickling.

"Thank you, Sir!" she said through her escaping breath. She felt like she was swinging around. But she couldn't tell which way was down.

And then there came a slap on her cheek, but not from a hand. It was the familiar sting of Edward's member. His hand grabbed her hair to stop her momentum before he slapped her again. She dutifully opened her mouth in preparation for potential use.

"Good girl. But it's time for this cock to go somewhere else," he said as he spun her around.

"Somewhere else, Sir?"

"Mm hm."

She felt him between her legs pulling downward to position her horizontally. His elbows spread her thighs with his hands on her hips.

"Are you ready for me?" he asked as he used his member to slap her labia. Now there was no doubt what he meant.

"Sir! Wait!"

He slapped her labia again. She tried to close her legs but the effort only pulled her arms. There was no way she could overpower him, with or without ropes.

"What's the matter, my charge?"

"Remember, Sir! You ask me to help protect your virginity!"

"It's been long enough. You don't know what it's like to have a girl as sexy as you and a pussy right here for the taking!"

"No, Sir! Stop!"

He laughed. "You know that doesn't mean anything!"

She tried their safeword. "Exonerate!"

"We don't have safewords anymore, remember?"

"I don't care, Sir!" she said, as she kicked at the air in panic. "I said I would help you stay a virgin until marriage, Sir! Please don't do this!" She repeated, "Exonerate!"

"You don't want this cock?!" he asked as he rested his member on her mons Venus.

"I do, Sir! But not like this! Please..." She became silent and still. "You are testing me, aren't you, Sir?"

Edward laughed and pulled her feet down, bringing her face to his. He pressed his forehead to the blindfold and whispered, "That's my good girl."

"Thank you, Sir," she replied with an exhale.

When her feet found the ground, Katrina stood upright again in position five. She grasped the bar in order to relieve some of the tension the ropes placed on her wrists and hands. The belts around her waist and thighs released. The ropes around her ankles and wrists loosened, no longer supporting her weight. But they were still tied tight otherwise.

Her hands were guided and placed on his shoulders. First the right, then the left. She gripped him for balance in her disorientation. There was the click of a leash being attached to the chain under her chin. Edward turned in place but she kept her hands on him. A tug upward on the chain caused her to step into him where she found more support.

He walked with small steps. She rhymed his stride, starting with her left foot, even though she could not see his feet. The leash held her to his back as she followed, ropes dragging behind, never breaking contact with him. She didn't know where she was being led. She didn't think about it. All she knew was her Dominant was leading by the chain that he had bestowed upon her. That's all she needed to know.

Their brief journey came to a halt when the leash fell slack. Edward turned in place again. With her hands in constant contact, she felt him lower and rise. Her right ankle was pulled up by the rope. She moved her foot in compliance until it rested in the cold dry tub of the shower. She shifted her weight onto it when she felt the same pull of the rope on her left ankle until it joined her right. She stood in the tub with her feet together. He pressed forward, pushing her back until she felt the edge of the bench and was gently set upon it. She naturally crossed her arms behind her back. He took the loose ends of rope from her wrists and pulled them around her, binding her arms behind with a knot tied in front, under her breasts.

She sat still, warming the cold bench with the heat of her own body. She heard Edward doing... something. It made no difference. She was fulfilling her purpose by waiting and existing... for him.

She didn't know how long she had been sitting there. She didn't need to know how much longer it would be. She didn't think about what was going to happen next. It didn't matter. Being in the moment had become innate to her. The water turned on to a trickle, enhancing her peace though she was barely cognizant of the silence in her mind.

Once again, her right foot was lifted by the rope. And then she felt something wet. One of Edward's hands was holding her heel while he used a sponge to wash from her ankle down. It slid over the top gushing warm water. The sensation was repeated after the sponge was wet again. There was scrubbing under her heel, a slight tickle at her arch, and a light pinch between her toes before her foot was replaced next to the other. She sat in the deepening calm of her mind. But there would be an interruption.

The blindfold was removed, but she kept her eyes closed so she could open them gradually, as trained. Her left foot was lifted by the rope as with the right. Soothing water flowed to the tips of her toes.

Through squinted eyes, she began to take in light. The crown of Edward's head came into perception. Then she saw a blurry sponge in one hand and her foot in the other. She beheld the image of her Master ...on his knees before her ...washing her feet. Realizing what he was doing, she watched until her tears blinded her again. She knew what was going to happen next. She began to cry.

Edward finished washing all the way to her pinky toe and replaced her foot next to the other. He looked up into her weeping eyes with tears in his own. "Will you marry me?"

He hardly finished the last word before she replied, "Yes, Master."

With that, he reached up and pulled a loose end of the knot at her front, releasing her arms. She spilled into him. They held each other as the water rose around them.

"Now I can call you, 'Master', Master!" she said with her chin on his shoulder.

"That's right, my charge."

"Will you please *order* me to marry you, Master?"

"With pleasure," he said as he pulled her by the hair to lock her gaze with his. "I order you to be my wife, allowing me to own you and suffer through this life with me, that I may strive to earn the submission that you will unconditionally give me, until death do we part, through the sacred bonds of marriage."

"Yes, Master," she whispered as she latched her chin back over his shoulder. "Will you tell me why Adam loved Eve, Master?"

"Because she was made for him."

It was up to them to decide if they would be living happily ever after. Together, they would make it up.

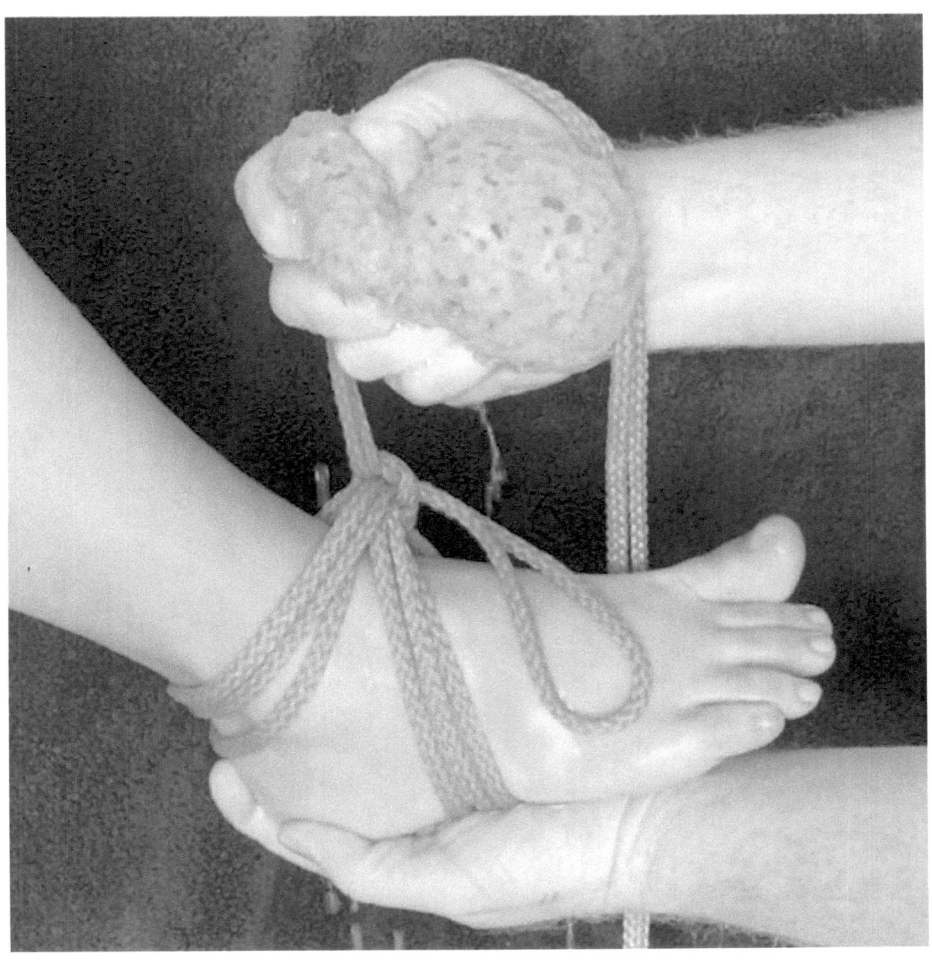

AUTHOR AMBITIONS:
 If the resources become available, the author would like to record an audio play version of this book and would also like to see a miniseries screen adaptation.
 In the meantime, it would be greatly appreciated if you leave a review and rating. Thank you so much for reading. Please share it with your friends and book clubs.

This is a work of fiction.
Any resemblance to actual persons, living or dead,
events, or locales is entirely coincidental.
No artificial intelligence was utilized in the creation of this book.

"To Earn Submission"
by Evelina Cortez
All rights reserved © 2019, 2023
ToEarnSubmission@gmail.com

"Unless I Wash You" cover photo
Models were age 43 (foot) and 40 (hands) at the time of the shoot.
Records on file. All rights reserved. © 2021

## COURTESY COPYRIGHT INFORMATION:
Although all references to intellectual property fall under "fair use", the author includes the following information as a courtesy and with respect:

Magician "Dyno Staats", name used by permission.

"JEOPARDY!" is a registered trademark of Jeopardy Productions, Incorporated and Sony Pictures Television. All rights reserved.
© Sony Pictures Entertainment Inc.

"Star Trek" is a registered trademark of CBS Studios Incorporated, Paramount Pictures Corporation, and CBS Interactive Incorporated, Paramount companies. © All rights reserved.

"Casino"
MCA/Universal Pictures © 1995

"Back To The Future II"
Amblin Entertainment/Universal Pictures © 1989

"Diamonds Are Forever"
United Artists © 1971

"Fight Club"
Fox 2000 Pictures © 1999

"The Grand"
Anchor Bay Entertainment © 2007

"Casablanca"
Warner Bros. Pictures © 1942

"The Terminator"
Created by James Cameron and Gale Anne Hurd
StudioCanal © 1984

"Love Shack"
The B-52's
Warner Records Inc. © 1989

"Paradise By The Dashboard Light"
Meatloaf
Sony Music Entertainment © 1977, 2012

"Hit Me Like A Man"
The Pretty Reckless
Interscope Records © 2012

Portishead's self-titled first album is on "Go Beat" records.
Go Beat © 1997

"Root Down"
Beastie Boys
Capitol Records, LLC, Grand Royal, and Beastie Boys © 1994

The music of Louise Farrenc is in the public domain.
Be encouraged to seek the copyright information of the recordings and performers of her music.

www.ingramcontent.com/pod-product-compliance
Ingram Content Group UK Ltd.
Pitfield, Milton Keynes, MK11 3LW, UK
UKHW042004230426
12048UKWH00009B/553